M000006567

Every Wickedness

Every Wickedness

A Kristin Ginelli Mystery

Susan Thistlethwaite

RESOURCE *Publications* · Eugene, Oregon

EVERY WICKEDNESS
A Kristin Ginelli Mystery

Copyright © 2017 Susan Thistlethwaite. All rights reserved. Except for brief quotations in critical publications or reviews, no part of this book may be reproduced in any manner without prior written permission from the publisher. Write: Permissions, Wipf and Stock Publishers, 199 W. 8th Ave., Suite 3, Eugene, OR 97401.

Resource Publications
An Imprint of Wipf and Stock Publishers
199 W. 8th Ave., Suite 3
Eugene, OR 97401

www.wipfandstock.com

PAPERBACK ISBN: 978-1-5326-1914-4
HARDCOVER ISBN: 978-1-4982-4527-2
EBOOK ISBN: 978-1-4982-4526-5

Manufactured in the U.S.A.

"a belief in a supernatural source of evil is not necessary; men alone are quite capable of every wickedness."

—Joseph Conrad, *Under Western Eyes*

Contents

Acknowledgments

The University of Chicago is, of course, a real place, but all the events, characters and locations on and around the university campus, with the exception of the iconic Rockefeller Chapel, are fictional and solely the work of my imagination. The characters in this novel have no relationship to actual events or persons living or dead. The events, buildings and personnel at the University of Chicago hospitals are similarly completely fictional, with the exception of the work of local activists to get a Level 1 Trauma Center opened at the hospital, an effort that has been successful. This life-saving center is scheduled to open in 2018.[1]

I wish to thank my husband, J. Richard Thistlethwaite, Jr., M.D, Ph.D., for his unfailing support for me in every endeavor I undertake, and for his feedback on parts of this narrative. Any errors are my own.

I would also like to thank W. Dow Edgerton, Professor of Ministry at Chicago Theological Seminary, for his helpful comments on the perils of sailing on Lake Michigan. As someone who has sailed those treacherous waters, this is a subject he knows well.

The character of the University Chaplain, Rev. Jane Miller-Gershman, is fictional, but is named "Jane" as a thank you to Rev. Dr. Jane Fisler-Hoffman, ordained minister of the United Church of Christ and retired Conference Minister, for her careful reading and critical feedback not only on this

---

1. Cassie Walker Burke, "U of C Medicine adult trauma center to open May 2018,"*Crain's Chicago Business.* http://www.chicagobusiness.com/article/20170607/NEWS03/170609908/u-of-c-medicine-adult-trauma-center-to-open-may-2018, (June 7, 2017)/

novel, but on the previous one, *Where Drowned Things Live*. The real Jane, like so many clergy I know, is a dedicated mystery fan.

The giraffe at the Lincoln Park Zoo, Morgan, who makes a brief appearance in this novel, was, in fact, named "Morgan" by the zoo after my dear friend, Howard Morgan, for his committed volunteer work to support this fine institution. Howard Morgan was also chairperson of the Board of Trustees when I was Chicago Theological Seminary President and over the years I have learned from him how volunteerism works to make the world a more decent place.

StreetWise, a Chicago-based magazine sold by people without homes and those at-risk for homelessness, is also real, founded in 1991, and the actual name is used in this novel. I want to thank Julie Youngquist, Chief Executive Officer of *StreetWise*, for granting me permission for that use.

StreetWise has one of the largest readerships of any street publication in the United States and it contains articles of national and local interest, as well as art, poetry and articles by actual vendors as well as others. I have been a supporter through purchasing and reading *StreetWise* since its founding. I have especially admired the poetry. Those poems inspired me to write and include the poetry in this novel. In the face of hard economic times and other challenges, *StreetWise* has continued to innovate. Go to StreetWise.org for more information and to donate.

The *StreetWise* vendors that appear as characters in this novel are completely fictional, however, and are not based on any person living or dead. I have, however, tried to portray the courage and resourcefulness of those who struggle with homelessness in the face of a society that is becoming more and more devoid of compassion.

In this novel, human connections are forged across chasms of race, class, disability and educational opportunity. These connections are the warp and woof of goodness. As theologian and ethicist Dr. Beverly Harrison once so wisely said, "God is in the connections."

Wickedness is the mirror opposite of such goodness. Wickedness works to deform and destroy human life especially for the sake of gaining power over others. Goodness can, at times, overcome the worst of the havoc wickedness can wreak, but often at great cost.

I write fiction because fiction can allow us the psychological space, within the pages of the novel, to explore these themes while we remain safely behind the boundaries of the written word. This may empower us to confront these conditions in the real world to help goodness thrive and make wickedness wither away.

No Suspects in Vendor Murder

Police claim they still have no suspects and no motive in the April 10 murder of James Maddox, a vendor for *StreetWise,* a paper sold by the homeless. Maddox was found in an alley in the 5200 block of S. Palmer Ave., near the campus of the University of Chicago. Maddox had been a vendor for *StreetWise* for eight years, making him one of the veterans of the business of selling street newspapers.

Hyde Park residents have expressed outrage over the lack of police progress in the case. "Jimmy was a great guy and we want to see his killer caught," a long-time resident told this reporter. *StreetWise* vendors and supporters demonstrated yesterday outside Chicago Police Branch 36 demanding more police action in the investigation.

StreetWise, May 15

1

I got gratitude
Not that old 'tude
See my face
It's no disgrace
To smile
"Gotta Smile"
Jarmal Jackson, #722
StreetWise

Wednesday, May 17, 6 p.m.

Coffee. Coffee. Coffee.

The word rolled around in his mind while he jingled the extra change joyously in his pants pocket. The chunk, chunk, chunk sound it made reminded him of Christmas bells, only worn down so the jingle wasn't very loud. Or, like Santa was still far away. Santa made him think of presents. He wished he'd gotten Christmas presents. But the change was a present, wasn't it? The last customer had given him extra money and told him to 'Get something for yourself.' Was that against the rules? He couldn't remember. So many rules. Nah. How could it be? Well, anyway, he'd drink up the evidence and then how could they tell? Drink up the evidence. That was good, really good. He was so smart sometimes.

But he had decided to wait to the end of shift to go buy the coffee. Waiting was good too. Knowing he could buy something when he wanted. Coffee. Sometimes it was bettern' drink and it didn't get you in trouble. Yes sir. Drink coffee. That was okay with AA. Coffee at all the meetings. Two, three, four cups he had sometimes. Couldn't sleep then, but he mostly didn't sleep anyway.

"StreetWise!" he called out. He'd better get back on the job here. He had papers to sell. The street was picking up. He called out suddenly, loudly and then laughed silently at the startled face of the suit walking by.

Whoa there! Fancy suit. The kind guys got married in, only this one even fit. Looked weird here where the students and even the profs slouched up and down the street all day in jeans and tee shirts.

Wedding suit shied away like a scared ole rabbit, actually thunking his hand with a little donk on the copy store window on the other side of the sidewalk. Wedding suit looked sideways at him, probably wondering if some bad, black dude was gonna hold him up for his fancy watch. He watched with glee as disbelief registered on wedding suit's pale face.

White dude? A homeless white dude? He could read wedding suit like he had the words printed on his face.

The vendor had to bend at the waist to keep the laughter in. It hurt his stomach. Damn stomach. Damn wedding suit.

Hate to see one of your own on the street? A few bad deals and wham! You'd need a corner of your own.

He bent over a little more. Took a deep breath, then straightened. Wedding suit was hustling away, shoulders squared up, smooth cloth getting even smoother on that snobby back. Smooth rich suit once more. But he'd been scared.

"StreetWise!" The sound floated down the street after wedding suit's back and got sucked into the ears of a bearded guy with a sweatshirt and jeans on. A regular. A guy who lived in the area. Bought papers. Not every day. Like mosta the regulars, had their days when they bought, days they didn't. This guy was a twice a weeker. Well, four times now since he'd had this corner only two weeks.

Bearded sweatshirt stopped. Looked at him. Direct, like he was a person.

"Seventeenth today," he said. "New paper?"

The vendor nodded. He could talk when he wanted to. But lots of the time it was so much easier to listen to himself in his head. Then he could say what he wanted. It came out so smooth, so cool in his head.

Bearded sweatshirt handed over two bills. No chit chat. He liked that about bearded sweatshirt. He passed over a paper.

"Any news about Jimmy in here?"

Oh shit, a question. Wait, wait. A shrug might do it. He bent his head and tried a shrug, but didn't look up to see how it went over. He looked down. Saw his shoes. His Nikes. Actual Nikes. Another regular had given them to him less than a week ago. He loved them. Checked them frequently to be sure no dirt had gotten on them. No, they were still fine.

The man waited a minute and then quietly said goodbye and left.

Okay. Okay.

Everything's fine.

"StreetWise." He said it softly to the emptying street. Just so he could show himself he'd got that word great. It'd come out perfect.

The *practice* he'd done with that word when he'd first heard about becoming a vendor from another guy at a free breakfast at the downtown Y. He'd even done that breathing they'd taught him so long ago in that special class in school. But Mama'd put a stop to that.

"My son's no retard. Get him outta that retard class!" She'd cut up somethin' fierce that day. He never did find out how she'd known they'd moved him to a special class. Special. Not retard. But there was no talkin' to Mama. He never talked to Mama. Course, he hardly ever spoke to anybody, but Mama was the one who'd belt him if he stuttered. Other folks'd just look embarrassed and impatient. Well, he'd fixed that.

"StreetWise!" He said it louder. Enjoying the word. Even Mama'd have to sit back and admire the way he said it.

"StreetWise!" Traffic was picking up. Talk louder.

From his corner across from the campus, he could see something was happening way down to the right, three blocks away from the big group of buildings in the middle. A new building was going up there—big, big sucker. Huge. The beams rose high into the darkening sky, looking like the bars of a prison built for Godzilla. But it was just a prison with bars and no walls. Prison bars so, so high. But no walls. It was a prison that would leak Godzilla out all over the city and the city would be destroyed.

He watched down the street as long, thin black cars stopped and more fancy black suits got out. If he squinted, they looked like really dressed up ants. Then the fancy black ants reached into the cars and pulled out lady ants. Expensive lady ants in all colors.

Why were all these fancy ants marching into the prison building that wasn't even finished? Because they're stupid, that's why. It was so funny it made his stomach hurt again.

He'd better get back to business. He hadn't done so well this last hour.

"StreetWise!"

Down the street the other way he could see another one of the fancy suits coming down the sidewalk. This one had his lady in tow. They musta parked around the corner. The woman was sure easy on the eyes. Young. A lot younger than fancy suit. He laughed his silent, invisible laugh. They were too close for him to risk any sound.

Her hair was long and blond. Not out of a bottle, he'd bet. The store lights made it look smooth like a veil over a church statue. Her clothes musta been painted on her they fit that good—and lots and lots of leg. And great shoes. He marveled at how women could stand up on those teeny, tiny kinds of shoes with the straps and the high, high heels. He loved those kinds of shoes. That was one thing bad about this corner. All the women wore Nikes like his. Shit, if he wanted to see Nikes, he could just look down.

"StreetWise." He said it again, but quietly. Just for the form of the thing. The rich never bought papers. Everybody knew that. They'd no money just loose in their pockets—and bring out that wallet? No sir, no sir. Let the poor dude see all that cash and them credit cards? No sir. No sir.

Besides, these two were not exactly honeymooners. She was angry in that thin woman pinched nose way they got. And the suit? He was real, real aggravated. Also tryin' to hide it. Walking like he had a poker up his butt. Stiff. All like, 'I'm bein' pushed and I don't let nobody push me.' Cept of course this little church statue could call the tune to any guy she chose any time. The legs alone could lead a guy straight to hell and he'd pay for the trip and enjoy it.

"Would you please hurry up!" She spoke without hardly moving her painted statue lips. Oh, if all church Madonnas looked and moved like that the Catholics'd be building churches instead of shutting them or letting them be turned into restaurants like what'd happened on the old street where he used to panhandle before he got to be a vendor. A restaurant. He still felt the shock of it when a construction guy had told him what was going on. Why'd God let that happen? God must be a chef now. Stop that thought right now, he told himself sternly.

The fancy suit moved like he was the rusted Tin Man. Oh how he *loved* that movie. In that hospital they'd called him a flit for liking it so much, but so what? He'd watched it anyway. Now he even *owned* his own copy, though the shelter had no VCR that worked. But still, he owned it. Locked up in his own locker. Safe.

He watched the rusted Tin Man walk of the angry suit. It wasn't the same, but he still enjoyed it. Poor rusted rich Tin Man. Bein' forced down the street toward a half-finished prison by a pissed off Madonna. Didn't that just beat all?

They'd passed him now without a glance. He watched their backs. Nah, he watched her butt sway and the Tin Man's butt stay put, kind of enjoying the contrast.

"Dwayne, how's it going tonight?"

He snapped his head around. His name!

He calmed some when he saw who it was. He'd seen her around a lot. Bought papers. A regular. His head just came up to her shoulder. Just like Mama. *Not* like mama. Push that thought right outta there.

What should he do? She'd asked him a question!

"StreetWise?" He made it a question like it was sort of like part of a conversation. That was so smart of him. He quivered with his own smarts.

Dwayne, though. His name. His name!

"I read your bio in the last paper. Dwayne Moorehouse, right?"

He nodded carefully.

Had he done something? Was she mad at him?

But wait. She couldn't be mad at him. She was all dressed up too, like a princess she looked. A cape thing hung from her shoulders to practically the ground for heaven's sake. He looked very carefully now, stunned. Her dress was all sparkles and it went all the way to the ground too. Glenda! The Good Witch of the North. Just like her. He looked down and sighed with delight. Red sparkle shoes. Dorothy's sparkle shoes. Oh, the shoes were so beautiful they put his clean Nikes in the shade.

He wanted to make her stay. He'd have to talk. Sweat beaded suddenly on his lip. But Glenda wouldn't hit him. She was *good*. It was even in her name. Good. He knew that.

"Yes." There! And it was a perfect yes. A beautiful yes. It matched the shoes and the dress it was so beautiful, so perfectly formed.

"My name's Kristin, glad to meet you."

She stuck her hand out from inside the cape and the cape made little flutter motions. The material was sorta stiff and shiny. He couldn't take his eyes off it. So beautiful. He watched until the cape was perfectly still again. He looked up at Glenda. What had she said?

She was just smiling now, but it was a sad smile. He hoped she was okay. She held out the money. Two dollars.

He took it and gave her a paper, doing his business the way it should be done.

"I'm so sorry about Jimmy," she said, looking even sadder, like Glenda the Good Witch should when somebody dropped a house on somebody.

And somebody *had* dropped a house on Jimmy. That was for sure. He shivered.

2

All the fears
From all the years
I see the streets
I know what's up
And down.
"What's Up?"
James Maddox, #965
StreetWise

Wednesday, May 17, 6 p.m.

I was just about to call the police and report her missing when Kelly appeared at my front door over two hours late. Kelly is a fourteen-year-old and the daughter of Tom Grayson, a surgeon at the University of Chicago hospital and my, I guess you would say, boyfriend. We're not lovers, not yet anyway. What other word is there?

I could see her smug expression through the leaded glass of our front door even before I yanked it open. She knew exactly how angry she'd made me, and that, of course, made me still angrier. 'Slow down, slow down,' cautioned an inner voice as I unfastened the deadbolt. 'She's a teenager. She's manipulating you,' it said reasonably. 'She's doing a damn fine job,' I snapped back at the inner voice. A friend of mine, mother of a teenage girl, had said to me that she was beginning to favor abortion up to age fifteen. I'd thought at the time she was just overreacting. I took a deep breath and opened the door.

Kelly slouched in, hiding her breasts under a Kurt Cobain tee shirt, complete with the dates of his birth and death. Great. Well, her baggy jeans

8

and clogs fit the grunge look. But no matter how much she slouched, she couldn't hide that she was nearly my height, and I'm just over 6 feet tall. I'd made my peace with being a tall, blond Viking. Kelly had not, though she had lovely skin and blonde hair as well. Well, it used to be blond, now there was a streak of purple down one side. She wore it dragged back and tied with a strip of leather. This, I suppose you would call it hairstyle, was designed to show off the double pierced ears, a stud and a ring, that had been newly acquired. Tom had been stunned when she'd shown up one afternoon with the pierced ears. He was a new, full-time custodial father, his ex-wife having died in a traffic accident a few months before. He was still learning teen culture, and in this he was a slow learner. I'd tried to console him by describing all the other things she could have pierced. He had become so pale I stopped my description.

Kelly was angry at her mother for dying, angry that she'd been forced to move to Chicago and leave her friends, angry at being so tall and angry at basically *everything*. Her eyes were blue like Tom's, only hers resembled lasers as she stood sullenly just inside the doorway and just looked at me. She wanted me to know how much she hated this witchy interloper in her father's life. I knew. And my twin sons, aged six, she considered the Devil's spawn.

I sighed and fed her my obligatory line.

"Why are you so late?"

She just shrugged while she dropped her backpack heavily onto the parquet floor of our entry.

"Dunno."

I knew. She (and privately I agreed with her) thought she was old enough to stay home alone for the evening, but her father didn't. Usually they compromised by having Mrs. Bronsky, their downstairs neighbor, 'keep an eye on Kelly' when Tom was out for the evening, or out most of the night in a long surgery. But Mrs. Bronsky was in Cleveland attending to her daughter and her new grandchild. Tom had cajoled me into letting Kelly come over while he and I went to a reception dedicating a new medical building in the hospital complex. Carol and Giles, a live-in couple, both graduate students, help me take care of the kids and try to keep up with the cooking and the cleaning. I'd known when Tom asked that it was a bad idea, and it appeared I'd been right.

"Never mind," I forced out through my teeth. "Giles has dinner for you in the kitchen."

"I've eaten."

She addressed this snotty remark to the hat stand that graces our Victorian hall.

"Fine," I managed. Though it wasn't fine. Giles, a math Ph.D. candidate, who had emigrated from Senegal, did all the cooking and he took it very personally when someone didn't eat what he had prepared.

Fortunately, my twin boys ate anything. At nearly seven-years-old they were approaching 4 ½ feet tall and climbing. I bought shoes nearly once a month.

The boys had heard the door and they came running down the hall with Molly, our Golden Retriever. Molly likes Kelly, God knows why, and she proceeded to jump up on her, wiggling with joy. Kelly swore and pushed Molly down roughly. Molly yiked, more in disbelief than in actual hurt, I thought, but Mike, my oldest by a few minutes, was hugely offended.

"Hey!" he yelled, grabbing for Molly's collar and pulling her into a hug. He looked up at Kelly like she was Eichmann in his glass booth on trial for war crimes.

"Yeah, watch out, you stupid, clumsy ox," contributed Sam, my less diplomatic son.

"Who're you calling an ox, you toad!" was Kelly's scintillating rebuttal. "And get that creature away from me!"

Kelly aimed a half-hearted kick in Molly and Mike's direction.

"That's enough!" I stepped between the would-be combatants and then turned to Kelly.

"You don't want to be here. All right, you've made that sufficiently clear. Take your book bag off my floor and go into the den. Close the door. Stay there."

I turned to Mike and Sam.

"Take Molly into the kitchen, and then go upstairs and do your spelling."

Having divided, but having no illusions I had conquered, I called down the hall to Carol that Kelly had arrived. I didn't include Giles in my announcement. A dedicated pacifist, Giles just hated conflict. His soft brown eyes, magnified by his horn-rimmed glasses, take on the look of a deer caught in the headlights whenever there is yelling. At the sound of Kelly's loud and angry voice, I'd heard the rapid flap, flap, flap of his flip-flops as he had hurried upstairs.

Carol came down our long, narrow center hallway, her short, rounded figure topped by a mop of hair cut exactly in a bowl shape. Giles's culinary skills at work, I always assumed. She looks like she was born swaddled by L.L. Bean. I believe everyone from Maine is required to wear corduroy clothing, and Carol is no exception. As she came down the hall toward us, her friendly, freckled face was calm, but her hazel eyes were assessing the situation.

"Kelly, let's get you set up in the den," Carol said. She has a lovely, clear voice, both concerned and yet authoritative. My chief fear for her in her chosen career of social work was that the overwhelming needs in our society would burn her out, leaving only a shell of concern. Making her a bureaucrat. But not yet.

For a second it looked like we were going to get away with separating the kids so I could leave in peace. No such luck. Molly, disliking calm in any form, slipped away from Mike's grasp as he had been slowly, oh so slowly, tugging her toward the kitchen. She dashed over to Kelly and licked her hand.

"Oh, gross!" Kelly yelled, holding up her hand like she'd been scalded instead of licked.

The boys laughed heartily at this reaction, causing Kelly to yell, "You suck!" at them.

I opened my mouth to remonstrate, but Carol made shooing motions at me with her hands, looking for all the world like a young and very intelligent Aunt Bea from Mayberry. It was cowardly, but I ran for it.

Well, I ran as fast as I could wearing a full-length formal dress, a cape and red sequined Ferragamo heels. I rarely wore heels. At my height I hardly needed to add to it and I was not good at walking in them, let alone sprinting. I got out the door in record time, however, and then teetered down our brick walkway toward the sidewalk.

The screaming inside the house followed me. A couple walking by, white, conservatively dressed, middle-aged, probably prospective freshman parents, glanced up at the sound of the screaming and then shuddered. Was it just the screaming or was it also the color of my house? It was hard to tell from their quickly shuttered faces.

My old Victorian house is only two blocks from campus and when I bought it, it had been painted a drab gray that was peeling off in sections. After the kids, Giles, Carol and I had failed to do more than dab on about ten square feet of paint in several months of effort, I'd hired a professional painter and it was now red with yellow picking out the trim like the San Francisco "Painted Ladies." This was designed as a deliberate insult to the constantly gray skies of Chicago. People noticed. From the windows of my study on the second floor, I often saw people stop and point. Well, it made it easy to give directions to my house since every other house in this row of tall, thin Victorians was either gray or brown. The kids liked it a lot. They said it was a cartoon house.

The passersby shuddered briefly and hurried on down the street. Small-town parents often looked shell-shocked after visiting Hyde Park. The recruitment office should keep them on campus.

Safely on the sidewalk in my stiletto heels, I took a couple of breaths from my diaphragm like the kids and my Tae Kwon Do instructor had us do in classes. It was supposed to increase your life force. God knows I needed to do that. My life force was running close to empty.

Despite my love of getting really dressed up, my schedule had made me want to back out of this mid-week reception thing. I really couldn't spare the time. In addition to two kids, I worked in the Department of Philosophy and Religion as an instructor while I was supposed to be finishing my dissertation. I had cut a deal last semester to teach half-time, and I had thrown out my old dissertation and launched a new one.

Right out of college I had become a cop; that's where I had met my future husband, Marco. But he'd been killed in a traffic stop that had gone hideously wrong, and there'd been suspicions of police misconduct in his death. I'd run as far and as fast as I could from police work. Philosophy and Religion had seemed far enough, but oddly my previous life kept catching up to me. Finally, I'd decided to quit running away from what I knew from police work, and I'd decided to dig deeply into the kinds of contradictions of power that were not only what policing was like, but it had turned out, what academic life was like as well. This had led me to work out an agreement to do some consulting for the campus police. I wasn't really doing much of that, though, and I had made almost no progress on the dissertation re-write. In fact, right now I should probably be making notes and trying to write, not hobbling down the sidewalk swathed in sequins and satin.

I teetered along in the unaccustomed heels, vaguely registering the odd looks of passersby. You could wear nothing but a loincloth and a lot of tattoos on the campus, like the young man I'd seen escorted off the main quadrangle just last week, and not rate a second glance. But a formal length gown and cape stuck out like jeans on the Pope. That's university culture.

University culture was not turning out to be what I expected when I chose it as a refuge from police work. It was much more violent than I had imagined. I'd sought academics like a wounded animal would seek a dark, narrow burrow as a safe, quiet place to lick its wounds, but I'd been quickly made aware that the burrow was nearly as bad as the Chicago streets. The university was ringed by urban poverty and a lot of the crime was petty theft. The surrounding poor saw the casual affluence of the whole place as both an insult to their existence and an easy target. And the students, faculty and staff were not exempt from the tendency to steal from and even inflict bodily harm on each other. In the Middle Ages in Europe, members of universities had been exempt from prosecution by civil authorities and some of that attitude still persisted. City cops were kept at arms length for crimes committed on campus, especially theft and sexual assault. The campus police had to walk a fine line between the see-nothing attitude of the administration and the outrage of the campus community when it was suddenly revealed that such and such a crime had been treated too lightly. Some administrators were trying to bridge the gap, but they were still too few.

As I turned the corner, I spotted the new guy who was selling *Street-Wise*, the newspapers sold by the homeless or nearly homeless to work themselves out of poverty. Speaking of crime, his predecessor had just been murdered in an alley not far from campus. Jimmy Maddox, disabled veteran, recovering addict and full-time comedian, had been well-liked in Hyde Park. People were upset and angry over his death and what seemed to be the lack of police progress in the case.

By now I was approaching Jimmy's old corner. I'd passed the guy who'd taken his place two weeks ago quite a few times on my way to and from work. I'd bought papers, but it occurred to me to stop and talk. I wanted to see if there'd been any developments in the Maddox investigation that weren't in the Chicago papers. Since Jimmy had been one of their own, *StreetWise* had better updates. The paper came out twice a month and there'd be a new one today.

I'd read the new vendor's bio in the last paper. He was 28, but seemed much younger. He was also so fair he was almost an albino. He had long, lanky hair pulled back from a thin, mousy face. His skinny limbs seemed tight, like he was wired. I had wondered, as I walked back and forth to campus, whether he was scared of his new job or if he was on something. Unlike Jimmy, this guy rarely spoke. But his mouse face was appealing, a kind of Disney mouse face.

I knew I had bills in my tiny evening bag and I approached him. The bio had included his name, Dwayne Moorehouse.

He was looking away from me down the block toward the campus. I spoke softly, sensing I might startle him.

"Dwayne, how's it going tonight?"

His small head snapped around and he hunched his chin into his shirt, like the little turtle that, in a moment of insanity, I'd let the kids buy in a pet shop. The tiny thing had only lived a month and had rarely stuck its brown head out of the shell, much to the kids' disappointment.

After a pause, his pale eyes glanced up at me.

"StreetWise?" he asked in almost a whisper.

"Hi, Dwayne. Yes. I'd like a paper. I read your bio in the last issue. Dwayne Moorehouse, right?"

A longer pause, then the turtle head popped out briefly for a nod, settled back in his shirt. A barely audible "yes" followed after another delay.

Gradually his shoulders relaxed a little but he was looking down. He seemed fascinated with my shoes. I decided rushing would spook him, so I just stood there. I slowly put out my hand.

"My name's Kristin, glad to meet you."

My hand remained solitary in the air until I pulled it back to my side. Dwayne continued staring at my shoes.

I held out the money where he could see it and he took it quickly, pulling a paper off the pile he held with a practiced motion.

I tried again.

"I'm so sorry about Jimmy."

The narrow corners of Dwayne's mouth had been tending up, like a smile might even appear, but when I mentioned Jimmy, the corners sagged down into a sad little droop. He looked so much like a Disney mouse I imagined I saw whiskers drooping too. Then he looked directly at me with his pale, almost unlashed eyes and nodded. For a moment, there was a flash of quick intelligence, I thought. Though was I imagining that?

I moved on, a little unsettled by meeting Dwayne. I'd gotten used to bantering with Jimmy, and except for that brief eye contact, Dwayne seemed like he might have developmental problems, or perhaps he just had a speech impediment and was consequently shy about speaking.

Well. I shook myself. Whatever problems he might have, selling papers was better than making brooms in some protected workshop, inside all day. Despite being so shy, he was out in the public, meeting people, doing a hard job. Behind me I heard "StreetWise" again.

The ordinariness of courage. It's easy to miss it.

3

The rat likes the cheese
Not the trap
But rats gotta eat
Don't they?
"Traps"
Abigail Collins, #584
StreetWise

Wednesday, May 17, 7 p.m.

I was late to the reception, of course. That's what Kelly had intended. But what she didn't know, and I had no intention of ever telling her, was that it didn't really matter all that much. Her Dad would probably have an emergency and be later still, if he made it at all.

You have to have a pretty thick skin to date a surgeon. I'd discovered that nine times out of ten you were left at the restaurant, reception, dinner party, opera (pick one), either dateless or abandoned after he got an emergency call.

Oddly enough, it didn't seem to bother me, a fact Tom found astounding. I've always liked surprises—it was the unpredictability I actually liked. Will he? Won't he? And the times we did get together became all the sweeter for it. Augustine of Hippo, a really randy Christian saint, wondered why, when he was a kid, pears he'd stolen out of an orchard tasted the sweetest. Why is stolen pleasure sweeter? Augustine couldn't figure it out (well, actually he thought it had a lot to do with human sin, but I couldn't buy that convenient out). I did respect his insights into the perversity of the human soul though. A lot.

The Anderson building was directly in front of me now. Ames Anderson was a wealthy racetrack owner and he'd bankrolled this hospital construction project with a single, fifty million dollar donation. Atonement? Tax write-off? Probably both. Though, can one genuinely atone while also reducing your tax bill? Kind of ruined the sacrificial aspect of atonement, I mused.

Tom had told me this pile of steel and concrete was going to double the number of beds at the hospital. His voice had carried both awe and worry. The clear trajectory in medicine these days is to reduce both health care costs and delivery, and thus increase profits. Eventually, I thought, health care could completely disappear for all but the rich. So why expand the in-patient capacity when reducing costs and increasing profits meant sending people who'd had surgery home before they passed go? Who knew? Privately I thought the honchos who ran this university hospital thought so much of their august brand ("First in Medicine!") that they figured they could buck these obvious trends. Well good luck with that. The titanic plates that were moving under American society these days were crushing all kinds of human care, and health care was sitting right on a major fault line and the cracks were getting wider.

As I turned the corner on University Avenue, a concrete truck was just pulling out from the ramp that divided the block-long building into two sides on the ground level. Above, an arch on the second level connected the two halves. It seemed to me that these construction guys were cutting it a little close, since not a hundred feet further down the block, long black limos were discharging formally attired attendees under a rented marquee. Even though the month was May, the covered walkway was a smart idea. In Chicago, it could have been snowing. And just because it wasn't snowing this minute didn't mean that this clear, fairly warm night would remain so. It was common for a front to surge down Lake Michigan from the North Pole and drop the temperature 30 degrees in an hour. Well, make that half an hour now as abrupt and violent climate change was accelerating and aggravating our weather patterns.

As I got even closer I could see some demonstrators on the sidewalk across from the entrance the reception-goers were using. I'd read about these protests not only in *StreetWise*, but also in the big Chicago papers. The people of the neighborhoods surrounding the university wanted a trauma center to be included in this multi-million dollar medical skyscraper. Nightly shootings in these areas took lives that might have been saved if there had been an adult trauma center close by. And so far there was no adult trauma center planned here, or anywhere in the hospital complex that I knew of. Signs read "Save Our Youth" and many were wearing "Trauma Center Now" tee shirts. I knew negotiations had started, but if demonstrations were still going on, no trauma center deal had yet been struck.

I just stopped walking and looked at the faces. I wondered how many of the older African American women and men who were demonstrating had lost children to gun violence. Their faces were grim, and determined. A small group of what looked like students, many of them white, stood behind them, partially hidden by the signs carried by the front line of demonstrators. Good for them. They knew where to stand, too, behind those who were literally on the front lines of this battleground. But they were up against not just the money and power of this particular hospital, but a whole national shift toward health as a profit center. And if it wasn't profitable, death of the unprofitable was clearly the preferred business plan. I made a mental note to check if these protestors had a website, see how I could help.

Finally, I turned in at the marquee and approached a reception table. I presented my invitation. Much to my amazement, the young woman behind the table in black sheath, pearls and a vacant face plunged her hand into a large cardboard box next to her chair and pulled out a white construction helmet with the words "Anderson Building" printed across the front in maroon letters. She handed this to me, showing no embarrassment at all. I took it from her, too bemused to do anything else. With my construction helmet dangling from my hand along with my tiny evening purse, I walked into the building. I stopped walking again, my stomach churning from the contrast between the needs of the demonstrators outside and the obvious luxury here.

Nearly a hundred people in formal wear carrying hard hats in one hand and drinks in the other were milling around. Waiters circulated with trays of hors d'oeuvres, but there were few takers. Unless the waiter dropped the crab puff or bacon-wrapped scallop into your construction helmet, there was no way to get the food and hold a drink as well. That was currently fine with me, and with my upset stomach.

The area where the reception was being held was obviously going to be the main lobby of the new hospital building. It was several stories high—and it seemed from looking up that this would continue—and was an impressively large space. Of course, the lack of walls helped with the sense of immensity. The concrete floor had been swept and all the construction equipment pushed back behind ropes along what would be the outer wall of this area. Above this atrium-like lobby, I could see floors rising in tiers—ropes had been strung along them to keep people from falling off. The effect was rather like the back of a huge doll hospital, a Barbie-becomes-a-brain-surgeon set. Now that the toy manufacturers had Barbie stop saying she hated math, there might be a chance of that. I stood still and marveled at the size of this lobby. The architect must be aiming for a Hyatt-hotel kind of effect. I'd heard, in fact, that this atrium would contain a Starbucks coffee shop, a decent restaurant and even a few shops. Now that airports are virtually indistinguishable from malls, maybe hospitals would also begin to resemble malls. The future promised that the whole country would become one giant mall called "Everywhere U.S.A," though since more than half the country couldn't make a living wage, how all this buying would take place with no money was a mystery. I pulled myself away from these morbid cultural reflections and began to look for Tom.

I was amazed to actually see him. He'd made it. I'm tall, but Tom is taller still and it's relatively easy for us to find each other in a crowd. Tom was standing with a small group of men, listening.

Tom's ability to listen continued to move me—his tall figure bent toward whoever was speaking, giving them his full attention. Even though I was too far away to see him distinctly, I knew his clear blue eyes would be focused in thought behind his wire-rimmed glasses. The skin at the corner of his eyes was permanently crinkled from that intent look. His sandy hair, graying a little at the temples, was too long and fell forward over his forehead when he bent his head. Tom's gaze was total—he was never, like many doctors, or academics for that matter, obviously mentally elsewhere. He was more like a cop in this. He was always present. And his look made you (or at least made me) want to trust him and tell him everything, a trait I'd found uncomfortable a couple of times already. I felt the rush of pleasure I always have when I see him. I wondered if I would continue to feel it.

I approached the group quietly and slipped my arm through Tom's. He gave it a squeeze and continued listening. I glanced over at him and noticed his bow tie appeared to have been tied by a monkey. An inept monkey.

The man holding forth in the group could only be an administrator. He was so smooth he appeared to have been lacquered. He was short and his baby smooth, pale face, immaculate hair, and buffed nails positively glistened in the glare from the bare bulbs strung over our heads. His bow tie, I noticed, was perfectly symmetrical. Of course, he probably slept in formal wear and therefore had a lot of practice tying the tie. He looked remarkably like Fred Astaire; I hoped he didn't dance.

"The additional beds will not *ever* be a financial *drain*—they are a wonderful source of *revenue*," he was saying with that palms up, 'trust me and buy this Edsel' gesture that dishonest car salesmen have. His speech was audibly italicized.

"But why are there nineteen operating rooms? The original plans we saw called for forty," said an older man with a completely gray head, his stoop and his tired eyes labeling him a surgeon. His tone wasn't hostile, but it was not a tone I'd like used to me. It conveyed very clearly that he knew he'd been lied to, he was being lied to now, and he expected to be lied to again in the future. It was both weary and contemptuous.

"I'm sure the hospital planning committee took all the departments' needs into account," said Fred the Administrator, doing a little administrative two-step. I was wrong. He did dance. He looked around the circle, making excellent eye contact. The gray-haired doctor gave an audible groan.

I looked around the group as well, since I couldn't quite make out what they were talking about. Next to Fred the Administrator was the tired doctor, then another older man, this one heavy-set and running to fat in the stomach area. This is not the physique that men's formal wear flatters. His cummerbund looked like it was a large bandage around his middle, keeping his stomach from exploding. Despite his weight, his carriage was very erect, almost stiff. This rigidity extended to his face. His lips were pursed so tightly they were white and his eyes behind his authoritative black eyeglass frames stared straight at Fred. He was probably struggling to hold on to some very choice words.

And holding on to the rigid guy's arm was a stunning young woman, easy half to a third of his age. A trophy wife? Her long blond hair flowed like a veil down her back, nearly reaching the hem of her tiny little black skirt. Below the skirt, tanned, slim legs led gracefully to high-heeled sandals. Her spaghetti strap top revealed she was thin, way too thin in that anorexic fashion model way that's come back into style to encourage girls like Kelly toward depression and eating disorders. I know it threatened me and I'm supposed to be a grown-up. I sighed. She was exactly the kind of woman, well, girl, really, who had always made me feel like I was a hundred-foot-tall freak. She was none too subtly pulling on the rigid guy's arm, trying to move him away from the circle. He was plainly having none of it. The fact that he wasn't budging, and that none of the other men appeared to be drooling over her, was revealing. Despite the empty phrases the administrator was rolling off his tongue with practiced ease, the docs were very nervous about this construction project.

I thought I'd make the lacquered administrator nervous instead.

"What progress are you making on opening an adult trauma center?" I asked, loud enough to be heard over the cocktail party noise and, if truth be told, even a little louder than necessary.

What people call 'an embarrassed silence' ensued. But only briefly.

The lacquered administrator was more than a match for my pushy question and me. He made a move worthy of Fred Astaire in his suave *Top Hat* film and made his escape without even looking at me, let alone answering my question. He turned gracefully and glanced across the room, and then he swiveled back and made little depreciating 'sorry about this' and 'need to see about that' murmurs all accompanied by backwards motion and hand-waving. He was gone in the twinkling of an eye.

Tom and then other men looked at each other and frowned. Then by mutual consent they gave up and the group dispersed. Tom turned to me.

"Was that one of the lower-level administrators?" I asked, having never seen him before.

"There's no one lower than Mandel Griffiths," Tom said dryly.

"So no progress on a trauma center?" I asked.

"We need that here. There's no doubt," Tom said seriously. "But adult trauma centers are very expensive and you see what kind of compassionate, visionary leadership we have to deal with." Tom nodded his head in the direction Mandel Griffith had taken when he'd danced away. "I'd say the odds were slim, but the community pressure is getting to them."

Good, I thought. Now I'll definitely look for that website.

"Did Kelly get to your house all right?" he asked, obviously wanting to talk about anything other than Mandel Griffiths, the lowly administrator, and his complete lack of vision and compassion. Of course, Kelly would not have been my choice as a new topic of conversation.

I steered him toward the bar that was set up along the wall on the far side of the room while I pondered how best to answer the question.

Honesty, I thought, stick to honesty.

"She was late, but she made it finally. I really don't think she likes having to come over when you're out, Tom. It makes her feel like you think she's a baby." Somebody had to tell him and Kelly wasn't having much success.

Tom stopped walking and disengaged his arm from mine.

"She's a young girl and this is the city." He even stuck his chin out.

He'd actually used those same words when we'd talked yesterday about Kelly's coming over. Did I say Tom listened? I take it back. Where his daughter is concerned, he's just as thick as any other father. Maybe more so as he was a new custodial father. I started to argue and then stopped. Not with a hundred over-dressed people surrounding us all carrying hard hats. It was not the time for this conversation.

"Come on," I said, taking his hand. "I'm thirsty."

He came along reluctantly, but loosened up a little as I played surreptitiously with his fingers. He greeted friends and made brief introductions along the way as we struggled through the crowd to get two watered-down drinks. As I weaved my way through the crowd, saying hello six or seven times to people I would never remember, my mind was on Kelly and Tom. Tomorrow. Tomorrow I'll tell him that how he raises Kelly is his business, but no more leaning on Carol, Giles and me. Right. I knew I sounded like Scarlett O'Hara.

We finally obtained our drinks and escaped from the crush close to the bar. We wandered around and joined a small crowd clustered in front of some sketches of what the final building would look like. The proposed outside wasn't too bad as it was drawn, with raised columns drawing the eye upward and masking the sheer size of the building. Of course, it was also surrounded by beautiful landscaping and happy, healthy people strolling in and out. It didn't exactly say 'sick and injured people welcome here.'

Two men up front were answering questions.

"Yes, that's correct. There will be valet parking. Here." A very large man pointed with a blunt finger to the sketch. "And you do have to tip," he said. A ripple of laughter went through the crowd. The guy seemed witty; perhaps that was a way he'd learned to deflect attention from his sheer size. He was huge. Probably about six and a half feet tall and he had flaming red hair. His large frame was carried by enormous shoulders. Really, he had wrestler or weightlifter shoulders and was still in pretty good shape, though he could be in his mid-forties or even older. Still the shoulders were impressive for someone who probably now spent a lot of time behind a desk. People call Chicago the "City of Big Shoulders," probably because of its brawling, up-start history. Boy, did this guy fit right in. He gave the impression of leashed power and his civilized formal attire only served to underline that contrast. He should have been wearing a fur vest and a helmet.

Next to him stood another man who looked like a midget, but in actuality was probably no shorter than Mandel Griffiths, the lowly administrator. He was slender, almost reed-like compared to the beefy-barbarian guy. Architect and contractor, I'd bet. The reedy man was answering a question from someone in front, but so softly I couldn't hear. Tom and I moved wordlessly away.

Tom was almost immediately buttonholed by a tall, gray-haired man in a dark suit, no tux. He was about Tom's height and spoke rapidly into Tom's ear, his agitation evident in his tense body. Tom smiled apologetically at me and listened. I let my attention wander over the room and spotted one person I knew, the new head of campus security, Commander Nicolas Stammos.

I had wrangled some release time to "consult" with campus security as part of my new employment arrangement, but it was still not clear exactly what that meant. My new department chair, Adelaide Winters, had decided what that meant was I was on the faculty committee that was a liaison to the campus police to handle student complaints and so forth. I'd been to two meetings now, and at the second I'd met Stammos when he'd come to answer questions about the Maddox investigation. He'd looked to me like a Greek resistance fighter from World War II. He was short, but he could have given the contractor a run for the money in the shoulders area. He had pockmarked, swarthy skin, and black hair with no trace of gray. He was probably pushing fifty, and I found that a tad suspicious, but I also couldn't imagine Stammos putting dye on his hair.

I watched him as he moved across the room, away from where Tom and I were standing. He went toward the rear wall where there was a staircase. His tux fit him well, must not be a rental, and he moved rapidly, with purpose. He was no mingler. I took a sip of my drink. I had no intention of crossing the room to speak to him. I found him immensely intimidating.

That intimidating manner had alienated the faculty on the liaison committee too, though his presentation had been excellent. His deep, slightly accented voice had been gripping when he had claimed Jimmy Maddox was 'one of ours' and that the campus police were working closely with the city police to find his killer. But most faculty had been critical of him after he'd left. In Chicago, the level of trust in the police would not have filled a shot glass, and with good reason. That attitude of suspicion and even hostility spilled over onto the campus police as well. There were mutterings about an unspecified 'cover up' or snide remarks about the campus police as 'glorified crossing guards.' Stammos was no crossing guard. He was a decorated former New York City police captain. The campus police in general, at least the ones I'd met, were competent professionals. I'd made a friend on the force, Alice Matthews, and we grabbed coffee together on campus when we could squeeze in the time. I'd tried to stand up for the campus cops, and draw their attention to what Stammos had said rather than vague stereotypes, but I had not endeared myself to my faculty colleagues as a result.

I continued to scan the room, but I didn't see anyone else I knew, except a tall student working as a waiter. For campus cops, I knew there would be a duty roster for a big reception like this. Today, big gatherings were by definition security risks, and not just because free food and drinks were being served. The fact that the university hospital was spending so many millions on a fancy new building when health care services for the surrounding poor communities were almost non-existent was generating a lot of ill will and even protest, witness what was happening outside. I didn't see any of the university teaching faculty I knew either. Not surprising though. The hospital circle and the teaching university circle did not often overlap and I doubted they'd socialize.

Besides, this was in the nature of a fundraising event and even the highest ranks of academics today don't command the salaries they once did. I imagined the tickets for this event were in the neighborhood of $500 each.

As Tom's guest I hadn't paid my own way, but I guessed the cost from the fact that both crab and shrimp were on the trays of the circulating waiters.

The tense guy was still hissing in Tom's ear, so I turned slowly around to look at the shape of this building in the making. It was kind of interesting to see the bones of the thing before the actual plaster smoothed over all the innards. At the opposite side from the stairs Stammos had approached was another, obviously temporary staircase that led up to the first tier of the floors that surrounded the atrium. A crowd was gathering at the foot of the stairs and they were donning their hard hats. Probably a guided tour. Suddenly, Tom took my arm, startling me out of my reverie. The agitated man had disappeared. Tom looked where I was looking.

"I'd like for you to see this place, but not like that." Tom nodded his head in the direction of the tour group, and I could see that Mandel Griffiths was preparing to lead it. I agreed. That was an item on the evening's program to be avoided at all costs.

"You've seen it? When?" I asked.

Tom shrugged.

"I came through with the Dean last week. This operating room thing is a fiasco. How can we even think of doing Level One Trauma and have so few operating rooms? We have our operating suite cut in half, but have our own private elevator. It's insane."

Tom's face was grim as he gazed at the upper tiers of the exposed building, obviously contemplating riding up and down in his private elevator with no place to operate on patients.

"Come on," I said. I drew him toward the place where I'd seen Stammos head to another set of stairs, nearly hidden behind a roped off area with small machinery and tools. I gestured in that direction.

"Show me. Give me a private tour."

I didn't have to tug him very hard. We deposited our wine glasses, still mostly full, on the tray of a passing waiter, walked over to the roped off area, and quickly ducked under. Nobody stopped us, so we continued on up the stairs.

When we'd climbed halfway, I felt a tug on my cape.

"Let's say hello as long as we're up here," said Tom, drawing me back down a step and into his arms.

"Let's," I agreed, leaning into his warm lips. This evening was improving by the second. When we freed ourselves, I took a second to retie his bow tie that had come completely undone. I felt a sudden pang for my dead husband, Marco. How many times had I done that for him? I turned, confused and curiously ashamed. I tried to shutter my face, smoothing it out so the pain wouldn't show and hurt Tom. Even touching Tom had, at first, elicited the same jolt of guilt, but I was overcoming it. Gradually, I guessed, intimacy with Tom would seem normal. That would be the ultimate betrayal then. I shivered and tried to focus on climbing unfinished stairs in heels in the semi-dark.

"The surgery suite is on the third floor," Tom said quietly as we continued our climb. I wondered if he'd seen my sudden discomfort. I could feel his eyes on my back.

We took a quick peek out of the stairwell as we turned to go up the next fight, but we didn't stop. When we got to the third floor, Tom took my hand. Used coffee cups and fast food wrappers littered the floor along with loose nails and stray boards. This area had not been cleaned up for the tours, obviously. We probably shouldn't be up here at all, but as long as we stayed near the outside where there was some light, I figured we were okay.

"Where exactly will your clinics be?" I asked, peering around the shadowy space that was punctuated by pillars that would contain not only the heating and air conditioning ducts, but with the addition of the extensive wiring and gas pipes that hospitals need. Duct work also radiated out overhead, looking like the intestines of the building, exposed for their own surgery.

Tom pointed over to the left and I could dimly see rooms framed in lumber that would eventually be the small examining rooms.

"But this is what I really wanted you to see," Tom said, holding on to my hand and leading me toward the east end of the building.

I gasped in delight. There was framing for a huge, two-story picture window. The height of the building raised the window level above the surrounding buildings. Several blocks away, Lake Michigan stretched out like a silvery-gray invitation to infinity. If you stood back about twenty feet from the window, the line of the lake seemed to meet the bottom of the window and draw you toward the gray horizon. The sense of expanse was immense.

My respect for the reedy-little architect guy rose if he was indeed the one who'd designed this. There was a serenity to this design that might be of comfort to those who would spend anxious time in this lounge in the future, whether a patient awaiting treatment or a concerned family member or friend. I tried to empty my mind and let it move toward that horizon.

Tom came up and stood next to me and silently we just looked at the silver water blending into a silver sky.

The silence was broken suddenly, horribly, by a scream and then a sickeningly flat thud coming from somewhere behind us. Tom and I started. I know my mind had been so far away that it took me a minute to react. We turned and as another scream reached us, we started to pick our way as fast as we dared toward the direction from which the sounds had come. It was from somewhere in the middle of this floor. Even now we could still hear muffled groans and cries that were becoming more faint.

"Watch it!" Tom yelled at me as I darted ahead of him. "The elevator shaft is somewhere right near here."

Since we were further into the center now, we'd lost a lot of the light. The sounds were growing even fainter, but I could still hear them. Clearly we were getting closer. I continued to speed up and I stepped on a small piece of pipe and almost fell. Tom grabbed my arm to steady me and took out his cell phone with the other. He turned on a spotlight app on the cell and a beam of light showed us more scattered pipe and lumber on the floor. And then I saw a huge black column with an even darker square in it about twenty feet ahead.

"I think that's where the noise is coming from. Let's take a look." My voice was loud in the cavernous space. We held hands and advanced as rapidly as we could, stepping over or around the debris.

We got to the dark square open on one side of the concrete shaft that went up to the ceiling. The opening, where the elevator doors would be, was blocked by a single two-by-four railing nailed to sawhorses on either side. I kneeled down at the edge, oblivious to the sequins that scattered as the long dress was rubbed by the rough concrete floor. Tom shone his cell phone beam into the hole. It was the elevator shaft, and about three floors below us a pale object writhed on an opaque surface. I looked at Tom and saw my horror mirrored on his face. The object was an arm, part of a shoulder and a cheek. The hand attached to the arm was moving. The problem was, it was moving on the surface of what was obviously still-setting concrete. Someone had fallen into this elevator shaft and had landed on the just-poured concrete base. The person was drowning in concrete.

I gazed dumbly into the shaft for a moment and began to think. How to reach this person? There were shadowed areas in what must be the entry for each floor's elevator entrance, but they were boarded shut. It would take too much time to run back down to the first floor and try to find something to pry those boards loose.

What then?

I looked around frantically and my eyes lit on a big coil of rope bunched over and around some of the lumber. I grabbed Tom's hand and yanked him toward the rope. Seconds counted. If the person wasn't pulled out soon, he or she was surely dead.

Tom let go of my hand as I started to tug on the rope. He yelled, "Are you crazy? We need to get help." He quickly dialed the campus emergency number and efficiently gave our location and a description of this tragedy in the making.

I paid him little attention. By now I had freed the rope where it had been looped around the lumber and I was pulling it over toward the shaft.

"Help won't come in time," I puffed as I continued to tug on the heavy rope. It had bits of concrete encrusted on it and it was unbelievably rough and stiff in my hands. I thrust a coil of it into Tom's unwilling arms.

"Pull!" I grabbed the rope further down and yanked. As it uncoiled it was clear it was very long. But was it long enough? I estimated 3 floors at perhaps more than 20 feet per floor. Maybe. Maybe it would reach.

I pulled the end over to the closest pillar and started looping it around. I swore as my long dress nearly tripped me up. I'd already lost the cape somewhere. I made a double loop and a slipknot. I pulled on the tied rope and it held. I went over to try to see down into the shaft. Without Tom's cell phone light, it was a black hole. Tom couldn't hold his cell phone light on me and also hold the rope. I frantically looked around again. About 25 feet away I saw a tripod with two work lights. I ran over. It appeared to be cordless. Battery maybe. I turned it on. Bright light blazed out. Great. I picked it up and hurried back. I positioned it so the lights pointed down into the shaft. I took a quick look. The shoulder had disappeared. The fingers on the hand were still moving.

I handed part of the rope to Tom.

"Lower me down as fast as you can manage. If I can reach the arm, I'll tie the rope around it. There's an opening about two or three feet from the bottom. You can't drag us both up. I'll climb in the opening and wait."

"No, Kristin," Tom said firmly. "I'll do it."

I faced him and looked directly into his face.

"Have you ever rappelled?"

"No." Tom looked back unflinchingly at me. "But look at how you're dressed. I need to do it."

I realized he was right. Well, about how I was dressed. I had already kicked off my shoes. I pulled down the zipper of my dress, shrugged it off my shoulders and it fell to the floor with a clatter of scattering beads. I kicked it aside and looked back up at Tom. I was wearing only panty hose and a teddy. Well, this was not the way I had imagined undressing for Tom. Too bad.

"I have rappelled. Lots. Besides you're stronger in your upper body than I am. You need to work the rope. Wrap it around your waist twice and brace yourself on the pillar."

I have to say this for surgery. It trains people to think quickly in life and death situations and Tom didn't argue any more. His face drew in on itself and he focused on the task. He moved to the pillar and wrapped the heavy rope around his dinner jacket.

I made a loop in the rope around my waist and padded to the edge of the shaft in my stocking feet, dragging the rest of the rope behind me. My eyes fell on the construction helmet I'd dropped in my haste to get the rope. What the heck. I reached over, picked it up and slapped it on my head, fastening the strap below my chin. I turned back toward the shaft and called out to Tom.

"Let out about 3 feet at a time. We don't have time for a slower descent. I'm ready now."

I fit my body under the two-by-four, turned my back to the shaft and leaned back. As I went over the edge with the slackened rope I saw Tom's pale and intense face watching me.

A second later the rope slackened again and I bent my knees and pushed out from the wall. The surface was pitted and pockmarked with recently poured concrete and the soles of my feet burned. My hose had already shredded. Again the rope slackened and again I pushed out. Too much rope this time. I skidded and missed the wall with my feet as I came back in. I hit the wall and the helmet took the brunt of the blow that would have otherwise probably broken my nose. What do you know? These helmets had been an excellent idea after all. Despite its protection, however, I'd had the wind briefly knocked out of me. I scrambled to regain my footing and lean back out. My bare feet could get little purchase on the wall and I scrabbled in vain for what seemed like minutes until I had my balance again. Good thing. Just as I got my footing, Tom let out another length of rope. I jumped and landed, this time with my feet hitting the wall. I jumped, landed, jumped, landed. I looked down on the next landing. I'd come a fairly long way. I needed another 6 feet and I could reach.

The work light was doing its job, though it made looking up difficult. Looking down I could still see part of the hand on the congealing surface, but it was still, as though imprinting the jellied skin like some hideous parody of the plaster molds the kids had made of their hands in kindergarten.

Two more jumps and I was hovering about a foot above where the body had landed. My hands burned from the rough rope, but this would not be a good time to lose my grip or I'd fall into the same suffocating muck.

I shouted up to Tom to stop letting out rope. I hoped to hell he heard me.

I was now almost horizontal to the surface and above the arm. I had to tie the rope around the person's wrist with one hand while not losing my grip on my part of the rope with the other. I felt the rope around my waist. It seemed secure. I let go with one hand and picked up the trailing end of the rope. We'd cut it close with this rope. There wasn't much left.

I made a loop and tried to lasso the hand as it sank deeper into the sludge. This wasn't working. I needed two hands. Could I risk letting go with both hands for a second? Would the coil around my waist hold me? It was now or never. I was going to have to dig the hand out of the surface as it was.

I let go with my other hand and reached into the slimy concrete. I felt the hand. It was freezing cold. I held on to it with my left and wrapped the rope around the wrist with my right. I had her. For it was a her. The hand I held above the surface was manicured with long red nails and several rings. Rings that had scratched me when I'd reached under the surface to grab the hand. I tried to make a secure knot and sickeningly felt myself slide closer to the surface. My torso was now only inches from the glistening veneer that appeared to be a floor but was really a death trap. If I slid further, the floor would swallow me whole.

"Pull up!" I shouted as loud as I could. "Pull up about twelve inches." I was now about fifty feet below where Tom was straining with the rope and the part looped around my waist was tightening. My thin teddy had already shredded and the rope was cutting directly into my skin.

There was no response. I frantically pulled the knot tight around her wrist, prayed it would hold, and screamed again, "Pull up! Pull up!"

At first there was no motion and I felt panic start in my chest. Then the rope started to move. I was rising.

As I started to rise, I bent my knees and inched my now bleeding feet into an opening about just over a foot above the clotted surface. My feet slid in and I bent my knees more to get my whole body into the indentation left in the shaft for another elevator door opening. It was only eighteen inches deep and a plywood board met my feet as I slid into the crevice. I could feel countless splinters pierce my scraped feet. It hurt like hell. I scooted my butt sideways into the opening and slid in as neatly as you would slide a corpse into a medieval wall burial. Well, nice image, I thought.

When I could sit up, I yelled to Tom to just hold on. There was an answering yell that I took to be assent. I tried to quickly shrug out of the looped rope around my waist, but its concrete encrusted surface resisted my efforts. Finally I got it off me. For a minute I felt the panic again. If I fell off this narrow shelf, I would be drowning in concrete too.

I took a breath and let go of the rope. I yelled to Tom to pull up. Pull up hard.

The rope started to ascend more quickly and the hand came out of the slime. She had sunk some while I was getting the rope off of me. Then came the arm, a shoulder and a torso, the concrete seeming to pull back on the limp form, resisting letting go of its prey. The body moved slowly upward, past where I crouched on the ledge, in a hideous parody of the resurrection of the dead.

4

They are thrown away
The trash people
People Nobody Wants
They picked up the trash today
Dwayne Moorehouse, #2165
"Trash Man"
StreetWise

Wednesday, May 17, 9:00 p.m.

A few minutes after the body disappeared over the edge of the shaft, the rope was lowered and I grabbed it. I looped it around my bleeding waist and yelled again, "Pull up!" The rope tightened, I pushed out from the crevice, and I made a painful ascent, my abraded feet leaving bloody footprints up the wall.

When I'd climbed to about a foot below the edge, I was startled to see Commander Stammos above me. He reached down and lifted me under the arms like I was a child who had just fallen off her bike. When we'd both stood up, I topped him by a head, but the strength in those shoulders and arms was impressive. I am no lightweight. Tom had not helped pull me up; he was with two paramedics about twenty feet away, bending over the prostrate body of the young woman. Mel Billman, a campus cop I knew well, was handling the rope, pulling it completely away from the shaft opening and coiling it up out of the way.

Mel nodded to me, looking unsurprised at finding me barefoot, nearly naked, bloody and smeared with concrete. Mel's features rarely ever registered emotion, and he and I had been through a hair-raising event in the fall that hardly put a crack in his carved features. Alice Matthews, my campus cop friend, was often partnered with Mel and when we happened to be all together, she and I teased Mel, trying to get a rise out of him. If this act of mine didn't do it, I thought I'd have to tell Alice nothing would. I looked around, hoping to see Alice, but she didn't seem to be here. Two guys in campus cop uniforms were visible and a third was just coming up the stairs on the outside wall leading two city cops.

Mel wordlessly held out my ruined dress to me and turned his back. I stepped into what was left of it, wincing as I eased the zipper up along my scraped waist.

"Thanks, Mel," I said and he turned around. He reached down and handed me my shoes as well. No way I was going to be able to get them on my swollen feet.

We both looked over at Stammos who was standing near us. He was looking toward the body. His craggy face registered absolute fury. I thought again what a passionate guy he was, though he had clearly taught himself to keep it under control. Mel, on the other hand, was banked down and you couldn't tell what he was thinking or feeling. Stammos's face was so darkened with rage you could practically hear distant thunder. I hoped his anger was only for what had happened to this young woman and did not include me and my jumping into an elevator shaft to pull her out.

I was suddenly exhausted and I turned away from them. I saw my dirty cape lying next to the pile of lumber where I'd found the rope. That moment seemed like days not hours ago. I picked up my cape, pulled it around my shoulders, sat down on a stack of boards, and shivered.

Mel came over and pulled off his own jacket, putting it around my shoulders for additional warmth. I would have thanked him, but my teeth had started to chatter.

"You hurt in any way?" he asked.

I shook my head no. All I was capable of at the moment. Sure, my feet, my hands and my waist were bleeding, but that was nothing compared to having your every body orifice filled with concrete. I shuddered. A waking nightmare. I was still cold, but Mel's jacket was helping.

I looked over at Stammos, still fixed like a hawk on the medical personnel working over the body.

"Is she alive?" I called to him, braving having him turn his hawk's eyes toward me.

He came over and I decided to stand. I figured I needed every inch of height to talk to him.

"Wasn't breathing. CPR now for . . . ," he paused and looked at his watch. "Four minutes."

That didn't sound good at all.

Stammos turned toward the city cops who were walking toward where we were standing. He wouldn't waste time asking me questions I'd just be asked again in a minute. As they came up, Stammos introduced himself and then told them who Mel and I were. They gave their names and I was very glad I didn't know either of them. A certain Chicago detective and I have a nasty history and he had been the one to investigate the last serious crime we'd had on campus.

These two guys were in uniform, anyway. The detectives would follow shortly. Even in the dim light I could see their names on their badges. G. Gwynne and F. Kaplan. Kaplan was black, Gwynne was white. Both on the young side, still probably in their twenties. Gwynne was fair and had a mustache so faint it could just have been the product of a dull razor. Kaplan had an earring in his right ear. They were probably just the closest when the call came in. They looked at Stammos.

He took the cue, turned to me, and led me through a description of what Tom and I had been doing up here (I edited that slightly), what we'd heard and done. He went very slowly over whether we'd seen her before she'd fallen, whether she'd been with anybody, whether we'd seen anyone at all on this floor. I told them we hadn't seen anybody up here, in fact hadn't even seen her, just heard noise and cries. I told them I'd seen her on the first floor at the reception and described the guy it seemed she had been with as thoroughly as I could. I told them who Tom was and that he probably knew whoever had been her husband, lover, date. I said I didn't know if Tom knew her as well. I went carefully over the fact that we'd seen no one and heard nothing once we'd left the reception until we heard the scream and the thud. We went over that three times before my repeated 'no's' about seeing other people or anything else suspicious seemed to be enough for them. Both Kaplan and Gwynne took copious notes.

Of course, Stammos was zeroing in on the key point. Had it been an accident or had she been pushed or even thrown in? An accident was possible, though there was that one row of two-by-fours as a guardrail. I guess she could have tripped near the edge on those tiny, teetery sandals and slipped under it, but then why was she up here in the dark and alone? If she'd been with someone and it had been an accident, that person would have been yelling, calling 911, raising a ruckus, something. Unless he, or she, but I was betting a he, given what she looked like, had deliberately pushed her in. Of course, there were other possibilities. She could have come up here to meet someone, been stood up and then stumbled in the dark as she went by the shaft. Then it could have been accidental and he didn't know. 'He' again. Yes, I was jumping to conclusions based on what she looked like. But that kind of knee-jerk reaction can really throw off an investigation. She could be bisexual and have thrown over the fat doc for a female lover. Then they'd quarreled and . . . .

Stammos spoke sharply to me, interrupting my train of thought. I needed to quit this speculating and concentrate on what was happening right in front of me. Stammos wanted me to explain how I'd gotten to her.

I talked about seeing the rope and using it to rappel down into the elevator shaft. Gwynne looked up and broke out with a 'No way!' Stammos quelled him with a glance. I ignored him and described as efficiently as I could how Tom had worked the rope and I'd gotten her arm lassoed.

"That's Dr. Grayson over there, right?" Stammos asked, his large head tilting in Tom's direction. I nodded and all of us turned and looked at him, and the paramedics. Two more paramedics had arrived with a stretcher and it was clear they were preparing to move her. Since the hospital emergency room was literally across the street, the only tricky part was getting her down the stairs. She was moved to the stretcher, one of them holding an IV bag above her, the other steadying what looked like an oxygen tank, and they strapped her in. They departed rapidly, accompanied by Mel and the other campus cops. Tom's eyes followed them to the stairs and then looked for me.

I walked over to him, the cops and Stammos coming along. Tom's black tux jacket was torn around the waist and his tie was missing. No. I glanced down. He'd wrapped the tie around one of his hands. His hands! A wave of guilt washed over me. If my hands were sore from contact with the rope, what must all that pulling have done to Tom's surgeon hands? He saw where I was looking and he grimaced.

"Yeah. They're pretty bad. I'm going over to the ER and see this through and get my hands treated as well. You coming? You could use some patching up too. As usual," he finished, looking at the state I was in.

Tom hadn't even registered Stammos and the two city cops. Stammos was so close to me on my left I actually felt him stiffen. He certainly didn't like being ignored.

I hastily made introductions and the city cops dutifully flipped to new pages in their notebooks.

Tom nodded briefly but just took my arm and turned. He said over his shoulder, politely but firmly, "I want to be there when they examine her. You'll just have to follow I'm afraid."

And then we were walking at Tom's race-walking pace toward the stairs. When he gets going, he walks faster than anyone I've ever known. He doesn't actually exercise that I've ever been able to discern, but he's very trim. I have concluded that's because he race-walks the miles of hospital corridor, loping up and down the stairs, disdaining the elevators as too slow. We were actually at the stairs before Stammos and the city cops got moving. I heard a deep voice say, "Now just a minute, Doctor," but Tom just kept going. I doubted he'd even heard. Well, Tom was somebody Stammos didn't intimidate. Thank God my feet felt numb as we hurried down the wooden stairs and across the street.

# # # #

When Stammos and the city cops had finally caught up with Tom in the Emergency Room, he had paused, impatient, but had identified the surgeon who had been with the victim at the reception. The guy's name was Dr. Russell Wagner.

The city cops would get his name and contact information from the hospital operator.

I waited my turn to check in and get treated. I was still waiting when Stammos came back to the ER waiting room to tell me he was leaving. He'd grimly recounted that when the city cops had reached the doctor at home, Dr. Wagner had been offhand about not knowing much about a young woman he had identified as a 'date' he'd met at a party earlier in the week. Her name, he'd said, was Courtney Carlyle and he 'didn't really know anything about her.' The city cops had left immediately to question Dr. Wagner at home. They were likely there now, politely but firmly interrogating him about his apparently casual willingness to misplace his date.

They'd also told Stammos they'd found no 'Courtney Carlyle' in their first, citywide records search.

It was 2 a.m. before I'd been able to get Tom to leave the hospital. Courtney was likely not going to benefit from his further attention. In fact, Tom said, a neurologist would be coming to examine her and determine if any brain function could be detected or whether she was brain dead.

I'd already had my superficial cuts and abrasions treated in the ER while Tom had gone with the paramedics. Since the triage nurse had seen me come in with a surgeon, I'd actually been treated relatively quickly. That made a nice change from a previous time I'd had to come to the ER when I'd been made to sit for hours in a freezing white-on-white cubicle. This time when I was ushered into a treatment room, I'd gotten a warm blanket wrapped around me right away, and my cuts had been cleaned and bandaged efficiently.

After I'd been treated, I returned to the waiting room. Earlier, I'd called Carol and Giles to let them know a guest at the reception had been injured and I'd accompanied Tom to the hospital. They (and my boys) worried about me a lot, especially after what had happened this past fall, so I made no mention of my own injuries. I told them to make up a bed for Kelly in the den as we'd be very late.

After a while, I checked my email on my cell phone. The corner was a little dented from having been dropped, along with my tiny purse, when Tom and I had been rushing around trying to save Courtney, but it still seemed to work okay. Nothing to interest me there, and the current news was so ghastly I decided to avoid browsing the Internet. The TV hung on the wall in one corner was either broken or turned off. I left it alone.

Instead, I read the pamphlets on safe sex, which rightly should be called 'safer sex', drug and alcohol abuse, domestic violence and preventing pregnancy that were displayed on racks over the chairs. I'd had a cup of coffee, at least I think it was coffee, from the vending machine down the hall.

I was horrified at what had happened and bored out of my mind at the same time. And I was incredibly uncomfortable. The orange molded plastic chairs ranged around the florescent-lit waiting area had not been designed for long-term occupancy. In fact, since I had so much time to think about it, I realized they were designed to discourage occupancy.

My entire torso was starting to take on the same molded shape as the chairs before Tom returned. He'd come out earlier to tell me about the clinical diagnosis. The skin of his face was almost translucent with fatigue and drawn so tight over his cheekbones it looked like it might tear.

I knew. We hadn't saved her life. We'd just saved her body.

We left the ER and walked slowly across the shadowed campus, the stone shapes of the buildings rising stone upon stone, lit by the blue moonlight and the halogen floodlights installed to deter crime, though crime still regularly occurred. Gargoyles regarded us passively from the edges of the turrets above, not caring one way or the other if we were mugged.

But we walked safely on. My feet still hurt, but I was not wearing my badly scuffed spangled heels. I carried them in one hand, the remaining sequins hanging by barely a thread. I thought they were probably damaged beyond repair. Instead I was wearing the soft hospital socks and slippers they'd given me.

Tom's hands were bandaged, as were mine. He must have allowed someone to treat his hands, or more likely, he'd done it himself. There's nothing doctors seem to hate more than letting other doctors touch them. I'd been afraid he'd ignore his injured hands, but then, as we gingerly touched bandage to bandage at the tips of our fingers, I realized his hands were his livelihood and he would not have neglected them.

We walked on, saying nothing. What was there to say?

Finally, we arrived at my darkened house.

I had wondered, as I'd been sitting and waiting, whether Kelly might have talked to Carol, opened up a little about the tragedy of her mother's death, the sudden move to Chicago, having to change schools and then live with her Dad. When I got away from Kelly's smoldering presence, I could sympathize with her hurt, even identify with it a little. I hadn't lost my parents, it's true, they'd lost me, but the loss of Marco was something I'd never get over and I still alternated between grief and rage about it.

I unlocked our front door and disengaged the security system before it started wailing and waking everybody. The scene in the front hall earlier with Kelly, the boys and Molly seemed to have happened years and not just hours before. I shut the door behind Tom and me and he put his arms around me. I rested my head on his chest for one moment of peace before we had to face waking Kelly.

The overhead light snapping on made us both jump. I turned and saw Kelly's accusing face regarding her father and me. I felt Tom start and move quickly away from me.

Too late.

Kelly had seen us embracing.

Kelly's Online Journal

Thursday, May 18, 8:30 a.m.

Spanish is so dumb this morning and the asshole teacher thinks I'm actually taking notes on my computer. Nah. She's just too lazy to care what any of us are doing. Well, like I'd care about Spanish verbs with the night I had last night. I can't even function this morning.

Well, first, the Amazon struck again. She and Daddy were supposed to be at some hospital thing and then I find out she jumped down a hole—she's the hole—yeah, and she saved this woman only she didn't save her anyway. She died. Well too bad. Dad, Daddy, my darling Daddy. You suck. You couldn't keep your hands off her.

I don't care. Nothing here is right for me. I called Alison again last night. At midnight! I texted so her idiot parents wouldn't hear her cell. Alison never goes to bed. She always says she sleeps all day in school, that's what it's for. Ha. That's right. We talked for an hour!!!

Alison said she's going to go out with Scott, but I think she's lying. He never even talks to her. I so don't think so.

Anyway, screw them. Besides, he's only a kid. Fifteen. No big deal.

I told Alison all about this guy at the idiot Amazon's house. His name is Giles—is that cool or what? He's from a French place in Africa and he has the most darling accent. He's married. Doesn't it just figure? To this American named Carol. She's okay, but she seems so way older than he is. Alison wanted to know everything. Well, Giles is this sweet mild chocolate color with these killer brown eyes. He's not real tall, but he has muscles where it counts.

Dad totally forced me to go to the Amazon's house while they went to the hospital thing, and I was so pissed I showed up late and then went in their den and locked the door. Her kids are fiends.

So Giles comes and knocks on the door and says so softly, 'Kel-ly?' Oh, it's to die for the French way he says it. Anyway, I opened the door and he has espresso coffee for me and him. Decaf, but hey, espresso! He must think I'm much older than 14. Well, girls mature much faster than boys, everybody knows that.

So I talked to him, really talked, and he listened and didn't say I shouldn't swear or that I should try to see Daddy's side or anything. He just listened and nodded and once he called me "la pauvre." It means poor thing. I looked it up. I wish I was taking French. It's way cooler than Spanish.

And he cooks. After a while we went in the kitchen and he gave me some black bean and rice dish he'd made and it smelled so good and I realized I was starved. Usually I hate that kind of vegetarian bean crap, but this was really good. I ate a ton of it and had a coke. The espresso was great, but maybe it was a little strong.

Giles was so sweet I wanted to figure out a way to let him know that I'm not a kid and I can tell when a guy is interested. So when we were putting the dishes in the dishwasher I accidentally on purpose brushed against him twice. When he didn't seem to get it, I pretended to trip and fell toward him so he'd have to catch me.

Well, can you fucking believe it??? He catches me by the arms and holds me at arms length. His face looks like a mask and he says, "No, Kel-ly, no. Be a child. It is okay."

I was so humiliated I wanted to die. A child! What does he think these breasts are, balloons under my shirt? I ran back to the den and locked the door again.

Well, of course I didn't tell Alison that part. I let her think things got a little heavy in the kitchen. Whatever. I could tell she was just so jealous.

But then I heard the front door open. I went out and the Amazon and Dad were in the dark in the front hall groping each other for crap's sake. Oh, who gives a shit? Everybody's got somebody but me. I wish I was the one who'd fallen into the hole and the hole had no bottom and I could go on falling.

Forever.

5

Good morning street!
The street wakes up.
I wake up the street.
Don't run Alisha!
I wave at the bus to wait;
She makes it.
Alisha's grandpa waves at me,
Taps his cane twice,
And makes his way back home.
"A Good Morning"
Charlie Bruin, #876
StreetWise

Thursday, May 18, 8:00 a.m.

He shivered in the cold, damp morning air.

StreetWise!

It was an okay day. The sun was creeping up the street like it hoped it could sneak up behind him and yell, "Gotcha!" Fat chance of that. Just hurry up sun. Warm my street and warm my feet. Ha! Another poem. He'd written poems at the workshop. It was amazing. Not supposed to hafta rhyme. No more "Roses are red, violets are blue, sugar is sweet, and so are you." Blue, you. That's a rhyme. Don't hafta rhyme. You can just put down what you're thinking. Yeah. Okay. But he liked blue, you, street, feet. More like a song. But songs didn't hafta rhyme anymore either. He sighed.

StreetWise!

The train was just letting out and the steady tramp, tramp, tramp of morning commuters' feet made the street wake up.

He sold a couple of papers. No big deal. Easy sell these morning commuters. Still wakin' up. Didn't talk much.

A couple of kids came by, going the other way, toward the school around the corner. One tall, skinny, dark-skinned kid, not a black, another kind, dug in his pocket and pulled out some bills. Bought a paper. His friends raced on into the little store next to the copy shop—shrieking even before they got their sugar. Sugar's bad for kids, Mama'd always said that. Makes 'em wild. But this dark kid. No sugar for him, he'd bought a paper. Didn't say nothin', just stood there till his friends ran back out. Then they all moved off toward the school like they was joined at the hip.

You see anything, everything on the street.

Couple of regulars came by. Said hi, catch you next time.

Was okay.

A campus cop came by, rode a bicycle. Looked like a student, young, shiny brown hair. Glasses. But a uniform. The bicycle cop was mean and looked through him like he was invisible. Like he was wearing that cape the Harry Potter kid had. They'd showed that movie at the shelter one night. Scary flying things. He shivered.

He watched the cop who couldn't see him. Bicycle cop crossed over the street, headed to the campus. Cut through two parked cars, for Pete's sake. Didn't cross at the crosswalk. Cops don't think they hafta follow the rules. No sir, no sir.

StreetWise!

The train people had passed. Next train in a few minutes.

He watched the young cop some more. Got off his bike, talking to a student. He watched more closely. Was the student in trouble? Nah. They were both laughing. Shook hands. Okay. Okay. Nothing to worry about there.

StreetWise!

The sparkle shoes lady turned the corner and came down the block toward him. He squinted. He thought it was her, but where was her sparkle dress? Where were her sparkle shoes? Today she was all in black, her long blonde hair pulled back like an old school teacher. Well hell. But it *was* her. He looked carefully. Couldn't be two of 'em that tall with blond hair. From the neck up she was still more than okay, 'cept she did look sad. And the black dress. She didn't look like Glenda now. No sir. All that black she could be the Wicked Witch of the West. He hated black. Funerals and cold meat and people crying. He shuddered. Street needed to pick up. He looked at his own shoes.

He took a quick look up, hoping the Glenda/Wicked Witch had gone, but she'd stopped. Met somebody. Black woman. A campus cop, her uniform kinda tight on her short round body. Kind round all around. He smiled at the rhyme. Maybe he'd use it. Poems could rhyme if you wanted to, right? Kinda round all around cop even had round hair. She only came up to Glenda/Wicked Witch's chest. Looked like Abbott and Costello. 'Who's on first?' He chuckled. But he still didn't like all that black. Good. They were moving down the street. He looked back at his shoes until they passed out of sight.

StreetWise!

Good. The next train had come.

Oh shit! That guy was hangin' around the station. No good panhandler. Hustler. Scared people. Bad for business. He put on his meanest face as the guy walked by tryin' to hustle a commuter. Givin' him a hard luck story. Commuter didn't even look up. No dice. He'd heard it all before. We'd all heard it all before. Hustler gave up.

He smiled.

6

Her life is in a bag
All she has
It's very sad
"Bag Lady"
Dee Dee Robinson, #471
StreetWise

Thursday, May 18, 8:00 a.m.

A chill wind razored down the street directly off the lake four blocks away. I shivered in my thin jacket as I stepped out the front door. May in Chicago. I briefly contemplated going back in for something warmer, but it was too much effort. Besides, it wasn't the freezing gusts that were chilling me. It was fatigue. Memories from the previous evening had kept me awake most of the night. That image of the mouth and nose clogged with concrete rising slowly in front of my eyes had been with me ever since, waking and sleeping.

At first, of course, I'd been charged up by the adrenaline rush that comes with a rescue. Jumping into the elevator shaft, acting heroic. But somehow the horror of that gray clotting matter holding on to its prey had gotten right down into my bones, turning them to jelly. 'Preserve me from this' had been a prayer I'd silently breathed through stiff and frightened lips more than once last night.

I doubted Courtney's death had been an accident and in my mind's eye the memory of that dark gaping mouth of the elevator shaft had included monster shapes, feeding the mouth, feeding her to the dark maw. Those monster shapes were the shadowy outline of a murderer.

These charming thoughts accompanied me as I walked slowly on my sore feet toward the corner. When I turned, I brightened, seeing Alice Matthews coming down the sidewalk. She must have taken the train. I could see a brief flash as she lit a cigarette and inhaled slowly. I waited.

Alice was hatless and she only had on a light jacket that wasn't even zipped despite the cold. Both the jacket and her hair whipped in the wind. She seemed lost in thought and she was almost next to me before she glanced up.

"Who died?" she quipped. My mood was none too subtly reflected in my choice of clothes this morning. I was in black from head to toe and I'd tied my hair back, too tired to do anything else.

"A young woman about twenty years of age, I'd say," was my curt reply.

Alice's deep brown eyes flashed up at me, and I was brought up short, ashamed of my self-dramatizing. I flushed.

"Sorry, Alice," I said. "Really bad night."

I proceeded to give her a quick run through of what had happened while we walked down the street toward the university. We passed Dwayne, the *StreetWise* vendor, to whom I'd spoken last night. He seemed to be concentrating on his shoes again.

While I gave her a blow-by-blow description of the demonstration, the reception, the so-called rescue and then the time in the hospital, Alice kept running her free hand through her blowing curls, pushing them back from her face. The wind at our backs kept pushing them forward. With the other hand, she took short, quick drags on her cigarette. She finally threw it down on the sidewalk and ground it out with her heel. She was probably afraid of her hair catching on fire. But her attention was clearly on what I was saying and when I finished, she groaned.

"Jane Quixote rides again. God, Kristin, don't you ever quit jumping in where you don't belong? This time into an elevator shaft for Christ's sake? And you say Stammos was there and saw you pull this stunt?"

I nodded.

"Yep. He helped pull me out of the elevator shaft." I remembered the power in his arms and shoulders.

Alice sighed.

"Sounds like you're making friends in high places as usual. I'll see what they say at morning briefing. You teaching today?"

"Yes. I have a morning class, heaven help me. Want to meet for coffee later?"

Alice nodded.

"Sure. Later is right. I'm on for ten stinking hours today. Last night was the first night I didn't work in four straight days."

She reached into an outside pocket of her shoulder bag, pulled out a pack of cigarettes, shook one out and had it lit before I could blink. She had lots of practice. She watched me watching her.

"Don't say it. Don't even think of saying it. If I didn't smoke I'd be one of those crazy cops who go home and shoot the family and then themselves." Her plump shoulders sagged.

"Jim still having no luck?"

Jim, her husband, was an out of work firefighter, the victim of budget cuts in their small, south suburban town this past fall. That made six months he'd been out of work. The strain on their family had been enormous. Alice worked over-time, Jim stayed home and got depressed, and their daughter Shawna, who'd seemed to me to be a happy, energetic child when I'd met her with Alice on campus one day, was now wetting the bed. A typical and tragic story in the 'not so great' American local economy today.

Alice stopped. We'd reached the middle of the campus. My faculty office was straight ahead, the campus police station to the right and a few blocks further. Her eyes didn't meet mine.

"Nothing. Just nothing. He hardly even looks now. He . . . " She broke off. "Let's just leave it, okay?"

"Okay. But if I can help in any way, let me know."

Alice glared at me.

"What, you got a fire that needs putting out?" She threw down her second cigarette and ground it into dust. The slicing wind took the tobacco flakes and the paper and spread them across the grass in an instant.

I looked down at her. No, I didn't have a fire that needed to be put out. What I did have was a huge trust fund. When I'd married my husband Marco, we hadn't wanted to touch the Hilger wealth. I was rebelling against my family and he was too proud. After he had been killed, I'd had no energy either for rebellion or pride. I'd used the money to help support myself and the boys. No, I didn't have a fire. I had Hilger shipping stock. But Alice would never take my help and so I would never offer it.

Time to change the subject.

"Well, no, but I might burst into flame when the Dean of the Faculty gets wind of what I did last night," I said dryly.

Alice and I both knew the Dean would just love to see me kicked off the faculty because of my meddling ways, and because I'd effectively blackmailed him into giving me my current release time from teaching one class and doing "consulting" for the campus police that seemed, so far, to mean sitting on a committee and also having coffee with Alice. Could be worse.

Alice shot me a forced smile, erasing the pain from her face by sheer will power.

"Man, that's the truth. If I was you, I'd sneak in to work, wear a disguise, do what you can to be invisible." As she said this, she looked me up and down, clearly noting my six-foot frame encased in black. She shook her head.

"But there ain't no way."

"There's no way I'm going to be on time for my class either," I said, glancing at my watch. "What do you say I call your cell around 1?"

Alice nodded and started to turn toward the campus police station. Then she stopped and turned back.

"What're you teaching them today?" Alice was endlessly curious about my switch from being a cop to being a professor. Or maybe incredulous was more accurate.

"The course is called 'Good and Evil,'" I said, trying to keep a straight face.

Alice snorted.

"You kill me, girl. You purely do." Her shoulders were shaking with laughter as she hurried away.

I trudged on toward the building where the department of Philosophy and Religion was housed.

It was killing me too.

7

You have no heart
You make me sick
You're a robot
Not a person
You took away my mother
In your van
She looked back at me
Crying
"ICE-Y Hearts"
Valerie Hernandez, #998
StreetWise

Thursday, May 18, 8:45 a.m.

I clumped up the three flights of stairs of Myerson Hall to our offices and classrooms. Our medieval-style building was gray stone with turrets holding down the four corners. Philosophy and Religion had one side of this top floor, history had the other. Academic backwaters, both relegated to ancient and unrenovated buildings. The elevators never worked.

The faculty office door was open when I entered our corridor. Good. Maybe that meant our faculty secretary, Mary Frost, was out.

I cautiously stuck my head through the door. The office seemed empty. I could grab my snail mail and get going. But as I moved further into the room, Mary backed out of the closet in the far corner carrying a stack of large manila envelopes. Her thin, elderly face was flushed even with this small effort.

"Professor Ginelli. Good morning. How are you this morning? Can I get you some tea? I brought some Lapsang Souchong from home and it's still quite hot."

All of this was said in a rushed, whispery tone as she bustled over to her desk. She placed the stack of envelopes hurriedly on top of an already precarious stack of papers and reached for a paper-thin teacup next to the stack that would be crushed if the pile slid that way. As she picked it up, the delicate china cup rattled on its saucer. She literally jumped at the sound and put it back down. She placed both trembling hands around a shining, stainless steel thermos that was next to her computer, more to still them, I thought, than to get me any actual tea.

This is what I had been trying, coward that I am, to avoid. Mary Frost had been the faculty secretary for Philosophy and Religion for more than twenty years. She'd had a breakdown, what she referred to as a 'spell,' when our former department chair, Harold Grimes, had died and his various misdeeds had come to light. I'd always thought Mary had idolized her old boss and yet her almost collapse had seemed extreme. I had often wondered if she'd also been a victim of his misdeeds, or perhaps a silent witness. She'd been given medical leave until the middle of April and then had returned to work. Astonishingly, given the role I'd had in exposing her old boss, she had switched her devotion from him to me. It was so unnerving.

"No, thanks, Mary. That's the good stuff. I'll just have some coffee if there is any left down the hall." I mumbled this while shoveling into my backpack the amazing amount of paper that still accumulated in my mailbox despite the advent of the digital age. I hefted it and turned to look at Mary. She was bent over the messy piles of paper and files that six months ago would have appalled her; she was simply moving papers from one stack to another.

"Well," she said in that whispery rushed voice, "you know best, though coffee is bad for the heart. I just read an article on that. In fact I have it right here," she said as she rummaged around even faster, going through one of the piles. The pale May sunshine from the window behind her shone through her thinning gray hair and piteously illuminated her pink scalp. I stood helplessly watching her shuffle papers, now unwilling to leave her and just walk out.

"Lose something, Mary?" A robust voice coming from the doorway was both brisk and yet held an undertone of compassion.

My boss, Dr. Adelaide Winters, newly appointed department chairperson, came into the office. She glanced sharply at me and I jumped in as bid.

"Mary has an article she wants me to read, on how coffee is bad for you. But just now she can't seem to locate it." Mary continued shuffling papers, seeming oblivious now to both of us.

Adelaide might have been a large woman, but she was always quick on her feet and she swiftly reached Mary's side, putting one of her soft hands over the thin, restless ones—delicately stilling their motion.

"I'm sure that article is excellent, but right now I need something copied," she said briskly. I had also noticed that Mary spent a lot of time standing over the copier, watching its rhythmic flash. It did seem to calm her.

Mary's watery blue eyes looked up from the desktop and seemed to focus. She suddenly jerked her hands out from under Adelaide's. She grabbed at the file that Adelaide was holding in her other hand.

"Fine, Dr. Winters," she snapped. "How many copies?"

I never thought I'd be glad to see a glimpse of the old bitchy Mary, but I was. The snap of her eyes and frigid tone was a frank relief, much to be preferred to the delicate wraith that moved around the office with no seeming purpose. That glance and tone used to be called 'getting frosted' by the students and faculty alike. We all used to tiptoe past her office trying not to draw her attention. Now we still tiptoed by, but for very different reasons.

Frost did not like it one bit that Adelaide had replaced her old boss, but her anger at Adelaide seemed to wake her up.

Adelaide knew this, of course, and used it to try to bring Frost around. She kept her Mrs. Claus face on, the one that fooled people into thinking that her halo of graying hair and her round face meant she was a sweet older lady. Adelaide was far more likely to give you a verbal kick in the pants than a cookie, however. She was probably counting on Mary's animosity to snap her out of the repetitive behavior.

"Twenty-five," Adelaide snapped back, matching Mary's tone. "By 11 o'clock."

"You'll have them by 9:30," Mary said with a trace of her former asperity, her frame erect in the faded floral dress that now hung on her thin frame. She walked steadily over to the copier, keeping her back ramrod straight. Once Mary's back was turned, Adelaide allowed her concern to show on her face, and then she took my arm and hustled me out the door.

By unspoken consent we went down the hall toward her office. She had set up a table with a De'Longhi combination coffee/espresso machine on a table in the hall outside her door. Ground the beans and everything. I had one at home. Adelaide was clearly leading us in a new direction, a place where faculty and students all had access to good coffee. I put my money in the donation jar and made a cup of espresso. Adelaide did the same. Then we walked into her office. In contrast to the former occupant, who always kept his door shut and often even locked, doing God-knows-what behind that closed door, she almost always kept her door open.

"What is it about me that sets her off?" I asked as we sat down. Even to my ears I sounded like I was whining. But Mary's condition rattled me.

"Kid, who knows? Whatever her affection for the old bastard was based on, I have come to think there was a healthy dose of hatred there too." Well, Adelaide should know. She had good reasons to have thoroughly hated our departed and unlamented department chair as well.

"At some level," she said, pausing to take a sip of the really excellent espresso, "she must be glad he's dead and you are St. George, the hero. The dragon slayer. But me? I'm the replacement for the love object, so she hates me."

I narrowed my eyes and glared at her.

"Did you talk this over with Willie?" Donald Willie was our colleague in Psychology and Religion and I thought he was a superficial idiot.

Adelaide chuckled.

"Not even close. No, you know there's a lot of myths about conflict that feminists use to dive into the origins of patriarchy. My own psychological brew, if you will. No point in teaching Women and Religion if you don't actually believe the stuff. Don't worry about it. I think she's beginning to realize she needs to retire this summer."

She patted me on the back with her free hand as she said this, causing me to nearly spill my coffee. She calmly steadied my arm and then seemed to take a hard look at me in the process.

"Say, what's with the cheerful black ensemble? Halloween is in October and this is May."

Her shrewd eyes seemed to take in my washed out face and limp hair as well.

I gulped down the rest of the coffee and said, "Let me just put my head into my class and let Hercules know I'll be late. I'll be right back. I think you need to know what happened last night before you hear it from somebody else."

Hercules Abraham, already retired Professor of Judaism who taught for us part-time, was team teaching the class with me. Or rather, I was learning a ton from Hercules and so were the students.

After I got back, I gave her a quick run-through of what had happened. I described the reception, Tom's and my private tour up to the floor where the operating suites would be, hearing the thud and the cry, our trying to rescue her, and then the tragic end result. I described the young woman, whom I now thought of as the victim, as I had seen her at the reception. Her long blonde hair, her supermodel figure, her tight, determined face. And then her waxed features above the blanket on the hospital gurney as I'd last seen her. I couldn't help but shudder once again at what it might feel like to drown in concrete.

Adelaide frowned. "You said the name was Courtney Carlyle?"

"Well, that's the name the doctor who was her date gave the police. She had no identification and I suppose her purse is now encased in several tons of hardened concrete."

"I wonder if that's Karen Carlyle? She insisted people call her Courtney."

Adelaide got up abruptly and walked over to gaze out the window behind her desk.

"You think you knew her?" I asked, amazed. "How?"

She spoke almost absently, without turning around.

"Well, if it's the same young woman, she was a student here and she took my 'History of Feminist Theory' class last year. She was very distinctive looking, pretty much just as you've described. And, as I said, she insisted she be called Courtney instead of Karen." Adelaide turned, put down her coffee cup on the desk, and moved slowly, almost reluctantly to her computer.

"Let me just pull my records and notes up."

Tempted as I was to follow this up right now, I really needed to get to my class.

"Listen, Adelaide, I need to go. Can we meet after? Go over the records?"

She spoke without looking up from the screen.

"Sure. Here. After class." And she kept staring at the screen.

Student? If Courtney Carlyle the doctor's date was Karen Carlyle the undergraduate we had to get that information to help the investigation into her death. My curiosity was so strong I had to force myself out of Adelaide's office and hurry down the hall to the seminar room.

# # # #

I slowed down as I reached the classroom door. I could hear voices and I didn't want to interrupt the discussion more than my tardy entrance would already do. I entered quietly and navigated around the backpacks littering the floor by the students' seats around the seminar table. I took a chair next to Hercules.

He had stopped speaking as soon as he'd seen me enter, however. Naturally he did. He was far too polite to keep talking while I entered.

Hercules was over 80, but you'd never know it. He was small and wiry, a French Jew who, as a young child during World War II, had been hidden from the Nazis in a small town in France with his mother. He taught Jewish studies and was a well-known scholar of the Talmud. He had approached me with the idea for this course, and even though we were understaffed this spring (I'd moved to part-time, we'd had one resignation plus the death of our department chair and another colleague, Donald Willie, the Religion and Psychology guy, was on sabbatical), Adelaide had agreed. She said it would be good for both of us. I didn't know what it was doing for Hercules to teach with me, but I know it was helping me in ways I didn't even know I needed. Plus, I adored him.

Hercules spoke gently as I wrestled my tablet out of my backpack.

"My dear—you take a moment. The time is only just at the 9. Begin when you are ready."

Since it was already more like a quarter past, I appreciated the sentiment. I opened the tablet and scrolled to the lecture notes I'd prepared last week. That was pretty much a record for me as a new teacher. Usually I was just hours ahead of the students in terms of class prep. But I loved the current topic and the book we were using, a modern interpretation of Aristotle called *The Fragility of Goodness*. Well, that was right. Goodness was fragile and a big part of that was the fragility of human life. I glanced down at my carefully prepared notes and shut the tablet.

"Last night I had the misfortune to watch someone young die."

Coffee cups were put down abruptly, hands stilled over notebooks and laptops. There was one soft exhalation from a young woman on my right. Fair-haired and slight, her name was Karen. The name jarred me. The other Karen who liked to be called Courtney might have sat in this room just last year.

Several of the students wouldn't meet my eyes. I could hear their silent protests. This was philosophy, for Pete's sake. Why all this reality so early in the morning? This course met a distribution requirement for the Humanities Division, so we were blessed with the appearance of several science majors who clearly conveyed they were going through the motions. Well, no 'going through the motions' would work this morning.

"You felt pain when I said that, didn't you?" I looked at each person around the table, one at a time, waiting until she or he made eye contact. It took a while, but it was worth the time. No holding back here.

"So feeling that pain also makes it possible for you to know that love, commitment, and, in fact, being in a relationship are good things. You know that's good because you also feel bad about loss, maybe even the loss of someone young whom you didn't know. But it's loss, it's real."

One hand rose slowly. Isabelle Oliveira, an international student from Brazil. Second year science major.

"I didn't understand this reading on Aristotle at all. I thought after last week that we'd said pain and loss were the definition of evil from that other reading. Now we're supposed to think they're part of good?"

Her voice gained in strength as she voiced her grievance. Science majors thought definitions should hold up, not be offered one week and then unsettled again the next week.

Beside me Hercules lowered his chin to let his mustache hide his smile. Unsettled questions and ambiguity were his philosophy of life.

I glanced around the room, still trying to hold eye contact. It was heavy going.

"Anybody care to take a crack at answering Isabelle's question? The reading we had last week from Nel Noddings did say pain and loss define evil. So how can they also be part of good according to Aristotle? Do these thinkers disagree or is there a way these ideas can go together?"

I primed the pump a little by giving them the name of the author of last week's reading. Smart they might be, but in a school where the sciences and economics held supreme, philosophy came way down the list of things that needed to get read. They looked at their computer screens, or down at their backpacks contemplating whether they'd even brought that book from last week along (probably not) or they just took a sip of coffee. One student blew his nose in a wad of tissue.

They weren't going for it. Teaching can be threatening to one's self-esteem. I felt like a feminist stand-up comedian trying to get a bunch of Christian fundamentalists to laugh at her jokes about patriarchy.

The key is to wait.

Finally a large hand went up at the far end of the seminar table. Edwin Porterman, African American, six and a half feet tall, a brilliant economist. Edwin had one of the few athletic scholarships at this school, playing football to keep himself debt free. I'd met him in the fall. Playing on our Division III football team seemed not to tax him at all, and he was a straight A student in this university's challenging economics department. He must also have a campus job to earn extra money. I suddenly remembered he'd been one of the student workers helping to pass the canapés at the reception last night.

This class filled no distribution requirement for Edwin. He'd signed up at the beginning of this term as an audit. Edwin and I had a history. I'd been useful in preventing him from being accused of murder. But there was more about 'Good and Evil' that he was clearly working out in his own mind from the events of the fall. As I saw his serious brown eyes fixed steadily on me and Hercules each week, I wondered how he was doing with that self-imposed task. Edwin did nothing without deliberation.

I nodded at him and his measured voice rumbled out over the class.

"Aristotle and Noddings aren't disagreeing. They're saying that good is connected to evil and vice versa. The Stoics in Aristotle's time were saying you had to avoid all attachments to achieve happiness, because attachments bring pain. Aristotle said, 'right,' but attachments are also how you can know happiness. There's no ducking it."

He placed his large hands with their long, graceful fingers on top of the *Fragility of Goodness* book.

"This here is a philosophy of what life is really like—damned if you do, damned if you don't." His hands moved to grip the book as he ground out these words.

The other students stared. Not only pain but passion in the classroom. This was going from bad to worse. Physics did not normally include a punch to the solar plexus. And Edwin was the only African American in the class. Most of them tried to disguise it, but they were afraid of him, well indoctrinated by the drumbeat of white supremacy in this country. But they were also intimidated by his brilliance. Some of them probably secretly wanted to see his birth certificate.

The waves of discomfort that went around the room were nearly visible like heat in the desert.

Into the silence, a gentle voice spoke.

"Is this our damnation as humans, or is it our only salvation?" Hercules asked, easing the tension caused by their fears.

"If I cannot feel, am I not already a dead person, a thing of no passions?" His softly accented voice still had no trouble carrying around the whole room.

Hercules stood and walked unhurriedly to the other end of the seminar table where Edwin sat. He put a thin, parchment-colored hand down by Edwin's big brown one on the top of the book. He waited, their two hands resting side-by-side, liver spots and wrinkles next to dark youth and strength.

"Here is difference, and here is the same. Blood, muscles, nerves, same pain, same pleasure. Look carefully please." He paused, every eye on him and Edwin. I was holding my breath. I knew I was not the only one.

"When I do not see the same, only the different, I lose my own humanity. When I make a friend," here he slowly grasped Edwin's hand and shook it, "my life becomes richer. I have the good of friendship. But good is not without risk, because my friend is different from me. But that is also a pleasure."

I would give a lot to become the kind of teacher that makes the classroom a real place. I met Hercules's eyes down the length of the seminar table. Under his bushy white eyebrows, a brown eye winked at me. I laughed aloud with pleasure in this friendship. The students looked at us like we were crazy. All except Edwin. He shook Hercules's hand back so vigorously that the little man's whole frame moved up and down.

But the ice was broken. Hands rose all around the room. Friendship as both pleasure and pain is something young people trying to live in community are deeply concerned about.

8

I need to get out of here
Go somewhere
Get away
From myself
"Escape"
Amber Brown, #1100
StreetWise

Thursday, May 18, noon

By the time class ended, I was on such an adrenaline high I could have set rebounding records for the Chicago Bulls. Especially this year's Bulls. I headed down to my office, trying to process what had just happened in class.

When I'd run away from being a cop to being a graduate student in philosophy and religion, I'd not thought much at all about the teaching part of that career. I'd imagined myself sitting at a desk in a beautiful library made golden by light streaming in from stained glass windows while I did abstract scholarly research. In other words, I wanted to make a clean break from my former life. I'd tried that for a while and it was really boring. Not enough human contact for me. So I'd signed up to be a teaching assistant while I was doing my graduate classwork and I found I liked it. Liked it a lot, but I knew I needed to get better at it. Now, teaching with Hercules, I realized I needed to get a lot better at it. So far I had been taking the ideas from my notes and trying to pass them on to the students to put in their notes. But teachers like Hercules were—I dumped my books and bag on my desk—well, what were they? Soul shapers?

I shook myself briefly. Nah. Too romantic and sentimental. Well, Hercules was amazing in the classroom, whatever you called it. I checked my watch and could hardly believe the time. Adelaide was waiting for me. I grabbed my keys from among the pile on my desk and quickly locked the door behind me though I knew it wouldn't do much good since these doors all opened with the same key. But I was still on edge from the events of the fall and I dutifully locked up.

I hurried down the hall, but slowed down as I passed the coffee machine, tempted by its glorious coffee. But I thought I'd better hurry up. Adelaide's door was open so I knocked softly on the door jam and looked in.

Adelaide was seated on her couch. She really had changed the office to a much more welcoming set up. There were piles of paper on her desk and on the coffee table in front of the couch, along with books and a bowl of some kind of potpourri I hadn't noticed before. The feeling was more like visiting your favorite aunt who also just happened to have a Ph.D. and who was your boss. Much better than the former occupant who had decorated for intimidation.

Adelaide had not even raised her head in response to my knock. Her graying head was bent over whatever she was reading on her laptop. She also had a paper file folder open in front of her on the table. Next to the file were two brown bags and two coffee cups. I smelled turkey and, I took a really deep sniff, cappuccino. It seemed like lunch in the office was the plan.

I walked over and took one of the side chairs. Adelaide still didn't look up. She seemed totally engrossed in whatever she was reading.

I reached over and took one of the coffee cups—a logo on the side let me know the cup had come from the basement coffee shop of a seminary down the street, probably where Adelaide had gotten the sandwiches. "Where God Drinks Coffee" was their rather overblown motto. They were surely committing the sin of pride, though their coffee was actually quite good. But Adelaide had filled the cup with her own brew, I thought, as I sipped blissfully. God should try getting a De'Longhi.

I took a couple more sips and started to register that Adelaide's silence was continuing unabated. I studied her over the rim of my cup, and I didn't like what I saw. Adelaide is a large woman who usually sat with a strong upright posture. Now, she had drawn her shoulders in, her back was hunched, and even her knees were drawn in. She looked shrunken. I'd swear even the flowers on her dress were smaller than they'd been this morning. The hands gripping the sides of the laptop were white, fingertips red from the force of her clenched fingers.

What was this all about?

"Is that Karen who liked to be called Courtney's paper?" I asked in what I hoped was a neutral voice. I took another sip of the coffee and waited.

Adelaide shrugged her shoulders to release some of her tension and let out a long sigh.

She ran a hand over her eyes, as though to erase what she had been reading.

"I guess I'd forgotten, or probably repressed really, all the problems with this—with her. How extreme she was." She paused. "You know what that class covers, don't you?" she asked me.

Actually the history of feminist theory was not my forte.

"Give me a summary of how you approach it, would you?"

Adelaide gave me one of her 'you're not fooling me' looks, but she obliged.

"It's a huge field, from early women's rights work in the 18th century to postmodernist critiques of gender and sexuality in the 21st. Art, politics, science, psychology, language, and, yes, religion, are all part of it. So I just took themes and tried to trace their development. One big theme is the body. Students could choose to read two books from a list, and compare and contrast them. Some of these older works are so oblivious to race, to sexual orientation, to cultural differences, that I make the students deal with that by contrasting a more contemporary text." She paused again and gazed at the screen. "Karen chose *The Beauty Myth* by Naomi Wolf. She didn't choose a second book."

Even I'd heard of that book. It was older, but it came up all the time in the press, especially when a model died of anorexia. It was a broadside against the beauty industry.

"Yikes, Adelaide. What a topic for her to have chosen, given her looks."

"Exactly so." It was almost a groan.

Adelaide passed over her laptop. I put down the coffee cup and started skimming the paper. I was curious how someone so very beautiful would feel about Wolf's searing depiction of the way the beauty industry exploits women's deepest fears about their bodies. Even, really, creates those fears. Of course, that argument was always met with a barrage of denials and hostile counterattacks not only from the industry itself, but from conservative politicians and religious types. 'Women should dress like women' was the latest version of this.

I kept scrolling down the pages. Carlyle had been equally hostile. Phrases such as "sweeping generalization" and even "conspiracy theory" leapt out at me.

I glanced up at Adelaide. She had closed in on herself again, sitting hunched on the couch, looking down at her hands.

Carlyle had been more restrained in her critiques of Wolf in the first few pages of her paper, covering the sections of the book on culture, work, and religion. It was well written, and she had cited extensively from the text to show that, in her view, the argument was one-sided and biased.

But the chapter on sex had come in for a frenzied set of denials. The last page of the paper contained the conclusion and it fairly jumped off the screen. She had chosen to write it all in caps and it was astoundingly crude and explicit.

BEAUTY IS NOT ABOUT SUBMISSION, IT IS ABOUT CONTROL. THE AUTHOR HAS OBVIOUSLY NEVER IN HER LIFE EXPERIENCED THE POWER THAT COMES FROM THE ABILITY TO STIMULATE MEN'S SEXUAL FANTASIES. SHE RUNS ON ABOUT SADOMASOCHISM IN ADVERTISEMENTS SHOWING "WOMEN BEATEN, BOUND AND ABDUCTED, BUT IMMACULATELY TURNED OUT AND ARTISTICALLY PHOTOGRAPHED." BUT WHO LOSES CONTROL IN VIEWING SUCH PICTURES? NOT THE WOMEN POSING. THEY KNOW IT IS ALL ACTING. THE MEN LOSE CONTROL. THEY CAN'T KEEP FROM GETTING HARD. CLEARLY THE AUTHOR IS A DYKE AND THE PORN MAKES HER NIPPLES STAND UP AND PAY ATTENTION—BUT SHE'S TOO UGLY AND FAT TO BE ABLE TO GET A RISE OUT OF ANYONE, WITH ANYTHING.

"Yuck, as my kids would say. I'd hate to have been faced with this paper. What kind of grade did you give her?"

"I couldn't grade it. It's so—erratic, I guess you'd say. There are parts that deserve a D or even an F, but I could have given her a B on other parts. Though, of course, she only did half the assignment."

She reached out a hand for the laptop and I passed it over, the paper still on the screen. She skimmed up to the beginning.

"This first part isn't too bad. Wolf is a little broad in her characterizations. If she'd picked a book from the second list, it could have served as the basis of that critique."

Adelaide trailed off, reading the words again. She was frowning so deeply her usually plump, round face looked like one of those dried apple dolls, shrunken in on itself.

"So then what did you do?"

She closed the computer and put it on the table. She reached for her coffee and took a long drink. It must have cooled considerably by now.

I wasn't used to dithering from Adelaide. Even when she'd told me about a traumatic event in her early years of teaching, she'd been less skittish. Well, the only thing to do was wait her out. I picked up my own coffee and tried not to look impatient.

Finally she put down her cup and reached into the paper file folder that was on the table next to our uneaten sandwiches. She extracted a printed copy of an email. She passed it silently over to me.

> Dear Karen: You make some good points in your critique. Wolf does not pretend, however, that she is giving a "balanced view," a criticism you level. This genre of writing is guided more by the nineteenth century women's movement and its use of muckraking to force certain issues into the public arena where the barriers to their being heard are almost insurmountable. This is clearly Wolf's view. She contends the media is engaging in a cover-up of how the control of women's bodies through ideologies of beauty harms women.
>
> But before I can give you a grade, I'd like you come in and talk to me. Your class attendance has been sporadic and so perhaps you missed the instructions for this paper. You were required to compare the Wolf book to one of the other texts on the list I provided.
>
> I know we haven't seen eye to eye in this class, but I'd really like a chance to discuss this paper with you, particularly the conclusion.
>
> Please email me for an appointment.
>
> Sincerely, Dr. A. Winters

"You were a lot nicer than I would have been. Did she call?"

"No." A put off 'no' if I'd ever heard one. But I'm not that easily put off.

"Did you ever get a chance to talk to her about this?"

"No." This time uttered as a sigh that came practically from her arches.

"She'd already dropped out of school. I know. When I didn't hear back and she missed the next class, I called her dorm. Spoke with her roommate. She didn't know where Karen had gone. The roommate said she'd just come back to the room one day and a lot of Karen's stuff had been cleaned out. She'd left stuff behind, but had taken some items at least. I tried at the Dean of Students' office, and then at the Registrar. Just gone. I did get a home address and phone number from the Registrar. Minnesota some place. I called the phone number and whomever answered, father I assumed, though he didn't identify himself, said he'd no idea where she was and not to bother him again. He hung up. A real charmer. I took it she wouldn't have gone home."

Adelaide paused and took a sip of her coffee. Then she spoke again, but not looking at me. She turned slightly so she could look toward the large window on the far wall. The light faded her blue eyes to mirror gray, and I imagined I could see faded memory reflected there.

"She was so hostile in class. From day one. I don't know why she signed up for the class, or why she didn't just drop it when she saw what it was about."

She shrugged her large shoulders and then looked over at me, grimacing.

"I didn't handle her very well, I must say. But I'd never had a student even remotely like her. She was so brittle and she challenged everything I said, everything anyone said. I must say I felt relief when she started missing classes. The other students really disliked her, but she intimidated them too. If Karen and Courtney are the same person, then you've seen how stunning she was and she was always so beautifully dressed. It was so odd here where everyone tries to look like an unmade bed. She looked like her bed was made with those 1,000 thread count Italian sheets."

She put down her coffee cup and opened the computer again, turned it so I could see the screen, and scrolled up from the ghastly Wolf paper.

"She didn't like any of the reading, really. Her earlier work was a trifle better."

She stopped scrolling and looked at the screen.

"She was least hostile to Heilbrun, disliked MacKinnon, but it really was Wolf she detested. She actually said in class that Wolf's picture on the back of the book must be a fake because that woman was too good-looking to be the author."

Adelaide even cracked a small smile at that outrageous stereotype. Good. A little more perspective.

"What was the roommate's name?" I asked.

The wry smile turned into a rumbling chuckle.

"What?" I said, not getting what she was laughing at.

"Kid, you are still so much the cop, you know? You don't try to sympathize with me, you just nose in on whatever facts there are. It's rather bracing, like watching old TV shows like Dragnet."

She sat up a little straighter.

Well, I can be sympathetic. Sure I can. I just find it kind of wimpy.

"You know, Adelaide, if you'd like me to act like Donald and use some empathetic identification with you, I can try. But personally I always want to punch Donald when he tries that on me."

Despite being on sabbatical, my colleague in psychology and religion was apparently still irritating me. If you weren't careful, Donald would start identifying with you. I hoped he was using his leave to look for another job.

"Now don't get all huffy about it."

Huffy? I opened my mouth to protest and Adelaide cut me off.

"Let's see what I kept in her file. I may have the names and numbers of the people I tried. If you have any luck getting contact information for her, let me know. Karen should see my comments on her work, I mean, should have seen . . . " She paused, remembering.

"I mean, well, just let me know if you find out where she went after she quit."

I thought Adelaide was too smart to blame herself for Karen/Courtney leaving school, but obviously she did harbor some guilt, probably over her relief when the beautiful bitch had started skipping class.

I watched as Adelaide's plump hands moved carefully through the papers in the file. What kind of a person ridicules the unlovely to a person who looks like Adelaide? Was it calculated cruelty? A power trip in the classroom, queening it over the large, older woman teacher and her collection of badly made beds? Or had Karen/Courtney been so self-centered she'd not even been aware of her audience? No, I thought it was a power trip, remembering that gloating paragraph on beauty as sexual power. Maybe she'd quit school to try to find a rich husband. Hence the distinctly unlovely but very possibly well-off Dr. Russell Wagner. Apparently ugly in men hadn't counted for much with Karen. I mean Courtney.

Adelaide plucked a yellow memo sheet from the pile and handed it to me.

"Here it is—the roommate's name from last year, Bonnie Roddenberg. This is last year's number, of course. I don't know where she's living this year, or even if she's still a student. Below that is the address and phone number in Minnesota."

She gathered the papers back into the file and started to shut down the computer file of Karen/Courtney's work.

"Wait a minute, Adelaide. Could you email me a copy of those papers she wrote? I'd like to look at them again."

"Sure. I guess. I'll do it now so I remember."

She lifted the computer on to her lap and started tapping keys.

I assumed the young woman who died had been identified by now, but I didn't know. I also didn't want to bring it up right now, but if Karen and Courtney were the same Carlyle, and if her death was not accidental, her student work was evidence. I would like to read the papers, and if Adelaide had kept that file this long, I was sure I could trust her to keep it longer.

Adelaide closed the computer with a snap.

"I'll tell you this, Kristin. That was a brilliant young woman who was cursed with how beautiful she was. Her brains got her into a first-class university, but here, her beauty counted for nothing. Or less than nothing. It actually counted against her. Beauty here means dumb. Just another damn stereotype Wolf could have helped her see if she'd just let her in. But no.

"And the other students, they didn't see it either. They just channeled the dumb blonde stereotype as their defense against Karen. If she'd had contempt for them, they gave it back to her in spades."

A pause.

"Me too, I'm afraid."

Adelaide reached for her turkey sandwich.

9

I know what that means
Dead and Buried
Nobody cries
Nobody remembers
No body.
Pamela Green, #1121
"Funeral"
StreetWise

Thursday, May 18, 1 p.m.

I walked to my office on autopilot, trying to process my conversation with Adelaide. I was actually surprised when I arrived at the door since I had no memory of getting there. It took me a few seconds after I had unlocked the door to register that the phone on the desk was ringing. I scrambled through the outer part of the office, banging my hip on the desk of my former office mate who'd quit Philosophy and Religion for the higher pay scales of the computer sciences. I jerked the phone off the hook, hoping voicemail had not picked up. I hated our office voicemail. It malfunctioned frequently, giving back only half a message or not even letting you access your messages. And you couldn't turn it off. People left messages you couldn't get and then they got furious at you for not returning their calls. They would call back, leaving an irate message that you couldn't get and so on. But I gave my cell phone number to very few people, so I'd have to live with this phone system.

"Yes!" I grunted into the phone, using my other hand to rub my hip where I'd bumped it.

"Kristin? It's Tom. I was just about to leave a message."

"Thank God you didn't," I breathed.

"What?"

"Nothing. How are you? How are your hands?"

"Fine. Fine."

Sure they were.

"How are you holding up?" Tom asked.

"Actually, it's the most amazing thing. I was going to call you. I think I got some information on the victim. Have they definitely identified her yet?"

"Who?"

Oh yes, Tom would think of her as a patient, not a victim.

"The person we hauled out of the cement last night."

Voices on Tom's end.

"Wait a minute, Kristin. Just a minute."

I could hear more voices, all talking at once it seemed. Tom seemed to be surrounded with people who had questions that couldn't wait apparently. Probably medical students and residents. I hit the speakerphone button and sat down to try to make some order out of all the detritus of paper that kept accumulating. I reached into my backpack for the stack I'd picked up from under the nervous eyes of Mary Frost this morning. I added them to the pile of paper that was clinging precariously to the edge of the desk with the same dogged tenacity as those who sent snail mail in the age of the Internet. I took a bunch at random and plopped them in front of me. I pulled over my blue recycling bin and began skimming and tossing, skimming and tossing. It was so rhythmic I was startled when Tom's voice suddenly came out of the speakerphone.

"Kristin? You still there?"

"Yes, I'm still here." And I've lost several pounds of trash.

"Sorry about that. Listen. I've only got a minute, but the Chief of Surgery's office called and the guy who's in charge of the Anderson building project, the contractor? Do you remember him? I think he was the tall one speaking at the reception."

The barbarian.

"Yes, I remember."

"His name is Cullen O'Shea. He's president of O'Shea Construction and he's got a box at the United Center. We're invited for Saturday night. Can you make it? I need to call them back right away."

Tom sounded like a kid. Well, it was the homestretch of the basketball season and while these were not the Chicago Bulls of the Jordan era, it sounded like fun. It used to be easier to get plutonium than tickets for the Bulls. Maybe it still was. I didn't know. Not something the boys were old enough to enjoy.

"I'll have to check with Carol and Giles, but I think it will be okay. I'll call them and then just text you."

"Good, then that will take care of Kelly, too."

"No, Tom, wait. About Kelly coming over. I told you it didn't work the other . . . "

"Just a minute, Kristin." Damn. More voices. I went back to working on my pile of paper.

"Kristin, you there?"

"Yes. Look, Tom, Kelly does not like . . . "

"Wait, Kristin." A pause. "That's the hospital attorney paging me. The neurologist has seen the Carlyle woman and there is no evidence of brain function. They still can't identify her and locate any family."

I yanked up the receiver of the phone and fairly shouted into it.

"Stop for a minute and listen to me! I was trying to tell you. I think I know who she is and who her family is. And since you are saying they have not been able to find out, this is crucial."

"What? What do you mean you think you know who she is? There was no identification beyond the name Russell gave the police and they haven't been able to trace that name at all."

I gave Tom a quick run through of my conversation with Adelaide. I fairly tripped over the words thinking we'd be interrupted again. I heard the buzz of voices around him. It sounded like he was standing in a beehive.

But he listened.

"Kristin, I'd better have the attorney call her directly. Your Dr. Winters will need to come here and make an identification."

Oh, great. Just what "my" Dr. Winters needed right now.

"Okay, Tom, but give the lawyer my cell phone number. I'll walk down to Dr. Winters's office and wait there for the call."

"Fine. The lawyer's name is Rachel Koppelman."

"When she calls, I'll answer and then hand the phone over."

I hoped Adelaide was still in her office.

I grabbed my cell phone and slammed out the door. As I hustled down the hall, it dawned on me that Tom and I still hadn't had the Kelly conversation. Not good.

# # # #

I hadn't even given a thought to what I'd do if Adelaide had gone out, or had a class, but as I reached her open door I saw she was still in her office, still sitting on the couch, in fact. I just stood opposite her and brought her quickly up to date.

"Identify her? Now?" Adelaide heaved herself off the couch and stood. She glared at me, her hands clenching into fists at her sides. Her whole body was tense. You can see why it's always the messenger who gets killed in Greek tragedies.

I stood my ground, literally, and spoke in what I hoped was a level tone of voice.

"Somebody has to. The family needs to know. You know that."

Her shoulders slumped and her whole body shrank again.

"Yeah. Sure. I know." A pause. "Come with me?"

"Absolutely."

Just then the cell phone in my hand rang. Ms. Koppelman, I presumed. "I think this is the hospital lawyer." I answered.

It was indeed Ms. Koppelman. I identified myself and said I was with Dr. Winters. Koppelman asked to speak to her and I handed the phone over.

"Hello. Dr. Winters here." Adelaide listened.

"Well, I don't know for certain, of course, but I am willing to go visit this young woman."

More listening.

"Oh, yes. For at least half a semester."

Pause.

"Right now? Fine. Meet you there. I'll bring what I have." She sat down and wrote on a pad on the coffee table and hung up.

She looked up at me with eyes that had again turned cloudy and old.

"Surgical Tower, room B317. Know where it is?"

"I think so. I know where the Surgical Tower is."

"Good. Get your stuff and meet me in the hall . . . Oh, and Kristin?"

I paused in the doorway.

"You'll never get tenure. I swear."

Adelaide picked up Karen/Courtney's file and started for her office closet.

I hoped Adelaide was kidding about the 'no tenure'. On the other hand, she didn't seem to be in the mood to joke around.

# # # #

It was only a few minutes walk from our offices to one of the entrances to the university hospital, but then it took another fifteen minutes to reach the surgical tower. The hospital is huge, covering several large city blocks. The addition of the Anderson building would add another block.

That hospital smell—sweetly cloying antiseptic covering God-knows-what—had saturated our clothes and hair before we'd walked even half the distance. Adelaide didn't speak. She just walked steadily along, her head down. I felt kind of like a rat for involving her in this. It was a feeling I had rather a lot in my life.

We finally reached the surgical tower and took the elevator to the third floor. Signs pointed to the Intensive Care Unit and those numbers matched the ones on Adelaide's paper. Tom met us outside the ICU. He was standing with a small, dark haired woman of about thirty. She had a skinny little jogger's body stuffed into a skinny little gray three-piece suit complete with vest and a small tie. Must be the lawyer, I thought, though I thought this dressing like a guy would if he were a woman had gone out of style. Not with women lawyers apparently.

She stuck out an arm the size of a stick and the little hand at the end of it grasped my hand.

"Dr. Winters?"

"No." I let go of the bird hand. "This is Dr. Winters," I said, indicating Adelaide. Maybe I shouldn't overreact. We'd just been discussing Naomi Wolf who argues that women who are older and overweight are literally invisible in our culture. Maybe Ms. Koppelman had just made a mistake.

"Really?" she squeaked.

Maybe I wasn't overreacting. Adelaide and I said nothing.

Tom put out his hand and spoke into the frozen silence.

"Hello, Dr. Winters. I'm Tom Grayson. Kristin talks about you all the time. I'm glad to make your acquaintance at last."

Adelaide, despite the stress she must be feeling, shook Tom's hand and took a long moment to look him over carefully. He actually blushed a little.

"Pleased to meet you. I've heard so little about you, but I'm sure that will change, right, Kristin?" Adelaide let go of Tom's hand and gave me a sideways look.

I mumbled something. I had a feeling I'd be paying for my detective work on Carlyle for a long time.

Koppelman contented herself with a nod at Adelaide. Then she turned and clicked on her tiny spiked heels to the door of the ICU and held the door open. We went in.

I don't make it a point to hang around medical centers, but I'd been in an ICU before to visit a cop friend who had been severely wounded on the job. He had fortunately survived. I had been startled by how much an ICU looks like the deck of the Starship Enterprise. Tiers of computer screens and monitors wink in the subdued light. They are arrayed in a semicircle with swivel chairs in front of them. This was the same kind of set-up. Most of the chairs were occupied, but all we could see were white-coated backs intent on the screens in front of them, or typing on computers arranged on the desk.

Tom and Koppelman moved ahead and Tom spoke quietly to one of the figures at the desk. That white-coated figure got up and led us to a glassed-in room a short way from the command center.

Through the glass, I could see a figure on the bed, motionless and supine, the small frame barely lifting the blankets. The golden hair was hidden by an opaque cap and tubes entering her nose and mouth distorted her features. Leads from under her gown snaked from her chest to monitors that blinked beside the bed, lines and data running across them. The sound of the air being pushed in and out of her lungs was loud and jarring. Her skin was alabaster in color and looked to be as cold. Would Adelaide even be able to recognize her beautiful student in this fragile husk of humanity? We silently trooped into the room.

"May I touch her?" Adelaide asked in the hushed tones the eerie surroundings seemed to demand. If anyone spoke in a normal tone of voice I think I would have jumped out of my skin.

Tom nodded. I glanced at the energetic Rachel Koppelman, but even she seemed subdued by the setting.

Adelaide spoke as she moved toward the bed.

"Karen Carlyle had a distinctive scar inside her right wrist. She tried to keep it covered, but it is quite large and I saw it several times. It looked like a burn scar."

She fell silent and drew back the covers to reveal the right arm with its IV tube taped down on the pale skin. As she did so, the short sleeve of the loose hospital gown flopped to the side, exposing the upper part of the arm. A bruise circled her bicep. A bruise with four distinct circles. Four fingers. If we raised the arm, I suspected we would see the thumb print too. I knew that bruise hadn't been on her arm at the reception. The spaghetti straps of her gown had left nothing covered on her upper arm and this ugly stain of bruising had not been there then. I had not touched that part of her arm as I was trying to lasso her wrist in the concrete. And I very much doubted the hospital personnel handled their patients roughly enough to leave bruises.

"Yes, here it is." Adelaide had turned the wrist slightly and she touched it ever so softly. We could all see the puckered scar. I hadn't seen that before.

Courtney/Karen had worn long gloves to the reception. Now I understood why. Adelaide slowly, carefully, turned the wrist back and covered the arm with the blanket.

Adelaide, Tom and Koppelman turned wordlessly and headed back to the corridor. I waited until their backs were turned and then quickly pulled down the blanket covering the other arm and lifted the sleeve of the gown. Identical bruises circled it. I uncovered the arm with the scar as well, reached into my pocket where I'd tucked my cell phone and took several quick photos of both arms, and then a full body shot. I was sure that was totally against hospital rules, but I wanted a record. Then I drew the gown and the blanket back up over both pale little arms with their purple stains. I hustled out into the hall.

"Well," Ms. Koppelman was saying brightly. "Thank you, Dr. Winters. You said you had her home number and her parents' names?"

Adelaide dug silently in her large purse and pulled out Karen's file. She extracted the memo sheet with the contact information and handed it over.

"So, I'll contact the family and also let the police know. They'll contact you directly, Dr. Winters. Could I have the best number for them to reach you?"

Adelaide stoically recited a phone number and Koppelman typed it into her cell contacts directly. She pocketed her phone.

"We appreciate your help." Without saying good-bye she turned and clicked rapidly away.

Adelaide looked up at me and cocked a gray eyebrow.

"Police too? It's so educational knowing you, Kristin."

I really hoped she had been joking about no tenure.

Adelaide solemnly told Tom good-bye and trooped away down the corridor, the blinking lights from central monitors making her look like a figure from a silent movie, fading in and out.

"Tom," I said, watching her. "I'd better go with her."

I touched his hand and hurried after her. When I caught up, we walked slowly side-by-side. Adelaide steadily and determinedly talked about the faculty searches we had underway for our department.

I wasn't really listening.

Neither was she.

# # # #

As I unlocked my office door, I heard the phone ringing again. As I raced to pick up the phone, I did manage to avoid hitting my hip on the corner of Henry's old desk, but then I was too late to get the phone. I labored through the access number, my security code and the menu, chose messages and finally got to hear Alice's voice telling me she was waiting at the new coffee shop next to the hospital and she'd be there for the next 20 minutes. Swearing under my breath, I texted her I'd be there as fast as I could. Why did people just not text in the first place? I loved texting for the same reason the original Sherlock Holmes had preferred telegrams. Short and to the point. No chitchat.

I raced back down the stairs and headed back toward the hospital. The new coffee shop was right next-door, run by a chain bookstore. The most famous academic bookstore in the country, perhaps in the world, was the Seminary Cooperative Bookstore, located on the opposite side of the campus across from the Oriental Institute, a museum created with effectively all the loot the colonial era of archeology had been able to collect and then hold on to despite protests from the original countries where they'd been 'found.' The Seminary Coop, as it was called, did not serve coffee. In fact, they'd hung a cartoon on the door of an irate man in a bookstore, yelling at a clerk. "What do you mean you don't serve coffee? What kind of a bookstore is this?" One that sold books, apparently.

The coffee conflicts on campus were symbolic, I mused, as I hustled toward where Alice was waiting. This new coffee shop had replaced the original student hangout, the "C Shop." The C Shop had been dark and dirty, with cracked linoleum floors and scarred wooden tables with uneven legs. Faded photos of the legendary past of the university had lined the walls, from graduation in 1919 with women in long white dresses with ivy trailing from their hair to, of course, the football games at the old field. Horse-drawn carriages in faded black and white were shown circling the stands, the horses' breath rising as steam in the freezing cold. It had been marvelous.

The new coffee shop was bright and cheerful, with faux wood paneling below a chair rail, and golden, marbled wallpaper above. Faux Tiffany lamps hung down over faux French wrought iron cafe tables, and all their legs were even. You could get a skinny latte with cinnamon. It was ghastly and it boded ill for the future of a university that had permitted it.

The essence of the University of Chicago and in my opinion its very best thing for a long time was a kind of genteel seediness, conveying quite distinctly, 'don't bother us with material reality, we're thinking here.' Now that culture was being diluted and even distorted by chain bookstores and bright, shiny faux everything. Who are we now? I wondered as I approached. It depressed me to think about that so I usually avoided this new coffee shop. So did older faculty and some graduate students. Others, like hospital administrators, doctors, staff and campus cops loved it. It was clean, warm, the coffee was hot and the service was fast. Alice liked it and compared it favorably to that 'other dump.'

I entered and saw with relief she was still there, but outside in a garden area complete with more little faux French garden furniture. She was smoking and staring off into space. I went by the coffee bar, got myself a plain black coffee without vanilla, cinnamon, hazelnuts or other additives. I tapped my ID on the scanner and was out the door in less than a minute. It was fast, I'd give them that.

I hurried over to Alice's table.

"Hi, lady."

She looked up at me almost without recognition for a minute. She'd clearly been very much elsewhere. She ground out her cigarette in the little box of sand she carried in her purse. She put it away.

"Yeah, Kristin. Hey—didn't know if you'd make it," she said slowly, without her usual energy.

I knew better than to ask what was wrong. If Alice wanted to tell me, she'd tell me, but she was a very private person so I knew from experience not to pry. Before I'd even gotten my butt into the little chair, I started talking, not knowing how long she could stay.

Alice went from brooding to all cop in about sixty seconds when I mentioned the woman I'd pulled out of the elevator shaft. She started digging around in her jacket pocket for her notebook, and as I brought her up to date on my conversation with Adelaide, the class the young woman had been taking with her and the student's difficulties in school, she was taking furious notes. When I moved on to going to the hospital for the identification, she held up a hand, the blunt-tipped fingers stained with nicotine.

"Wait a minute, girl. Slow down here. You say this teacher friend of yours," she tapped the notebook, "Dr. Winters, made a positive ID? The victim is a student?"

"Had been a student. She dropped out last year."

"And there's a family? Hospital got that info?"

I nodded.

"Do the city cops know?"

"The lawyer said she'd notify them."

"Okay then. So what's all this mess about her troubles with the schoolwork? Some book she didn't like, you said? What's that all about?" Alice raised her eyebrows and her shrewd brown eyes reflected her skepticism.

"The book is by a woman named Naomi Wolf. Well, to back up, it's an older text in a sort of survey course Dr. Winters' teaches on the history of feminism. This Courtney Carlyle woman, whose real first name is Karen by the way, was in the class. Wolf wrote a blistering critique of the beauty industry, how they promote impossible beauty standards for women, causing them to starve themselves, use cosmetics they don't need, get plastic surgery and so forth. The kid took on the book to review and just hated it. The paper's so angry it's frightening."

Alice put down her notebook and pen, and picked up her coffee cup with such force she actually bent the cardboard. She frowned down at the lid.

"Why'd she care? She was a honey—you said so—so why get so pissed? She's got no reason. Now somebody like me . . . " She stopped. Raised her head and her eyes were no longer skeptical, they were narrowed in anger.

"That's all we see, you know? Skinny white blond with a tight ass. Nothin' like the wide hips, big lips and natural hair need apply. You know that fuss the media made about Michelle Obama's arms? Or for Christ's sake, Serena Williams?" She slapped her abused coffee cup down on the table again.

"So this woman Wolf, she's white, right?"

I nodded.

"What does she have to say about that?"

Nothing. Just nothing.

I took a breath.

"Well, she doesn't exactly address race."

Alice looked up at the trees and slivers of sky. I didn't know if she was asking heaven for help or she just couldn't stand looking at me for a minute.

"All right," I said. "Hell, you're right. Nothing. She's white and she's talking to white women. And this young white woman got hysterical about it. Why? I don't know. I do know she's over in the hospital and she's brain dead. Maybe the paper has something to do with it. That's all."

"Uh huh."

Alice pulled her purse toward her and took out a pack of cigarettes and her lighter, looking at me the whole time, daring me to make a comment. I kept my mouth shut, but I glared right back. She took out a cigarette but didn't light it. She twirled it between her fingers.

"Maybe, maybe not," she said slowly. "I'll pass this on. Stammos wants everything given to him personal." She was talking like the earlier words had not been said. But they had. I could see them hanging in the sunlight filtering down on us through the trees. She continued without a break.

"Said at morning meeting, anybody hear anything, bring it to him. No word yet if it's accident, suicide or murder—though Chicago homicide came by to see him today. I heard, anyway. They talk to you yet?"

I shook my head no.

"They will."

She gulped the dregs of her cold coffee from her ruined cup and started to shrug into her jacket.

"Alice."

"Leave it, Kristin. Just leave it. There's nothing you can do about it."

I hate it when people tell me there's nothing I can do about something.

"I don't believe that, Alice."

She stood and looked at me. Standing, Alice is not that much taller than I am sitting. She barked a laugh.

"I know, girl. But race ain't somethin' you can think your way out of. I don't care how many books you read."

She took out her lighter and lit the cigarette she was still holding.

She left, trailing smoke and resignation.

I sat for a moment and contemplated the racks of books that I could see through the big windows of the coffee shop/bookstore. They seemed cheapened by their proximity to the faux marble and the fake wood paneling. I jumped to my feet. I'd better get out of here before I became as faux as this coffee shop. Though maybe what Alice saw is that I already was.

10

More buildings go up, up, up
The homeless still sleep in the doorways
Their lives go down, down, down.
"Down But Not Out"
Mrs. Eliza Hayes, #596
Streetwise

Thursday, May 18, 3 p.m.

I left via the garden area rather than go back in and have to pass the coffee-tainted books one more time. As I turned the corner, up the street I saw a small group of people gathered in front of the Anderson building construction site. One campus security car was pulled up, its lights flashing. I was still traumatized by my last experience on this job site and I immediately started to wonder if someone else had had a fatal 'accident' here. Instead of heading back to my office, I slowly walked down the block toward the crowd, fearful and yet curious as to what I would find.

A large wooden fence, broken occasionally by industrial chain-link, had been put up around the square block where the building was going up. The sections of wood did not have the kind of graffiti you normally found at a construction site. This was, after all, the University of Chicago. One, quite neatly spray-painted message read "God is Dead—Nietzsche." And directly below it, another said, "Nietzsche is Dead—God." Two other scrawls were in classical Greek. At least I thought it was classical Greek. Could be modern. That graffiti was less neatly painted and the paint had dripped. I felt a little philosophical pride at the neatness of those dueling over Nietzsche.

There were gates in the chain-link with "No Trespassing!" signs hung on them.

The gates ahead of me where the crowd had gathered were open, and as I got closer, I could just see the front of a car parked on the street, blocking that entrance. Next to the car, blocking the street, was a concrete truck. I almost turned to head back to the office. Just another parking dispute. There is never enough parking around the campus and parking disputes were common. The parking conflicts were usually not violent, as was often the case in Boston, where it was scarcely unusual for people to duke it out over a parking space near Harvard Yard. Here, an exchange of biting remarks was more the norm.

Just then, the group of gapers parted slightly and I could see that the car, an older Chevrolet convertible, with the top down, was filled with concrete. The chute from the concrete truck was still poised over the back seat and small globs of gray matter were sliding down and plopping onto the load in the already filled car.

This is not something one sees every day and I walked closer, wondering how on earth such an accident could have happened.

I was now at the rear of the group of onlookers and I could see a red-faced twenty-something man, wearing a maroon "GSB," for Graduate School of Business, sweatshirt waving his arms and yelling. The rumble, rumble, rumble of the turning drum of the concrete truck made it impossible to hear what he was saying, but his long narrow face was contorted in rage. A young campus cop was standing ineffectively by, as nonplussed by what was, I have to admit, an unusual development in a parking dispute.

The GSB student's ire was being directed not at the young cop, however, but at the tall, red-haired man who'd been speaking at the Anderson reception. Tom had called him Cullen O'Shea. O'Shea was easily a foot taller than the irate grad student who, I guessed, was the owner of the car. O'Shea was just looking down at him while he ranted, plainly trying not to laugh, which was, of course, enraging the student even more.

Suddenly I realized I recognized the tall, thin back right in front of me. I'd just seen that frayed khaki jacket and long black ponytail. Jordan Jameson, a student in Hercules's and my class. Math major.

"Jordan," I said. No answer. He was still intent on the action. I touched his shoulder lightly. "Jordan!"

"Yeah?" He turned, a little startled. His pale, oval face was blank for a second. Then I saw recognition. He had his cell phone up and I could see it was still recording. He kept it pointed forward, even as he looked sideways at me. I registered that almost everyone in the crowd of onlookers had their cell phones out, also recording the scene.

"Oh, it's you, Professor Ginelli."

"Hi, Jordan. What happened here?"

"Oh, it's rich," said Jordan, his narrow chest contracting as he chuckled. I got most of it here on video. Wanna see?"

"No, thanks, Jordan. Just tell me."

"Well, okay. With the noise of that concrete truck now I'm not getting the audio anyway. So that guy there," and he pointed with the hand not holding the phone to the agitated young man in the GSB sweatshirt, "Well, he parked his car in the loading zone for the construction, see?" He pointed again.

I nodded. I saw.

"Well, I was crossing the street up there on my way to work in the computer lab."

Naturally.

"And I saw the whole thing. Good thing I pulled out my cell phone right away and started getting it, though I never thought . . . well, anyway, you see that other guy, the real tall guy with red hair?" He pointed again. His mother must never have mentioned pointing was rude.

"Well, he yells at the kid, 'You can't park there you blankety blank, but the kid ignores him." Here Jordan blushed slightly. I take it back. He must have been raised right. You didn't repeat swear words in front of women or women profs. Of course, it was all on the video.

"The guy whose car it is just flips him the finger and starts walking away. So the tall guy yells again, 'The concrete truck can't get in!'"

Just then another campus police car pulled up. Jordan checked the frame on his cell recording, not wanting to miss anything, but he continued.

"So anyway. The guy whose car it is flips the big guy the finger again and walks even faster down the street."

I could see what was coming, but I couldn't quite believe it.

Jordan started chuckling again.

"So calm as you please, the big guy goes over to the concrete truck, says a few words to the driver, the concrete truck starts rumbling, and the big guy unhooks that chute thing there and swings it so it's over the front seat of the car. The guy whose car it is has gotten about halfway down the block by now, but then he glances back. He stops. Can't believe it. Takes a few steps back. Right then, the big guy says to the truck driver, 'Hit it!' Concrete pours out and fills the front seat. Then . . . "

Jordan has to stop he's laughing so hard.

He wiped his eyes with the back of his hand and continued.

"Then the GSB guy starts yelling and running back. The big guy pays no attention. Still calm as you please, he moves the chute so it's over the back seat and it fills up too. Then he says, 'Hold it,' to the truck driver. The concrete stops pouring out. Then bang! bang! Two of the car's tires go flat."

Jordan checked his screen again to be sure the scene in front of us was still well-framed, concerned not to miss recording anything, though what else could top that I couldn't imagine.

Well, I was wrong. Commander Nick Stammos got out of the second police car. He marched directly over to O'Shea and started speaking. He only came up to O'Shea's chest, but clearly was getting his respectful attention where the GSB student had failed. The GSB student was, of course, still on the scene and now was making the mistake of trying to yell at Stammos. He was quelled with a glance.

Well, I'd nicknamed O'Shea well when I'd called him the barbarian. Though clearly a barbarian with a great sense of humor, kind of an Attila the Comic. Stammos, on the other hand, had no sense of humor that I'd ever been able to discern. His square back in its blue uniform jacket was rigid and he was standing, legs akimbo, and arms by his side with fists clenched.

Stammos seemed to have finished with O'Shea and he turned toward the irate GSB student. A curt gesture cut off a renewed stream of complaints. Calmly, Stammos extended a hand to the young cop who, I'd observed, had said exactly nothing and took his pad from him. He then proceeded to write on the pad. It looked like he was writing GSB a parking ticket. GSB took what Stammos handed him and read it. Disbelief spread over his red, shiny face, rounding his little eyes behind their horn-rimmed glasses to probably twice their size. He looked stunned. I know I'd think twice from now on about parking in a construction loading zone.

GSB looked up from the piece of paper in his hand to protest, but Stammos was already gone, over talking to the driver of the concrete truck. The truck moved on down the street and turned the corner. I saw a tow truck pulling up on the street it had vacated. The show was over. Jordan glanced over at me briefly, and smiled a sideways smile, reminding me of Disney's Goofy.

"Gotta go," he said, and loped off down the street.

I bet he was going to be late to work. First he had to upload his astonishing video. It was going to go viral, that's for certain. Along with all the other videos of this unbelievable event that were even now being sent into the cloud and out to other phones, iPads and computers.

I looked back over at the construction site. O'Shea was negligently leaning one of his huge shoulders against the fence with his arms folded across his chest. St. George taking it easy after having slain the dragon right on the drawbridge of his castle. I hoped the fence wouldn't leave a stain on the beautiful camel hair jacket he was wearing. It was obviously custom-made.

The soft tan of the jacket was set off by a rust-colored mock turtle cashmere sweater (I assumed it was cashmere, I mean, wouldn't it be?) underneath. Perfectly pressed pants fell unwrinkled to the tops of his calfskin loafers. Bruno Magli? Could be. Kind of over-dressed for a construction site.

Suddenly I realized he had become aware of my scrutiny and was looking at me. He smiled. I smiled back. I had to. In a world of Mandel Griffiths, we were both people who just acted and damn the consequences. The last of a dying breed. The Barbarian and the Viking. It sounded like a romance novel.

He moved away from the fence and crossed the street behind where the concrete-filled car was being loaded onto the flatbed tow truck. As he came toward me, he glanced back at the mess he'd made. The tow truck operator was shaking his head as his winch whined in protest at the weight of loading a car filled with concrete. O'Shea smiled again.

"Hello," he said, his smile widening. He extended a beautifully manicured hand.

"I'm Cullen O'Shea."

I took his hand. It was warm and dry. No sweaty palm to betray that his casual pose was an act.

"Yes, I'd assumed so," I said. "Only the boss would have taken such a novel approach to the parking problem around here."

I nodded to the huge sign on the fence down the block that said, "O'Shea Construction" in large green letters on a stark white background, and below, only slightly smaller, "Cullen O'Shea, President." In the upper left hand corner, a leprechaun in a hard hat operated a crane. His smile was nearly as infectious as the one O'Shea was directing at me.

"Ah, well, I know the lawyers will have a jolly good time over this one. It's not the first time that little jerk has parked in our loading zone, causing us delays. He won't do it again. And I did enjoy myself there, I did. And you are?" he prompted, giving me the full Irish treatment, blue eyes twinkling, tanned face breaking into a smile that followed grooves made by years of laughter, while his white teeth sparkled.

"My name is Kristin Ginelli. I teach here. Actually, I'm supposed to be at your Bulls game party tomorrow night," I said while extracting the hand that he had kept holding.

"Wonderful. Wonderful," O'Shea said warmly. "I've loved your Chicago Bulls for a long time now, even though it betrays me own New York Knicks. Since I'm in Chicago now a while for this little project I thought I'd start to enjoy the lads in person. I'll hate to give it up!"

I was still impressed by his clout, as he meant me to be. You can't just waltz up to the Bulls team office and rent a box for a season.

His smile suddenly dimmed.

"Ginelli?" He paused, clearly thinking. "Ah, you're the lady who witnessed our unfortunate accident here now, are you not?" His Irish brogue seemed to come and go, depending on how charming he wished to be. Now it was more subdued, there only in the rhythms of his speech.

"Yes, I am." I looked up at the skeleton of the Anderson building rising behind his head and shoulders, the beams black and silver against the increasingly cloudy sky.

O'Shea turned to follow my gaze.

"Such a cryin' shame that was. Young woman like that, off on her own. These construction sites are dangerous places when ye don't know what ye're doin'." The brogue was back, big time.

Before I could reply, Commander Stammos came up to where we were standing.

"Good afternoon, Professor," he said formally to me. He turned to O'Shea and gestured for him to walk a little away from me.

"Cullen, you'll need to make a statement later. I'll call you." Even though they'd moved away slightly, I could tell Stammos was still smoldering with anger. His dark brows met in one continuous line across his brow and his eyes were slits. But O'Shea scarcely seemed intimidated.

"Fine, fine, Nick. Anything you say." He slapped Stammos on the back. He might have been agreeing to meet for an after-work drink.

O'Shea came back to where I was standing and took my arm and led me across the street. I normally don't tolerate such 'lord of the manor' behavior, but I wanted to see where this was going. I glanced back and looked at Stammos. He was still clearly pissed off, perhaps even more so that he had been dismissed so abruptly by O'Shea. I saw that he was looking at us, so I turned away and kept walking.

"That Nick," O'Shea was saying, laughing and shaking his big head. "That boyo does not know how to take a joke. Not for anything would he laugh at the face of that little bugger and his car all loaded up like that." O'Shea chuckled.

"I take it you know each other?" I said, smiling back. I wouldn't admit it to O'Shea, but I also found Stammos to be too rigid from what I'd seen of him.

"Oh, my yes, for a dog's age now. When I was hauling bricks for me uncle in New York, Nicko was the new kid on the block—just come out of the academy. Brave and strong he was in his fine, clean uniform, star always shined up pretty. We'd put away a flock of beer before he'd start to bend his back a little." O'Shea stopped at the stairs of a construction office trailer and turned to me. "But he's a good man in a fight, is Nicko. None better." He looked down the street pensively as the police car with Stammos in it was moving away. Then he turned and looked down at me.

"Would you do me a big favor, now, Professor? Would you come with me and show me where you were when that young lady fell? Sure and it's gonna cost me—these bloody, sorry, these penny-pinching insurance blokes have been all over me since that time. And now this." He nodded toward where the concrete-laden car had stood. He gave a rueful grin, still completely unrepentant about the stunt he'd pulled. His voice trailed off but his 1000 watt grin was back on as he gazed down at me expectantly.

"Please call me Kristin, and yes, I'd like to do that. I'd like to see that place again myself." Maybe I could shake some of the bad dreams if I saw that floor and elevator shaft again in the daylight.

All the shades of tan and rust and red made O'Shea look like a huge tabby cat. Now he looked like a huge tabby that'd gotten the canary. I wondered why. I didn't think I could tell him much that would help his insurance problems. Though, come to think of it, maybe I could. Accidentally tripping on some lumber or rope and falling into a shaft would be his liability. Murder would be somebody else's liability. Liability for life.

"And you must call me Cullen," he said, and then he bounded up the stairs into the trailer. In a minute he returned with two construction helmets. These were not the nice white ones with Anderson Building stenciled neatly on the brim. The Martha Stewart ones. The one Cullen held out to me had probably once been bright yellow, but now was so battered and stained little of the color remained. "O'Shea Construction" was printed in green on the front. So once again I put on a construction helmet and headed toward the shell of what would eventually be a hospital.

# # # #

We rode up to the third floor on an outside freight elevator. Its plank floor was splattered with hardened concrete and its walls consisted of a thick rope swung from corner to corner. Cullen helped me in and then grabbed on to the steel bars that, like an exposed umbrella, made a frame for the hoist to lift the box and its contents. I grabbed the bar above my own head and braced my feet.

Cullen was smiling down at me as he pressed a button on the hoist and we started to rise. Guys love to show off their head for height (if they have a head for height!) and frighten the little woman. I was amused. I had grown up with a family who were not only in the shipping business, but who also loved the ocean and loved to sail. It was about the only thing they did love. We sailed out of Old Greenwich Yacht Club near Stamford, New York.

Since I'd been able to walk I'd been scampering around rigging high above the decks of our ever-changing fleet of sailboats—ketches, sloops, yawls. Designing sailboats was my father's hobby. I'd climbed masts in races to free jib lines that had gotten tangled with the mainsheets, I'd climbed out on a bowsprit the width of an oar to coax a stubborn spinnaker to pop, and I'd swung out in a hiking chair of a sailboat heeled over so far the keel was a visible blade knifing through gray, swollen chop thirty or forty feet below me. Height doesn't bother me at all. I held on to the cold bar above my head and felt the wind as the freight elevator swung in its ascent. I realized with a pang how much I missed sailing.

I glanced at Cullen. His red hair, worn a little too long, was whipping back. He was braced by his powerful legs, letting them take the movement of the plank floor as I was. His hand was resting only lightly on the bar above his head. Now he was the Viking.

We came to a bumpy stop when the elevator swung level with the third floor. He helped me off and I thanked him. Then I had to ask.

"Do you sail?"

He turned deep blue eyes to me, startled.

"Sail? I was born swaddled in canvas. Why do ye ask?"

"It was the way you stood on the elevator," I said. "That's the way sailors do. My family's in shipping," I added, a little self-consciously. Cullen was looking at me like I'd sprouted wings and a halo.

"Ye're a noticing kind of lady. I love sailing. I sailed me own 12-meter yacht up the inland waterway when we got this land-locked job. She's the 'Stars and Bars.' She'd done right well in the America's Cup a couple decades ago. I bought her. They were rentin' her out for tourists in the Bahamas, can ye believe it? Got her overhauled. She's anchored at the Chicago Yacht Club. I sail on her as often as I can. But that lake now," Cullen glanced east, though the lake was barely visible through the forest of timber framing, snaking electrical cables and the overcast skies outside. Yet, there was a hint of gray expanse out there. "She's as fierce as any ocean I've ever sailed. Terrible, too. The currents drive and pull against each other like she wants to tear the boat apart and swallow us all. We're entered in the Mackinac." He glanced down at me suddenly.

"Are you?"

I shook my head.

"No, I don't even have a sailboat any more. No time. But I miss it."

"Come with me. Crew the race. I bet ye're right handy, the way you move with the wind, not against it."

He threw out the invitation to participate in one of the most coveted yacht races in the world like he was asking me for coffee. I looked at him,

standing with his back to the open edge of the building, seemingly uncon-
cerned that two feet behind him loomed oblivion. Cullen liked the edge in
all things, I imagined.

"Let me think about it, Cullen," I said. His faced registered such crushing disappointment that I almost laughed. It was hard to separate out how
much was blarney and how much the actual man.

I glanced at my watch.

"I'm sorry, but I do need to get to a meeting shortly."

"Yes, yes. Me too, I'm afraid. On land there's always someone waitin',
wantin', callin'. That's why I love being out on the water. He moved away
from the edge of the building and glanced around the cavernous space.

"Where did ye come up—was it with the tour blokes?"

"No," I said. I looked around myself trying to get oriented. The freight
elevator bisected the east side of the building. Tom and I had come up the
staircase that was at the back of the downstairs lobby, and then walked over
to to the big large window.

"I came with a friend, a surgeon here. We came up over there," I said,
pointing to where I could see the outline of the two-by-fours that marked
that top of those stairs.

Cullen only nodded and took my elbow, guiding me expertly over the
lumber and pipe strewn floor. The sides of the building were all open, and
there were places where the concrete floor was black from driving rain. As
we moved away from the open side of the building and the wind, the smell
of damp concrete began to rise from the floor and bile started to rise in my
throat. I wanted to go back to the swinging freight elevator and pretend I
could smell the ocean instead. I looked down, seeming to pick my way over
the debris, but what I really saw was that deceptively flat, milky surface and
the coiled fingers reaching out, reaching up for the help that came too late.

I shuddered and Cullen felt me tremble.

"Here, cold now, are ye? he asked. "I forget how these buildings hold
the cold. Like ruddy ice boxes they can be." He let go of my elbow and started
to put his huge arm around my shoulders.

"No, I'm fine," I said, stepping briskly away from under the arm and
moving forward.

"I was just remembering how she died," I said over my shoulder.

He made a clucking sound with his tongue and teeth that echoed for a
second in the gloom.

Keeping the staircase in view, I headed in what I thought was the direction Tom and I had taken. We came past the pillars. The huge round
window was still just an unglazed single eye above.

I stopped behind one of the pillars.

"We were about here," I said, "looking up at that window space when we heard a scream and a thud. We hurried as fast as we could toward the sound."

I fit action to words and moved quickly around the pillar where only last night I had stood still, contemplating infinity instead of paying attention to what was happening around me. Cullen had called me a 'noticing kind of lady' and usually I was. Why hadn't I paid more attention when it could have made so much difference?

I was surprised to find Cullen was right behind me. He was surprising light on his feet for someone his size.

"Then what?" he asked behind my left shoulder. I paused. There was no sound to guide me this time.

"Then we went over here, I think." I thought I saw the black shape of the elevator shaft, now reinforced with more timbering around the front. But the yawning mouth still broke the concrete column, seemingly hungry for more victims.

"Yes." I walked over to it slowly and willed myself to look down. The bottom had hardened and trash and boards lay strewn on the surface. Along the top front edge, yellow police tape hung down, tattered and limp. I took my time and looked around, trying to remember the whole scene. I saw a long coil of rope now neatly stacked to one side next to a pile of lumber. Probably the rope I'd used.

I pointed out the rope and described the repelling act to Cullen. He listened, passive now. When I finished, he took my hands in his and turned them palms up. The abrasions had not had time to heal, though I had used plenty of ointment on them last night. They looked purplish red and swollen. He bent his head and suddenly I realized his intent. I pulled my hands away abruptly before he could press his lips to my palms. I turned away, disconcerted.

"Ye poor thing," he whispered behind my back. "And she died anyway. It's a miserable, cryin' shame for an accident to happen to a pretty little thing like that."

I was more than a little irritated with Cullen and his attempt to charm me into God-knows-what at the edge of what was virtually a grave. I stepped further away from him and turned.

"Listen, Cullen. She wasn't a thing, she was a person, and it was certainly tragic that we couldn't save her, but she wasn't just clumsy." I was breathing hard in my remembered frustration and fear, and my growing rage at this complacent charmer's response to violent death. He clearly had a cruel streak, given what he had done to the GSB student's car, no matter how provoked.

"Her upper arms are bruised," I said through clenched teeth. "Those bruises weren't there when I saw her at the reception. She was thrown down that shaft, I'll bet anything." I glared at him.

His rust colored eyebrows rose at my tirade and his blue eyes widened.

"This is the first I've heard of this, now, I must say. Bruises. How'd ye come by that big of gossip, eh?" He gave me his most charming smile, further enraging me. Any minute he'll try to pat me on the head, I thought.

"It's not 'gossip,' as you put it. I visited her in the intensive care unit here at the hospital. She had finger-shaped bruises on her upper arms. Those bruises weren't there at the reception. She was wearing a sleeveless dress and I saw her arms quite clearly. And I pulled her out by her wrist, not her upper arms."

"Did ye now?" Cullen looked away from me and down into the opening and the hole below that was not less than two feet from where he was standing. "Did ye now indeed?"

His big head was lowered and those twinkly blue eyes were shuddered, effectively hiding his thoughts. Was he thinking of a young woman struggling for her life down there, or of the impact this bit of news was going to have on his insurance problems? I tried to be fair. Maybe some of both. Nobody takes the news of a possible murder in stride.

"And did you see this mysterious fella who was supposed to have done this?" he asked, without lifting his head from contemplating the yawning gash beside us.

"No, we didn't see anyone," I said quietly. I too looked at the mouth of the shaft, thinking. If Karen/Courtney had come up with the tour, someone would remember. If not, what route had she and her supposed 'fella' taken to get up here?

"Cullen," I asked suddenly. He focused those blue eyes on me, now dark and intent. "Where are the other stairs located?"

He smiled tolerantly, but the smile did not reach his eyes. He threw out his long arm and pointed in turn at each of the four corners of the building. Sure, that made sense. Fire stairs would be required for a space this big. I didn't see how Courtney and anyone else she was with could have come up the stairs Tom and I used. We'd have seen them, unless they were well ahead of us, which could be true, I supposed. I doubted she'd been with the tour. Didn't seem like that was something she'd do, and the tour hadn't come all the way up here anyway. But that left other access points. What was clear is that she'd been thrown into the elevator shaft while Tom and I were concealed behind that pillar. I shuddered.

I felt a tremendous urgency to get out of there and away from that hole and its solid bottom. It made a solid base that had a tiny black sequined evening purse buried within it. A purse preserved for centuries.

"I have to go, Cullen," I said abruptly. I turned and without waiting to see if he was coming, I walked toward the freight hoist. It was the fastest way out of here. I could hear him behind me, but he made no move to touch me again. Then someone called "Mr. O'Shea" and it startled me. I hadn't realized there were any workers on this floor. It came from a rough, shed-like structure I hadn't registered before as a construction office. A door was now open in the shed and a guy in shirtsleeves was holding out a roll of architectural plans. O'Shea stopped and then followed the guy into the shed. I contemplated just going on ahead, but O'Shea was back out in a minute, looking grim. I didn't wait for him to catch up to me, but just resumed walking toward the outside elevator.

On the way down we were silent. When we got off, I turned and handed back his construction helmet.

"Goodbye," said Cullen. "Thanks a whole lot for yer time and I look forward to seein' you tomorrow night at the game." The words were charming, but the affect was flat. Cullen seemed to have been subdued by the thought of murder, I speculated. Well, who wouldn't be?

"Thank you for letting me see the place again," I said. Though I didn't know whether I meant it or not.

He nodded. I turned to go.

"And Kristin," I turned back. "Think about sailin' with me. I think we'd sail much the same, you and me." The smile was back in full force and I took it as a broadside. I didn't trust myself to respond and I just inclined my head slightly, I hoped noncommittally. Then I walked as briskly as I could toward the sidewalk that led to the main campus.

I felt like I was in some existentialist novel where sex and death were twined together in a vicious symbolic dance. I increased my pace, anxious to get away from the smell of wet concrete and the slippery sensuality of the Irish.

11

What's the diff?
You're in jail or you're stiff.
I need a different riff.
"Life"
James Maddox, #965
Street Wise

Thursday, May 18, 4 p.m.

I left the construction site and walked as fast as I could toward my office, the wind and the smell of rain at my back urging me on. Way too much was happening way too fast. As I walked along the almost deserted side-walk, the wind tearing at my coat, I contemplated Cullen O'Shea. He was a powerful and troubling personality. Even when you could see charm like that being turned on and off, it still had a pull. I recognized the pull, and then I mentally shook myself. What was with me? Did anything in pants attract me these days (well, anything really good-looking)? Me, the still-stricken widow who wouldn't sleep with Tom because it felt like the final betrayal of my dead husband? Alice Matthews had told me to 'get men off my eyeball' and she was right. All men did was mess up your concentration.

I pushed hard on the big, ersatz medieval door of Myerson, the build-ing where my office and the Department of Philosophy and Religion is lo-cated. The unrelenting wind was pushing back. I managed to get the door open about 18 inches and squeeze inside.

What I'd really loved to have done instead was stop by the main li-brary and work in the library stacks. The clammy scent of concrete would be siphoned out of my lungs and replaced with the lovely library smell of dust and mold. Libraries smell like book compost that ferments level upon level above and below you while you are immersed inside them. But I'd had a really nasty experience in our main library and I was still anxious when I was there. I resented that anxious feeling tremendously, though I still avoided the library. Anyway, I comforted myself, the book smell is getting less pronounced and it's now tainted with the saccharine smell of slightly heated plastic produced by dozens and dozens of computer monitors humming away where the card stacks used to be. Libraries are already becoming obsolete as more and more books and articles are available online. Why go to a library when you can just download what you need from your home or office computer? Why? To touch a book, to smell a book. That's why.

I don't like cyberspace. I hope I've made that clear.

I trooped up the stairs to my office (no one in their right mind took the rickety elevator in Myerson), reached my door and opened it. Its narrow space was lined with floor-to-ceiling bookshelves that were now all mine since my officemate had changed jobs. I sniffed. There was a whiff of good book smell. I dropped my things on the spare chair where students usually sat, opened my computer and accessed the file on my dissertation.

I proceeded to stare blankly at the screen. What I saw instead were images of Karen/Courtney as the Vogue-dressing, angry student, then the sophisticated and pouty doctor's date, and finally the little white mound with the bruised arms. Why was she so angry, so beautiful and so dead at what, 19 or 20 years of age? And if you're the one who's beautiful, why do you go out of your way to make the unlovely feel bad about themselves? I'm not drop-dead gorgeous, but I'm nearly 6 feet tall with long blond hair, blue eyes, fair skin and pretty even features. I've even been called "willowy." I thought I'd gotten fairly immune to being stared at, my looks commented upon including subtle put-downs mixed in. 'Is your hair color real?' and so forth. I ignored the comments, but they did embarrass me. I used to be very uncomfortable with my height, but I had accepted it, even occasionally liked it when I could loom over jerks. So okay, I look Scandinavian. I am Scandinavian. It doesn't make me a sex goddess, I'll tell you that flat out. And it sure didn't make me want to lord it over Adelaide or Alice either. Far from it. It made me want to minimize the differences among us. What was it about Karen/Courtney that made her turn her beauty into cruelty? Her youth? No, it had to be more than just adolescent preening. That paper on Wolf was vicious and disturbingly erratic. There was too much acid and too much barely hidden pain. And the emphasis on sexual manipulation had been downright scary.

I closed my dissertation folder and called up her Wolf paper. When I'd first read it in Adelaide's office, possible suicide had occurred to me. Outside the package was beautiful, but inside was a tangle of self-loathing. But no, the shape of those bruises had tipped the scales in the direction of murder. The bruises had been four fingers that lined up over her biceps, the thumb, though I didn't see it, would have been at the back of her arm. That meant she'd been grabbed hard by the arms from behind. A quarrel might have produced a shake, but that would logically be from the front. A confrontation. But the grab was from behind and near an open shaft. I could see the scene unfold over the words on the screen, images freshened by my trip up there with Cullen. I imagined an argument, her turning away, the sudden impulse (though was it sudden?) to grab and shove or even throw. The edge of a dangerous elevator shaft was a curious place to take a date. Unless. Unless there were words that needed to be said in absolute private. Shadowed figures and menacing hands wavered on the screen. Karen/Courtney couldn't weigh more than a hundred pounds. It would be nothing for a relatively in-shape guy, though a woman could have done it too, to take her by surprise from the back and toss her like a rag doll into the shaft, into the still soft bed of concrete that had welcomed her with suffocating arms.

Ugh. I shook myself. When the image of that gaping mouth of an open elevator shaft began to invade my office, it was time to quit. I glanced at my watch. Nearly 5 o'clock. Time to head home for kids, food and bed.

I turned off the computer and even the black screen held an outline of shadowy memory. I snapped the computer closed, got my stuff and left.

# # # #

Coming up our brick walkway, I could hear a raised voice inside. When your house holds two six-year-olds, this is scarcely unusual. But as I started to put my key in the lock, I realized the raised voice was not that of a child, but of an adult male. The words, still indistinguishable, had the cadence of French and I realized with a jolt of real panic that the tone was not anger but fear. My hand shook and I fumbled with the lock and then pushed rapidly through the door.

The tableau in the front hall froze as I entered. Carol stood in the center of the hall, her brown eyes swimming with tears. Giles stood at the door to the dining room, his hands clenched at his sides. His chest rose and fell with the effort he was making to hold in whatever he had been yelling. This was amazing in itself. Giles never spoke above a calm whisper.

To my right, Mike, Sam and even Molly sat huddled together on the bottom step of the stairs, silent and staring. Three sets of brown eyes were huge and fixed on Giles.

"What?" I choked out.

"The police just called," Carol said, her measured voice contradicting her swimming eyes. "They said they are coming this evening to talk to you about some young woman student?" Her voice rose on the last in the form of a question, but it was no question. She looked directly at me, willing me to understand.

Giles stood silently while she spoke, his eyes on the floor, his chest still moving up and down under his thin tee shirt. His sinewed arms twitched from tension.

I thought I understood. But before I spoke, I needed to lower the emotional temperature in the room. I crossed to the hall closet and put my coat on the nearest hanger. So what if it already contained another coat? I tossed my backpack in behind it. As I turned, I caught a glimpse of myself in the mirror on the back of the door. I looked like a ghost rising above a black curtain. Well, black had been an all around good choice for the events of the day, apparently. I took a breath.

"Well, yes. That's excellent." I addressed this remark half to the mirror and half to the room behind me. I turned. "If they hadn't called, I'd have called them and invited them over." That was untrue, of course, but it was what I needed to say.

"So, Giles," I went on, turning toward him slowly. "What time are they coming and do we have time for dinner first?"

Giles raised his eyes to me. They looked sunken in their sockets, like his very eyes were trying to hide in his head. The skin around them looked darker, bruised. Like perhaps they'd looked when he'd been arrested by the police in his home country when he'd been a university student and had been part of a student activist group.

Giles looked at me, but still said nothing. I glanced at Carol. She was looking more in control of herself and I could see her gather herself to help out. She squared her shoulders and spoke.

"They said around 7 p.m. I'd better set the table."

"Good," I replied.

She turned and walked past Giles and down the hall toward the kitchen.

I went over to where the kids and Molly were still sitting. I petted the dog, and kissed each of the boys on top of his head. I wanted to gather them up and cover them with kisses and hugs, but I knew that would produce howls of protest.

"And how was your day? Spelling test go okay?"

They woke as if from a trance and started talking over each other. "Aced it." That from Mike, the older by only a few minutes, but in temperament, older by several years. "I didn't make any mistakes. Neither did Sam." Sam jumped up off the stairs. "It was easy!" he yelled, and he danced around in a circle. Molly let out a sharp bark as if releasing tension from having sat still for a while and jumped on Sam's back. They both went down on the floor to wrestle.

"Say, that's great," I said, and ruffled Mike's hair as he had come to stand next to me, his eyes still on Giles. I too looked at Giles, who was standing so still in the doorway he looked like he was taking root. "I know. Giles, while I talk to the cops, why don't you and the boys walk down to the corner store and get us a gallon of Rocky Road? I think 100% on spelling tests deserve Rocky Road."

"Whoa! All right!" said Sam and he jumped up off the floor. That got Mike's attention too, and the boys and Molly raced down the hall toward the kitchen, presumably to give Carol the good news and tell her to go light on the vegetables with dinner. I looked at Giles.

He exhaled. His voice came from far away, thousands of miles away and from several years previously.

"Perhaps it is best if we remain. You should not be alone."

"I was a cop, remember? I know what they're coming to ask me and it's all right. I just have to give them some information."

Giles's chest contracted as if from a punch. Oh. God. Information. Wrong choice of word. Information is what his arrest in Senegal had been about, I thought.

"I mean description." I hurried along. My tone of fake unconcern wouldn't have fooled the boys and it certainly wasn't fooling Giles. But it was the best I could do.

"I just have to describe what I saw and what I did. I didn't do anything wrong. Somebody hurt a young woman who used to be a student, and I'm going to help the police find out who did it. Here the cops are on our side. They try to help catch the bad guys and put them in jail."

Giles' mouth pulled sideways in a ghastly parody of a smile. He, Carol, the boys and I have marched for #BlackLivesMatter after every killing by police of an unarmed black man or woman. He knew I was lying. Now my chest was contracting. Giles is a black man. Suddenly it was imperative to me that he leave and go get the Rocky Road with the boys. But I owed him the truth.

"Yeah, yeah. You're right. I know, Giles. I know. But look. I'm a rich white woman. What're they going to do to me?"

He grimaced some more. I knew he knew I had a bad history with a cop sexually harassing me. Even being white and rich wouldn't protect some women some of the time.

"I tell you what. I'll call and arrange to meet with them at the campus police station. Maybe my friend Alice Matthews can sit in. You remember Alice?" A slight nod. "Good then. Give me the call back number, would you, and I'll arrange that?"

I realized just how much I didn't want the police in my house either. Carl Kaiser was a Chicago detective and he and I had a very nasty history. He was supposed to have been my husband Marco's backup the day he had gotten shot and killed. Two weeks before, I'd filed a formal sexual harassment complaint against Kaiser. Coincidence? I didn't think so then, didn't think so now. And then Carl had been assigned to the last crime we'd had on campus and he'd tried to get me accused of murder.

Giles nodded slowly and took a piece of paper out of his jeans pocket and handed it to me. He turned and walked down the hallway. His flip flops skimmed along the oriental runner that covers the long center hall. It's a Bokhara. Bokhara's have more than 500 knots per square inch. The heavy pile effectively muffled the sound of his footsteps. If you didn't know there was someone in the hall, you'd think there was nobody there.

12

Why do they leave the lights on
All night long?
Why are the showers cold and the beds hard?
They want to punish us
For the sin of needing
A safe place to stay.
"At the Shelter"
Alfonso Enrique Garcia, #1302
StreetWise

Thursday, May 18, 8 p.m.

The night was dark with dusky clouds obscuring the moon and stars. The rain had come and gone, but it was probably temporary. I could smell the lake, even though it was five blocks behind me. That meant the wind had shifted to the northeast and thus the rain would cycle around the lake and come back at us. The lake is a giant depository of moisture and when the wind swirls around it, it scoops up enormous quantities of water and deposits them on the city. Again and again and again.

I was heading to the campus police station. While Carol and Giles got dinner on the table, I'd called the campus police station and asked for Alice. She'd gone off duty, so I had asked for Commander Stammos. He was in and gracious about having the Chicago police meet me there. He even offered his own office for the meeting, and he'd volunteered to call them and arrange it. Was that a nod to my campus police "consultant" status (which seemed to mean very little as far as I could tell), or did he want to hear my report first hand? Probably the latter.

The campus police station is on the north side of campus behind a group of student dorms. While dark had fallen early because of the lowering clouds, the station is so well lit I could see it clearly from several blocks away. The building that houses the campus police force is an ivy-covered, graceful three-story brick structure. It sits nestled among tall trees. Now, with only the first buds of leaves covering their branches, they were black sticks silhouetted against the graying sky. It looks like any other charming older building in the academic landscape.

That is, until you get inside. I've had occasion before to simply marvel at how much the inside looks and feels like so many of the poorly painted, inadequately lit and odiferous Chicago police stations. It felt so familiar.

As I pushed open the carved wooden door at the entrance, I reflected on why this building so was schizophrenic. The outside was reassuring to the university community and also local residents. These campus cop folks fit right in. But if you were a suspected perp, then the inside would convince you, with its cracked linoleum floors and the mustard-colored paint that covered the walls like jaundice, that these were real police and serious business was about to go down. Alice Matthews and I had joked about this building and the stark difference between the outside and the inside the first time I'd visited her in her office.

I stopped at the battered desk in the hall, gave my name, and asked where I could find the office of Commander Stammos. The police officer on duty was a youngish guy with close-cropped blond hair and an earring. He smiled and a pretty row of straight teeth gleamed at me, testimony to his parents' ability to afford quality braces.

"Hello, Professor Ginelli," he said brightly. He'd been told to expect me.

"Hello," I replied and grinned back at him. Another charmer. Today was my day for charming males, apparently. Though I wondered who and what awaited me upstairs. I doubted charm would be their leading characteristic.

"Commander Stammos is expecting you. Go right up. Second floor, turn left, first door on your right. 204." I nodded my thanks. Stammos ran a tight ship here, as I had imagined he would.

I climbed the flight of stairs, registering the uneven slant of the steps and the worn rubber treads. Above, the wall color changed to a bilious green. The dim overhead lights in their protective metal screens made me contemplate taking out my cell phone and turning on the flashlight app. I squinted. Across from the head of the stairs the door did say 204.

I pushed the green-painted door open and walked into an office that could have been in a downtown law firm except that the framed diplomas on the left wall were not only from "Fordham University" but also from the "The New York Police Academy." A forest of honorary plaques surrounded these along with framed photos of Stammos with various prominent politicians in New York.

The outer office had a reception desk and a few chairs against the right wall for those who would have to wait to see the Commander. That desk was unoccupied and the door to the inner office was open.

Directly ahead I could see Stammos seated behind a mahogany desk with a graceful bowed front that was placed opposite the door and in front of the windows. He rose as he heard the door and gestured me to come in. Heavy maroon drapes hung in thick folds in front of the two banks of windows, I assumed both to muffle sound and also mask the dirty glass.

Two other men had also risen when I'd entered. They'd been sitting in a living room setting to the right of the inner door. A gold and green striped sofa was pushed against the wall and it was paired with two dark green leather armchairs. Lamps with maroon shades cast a soft pink light that softened the ceiling lights.

Stammos came around his desk and plunged right into introductions.

"Professor Ginelli, I'd like you to meet Detective Albert Brown," he said, indicating a tall thin man unfolding himself from the low sofa. I knew him. He had been homicide detective Carl Kaiser's beat cop minion last fall. I'd nicknamed him 'Ichabod' in my mind because he looked like that character in the cartoon version of the "Headless Horseman." Even though he was in his mid-thirties, I guessed, it seemed he'd made detective. As he stood to shake my hand, his jacket hung limply from his wire-thin shoulders and at least six inches of bony wrist and narrow arm protruded from the sleeve. I saw he had not shaken his diffident manner. He was probably destined to always be another detective's sidekick.

"Hello, Detective Brown," I said as I shook his narrow hand.

"And this is Detective Horace Williams," continued Stammos.

Williams was still in the act of rising from one of the armchairs. He was nearly as wide as he was tall. Mr. Five-by-Five. Former weightlifter or wrestler, I'd bet. Lots of muscle going slowly south from age and lack of exercise. He had a broad, flat face covered with hundreds of moles and freckles, so many that his pale skin between was almost completely obscured. Close-cropped graying hair was receding from his flat forehead. He moved slowly, deliberately, extending a hand also nearly covered with the peppering of moles and freckles. I got the distinct impression he never hurried to do anything.

"Nice of you to join us, Professor," he drawled out.

I knew I wasn't late and I resisted the urge to glance at my watch. So it was going to be that kind of interview, was it?

There are basically two approaches to interviews taught to detectives. Technique A is 'relax them by becoming their friend.' My instructor had said you know you've done your job right on this technique when you ask a suspect if they want to have a lawyer present and the suspect protests, 'I don't need a lawyer, I have you.' Technique B is the opposite. 'Put'em on edge and keep'em on edge.' With the soft ambience of Stammos's office, I'd almost made the mistake of thinking we were all going to have a friendly chat.

Williams was standing aside so I could sit on the couch next to Brown. Given that opening gambit, however, there was no way I was going to sink into the foam padding of that sofa and be 10 inches shorter than Williams when he sat back down in a high-backed Queen Anne leather armchair.

I smiled, turned, and in two long strides had my hands on the back of a third armchair that had been placed in front of Stammos's desk. I swung it around and moved it over between the other two chairs, facing the sofa. Only Stammos had reacted. He put out a hand to help me position the chair.

"Thanks," I smiled at him. "Those kind of couches just kill my back," I lied sweetly.

I sat and the men sat. I was now the tallest person in the room. I caught Stammos's eye. His stern lips were curved in a ghost of a smile, but it didn't quite reach his eyes. They were slitted under his bushy brows. Brown folded his long frame back onto the low sofa with a pained expression. In his case, I suspected that soft couch was really bothering his back.

Williams sat down heavily and waited almost a full minute without speaking. I said nothing, just folded my hands in my lap and looked at him. Finally he spoke.

"So, Mrs. Ginelli, how long have you been a professor here?"

The Mrs. was deliberate too.

"Almost two years," I said quietly.

"And before that?" His voice carried almost no inflection and his brown eyes appeared painted on his dinner plate shaped face.

"I was a graduate student in Philosophy and Religion at Northwestern University in Evanston." I was having trouble matching his deadpan tone, but I was giving it my best shot. Why, I wasn't sure. At this point, probably pure stubbornness more than anything else.

"And before that?" His mouth was the only part of him that moved.

"I was a policewoman, and had just made detective." Same tone, note for note.

"And then you quit the force. Why?"

Ah. Now I knew why we didn't have Technique A here. Police work is a tight fraternity, and I use the word fraternity deliberately. The danger and the tension of often unreasonable and conflicting demands—be the nice friendly cop on the corner and the ruthless secret agent who brings down the villain—produces a particularly strong culture of 'it's us versus them.' And once having been admitted to the fraternity, especially on sufferance as women still were, it was supposed to be for life. Quitting was treason. Period.

I knew what I had to say and I didn't want to. I never spoke of it and I knew what the reaction of each of them would be. I felt my hands go cold. I waited and they waited.

"Mrs. Ginelli?" Williams said.

Okay. Get it over with.

"My husband, also a detective, was murdered in the line of duty. After his funeral, I quit the force." There. They'd gotten their pound of flesh. I sat back, stilling my shaking hands on my skirt-covered thighs. I made no mention of the sexual harassment complaint, but I certainly knew Brown was aware of it. And given the way Williams was treating me, I thought he knew too. I was a traitor. I dug my fingers into the wool and held on, willing my hands to stop quivering.

But at the mention of Marco's murder, the atmosphere subtly shifted. Stammos made a slow, sharp noise in the back of his throat. I wondered if he didn't know about Marco's death. Brown stopped writing and looked at Stammos. Brown knew that too. Williams put his hands on his knees. I'd thrown him off a little. Sure, I was a traitor but I was also that revered icon, the police widow. Was that enough to balance out being police turncoat, maybe even tip the scales a little in my favor? Who knew? Who cared? Williams knew I'd been a cop before this so-called interview started. He had to have known that I had been married to a slain officer, Marco Ginelli. Williams had just wanted to make me say it. To cause me pain. And that was Technique B.

I despise Technique B. I don't even disagree that it gets results. I just know what it does to a person, to an officer, to deliberately seek to cause pain again and again. I looked at Williams. His flat eyes and closed face weren't his effort to keep me out, they were a way to try to keep the cruelty outside himself. I kept steadily looking at him and I saw his eyelids flicker. It doesn't work. That's what I wanted to say. Cruelty you inflict comes back at you and settles right inside you. Traditional Korean thought called that "Han," which doesn't translate into English very well, but it means 'a lump of coal in the soul.' All the cruel things you do, and interestingly, all the cruel things done to you, congeal and make this hard, nasty substance that corrodes you from inside.

"Why were you at the reception at the Anderson building on May 17th?" Williams asked, still in a monotone.

"I was the guest of Dr. Thomas Grayson, a surgeon at the same hospital. Have you talked with him yet?"

Williams did not reply and again went silent for another full minute. Witnesses are not supposed to ask questions. And it was clear he had made up his mind that Tom was my lover and he was trying to make me feel shame. Probably if Williams had his way, police widows would be forced to commit Suttee, the Indian self-immolation of widows on the bonfire of their husband's funeral. But in this, unlike many other things in my life, I was guiltless. I waited too. I started counting my breaths, five inhales, five exhales, and then trying to extend it to six, then seven. Excellent meditation technique.

And again I saw Williams's eyelids flicker. I wondered if he knew how his eyelids were betraying his tension as he tried to rattle his witnesses. The cruelty was costing him. Suppose I just said, 'Why yes, I did nearly curl up and die when my husband was murdered.' Would his eyelids flicker faster?

Time to rattle a little back.

"Have you talked to Dr. Grayson yet?" I asked. I thought I sounded pretty calm.

"No," said Williams, now willing to answer a direct question. "He's been unavailable today, in surgery."

He paused again and consulted a small pad I'd not seen before. It had been completely hidden in the palm of one meaty hand.

"What time did you and Dr. Grayson go upstairs?"

Williams made the question sound as sleazy as he could. Oh, please. Come up and see my etchings? I drew one corner of my mouth up slightly to show him that one had missed by a mile. Childish, I know, but Technique B has that effect on me. If Stammos had served us coffee from the carafe I'd seen on a credenza when I'd come in, I bet I'd have flung it at Williams at some point during this evening's interview. But getting the witness coffee is part of Technique A. Suddenly, I wondered if the three of them had discussed what approach they would use before I'd arrived. Of course they had. And I felt like the outsider they wanted me to be.

Now it was time to really speed things up and get out of here.

"It was about 8 p.m. Dr. Grayson's clinics, or future clinics, I should say, will be on that floor. We went to see them, and the view of the lake. We were at that far end by what will be the large round picture window when we heard a scream and a thud."

"Slow down, Professor," said Williams, imitating his own words. There was at least a second between each word.

"What did you see and hear before that?" Williams consulted his tiny pad.

"Nothing. I saw no one and heard nothing. I'm sorry. I really am. I wish I had seen whoever did that to a young woman." I also wished they'd seen us and been frightened off. I wished she hadn't come up there. I wished a lot of things.

Williams wrote slowly in his little notebook with the stub of a pencil. Then he raised his pumpkin head and looked at me, leaning forward slightly.

"If you saw nothing and heard nothing, how do you know she didn't just come up for the view like you did and then trip on something and fall into the open elevator shaft? Or jump in, for that matter?" Four rapid blinks.

"I've visited her in Intensive Care, Detective. Have you?" I sat up and leaned forward myself, able to look down on him.

That didn't seem to phase him. His eyes were back to being flat and he had his eyelids under control. Then he gave me a small nod. What'd that cost you, Williams? I glanced at Brown who was scribbling in silence, sitting on the soft low couch with his knees almost up to his nose. What was he writing? 'Detective Williams nodded and did not blink.' Probably. Brown struck me as plodding but thorough. Stammos sat like a Sphinx, hands on knees. It occurred to me that he was probably here on sufferance and had instructions to butt out. I bet that galled him.

"Then you probably saw the bruises on her upper arms," I continued. "Four-finger shaped bruises along the biceps. Those bruises weren't there when I saw her downstairs at the reception. She was wearing a spaghetti-strapped top with long gloves, but her upper arms were bare. I saw them clearly. Not a mark on them. Not much of a leap to imagine hands to go with those bruises, eh Detective?" I took a breath and sat back, trembling and trying to hide it.

"Those bruises could have been made before the fall or jump, Professor."

Why Williams. Positively argumentative.

"True, Detective. But I doubt it." I took a deep breath and leaned forward again. "And so do you."

I felt more than saw Brown stop writing. He hadn't recorded what I'd said. I revised my opinion of him as thorough. He was a lackey and he'd left that out of the record.

I turned to him.

"Did you get that, Detective Brown, or shall I repeat it?"

He looked up at me but did not write.

"Would you describe what you did after you heard 'a scream and a thud'?" Williams drawled slowly into the silence of Brown's non-answer, insinuating doubt into every single word. But his enormous shoulders had turned slightly in my direction. He was definitely interested in my answer.

Stammos had surely told him his version of what had happened and he wanted to catch me saying something different.

I didn't care. What happened happened. I gave him a solid ten minutes of everything from our hearing the 'scream and a thud' to Tom's cell phone call for help to the moment Stammos had helped me climb over the edge of the elevator shaft.

Williams clearly didn't like any of it. His shoulders hunched with tension the more I spoke. Civilians, especially women civilians, should not take matters into their own hands.

"Why didn't you at least wait for the campus police?" Williams ground out each word between his teeth.

Stammos stiffened at the words 'at least.'

I knew what I had done was right and the attack rolled off me easily.

"She was under the surface when we first looked down there, Detective. Seconds counted."

Williams couldn't take that from me.

"But she died anyway, didn't she, Mrs. Ginelli?" said Williams, ripping into my regret like a shark smelling the smallest amount of blood.

I tried to breathe into the pain and not give way. I looked at his face. I saw satisfaction in the upward movement of the flat plane of his mouth and jaw. He'd seen my pain and he'd liked it. Did he like to cause pain because he was so ugly? How had it been for him to grow up spotted all over? Was he just giving back the cruelty he'd received? Then I realized that in concentrating on him, I'd gotten past the worst of the pain.

"Yes, Detective, she did," I said firmly. I was still bleeding a little inside, but I was clearly not as wounded as he'd hoped. His face actually fell when he heard that.

"Do you have any questions, Detective Brown?" Williams threw out. This was not a real question and Brown knew it. He shook his head. In the police manual, there is a list of qualities deemed desirable in those who would try to make detective. "Critical thinking" is number one. I kid you not. "The ability to communicate clearly in oral and written form" is also on the list, but it's way down there. So Al had made detective for his writing reports skills, apparently, but he'd always be second banana because the whole 'critical thinking' thing gets past him.

I rose and looked at Williams. He rose too, more slowly but holding my gaze the whole time. I thought about that list of desirable qualities in a detective. Where was a 'taste for cruelty' on the list? It wasn't on any printed list, but it was a qualification. That had been clear to me long before this interview.

With a dry mouth, I thanked Commander Stammos for letting us use his office and I nodded at Brown. It was all I could manage.

I got out of the office without breaking into a run, but it was a near thing. I did run down the stairs and burst out into the damp May evening. I started to shiver. I'd been sweating for an hour. Thank God Giles hadn't been present for that interview, or even in the same building.

I set my face toward home and walked as briskly as I could, swinging my arms to warm up. I wondered, did the good of getting a witness off-balance to learn the facts of a case compensate for the evil of the deliberate cruelty it took to smell out each weakness, each little vulnerability and twist it until blood appeared? I swung my arms harder and wondered what Aristotle would say. I decided to ask Hercules. Then I brightened a little. With some judicious editing, I might be able to get part of a lecture out of this evening. The ultimate academic revenge. The accuser becomes a research subject. I felt a little better as I came up to our house.

But still I lay awake long into the night, remembering the touch of that cold hand, feeling my failure. Williams knew his stuff.

13

Wash, wash, wash my face
But the tears are still there.
Wash, wash, wash my face.
The tears make puddles on my face.
"Sad"
Dwayne Moorehouse, #2165
StreetWise

Friday, May 19, 7 a.m.

Wet. Wet. Wet. Slow street to wake up. He felt proud he was up and in his regular place on time. He was the only one on time. He was the only one on the street. He was a good worker. Everybody said so.

He looked around. Nobody in the copy shop. The lights were on, though. They stayed open all night. Stupid students—needing copies of their stuff at 3 in the morning, but would they get up at dawn? Nah. But he did.

No one in the corner coffee shop that he could see through the wet windows. He hoped the rain would stop and the street would pick up. He needed a good day, get some of that good coffee. The coffee at the shelter tasted like, like—he tried to think of a word bad enough that wasn't a swear. He'd made up his mind to be finished with them swear words. Drunks used swear words and he wasn't a drunk any more. He struggled for another word. Nothing came.

He looked over at the boxes of papers next to his corner. His competition. He chuckled. They needed coins to pop them open so papers would come out. Three separate boxes. Three more kinds of papers. Papers full of words, he thought. New words, words he didn't know. Maybe even a word he could learn, use in a poem or something. He bent over and brought his face close to the little window at the front of the box, trying to see through it to the words. The front page was pressed to the wavy glass window in the box. There was a picture and some words at the top.

For a minute he looked at the words until they started to make sense to him. ACCIDENT AT UNIVERSITY. WOMAN CRITICALLY INJURED.

Oh no!

Then he squinted at the photo of someone on one of them rolling stretchers like when Harry collapsed at the shelter and they took him away. Hair hung down over the side of the rolling stretcher. He squinted hard. Her hair! Her lovely hair hanging down all messed up and a little of her white, white skin where the mask on her face didn't cover it.

The church Madonna. It was her. How could this happen? She'd been okay. When was that? He struggled to remember.

What had hurt her? His brain screamed the question so loud he put his hands over his own ears and his papers fell on to the sidewalk. He didn't even see them. She was hurt. He hated it when somebody got hurt. He looked harder. Tried to read but the picture and the big words took up the whole top. The rest was folded under. He couldn't see the words. The rain rolling down the front of the box made it look like she was crying.

He grabbed the side of the box in rage. "Tell me!" he yelled. But the box was silent. He started panting, the fear coming in, coming in, coming in.

A voice sounded in his ears. It was an angry voice. A hard voice. But the fear made too much noise for him to hear the angry words yelling yelling yelling.

A hand spun him around and slammed him into the box with her picture inside. It hurt him. His anger became fear, fear at the memory of pain, fear of pain to come. He looked up at the angry face where the mouth was yelling angry words at him and he trembled.

"What the hell are you doing?"

He stood frozen, the back of his thighs still pressed against the wet box. A big hard finger started poking him in the chest.

"You stupid little shit. I asked you what you're doing."

The poking finger was still hurting his chest. He looked up at the angry face. There was a hat. There was a uniform. A campus cop. Why was he yelling at him? What had he done? He tried to make some words but only flecks of foam came from between his lips.

"Officer?" A soft voice came from behind the big angry campus cop. The cop stopped poking and turned toward the voice.

"What?" asked the cop.

"I know this guy. He sells the *StreetWise* papers." The vendor nodded vigorously but no one was looking at him.

"He doesn't talk much, but he's harmless. I think something just upset him. Can I just take him into the copy shop, quiet him down?" The soft voice was coming from a tall, thin guy with a beard and glasses so thick they looked like the bottom of coke bottles. He wore an apron.

"Well, get him out of here and clean up this mess!" The cop raised his voice again and the vendor shrunk back against the box. Then the cop grabbed his bike that he'd left leaning against a bike rack and rode on down the street. The vendor stood, still paralyzed with fear.

Coke bottle glasses spoke quietly.

"Here. You dropped your papers. Let's get 'em, okay?" The copy shop guy bent his long, thin back and started to pick up his newspapers from the ground. Oh! His papers. Oh. No. His papers! He'd had to pay for those. He fell to his knees, but it was too late. The guy had all his papers. He started to feel rage. He stiffened and his hands clenched at his side. He looked over at the guy's back, his shirt darkening from the rain. It looked like a big bloodstain.

The tall, thin guy stood up.

It was now or never. He tensed and got ready to grab his papers.

But the tall thin guy held out the hand that was not holding his newspapers to gently take him by the elbow.

"Come on. Come inside until the rain stops. Your papers can dry in there. Would you like a cup of coffee?" The man's calm voice smothered the rage. He moved away from the hand under his elbow, but he turned toward the copy shop.

He felt like he had been hit all over and all he wanted to do was run away and hide. His shoulders drooped like somebody had let all the air out of him. But coffee! He could get coffee. He stood up a little straighter.

Okay. Go inside.

He nodded and followed coke-bottle glasses into the warm copy shop. But she had to stay outside in the rain.

14

How can you walk with your eyes open and not see me?
How do you do that, look right through me?
I'm a human being, not a window.
I refuse to be ignored.
"I Am Here"
James Maddox, #965
StreetWise

Friday, May 19, 7 a.m.

I sipped a cup of coffee and stared out the kitchen window. Corridors of rain were being etched into the oil-slick grime that clung permanently to the pane like it did to every window in the city. The rain did not clean, it was a major transportation system for the dirt of the city. When the sun came out, if it ever came out again, the window would be streaked with a greater density of matter. It was a wonder such a fragile substance like glass could hold out against the grungy weight clinging to it.

Between the streaks I could see Molly's golden fur now darkened by the rain. It stretched over her arched back as she bent, absorbed in sniffing a single blade of grass. In our sliver of yard, there were not that many blades of grass, but she looked prepared to carefully examine every one, trying to extract every nuance of whatever her canine brain deduced from the smells released by the spring rain.

My brain deduced nothing. I sipped and stared, trying to work up the energy to go through a few Tae Kwon Do forms, the ritual patterns that formed the basis of the Korean martial art I practiced along with my boys. Repeating the patterns slowly and repetitively was supposed to increase your mental and physical acuity. I just didn't have it in me for the focus that required. My mind was too swollen, too bruised. I was spending far too much energy keeping the pain away from my consciousness. I knew I needed the mind-stilling rhythms and yet I was too fatigued to begin. And so I just stood, trying to be empty and not succeeding.

Images from the last few days wavered between the streaks on the window and flattened themselves out over the wet grass. I tried to keep them there, refuse them entry into my mind. I didn't want to think about young girls dead and kept alive by machines or about Giles reliving nightmares of being arrested because cops were coming or images of my dead husband Marco or any other of the wet, wavy scenes that refused to leave my yard.

Suddenly a simple and uncomplicated memory popped up and I grabbed for it and stuffed it into my brain, trying to make it big enough to fill my whole frontal lobe. Tom wanted to know if we could go see the Bulls. Okay. I can think about this. I can even do this because between bites of Rocky Road ice cream last night I'd asked Carol and Giles if they were free to stay with the boys Saturday night and they'd indicated that they were. Unfortunately, I'd made the mistake of telling them where Tom and I were going and I then I had had to fend off Sam's pitiful pleading to be taken along, and, more alarmingly, Mike's lawyerly arguments that the invitation really meant me and my *family*. If he argues that well at 6, what was he going to be like at 16? 21? After he passed the bar? And part of me had thought, 'Well, perhaps I can get Cullen to let us come to another game,' and that thought had set off a whole round of complicated thoughts about Cullen. Did I even want a guy like that near my boys? But I also couldn't deny his appeal to me. I tried to kick that thought out as well, but did not entirely succeed.

I turned and looked at the clock. Only a little after 7. Tom would certainly be up and might still be home. I picked up the landline. It felt cold and clammy in my hand. I had no trouble remembering his home phone number as numbers of all kinds stuck in my head, another thing cluttering it up. I dialed and pressed the cool handset against my cheek.

Tom picked up on the first ring. Who would call at 7 a.m. except the hospital?

"Dr. Grayson."

"Hi, Tom, it's Kristin."

"Just a minute, Kristin." Though he'd obviously covered the receiver with his hand, I could still hear a muffled, "No, it's not. Just my friend, Kristin. Go get ready." Kelly was already up too.

"Good morning," Tom said, coming back on the line. He'd really shooed Kelly out in a hurry. I bet she'd added that to her stock of resentment against me.

"Good morning to you too. I was calling about Saturday night. Giles and Carol can watch the boys, so I can say yes to the Bulls." And here it comes.

"Good. What time shall I have Kelly there?"

Okay. Now or never. Kelly wasn't in the room to hear his side of the conversation.

"Look, Tom. Kelly doesn't like to come here. She resents me and she resents your not trusting her to stay alone. Ask her."

Silence.

"Tom?"

"What do you mean, ask her?"

What do I mean? How complex a verb is ask?

"Talk to her. Ask her to tell you what she wants, whether she wants to come here or why she thinks she can stay home by herself. Maybe compromise. Let her have a friend come over."

"Where did you get the idea she resents you?"

Let me see. What was my first clue?

"Let's just say it's a normal response for a girl her age, and especially with what she's been through in the last year. Just ask her and listen to what she says, okay? Then decide together." I sounded like a radio shrink.

"Well, we'll see. I'll call you later."

Tom abruptly hung up. Before I could rouse myself enough to hang up too, I heard a second click. I doubted anyone at my house would listen in on a conversation, or if they did, be able to restrain themselves from giggling. That meant Kelly had deliberately listened in on our conversation. I wondered what Tom had in store when he 'just asked.' For a moment I contemplated calling him back, but decided against it. I was going to regret that decision, but I didn't know it at the time.

Kelly's Online Journal

Friday, May 19, 11 a.m.

Ha. Ha. Ha. Ha. Ha. Boy did I ever fix her today. Her who, you ask, my darling secret nobody? The ten foot tall Wonder Woman Witch, that's who. She calls like at dawn and tries to be soooo understanding. 'Talk to her, Tom. She doesn't like it here.' Right. Like she cares.

She doesn't want me around because of Giles. Probably he's been like talking about me and she's getting clued in. So she thinks up this stupid way of stopping me from seeing him.

Invite a friend over. Yeah. Really. What a dumb idea.

So Daddy comes into my room after the phone call and he looks all frowny and worried. Boy has she got him tied into knots. And he says humph humph a few times and then cough cough. Finally gets around to it. 'Do you like going to Kristin's?'

I clutch Morris the Bear to me and say, 'Oh, yes, Daddy. I love it! The little boys are sooo sweet. It's like we're one big family.' He starts to look all happy and relaxed. I put Morris the Bear in front of my mouth to keep from laughing or throwing up.

'That's great, honey. It's really like you're their big sister and besides it's good experience for babysitting jobs too.' I have to practically stuff Morris's head in my mouth to keep from being hysterical.

Daddy pats my head, swear to God, and tells me to 'put a move on.' Then he goes out all smiles. Mom was never this easy to fool. Well, shit. Never mind.

I can't wait to tell Alison. This is too rich. With chocolate sauce on top.

I have to decide what to wear. Giles said 'be a child.' But is that what turns him on? Some guys like that little girl look. But maybe I should dress older. I'll cut math class and go get some magazines. Cosmo maybe.

15

I'm one big beautiful woman
In a skinny ass world.
"Big is Beautiful"
Belinda Rogers, # 439
StreetWise

Friday, May 19, 7:45 a.m.

The rain pelted down on my umbrella as I left the shelter of our front porch. Sleet. It felt heavy on the umbrella and slick under foot. The grass of our city-sized front lawn looked oily with a grey/white sheen. The few brave daffodils we had planted lay collapsed under the weight of the slush pounding on their delicate heads. They looked like fallen soldiers, as indeed they were. Casualties in the war between winter and spring in a northern climate.

I trudged toward the campus. After Tom (and Kelly) had hung up, it had occurred to me to see if Karen/Courtney's old roommate, Bonnie Roddenberg, was still a student and if I could get in touch with her. She was there in the online directory and I'd called her current phone number in her dorm. Amazingly enough, she'd been in the room and had been gracious about meeting me for early coffee without any questions, especially once I'd identified myself as a professor. The amount of power professors have in the eyes of students always bothered me when I was reminded of it. Nevertheless, I was headed back to the faux marble of the new coffee shop. Well, as Alice said, it was warm.

I shook myself like Molly in the entryway of the building where the new coffee shop was located. I looked up and saw "Caution—Wet Paint" signs. I looked around. The hall clearly had just been painted and it looked like the rest of the first floor of this student union building was being given a face-lift. I walked carefully forward, avoiding the walls and doorways, but I glanced in the student lounge as I passed it and shuddered. Instead of the old lounge with its worn, over-stuffed armchairs and couches with the springs poking through stained fabrics of an unidentifiable pattern, 'groupings' of art deco-type furniture resided. Their sloped contours were swathed in vaguely vegetable colors called, I imagined, eggplant and avocado. More of the fake Tiffany light fixtures had migrated into this room. Against the gothic fireplace, its magnificent stone mantle a full ten feet off the ground and at least twelve feet wide, this décor looked as though King Arthur's castle had been captured and redecorated by the least talented of Frank Lloyd Wright's apprentices. I realized that when parents drop the staggering amount of money it now costs to attend such an elite university, they probably expected that the school won't look like the showroom of Goodwill Industries. But art deco with gothic? As an employee of an institution that was capable of approving decisions like this, it made me feel like the flagstone floor that appeared so solid beneath my feet was really thinly spread over a deep, deep well. What other decisions, less visible but perhaps with more lasting impact, were being made by the minds that approved this décor?

I averted my eyes and hurried into the coffee shop. I glanced around the room lit with the golden glow given off by the refracted light from the stained glass shades of the hanging lamps. They lit the room to almost a sunny brightness. I missed the old fluorescent lights that had made everyone look a little blue, like brand-new corpses. Since most of the student occupants would have been up most of the night, this being near the end of term, it would be appropriate if they looked like the walking dead. But the golden glow gave them shining hair and glowing skin. Was this the U of C or the set of Baywatch?

Yeah. Yeah. I was grumpy and I knew it. But underneath the grump was the feeling that something infinitely valuable about higher education was slipping away and I could not stop it.

I looked around and there was a tall young woman sitting alone. Brown, straight hair hung limply to large shoulders. She was hunched forward over a steaming cup in front of her. In the sunny glare, I could see a sallow complexion pitted with old acne scars. As I scanned the room, there seemed to be no other singles. This was the roommate of Karen Carlyle, the gorgeous, well-dressed student? Who chose whom as a roommate or had they just been randomly assigned?

"Bonnie?" I asked as I approached the table.

"Yes." A smile of incredible sweetness changed her face completely. For a moment, it was all I could focus on.

"Are you Professor Ginelli?" she asked. Still taken with her smile, I smiled back and indicated that indeed I was and that I'd get myself some coffee. I offered to get her a refill, but she declined.

As I read the labels of the coffee dispensers, trying to get French roast and not Raspberry Amaretto by mistake, I thought about this roommate pairing. Succeeding finally with locating the French Roast, I filled my cup and then slowly walked back to the table. As I looked at her, I tried to imagine this woman side-by-side with the delicate frame of Karen/Courtney, walking to dinner, to the library, even sitting together here in this coffee shop. How had that made Bonnie feel? If Karen/Courtney had made me feel like a giant at that reception, what had been her effect on Bonnie? Bonnie was at least my height, perhaps taller, and easily outweighed me by sixty to even eighty pounds. As she hunched over her drink, I could see her shoulders and one leg at the side of the table. She wasn't so much overweight as just large all over; the shoulders were those of a linebacker. She had taken out an iPad and was myopically peering at some text on the screen, her glasses now perched on the end of her nose.

I sat back down and the sweet smile reappeared.

"How can I help you, Professor Ginelli?" she asked, closing the iPad and placing it in a worn canvas backpack next to her chair.

I always hate this part.

"I don't know if you've seen the news, but your former roommate Karen Carlyle was fatally injured on campus two days ago."

"What?" It came out as a tiny whisper from between Bonnie's now unsmiling lips.

"Yes. I'm sorry. Karen Carlyle died from a fall at a construction site on campus."

Bonnie swallowed and sat back in her chair. Even the golden glow of the lights couldn't give her face color.

"I didn't know it was her. I think somebody said there'd been an accident on campus, but, you know, exam time and all and I've just been holed up and pounding on this stuff." She gestured vaguely toward the backpack.

"No. I didn't know. I didn't think she was still around." She looked away from me and scanned the room like Karen Carlyle might just be getting some coffee. Then she took off her glasses and pushed at the tears forming in the corners of her eyes.

"So you and Karen were friends? It wasn't just a roommate assignment thing?"

"Courtney," she corrected, putting the glasses back on. "She liked to be called Courtney. She wouldn't answer to Karen."

"You were Courtney's friend, then?" I asked as patiently as I could. Patience does not come easily to me, but this had clearly been a blow to Bonnie. I suddenly regretted telling her this news when she had exams and papers approaching.

Bonnie didn't answer right away. She hunched further over her coffee cup and put her large hands around the cardboard heat shield covering it. She looked into the coffee like she could see the past in its dark, opaque surface.

"I haven't heard from her since she dropped out, but she was the one who asked me to room. Just one day in the fall of freshman year. I'd seen her around, of course. You know. You can't miss her." She stopped, cleared her throat. "Ah, she was so like, I don't know, a model should look. I was amazed she even knew who I was." Again the sweet smile transformed her face.

I smiled back, unable not to respond to such vulnerability. Is this what Karen/Courtney had seen? A large ugly duckling with no guile that would be stunned with gratitude by the attention of a swan? Or had Karen/Courtney really been seeking a friend and had sought out Bonnie because she looked past her appearance to the warm and caring soul inside? So far, from what I'd learned about Karen/Courtney, I leaned toward the first interpretation.

I stayed quiet, hoping Bonnie would continue.

"So, ah, she asked me to room. She knew my roommate had dropped out of school, and she said it wasn't working out where she was, so we applied together and got a double. It was nice it worked out that way."

Bonnie sighed and looked into her cooling coffee.

I raised my own coffee cup to my lips to give me a second to think what to ask now, and over the rim I spotted a familiar tousled brown head, the curls frizzed and gleaming from the damp. Alice!

I rose.

"Bonnie, I'd like you to meet a friend of mine. I'll be right back."

I got up and in three strides I was beside Alice who was dispensing coffee into a cup. I came up beside her.

"Hey. Listen," I said, keeping my voice down. "That's the dead girl's former roommate over there." I shrugged my shoulder toward the table where Bonnie was sitting.

"Bring your coffee, Alice, okay? I'll introduce you."

Alice raised her eyebrows at me.

"Introduce me? What are you up to, girl?" Instead of quietly following me like I'd hoped, she planted her feet and gazed up at me with what I'd come to call 'the look.' If I were her daughter Shawna, I'd never be able to keep a single secret. Students by the score were probably given 'the look' and whatever infraction they were committing on campus, or even thinking of committing, was stopped in its tracks.

I gave in immediately.

"I'm trying to find out what the Carlyle woman was like. You know that was no 'accident,' Alice." As I spoke, I made a sideways move toward the table, trying to nudge Alice along. She didn't budge. Sighing, I moved back to her side. I glanced down. If she planted her feet any more firmly, they were going to leave imprints in the fake marble floor.

"I know that," she said. "What I wanna know is what *you* think you're doin' in this mess."

"Helping?" I said with what I hoped was an innocent face.

Alice's snort probably cooled the coffee she was holding. But she started to walk toward the table where Bonnie was sitting. Bonnie had her iPad back out, but it didn't seem to me that she was reading what was on the screen.

I made introductions as we came up to the table and Alice shrugged off her slicker and sat down. Bonnie's eyes went to Alice's uniform.

"Alice is a campus policewoman," I explained. "She's also my friend." I ignored the second snort. "Naturally the campus police are concerned about this serious event on the campus."

I glanced over at Alice, who appeared to be holding in several choice words, but she stayed silent. Bonnie only nodded.

"What can you tell us to help us know what Courtney was like?" I asked.

Bonnie just frowned and pushed her unwashed brown hair back from her forehead with a heavy hand.

"I don't quite follow you."

Alice raised her coffee cup to cover her mouth.

"Was she easy to live with, for example? Was she a slob or a neat freak? Did she come in at all hours or was she in bed by 9? Did she study much or not at all?"

"I don't see how that will help you, but I'll try." She frowned again.

"Courtney was kind of, I don't know, kind of high-strung sometimes. She wanted to be left alone a lot. I didn't really mind studying in the library. It's quiet and I got a tremendous amount done. I waste more time this year because I study in the room. But it was okay with me to let her alone when she wanted to be." She smiled again and I glanced at Alice. Alice smiled back, registering the essential sweetness of this young woman, but her eyes were narrowed at what we'd just heard about the selfishness of Karen/Courtney.

"Was she with men in your room then?" I asked. Alice nodded slightly.

Bonnie's round face registered shock. Not something she'd thought about.

"Oh. No. I don't think so. No." Bonnie glanced down at her bitten nails. "She just needed to be alone. But you know, there were times when she'd come in later in the evening and she'd just talk and talk. She'd like to turn the lights down and she'd just sit there and talk to me about everything, like about fashion or classes or some of the profs. Just anything and nothing." She paused and got a faraway look on her face. To Bonnie it was a wonderful memory. Then she went on, remembering more. "Though sometimes she'd nearly sleep the clock around. Exhausted, I guess."

Alice and I exchanged a look. What Bonnie had just described was a person on cocaine, or possibly meth, or both. The high energy, the lights bothering her eyes, and then the crash. I nodded at Alice and she took the lead.

"Bonnie, did you ever see any little bags of white powder around the room? Did Courtney take any pills when you were around?"

Well, that was getting right to the point.

Bonnie looked stunned.

"No. No. You've got it all wrong. Nothing like that. Nothing." She paused. "Well, you know, sometimes I thought maybe she took some of the stuff people take to stay up and study, increases focus you know. But that's like legal, right?" Bonnie looked apprehensively at Alice. She pushed her chair back some and I thought for a minute she might just get up and leave.

Alice was on it.

"You mean like Adderall or Ritalin, you know, stimulant medications you get with a prescription?"

Bonnie cautiously nodded.

"But not everybody has their own prescription, right?" Alice continued in a conversational tone.

"I don't know anything about that," Bonnie said flatly.

"Now, Bonnie," Alice said in the same low key tone. "You know we have to ask. We want to find out why she died."

Tears formed behind the thick lenses of her glasses. She didn't even brush them away.

"You don't understand her at all. She was just really intense about studying. And, yeah, she needed to be alone a lot but that's just who she was."

She twirled a strand of hair around her finger, clearly pondering how to make us like Courtney as much as she had. She looked at Alice.

"She wasn't stuck up. I know that. I saw her across the quad a couple of times stopping to talk to one of the campus police guys, one of the ones who ride the bikes. He comes around our dorms too, I've seen him. He's really nice and Courtney was nice to him. See?"

Alice got a thoughtful look on her face. I'd had the same thought. What was up with that campus cop? I didn't buy the 'Courtney was really friendly' line. Was she dating him?

"Did you like her?" Alice asked suddenly. I looked over at her, surprised. She gave me 'the look' and I continued to keep my mouth shut.

"Did I like her?" Bonnie pulled her chair back up to the table and sat up really straight. Her tee shirt stretched over her large breasts. She was clearly as indignant as someone who is essentially kind can get.

"How can I explain this to you, Officer, but especially to you, Professor Ginelli?" She looked at each of us in turn. Her magnified eyes flashed at me.

"She never tried to change me, to get me to go on a diet or dress differently. Many pretty women do that, you know, to someone who looks like me. If we would just 'lose some weight,' or 'dress in solid colors,' or 'wear a little makeup,' and 'do something' with our hair, then we'd be beautiful too. Only it's a lie. The only purpose is to make *them* feel superior. Courtney never did that to me. She never tried to change me. And yes, I liked her. And not only for that."

Alice sat back, her round face shuttered. I wondered if Alice's girlfriends or even family had tried to get her to diet, to dress up, to wear makeup, whatever. And Bonnie had hit me too, where my childhood pain was from being told to 'stand up straight' and to 'wear solid colors' so as not to draw attention to my height. Bonnie might be sweet, but she'd certainly put us in our places. That 'especially you, Professor Ginelli,' wasn't lost on me. She saw me as I was now, not as the too-tall, skinny kid I'd been. And Alice. What was she thinking? I didn't know, but she looked grim.

"Bonnie," I said, needing to change the subject.

She looked at me, no trace of her sweet smile in evidence.

"Was Courtney unhappy? Why did she drop out?"

A few more tears.

"I don't know why she dropped out. The Dean of Students, the RA, the others on our floor, they all asked me that. She only took one suitcase, left all her books. All of them. She was an econ major and some of those textbooks cost a fortune. She took her cell phone, but she actually smashed her portable computer. Yeah, it was a cheap one that I think she'd gotten secondhand, but it looked like she'd thrown it on the floor and maybe stomped on it?" There was wonder and horror in Bonnie's voice.

"So she really was kind of stressed, then?" I asked slowly.

"Yeah, I guess."

"Stressed enough to kill herself?"

Bonnie looked appalled.

"The way she looked, how could she not want to live?" But then she stopped, considering.

"You know, sometimes I wondered. She had no calls from home or packages or anything like that. At least that I saw. And I asked about her family one time and you know what she said?"

"What?" I asked, though it was unnecessary. Bonnie rolled right on.

"She looked at me with this set, white face, and said, 'You don't want to know. You never want to know.'" Of course I never brought it up again, but I wondered about them. Wondered why she seemed to hate them so much. So maybe she was both stressed and unhappy. But I tell you, I never thought she'd just leave school like that. Not say anything to me." She hung her head.

Yikes. We were getting quite a picture of Courtney.

Bonnie sighed, her large chest moving slowly up and down. It was a deep sigh of disappointment and longing. Bonnie had liked Courtney. In fact, she'd loved the swan as only the ugly duckling can, purely, with no hope of ever becoming a swan. But what had Karen/Courtney thought of Bonnie that she'd leave without a word? Love that was hopeless could turn to hate in a flash. Could Karen/Courtney's abandonment of her have caused such hatred in Bonnie? Suppose they had met up by accident during the reception somehow? Suddenly I remembered the small knot of what I had assumed were students at the demonstration at the hospital entrance. If Bonnie had been one of those students, had she seen Karen/Courtney enter with her doctor date? Could she have gotten in to the construction site and sought her out somehow to talk and they'd had a fight? I looked at her large hands, seeing their strength and remembering the bruises on those little arms.

It suddenly occurred to me that there had been a tall white woman at the demonstration in the back row. I hadn't gotten a good look at the students, but I took a shot in the dark.

"Bonnie," I asked, I hoped casually, though it was a complete non sequitur, "I think I've seen you before. Did I see you with the trauma center demonstrators at the new hospital construction site?"

Alice looked at me like I had lost my mind.

Bonnie looked at me curiously.

"Yeah. I was there. I'm pre-med, you know. How can we not have a trauma center here when we're so close to where so many people get shot? I try to show up when I can. I didn't see you, though."

Awkward.

"Ah, well, I was attending the reception. Like Courtney was."

Bonnie looked stunned.

"She was at the reception? I didn't see her."

Maybe.

"Yes, Bonnie. That's where she died." Well, where she was fatally injured.

Bonnie slumped forward, folding in on herself. She put her hands over her face. Either she really didn't know that, or she was hiding her reaction. Tough to know. I leaned toward the first, but who knows how much rage was hidden inside that body that had been so despised by so many?

Alice and I looked at her in silence.

I suddenly noticed Alice had out her notebook and she bent to write something. Then she looked up and spoke briskly to Bonnie.

"What did she take in that one suitcase, do you know?"

Wow. Big time subject change. Alice knew her interrogation techniques.

Bonnie sat up in her chair and looked at Alice, seeming not to see her. She didn't speak. I noticed her eyes were dry.

Alice calmly repeated her question.

"Bonnie, I asked you what Courtney took in that one suitcase?"

She seemed to focus. Thought for a minute.

"Just her fanciest clothes, I think. I remember that from the packing."

"Packing?" Alice followed up.

"Yeah, I packed up the rest of her stuff in boxes when she didn't come back. The RA asked me to."

"What happened to those things?" Alice asked.

"The RA and I carried it down to the basement storage room in Stedman. That's where we roomed. We put it in the area where you can store stuff over the summer. But for all I know it's still there. I never thought about it again."

Too painful to think about, especially as Courtney had abandoned her without a word.

Bonnie glanced up at the wall clock and started.

"Oh, excuse me. I really need to go. I've got biochem. I hope I've helped."

I also hoped she didn't have a test today. We'd clearly upset her.

She pushed back her chair abruptly and stood. I stood too, as did Alice. Bonnie was taller than I am, perhaps an inch or two over 6 feet. I shook her hand as did Alice and we both expressed our thanks. Bonnie's sweet smile was no longer in evidence. She just nodded and started to turn away, then remembered her backpack and reached stiffly down for it. We really had rattled her. She walked quickly away.

Alice and I sat back down. She looked at her notebook, then at me.

"Yeah," I said. "Drugs."

"Right," she replied. "There's a sewer that carries a ton of drugs into Chicago, cocaine, meth, and heroin, primarily. Some of those designer things and the prescription stuff too. We try to keep them off campus, but the city is swamped with them. They get through. There's a whole lot of those prescription stimulants on this campus. Need to study all night? Take some of what they call lid-poppers. We're swamped with them here. And then they go on to something even worse." She tapped her pen on the notebook. "Could be just she was getting amped up on the prescription drugs, or a combination of that and something worse, either cocaine or meth or both." She stared down at her notebook. "But the pills, they're bad enough. Kids at other schools have died."

"Yeah. But Courtney didn't die of a drug overdose. I still think somebody threw her into that elevator shaft." I paused while Alice wrote something.

"So what about Bonnie here? What do you think? She was there, at least at the demonstration. Did she spot Courtney with her doctor date coming in to the reception, find a way to seek her out and they fought? She could easily have tossed Karen/Courtney around."

"I don't know, Kristin. I kind of think not, but I'll report all this," Alice said, tapping the open notebook with her pen.

I turned to look out the window toward the patio. Bonnie had left by that door and I could see her large figure moving across campus, her head and shoulders bent forward as many tall people did to hide their height. I'd been poked in the back enough to know that pose.

Behind me I heard a snap. I didn't need to turn my head to know what that sound meant. Alice had closed her notebook.

16

Jesus loves me
So they say
Then why won't Satan
Go away?
"A Prayer"
Deelon James, #595
Street Wise

Friday, May 19, 8:55 a.m.

I looked at my watch and stood up with a jerk. I had a class too. It was not a good idea to be late to class two times running. Especially since I was supposed to be a teacher, not a slacker student. I shrugged into my raincoat. It was still damp. I looked down at Alice. She was gazing intently at the brown, stained cover of her notebook as though the Rorschach test shapes could reveal the secrets of Courtney Carlyle.

"Gotta go," I said. "Class."

"Right," Alice said, looking up at me. I thought she was about to say something else, but she set her lips and kept whatever it was to herself.

"I'll call you later," I said, grabbing my bag. No answer.

I managed to get out of the building without getting any paint on me. I tried to check my watch again when I got outside. Mistake. I couldn't read it as the rain was now pelting down from a sky the color of gravel, a motley black and gray. I hoped the watch was waterproof.

I jogged along, trying to get myself to mentally shift gears. Thank God I didn't have to lecture today. I reached Myerson and pounded up the stairs two at a time, risking life and limb as the stairs were wet from the other feet, feet of those who were on time for class.

I took time to throw my wet raincoat into my office and then slowed down to a decent professorial gate. As I passed the door of the faculty office, I caught the flash of the copier and saw Mary Frost's thin frame bent over it. She seemed once again mesmerized by the pulsing light. I didn't envy Adelaide having to deal with Frost every day.

I slid into a chair just as Hercules was standing up to begin his lecture.

I looked around the room at the class. We were working on "Good" today. That's what the syllabus said. What they didn't know, yet, was that Hercules was going to tell them about the tiny French village, Le Chambon-sur-Lignon, where he and his mother had been hidden from the Nazis on a farm smack in the middle of occupied France during WWII. A screen was set up at the far end of the seminar table. First, we would be watching a film made by a French filmmaker who'd also been a child hidden by these amazing farmers. I loved the title of the film, "Weapons of the Spirit." In our current climate of "Fake News" and idiotic conspiracies, the story of the inhabitants of this remote village who had chosen to risk their own lives to follow their consciences was particularly apt. They had been persecuted as French Protestants in predominantly Catholic France, and rather than deciding they were permanent victims, they had developed a profound empathy with others who were being persecuted. And they had not been newbies at the business of saving the vulnerable. They had sheltered refugees during WWI. Their pastor, André Trocmé, a pacifist, had led them to combine sheltering refugees with resistance to religious persecution, and thus to rescue and hide hundreds of Jews. In that respect as well, it was also a contrast, even a judgment, on our own times when the persecution of American Muslims had become a cardinal tenet of conservative Christianity.

Hercules wisely didn't do any set up. He just nodded to a student who pressed play. I had seen the film many times, so I watched the faces of the students instead. In the parted lips and even the sheen of a tear on some faces, I could see the yearning to be part of something decent and even noble. Other faces had the pursed lips and narrowed eyes of cynicism and despair. Their thoughts were printed there. This story was 'too good to be true.' Or even, 'I won't admit this is true because then I might have to try to be brave too.' Why were some inspired and others hardened by the same story? Their own histories, their individual gifts, their views of the world and how it really worked all acted as filters, letting in only some parts of the story and refusing entry to other parts. And, I thought, Christianity has harmed many people, probably even people in this room. When so-called Christians have treated you like you don't even deserve to live as free and equal, why would you think they could be a vehicle for goodness? I thought about Karen/Courtney and what she might have thought of this film. I realized even with all I'd learned about her, I wasn't sure, but I suspected she would have been among the cynics.

I glanced at Edwin, wondering how this story of unselfish goodness fit with his experiences of racism. And how did it fit with what he was being taught about the rational choices of "Economic Man," the objective consumer so beloved of conservative economists?

Wait a minute, I thought. Economics. Bonnie had just told us Karen/Courtney was an Economics major. At least she'd had the expensive books. I watched Edwin's smooth bronze face as he gazed intently at the screen. His face didn't give much away, but I knew him well enough to know he was well versed in how to hide what he was really thinking. But he was too young to completely conceal the longing in his eyes. Edwin longed for a world where goodness reigned.

I made up my mind to corner him after class and see if he had known Karen/Courtney Carlyle. Then, as the film came to an end, I turned my full attention to Hercules and the impassioned class debate on how these farmers had done what the nations of the world would not, that is, stand in the way of the Nazi juggernaut of hate. I remembered a time in my own life when I'd wondered how hate could take over a whole society and poison it so thoroughly. I no longer wondered about that since I saw it on the news every day in my own country.

# # # #

As a subdued and thoughtful class filed out of the room, I moved over to Edwin's end of the table.

"Stay a minute, will you?" I asked as he started to rise.

One of his eyebrows went up a fraction. For a second he looked like Mr. Spock of *Star Trek*. I smiled inwardly. It would be like Edwin to have practiced that one eyebrow lift. He sat back down.

"Want some coffee or tea?" I asked gesturing toward the hall where the open door showed Adelaide's new coffee machine. It made both coffee and tea and I bet Edwin was a tea drinker.

He shook his large head no, but made no reply. He sat quietly, waiting. I sat down in a chair kitty-corner to him.

I looked at him for a second as I contemplated how to raise the subject of Karen/Courtney. He was very well dressed, as usual, in tailored gray slacks, a carefully ironed pinstriped Oxford cloth shirt and a cream-colored sweater vest. I briefly wondered if his Aunt Melda, who had raised him, had ironed the shirt. No, from what I knew of her, I bet she'd taught her nephew how to iron. On the back of the chair hung a forest green Abercrombie and Fitch anorak. A neatly-rolled umbrella lay on the seminar table parallel to his stacked books and his portable computer.

Come to think of it, he and Courtney were alike in their upscale dressing, though I thought for very different reasons. Courtney had dressed to attract attention and to further her sense of contempt for her peers. Edwin dressed to deflect attention. I was sure Edwin's immaculate grooming and Ralph Lauren ensembles were as carefully planned as everything else in his life. He hadn't chosen his race or his size, but he had read his environment with great precision. His look was designed to state, 'I am safe. I am not a criminal.' But a few times, since I'd known him, I'd glimpsed the considerable passion underneath his controlled exterior. And now I'd seen his longing for goodness as he watched the film.

"Edwin, I was wondering if you could help me?" I began.

He smiled faintly at that. Edwin does not consider me the safest person to know. I had wondered why he'd taken this class in fact. It would scarcely have fit in to his Economics major.

"I know, I know," I replied to that little smile. "But this shouldn't cost you, I swear. I'm just trying to get some background on a Karen or Courtney Carlyle. That's the young woman who just died after a fall at the Anderson building construction site. Did you hear about it?"

The smile vanished from his face like someone had passed an eraser over a chalkboard. A nod.

"Someone told me she was an econ major. Did you know her? What was she like?"

He leaned back in his chair and put his hands flat on the seminar table. Taking his time. Considering.

"Why do you want to know?" he asked slowly, turning his head away from me to look out the leaded glass windows that lined one wall.

"I was the one who found her and tried to save her. She was bruised, Edwin. She didn't just fall into an elevator shaft. Somebody pushed her or threw her, I'm sure of it. She drowned in the concrete. It's still giving me nightmares. I want to know why."

I paused, breathing heavily. Even this brief reminder of that suffocating death still bothered me. I reached out a hand toward the hand closest to me, still lying flat on the table. But I didn't touch him. As I'd hoped, my small movement made him look at me again.

"You know that about me by now. I have to know the causes. It's like breathing." And if I don't know, the nightmares will keep choking me.

Edwin frowned at me and then spoke.

"Yeah. I know. And yeah, I knew her. Not well, but I knew her. We're the same year. I mean, were the same year. Freshman year she was in a different section of Economics 100, the required intro, but last spring we were together in Macroeconomics."

Edwin looked down at his neat, square-cut nails. I could practically hear his self-editor click on, warning him not to say too much. I needed to give his self-editor the boot.

"Now don't shut me out, Edwin. I really need to know what she was like. Don't just tell me what you figure it's safe to tell me." I stopped. I had almost said, 'It won't go any further,' but he'd know that wasn't true. This wasn't a private conversation, it was my attempt to help with an investigation.

The frown became a grimace.

"You want to know what she was really like? Well, she was no Ah-seong, let me tell you that." Ah-seong had been a lovely Korean student Edwin had dated and who'd been murdered last semester. He was still plainly hurting from her death. As was I, in fact. He went on.

"Women like that Carlyle, now. They suck you in and make you pay. She had to be sure the eye of every guy in the class was on her the whole time. Even the prof. What am I saying? Especially the prof. I work the desk nights in the econ library and the hall that leads to the professors' offices runs right past the glass entry. You know it?"

He fixed me with a glare while I nodded and then he plunged on. It was like a dam had burst.

"So midnight? What's she doin' sashaying down the hall to a prof's office at midnight? Let me ask you that? What was she doin'? Well, you can guess."

Now I knew where Carlyle was at least some of the nights when Bonnie had said she was out so late.

Edwin stopped and took a shuddering breath. Well, well. Courtney had been visiting a professor's office at midnight and Edwin hadn't liked it one bit.

"Did you ever take her out?" I asked, watching his face.

Edwin's startled eyes gave me my answer. He looked so taken aback it was like I had poured a cup of ice water over his head.

"Me? Are you kidding? Do you think I'm insane or what? My Aunt Melda didn't raise nobody stupid enough to fall for that shit." His big shoulders shivered a little, like someone had walked over his grave. And someone just might have if he'd lived a few years earlier and tried to even look at a white girl. I mentally shook myself. What a dangerous delusion for me to have, that lethal racism was going away. It was obviously increasing in our times. Edwin knew that, but that didn't mean there was no attraction.

"But you thought about it, didn't you, Edwin?" I asked softly.

He looked back out the window and spoke without really seeing the view. He was seeing something very different.

"Thinking is all I ever do, Professor. All I can afford to do," he said, wearily. "But Carlyle made sure I thought about it all the time. When she'd pass the door to the library, on the way to that prof's office, she'd glance in, make sure I was at the desk, make sure I saw her and where she was going. She'd slow down. Give me a smile. She made sure I saw her and knew where she was going and why. Not because she wanted me. Because she knew that if I fell for her it'd fuck up my life. And that's what she wanted to do."

Now it was my turn to be startled.

"What?"

"Oh yeah." Edwin turned back to me and almost smiled at my response. Almost. He tapped a finger on the stack of books.

"You know that reading we had by that guy, what's his name, Poling? Where he said evil's a chameleon, it takes on the coloration of the good so you won't notice it's bad?"

I nodded.

"Well she took on the color of a harmless little doll. But she was evil."

Whoa.

After Edwin dropped this bomb, he leaned his chair back and folded his arms across his sweater-covered chest. He was an intelligent, sensitive man, but he was also enough of a kid to look a little pleased at how he'd related Courtney to the reading.

I decided to push back a little.

"Don't you think 'evil' is a little strong as a description of some who, I grant you, was flirting with every guy she saw?"

Edwin rocked his chair forward so abruptly the chair legs hitting the stone floor sounded like a gunshot. He pointed a long finger at me.

"Helen of Troy mean anything to you? How much was all that death and destruction her fault?"

Oh preserve me from the liberal arts educated. The Greeks, for God's sake.

"Now wait a damn minute here, Edwin. Guys, and that includes the Greeks, have always tried to blame the messes their desires lead them into on women. I seem to recall Adam blaming Eve because *he* wanted an apple."

As soon as the biblical reference was out of my mouth, however, I regretted it. For all his polish, I knew Aunt Melda was a staunch Baptist and Edwin had certainly been raised that way. Maybe he wouldn't take kindly to reinterpreting the bible from Eve's point of view.

Edwin leaned forward in the chair and the legs creaked in protest at all this action. He pointed his finger at me again.

"It's Eve's fault if she sets him up for it. She's bored in the garden, but she's too scared to go out on her own. So she uses Adam to pick a fight with God. Then while the two men duke it out, the gate's open and she waltzes on out into the world."

I was about to object, but then had to concede he might have a point. Of course, 'two men' included God as a guy, but hey, Edwin wasn't a biblical literalist anyway. But I wanted to get us back to specifics on Courtney.

"Listen, Edwin. I like biblical interpretation as much as the next person, probably more, really. But this argument isn't helping me get to know Courtney specifically. Let's shift gears. Tell me about her work in the economics classes. Was she a good student?"

It took him a minute to let go of both the anger and the desire that Courtney had inspired in him. To give him credit, I could see him exercise his considerable self-discipline to shake it off.

Then he looked a little puzzled. I wondered if he'd actually ever given a moment's thought to whether Courtney was becoming a decent economist. Well, this university, like most, had very few women in its economics department. I'd seen some stats on that a while ago. In fact, the sciences in general had very few women. I thought about that as I watched Edwin struggle to come up with some memory of Courtney that wasn't related to sex.

Edwin spoke suddenly, interrupting my reverie.

"She was pretty good, I think. Macro's tough. A lot of Calculus. It washes a lot of people out," he said, considering.

"So she was good at math?" I asked, my knowledge of Calculus being basically zero.

"Well, here, economics *is* mostly math. You'd have had to have gotten a B or better in first semester Calculus to even enroll in Macro, so she'd have to have done that."

Inwardly I shuddered. I'd hated Calculus and I bet at the U of C it was a bear of a class, designed to weed out the mathematically weak in homage to Darwin's survival of the fittest.

"Can you remember whether she participated in class, what she said? You said she liked to be noticed. That means to me she probably spoke up in class a lot."

Edwin's eyes held dash of humor.

"It was worse than you might think. Once a week we had a big lecture, but then the discussion sections would be in smaller groups. She was in my group. The prof, a guy named Nigel Southerland, liked to have people come up and graph problems on the board. You know, like supply curve versus demand curve?"

No, of course I didn't know, but I nodded anyway.

"So, the idea is to graph these curves and then translate them into equations. Ms. Carlyle would raise her hand and of course she got called on all the time. She'd be wearin' these heels and a short skirt and she'd take her own sweet time walking up to the board. Nobody complained." Edwin's voice petered out, I assumed remembering the short skirt and heels.

I snapped my fingers almost under his nose.

"Wake up, Edwin. What I want to know is, was she right or wrong, did she get the *right answer*?" Of course, none of these guys, including the professor apparently, seemed to have cared about that.

Edwin narrowed his eyes. He was really having to work at remembering whatever Courtney had written on the board apparently.

"Well, she was good at the graphic analysis, I think. Sometimes she stumbled over solving the equations, but that's pretty typical."

"And in the discussions? What did she contribute besides raising the room temperature?"

Edwin looked a trifle sheepish. He gave himself a little shake and tried to look thoughtful. God. Courtney had done a number on these guys. I was beginning to see her point in her paper for Adelaide. Why bother to fight for equal rights when you could just lead these guys around by their anatomy?

Edwin spoke up.

"Well, it seemed to me that she was good at the big picture. Like when we were discussing models of labor markets."

Edwin paused when he saw my quizzical look. He would make a good teacher some day, I thought.

"That's making a model of how people supply labor to the market, how they make job choices. I remember that the rest of us were struggling just to get the simple mechanics straight and wham she comes in with stuff about how the model isn't complete, that we haven't factored in how companies can strain people out in certain ways before they even get in, stuff like that. We were just getting the model and she'd seen past it to more complex problems."

So she had been smart. Ideas smart. Conceptions smart. Interesting.

I glanced at my watch. We'd been at this for nearly 40 minutes. I stood.

"Thanks, Edwin. And I'm sorry if I was a little tough on you. I have to know what is really what and who is, and was, really who to figure this out."

"No. It's okay. I guess I'd never let myself think how much she'd gotten to me, is all." He started methodically stacking his books into his briefcase. No backpack for Edwin.

I watched him carefully putting his things away. Proper Edwin on the outside, and a man who'd desired a woman on the inside. Had Edwin told me the truth? Was thinking really all he'd done with Karen/Courtney? Had he left the desk in the library one night and followed her to an empty classroom? He would never tell me if that had been the case. And what could she have done to him if they had gone to that empty classroom together? Had she threatened to screw up his life? It would have been child's play for Edwin to toss Courtney across a room let alone down into an elevator shaft.

Suddenly I remembered seeing him passing trays of canapés at the reception. That's right. He was on work/study in addition to having a scholarship. Working at the library must have been only one of those jobs.

"Edwin," I said. He paused in his careful packing of his briefcase and looked at me.

"That reception, where Courtney died. You worked it, right?"

He just nodded.

"Did you see her?"

"No, I didn't, Professor." He looked down and resumed packing his books, avoiding my eyes. He was lying. He'd seen her. Was this just self-preservation, or something more? Whatever it was, he was shut down now and he'd not tell me.

Edwin registered I was staring at him. His calling me 'professor' had triggered another question. That midnight professor.

"Edwin, that professor. The one she was seeing late at night. Was it that Southerland guy you mentioned?"

"Yeah, but it won't do you much good. He was visiting from the London School of Economics. He's not here this year."

I guess that eliminated him as a suspect. But his views on Courtney would have been interesting. And his views on Edwin.

We both turned and exited the room. I shut off the lights and closed the door.

17

My friend.
She's my friend.
When I see her on the street I'm glad
She's my friend.
"My Friend"
Marlena Myers, #1059
StreetWise

Friday, May 19, Noon to 3 p.m.

I worked straight through lunch. I had grabbed my paper mail when I figured Frost had departed for her lunch break. When I had finished throwing most of that in the recycle bin, I worked my way through my email. I scarcely took my finger off of the delete button. Every bureaucrat in this institution could now enter a tiny part of my mind by selecting 'list serve.' 'Orwellian' was already overused as a description of the first quarter of the 21st century, but that was because it was such a fitting description. I could feel the electronic tendrils with their sensitive cilia trying to attach themselves to all aspects of my life. After more than an hour, I started pressing 'delete' on my voicemail.

At this rate, eventually all we will ever do each day is send and receive messages without having time to think about any content. It was like an essay I'd once read by the great historian, Henry Steele Commager, written decades ago. He had been railing against the Xerox machine. All his students did now, he complained, was use a machine to pile up copies of material that they never actually read. He'd compared that to a time when one had had to copy references by hand. The laborious task brought one into intimate contact with the author. I shuddered to think what Commager would have thought of our era. Not only the metastasis of electronic messages, but Google searches? Wikipedia? Twitter? I pushed my chair back from the desk in a small, and fairly useless protest against contact with all this mind-numbing repetition. I was starting to feel like the kid's hamster in his little exercise ball. Rolling and rolling around to absolutely no purpose. I had never considered academic life could be this moronic. By contrast, in rosy retrospect, being a cop was looking pretty good.

I rolled my chair back to the desk and pressed the code to finish listening to my voicemail. Several students droned on about why their assignments would be late. Suddenly, I sat up as Alice's voice came on. She'd called a little after noon. Her voice sounded more upbeat than she'd seemed in the morning.

"This is Alice Matthews. I'm going to Stedman later. See if Carlyle's stuff is still in storage there. I should get there by about 1:15, 1:30 at the latest. Come if you want." I checked my watch. Damn. Probably missed her. But still. Faced with a choice of deleting messages or going to find Alice, it was a no-brainer. I was locking the door and racing down the stairs before the bureaucrats even knew I had escaped.

# # # #

The rain had stopped, but the sky was still laden with clouds. The wind from the west was whipping them into slate-colored streams running toward the lake. Small branches and leaves littered the paths between buildings, and puddles had become small lakes in low-lying areas, reflecting the racing, leaden skies. I picked my way around the water, heading toward Stedman, a dorm on the north side of the central quad.

It was a newer building, in the sense that 'new' here meant not 100 years old. It was part of the 1960's expansion of the undergraduate program. It was a typical '60's travesty of architecture set apart from the much older but still dignified Gothic. I could see it from several blocks away, sitting alone on a corner. Roughened concrete walls poked out in odd, hexagonal shapes connected by a slate-surfaced entrance. Glass punctuated the concrete in vertical slots, the architect trying for a modern rendering of the Gothic, I supposed. The windows were filled with the backs of torn posters, flowered sheets taped to the glass to cover areas left exposed by curtains half hanging off the rods, and quantities of books, papers, coffee pots and dying plants filling the sills. The concrete slabs between these cluttered windows had been streaked with long, brown stains, as though hundreds, no thousands, of gallons of coffee were dripping down from the roof. I wondered how long before this building was torn down to make way for some other modern architecture that would not last another half century.

As I hurried up to the glass and slate entrance, I carefully avoided the convoluted stainless steel sculpture in front of it. It looked like a giant, dirty silver-colored pretzel. Oddly enough, this place was still nicknamed "New Dorm."

I pulled open the glass door and crossed the white on white lobby. What a choice of color for an undergraduate residence. The white floors were covered with today's (and many other days') water and muddy foot-prints, the formerly white walls were covered with countless notices, the paint that was visible between them shredded when tape had pulled off the paint with previously discarded notices. The white, undulating reception desk was scarred at the bottom by many feet and dotted at the top with many dirty fingerprints. The whole place was making me feel like I wanted to run home, get some 409 cleaner and a rag.

I walked quickly up to the desk, resisting the cleaning impulse. The young woman sitting there had stringy, brown hair falling forward as she peered through wire-rimmed glasses at the text in front of her that was at least three inches thick. I addressed her twice and got no response before I saw the tiny earbuds leading to her cell phone that had been hidden by the hair.

I reached over the top of the desk and put my hand, none too gently, onto her reading material. She looked up at me with startled hazel eyes. She pulled one earbud out of her ear. Only one. I saw she was wearing a tee shirt with the words, "Sex Kills. Be a Physics Major and Live Forever" printed on it. How true.

"Yes?" she said in a tone of annoyance. Apparently she was only being paid to study.

"I want to find a campus policewoman who came in here probably about half an hour ago. Is she still here?"

"I have no idea, I haven't noticed anyone," she replied coldly. I believed her. The Mormon Tabernacle Choir all dressed in campus police uniforms could have been through here and she'd not have noticed.

"Which way is the basement storage room?" I asked, holding on to my temper by the scruff of its neck.

"I'm sorry. I don't know. I just started this job today." She put her ear-bud back in and looked back down at her book.

I quit wasting time with her. On the plus side, she clearly wasn't go-ing to try to stop me from searching for the entrance to basement. I slowly looked around the dirty white lobby, thinking. If Alice hadn't needed to check with someone at the reception desk for a key, maybe this dorm was on her route and she already had keys. Or she'd gotten keys from the campus police office before she'd headed over. But where was the entrance? Then I saw stairs going up to the second floor. Behind them was a door. Probably the basement.

I hurried over to it. It was not only unlocked, it was slightly ajar and when I opened it and the lights in the descending staircase were on. Good. Maybe Alice was still here.

White cinderblock walls, grimed from many hands touching the walls rather than the handrail, reflected the light from the overhead fluorescents. The garish light made the red, rubber treads of the stairs jump up at me. I hurried down them and paused at the bottom.

A central basement corridor was in front of me. Closed doors lined it on both sides. There were lots of doors. It was like a dream sequence or really a nightmare where an infinite number of doors are lined up along an infinite, receding corridor behind which subconscious fears lurked.

I shook myself. Basements do creep me out.

I listened for a moment and then called "Alice!" several times. No response.

Maybe the door to the basement had been left open by a maintenance person and Alice was already gone. I tried a more impersonal "Hello?"

Still the slightly clammy walls only bounced my own voice back to me. I drew my raincoat closer. It was not only damp down here, it was chilly.

Well, I thought, Alice had obviously departed, but maybe I could locate Carlyle's stuff too and we could compare notes later.

I started trying doors. The first door opened. It did not contain any neuroses, just a filthy sink and a large supply of cleaners and disinfectants. I wasn't surprised at the large store of available cleaners. They were plainly not using them on the building.

The next door opened too. Didn't these people know about locking doors in the city?

I flipped on the light and a pool table with a pitted, pale green baize surface and uneven legs leapt into view. A few battered sofas and a lot of chrome chairs with tattered, red vinyl seats were scattered around the walls. I'd found the basement lounge, apparently. I could appreciate the university's efforts to upgrade the lounge in the student union when this was the alternative. The air smelled of mold, stale cigarettes and a whiff of the sickly sweet smell of marijuana. I quickly shut off the light and closed the door.

The next door was locked, but the hum from behind it told me it housed the mechanicals. I looked down the hall. Soon I would run out of doors.

At the end of the corridor was a door with a red, electric sign above it that said, "Emergency Exit Only." Probably not the storage room.

I looked again and on the left-hand wall was another door that appeared to be slightly ajar. On the floor next to it was a black box labeled "Caution. Poison." Rodent bait. I bet the rodents were making tracks from outside to the storage room. Our house had a rodent problem too, but now I used traps after reading the label on the poison ones. The rodents eat the poison-soaked bait and then return to their nests. The poison works by stopping their blood from clotting and they bleed to death in the walls. I hadn't been able to stomach the idea of rats and mice hemorrhaging in my house walls. Probably hundreds of rodents were doing that right now in the walls of "New Dorm." Ick.

I quickly pushed open the door that was ajar and flipped on the light. Bingo. Wooden shelving rose to the ceiling. It was arranged in rows like a giant library. It made me a little anxious since I'd had a bad experience in a library, but I focused on the luggage, cardboard boxes, fans, sports equipment and even some bedding stacked on the shelves. Not a library. This was clearly the storage room. I walked toward the first rank and noticed each shelf had wooden dividers at about four foot intervals. Small, hand-lettered signs were tacked to each section. I peered at the one closest to me. "Bateson." The names of the owners, I assumed. Some of the little signs were faded and hard to read. I moved along slowly, having to read the top, middle and bottom of each section. No "Carlyle" so far. There was no attempt at alphabetical order. "Carlson" had followed "Winchester." I turned the corner at the end of the first rank, so intent on reading the signs I was startled when my foot struck something on the floor. I looked down. A small foot in a small, brown oxford. It was Alice, lying face down in the space between the next rows of shelves.

Bright red blood was trickling from a wound on her head. The part of my brain that was functioning registered that it hadn't even had time to clot. She was perfectly still.

"Alice! Alice!" I yelled, dropping down on my knees beside her. I fumbled around between her jacket and her hair, trying to get to her neck. My fingers found it and a small but definite pulse throbbed beneath my probing fingers. I sat back on my heels and tried to think.

I had rushed over here with only my keys in my pocket. I had no cell phone. I looked around for Alice's walkie-talkie but it was nowhere in sight. If it were under her, I could not risk moving her to find it. A head wound meant the neck might be involved. And the spine. I tried not to panic.

I'd have to go outside to call for help. I hated to leave her. Whoever had done this could still be around. I thought of that exit sign right outside this room. But Alice needed help immediately. I felt so helpless and enraged that my hands shook like I had MS. I ripped off my raincoat, tearing off a few buttons, and placed it as gently as I could over Alice. Then I raced into the corridor and jerked open the door under the exit sign. An alarm sounded. Good. It was an exterior door. A set of concrete stairs rose to ground level. I couldn't see anyone. I stepped back inside and pulled the door shut tightly. I went back into the storage room and took a look at Alice. She was in the same place and clearly still unconscious. I ran up and down the rows of shelving and saw no one. I went out of the room and ran down the length of the hall, throwing open the doors where I had not looked yet. Only two were unlocked and they were empty rooms.

I had to risk it. I pounded back up the stairs the way I had come and skidded up to the desk. I grabbed the landline from under the nose of the physics major.

I stabbed in the campus emergency number and quickly told the operator where I was and what had happened. I told them a campus police-woman was unconscious, had a head injury and an ambulance was needed immediately. I hung up.

"Take out those earbuds," I snapped at the startled face of the physics major. "Go outside and wait for the ambulance and the cops. Show them to the basement through the side door. I'll prop it open. An injured woman, a campus policewoman, is in the last storage room next to the emergency exit." She just sat there. "Hurry!" I yelled. She started to move.

I ran back down the stairs and down the corridor. I grabbed the poison bait box and used it to prop open the emergency door. The alarm wailed again. I ran back into the storage room. Alice had not moved. I put my back to the wall to stand guard over my friend. My friend. My friend whom I'd almost gotten killed with my stupid curiosity.

I bent over and checked Alice's pulse again. It was steady and did not seem to have changed.

Breathing a little easier, I stood up again and then I registered that the floor by Alice's feet and further down the row was littered with books, papers and even some clothes. I moved over to that section of the storage shelves and peered at the cards labeling the sections. I saw "Carlyle" in the middle section under some torn boxes. The papers and books were scattered on the floor directly in front of that area.

I frowned. Alice wouldn't have made this kind of mess in a search. The torn boxes and scattered papers were testimony to a hurried search, most likely by the person who had come up behind Alice and hit her on the head.

I whispered 'forgive me' to whatever god was poorly overseeing this catastrophe and went to my raincoat that was still covering Alice. I carefully pulled out my gloves and put them on. I did my own hurried search through the Carlyle section and also through what was scattered on the floor. I was tempted to take some of the papers with me, but decided I wouldn't tamper with evidence. Well, not any more than I had.

Then I heard the wail of approaching sirens and I went to the emergency exit to let them in.

I hated myself in that moment.

18

Rain rain go away
Papers won't stay dry that way
Rain rain go away
Sun please come out
Then it'll be okay
"Raining"
Dwayne Moorehouse, #2165
StreetWise

Friday, May 19, 3 p.m.

Rain and rain and rain. He wished this rotten day would just end. He tried not to think about her in that little box. He'd moved away from the box. Rules said you weren't supposed to move from your corner but he couldn't just stand there with people dropping coins into the slot, clang, clang, clang, and then the sound like a jail cell door opening and banging shut. Loud. Locking her in the box. He turned to look up the street opposite. Just forget it he told himself. Forget her. Why you getting all het up about nothin'? Mama'd said that when those puppies were drowned. They're nothin' to you. Nothin'. Right. He squared his shoulders. Nothin'.

He looked across up the street toward the campus, keeping that box out of his sight. Big building, where students lived. Stupid looking building. Looked like a big ole playpen. Big concrete bars holding in big babies. Big big babies those students. Maybe they spit up on the roof. He chuckled. Brown stains running down the bars like the giant babies had puked on the roof and the puke was running down the sides. He chuckled again. His stomach was bad today but he laughed his silent laugh anyway. And that statue in front. He shook his head over that. He squinted. He supposed it was a statue. What else could it be? Car crash? Another silent chuckle. Students sat all over it when it was nice but today the rain just ran down and down and down. Puddles on the ground. He paused. Hey, a rhyme. He hoped he'd remember it for a poem. He liked those rhyme poems.

A door opened low down on the side of the students' building. He looked harder. It was almost buried under the ground. He'd never seen any-body use that door. The top of the door was moving and a head came up, stopped. Must be stairs there. There were a lot of bushes so he couldn't see all that well. Then shoulders and a chest came up. He froze and his stomach clenched. That guy. One of them. That guy was so mean. The campus cop who'd shoved him. He scuttled over sideways like a crab and tried to hide in the copy shop doorway. He trembled. He squinted through the rain running down the windows looking to see if the nice copy shop guy was inside but he didn't see him. He huddled in the doorway trying to be invisible. He didn't want no more trouble with that guy over there. No sir. No sir.

He waited and then risked a peek over to the students' building. The guy was on his bike and taking off real fast. Movin' away. Okay okay. He came out slowly and went back to his new spot. He tried to stop trembling. Just a few more minutes he promised himself. Sell a couple more papers. He'd sold some. He patted his pocket. Probably enough to get some McD's.

Then he jerked. Wah, wah, wah. A loud noise. Awful noise. Comin' from the students' building. Like a car alarm but it wasn't. Then he saw her. Had to be her, the Glenda witch, the sparkly lady who changed to black. He hated black. Her head stuck up above the ground from the same place where that guy had come out. Her beautiful golden hair was getting wet. Looked almost brown but it was her. She looked around and then disappeared. The wah wah wah stopped. Then it started again.

He tensed waiting to see if she'd come back out. Then the screaming started. Scream. Scream. Scream. He felt it in his chest. In his stomach. Flashing lights came and hurt his eyes. He closed his eyes but it was worse. He could feel the screaming noise. He opened his eyes. An ambulance pulled up right by the side of the building where the door was. The screaming noise stopped so fast it was like somebody had choked it off. Some guys jumped out and ran to the door he'd never seen anybody use and now everybody was using it.

Oh no. Oh no. Ambulance guys coming meant somebody was hurt. Was the Glenda witch hurt? Had that guy hurt her? He wanted to run but he was too scared to move. Then he saw her head pop up again. Okay. Okay. She must be okay. She's not the one hurt.

Then more screaming. Cop cars coming. Lots of them. He put his hands over his ears and the plastic bag holding his papers fell unnoticed onto the wet sidewalk. Then his nerve broke completely and he ran the other way, his hands still covering his ears. He ran from the box and the noise and the hurt.

19

Night falls
And the stars come out.
They're hot,
But they look so cold.
And they don't give a damn.
"The Cold Stare"
James Maddox, #965
StreetWise

Friday, May 19, 8 p.m.

I could see Tom's tall figure walking toward me down the long green hall that bisected the emergency room. I tried to suck every nuance I could out of his walk, his face, his hands. He was carrying a large, brown envelope in one hand. What was that? Was he frowning? I concentrated. Did the slope of his shoulders mean bad news or just fatigue? I remembered another doctor coming down a long hall. It had seemed like he had been miles away, coming miles and miles, coming slowly. Coming to tell me Marco hadn't made it through the surgery. That Marco my husband was dead. I couldn't sit. I got up and hurried forward to meet Tom now, unable to stand the tension.

"She'll be fine," Tom said. For a second the words hung there but wouldn't change into meaning. I grappled with the sounds, afraid I hadn't heard him correctly.

"Fine?" I croaked.

"Yes. Fine." He looked closely at me and took my arm and led me back to the seating. As I sat, I registered that he didn't sit too. He squatted in front of me and was holding on to my left wrist. When I realized he was taking my pulse, I pulled my hand away.

"No. I'm okay. Tell me about Alice," I said jerkily. Tom still squatted in front of me, his intense blue eyes scanning my face like twin lasers, checking to see if I was okay. I squirmed. I wanted to get out from under those searchlights. I patted the cold, molded-orange plastic seat next to me.

"Just sit, Tom. Please. Tell me. You said Alice was fine. Fine how? How fine can she be when she was unconscious for so long and she was bleeding from a big gash on her head?" Despite my desire to seem calm, hot tears burned my eyes. I remembered Alice, all in a small lump being carried out on a stretcher.

Tom reached out a long finger and smoothed away the tears. His finger felt cool and dry on my hot, wet skin. Then he did get up and sit next to me. He placed the brown envelope on his lap. He patted it but left it closed.

"I can't show you this because of patient confidentiality, not unless Alice gives written permission, but this is a copy of her CT scan. I consulted with the radiologist and looked at it thoroughly myself. I can just tell you that the things that would concern us aren't there. She was hit from behind, but you already knew that. And she's regained consciousness. She's actually being moved to a room now."

His matter of fact voice was getting through to me. She was fine. She was okay. She was awake. She wasn't going to be a vegetable. She wasn't dead.

I realized I was gripping the top of Tom's hand that was holding the brown envelope so hard I was going to leave a mark on him. I let go and looked up at him. I looked at the lines that radiated out from his eyes, eyes that were looking at me now, not scanning me to see if I was going to faint. I'd ridden with Alice in the ambulance and had frantically called him during the short ride. He'd met us in the ER. I knew he would unless he was bending over some patient operating on them. But I knew he'd come as soon as he could. I knew that for certain. I knew I could count on him.

"Thanks for looking out for Alice, Tom," I said. I put my hand on his cheek and felt the scratch of a day's beard. He turned his face briefly into my palm and stood up.

"Let me check if she's in her room and then I'll take you to see her. They'll observe her overnight and it's likely she'll be released tomorrow. That's routine." He was already striding down the green hall.

What did he mean, routine? It must be serious to keep her in the expensive hospital when insurance companies kicked you out after brain surgery. I jumped up and ran after Tom.

He heard me coming and stopped so abruptly I almost ran into him.

"What do you mean, routine?" I panted.

"Routine. Normal procedure. Everything's going to be fine. Don't go ballistic, like Kelly would say." He chuckled at his own witticism and then was race-walking away. Okay. Sure. Breathe. Calm down, I told myself. But reminders of Kelly never helped me calm down. I hurried after him.

# # # #

The room was at the very end of a long corridor. Tom pushed open the door and it made a whoosh sound on its pneumatic hinges. The room was slightly too warm and darkened. The overhead lights were not on. The shade for the window was pulled up all the way, but the dark sky held only a few stars; the only light came from the windows of adjacent buildings and the streetlights below. As my eyes adjusted to the dim light, I could see Alice's daughter Shawna sitting in a high-backed chair of cracked-green vinyl, looking very small and scared. Her braided hair had little bows all over it. She had a doll clutched in one hand. It had the same color bows in its braided brown hair. Shawna was far too young to have been allowed in here. I wondered if Tom had fixed it so she could see her Mom.

At the head of the bed, facing the door, stood a tall man in jeans and a tee shirt. His face was as fixed as stone as he looked at his wife on the bed. Alice's eyes were closed. But they were holding hands.

He looked up as we came in.

"Hello, Doc," he said to Tom. "This girl's gonna be fine now." Fine. Clearly the preferred diagnosis. He squeezed Alice's hand and I saw her wince a little.

"Hello, Jim," I said softly.

He nodded. That was all. I felt a lump form in my stomach.

"I'd like to talk with you both," said Tom, addressing Alice and Jim. He glanced over at me and then at the huge eyes in the chair that were watching him like a sparrow watches a hawk. I took the hint.

"Hey, Shawna," I said. She dragged her eyes toward me.

"Let's go get some ice cream. I bet we can find out where the nurses keep it." Ice cream was my current response to children and crisis. This probably meant they'd all grow up with huge eating disorders as a response to crisis, starting with my boys.

Shawna just looked over at her Mom.

Alice's eyes opened.

"Come here, baby," said Alice, raising the hand Jim wasn't holding. Shawna got up obediently from the chair and walked slowly to the bed, never taking her eyes off this strange Mama with the bandage on her head. She stopped by the bedside and Alice stroked the braids.

"I'm okay, Shawna-baby. Mama's okay. Go get some ice cream with Kristin and in a few minutes Daddy will take you to Grammy's house. I'll see you tomorrow." She kissed her own hand and patted Shawna's cheek with it. I felt the tears coming back. I pressed my hands to my eyes to stop them.

Silently the child turned to me and took my hand.

We walked out together and headed for the small galley next to the nurse's station. I hoped there would be ice cream there, though I was sure, as I looked down at the silent little head next to me, neither of us would eat anything.

# # # #

"Don't you be stupid, now," Alice said from the bed. Tom, Jim and Shawna had all left. Jim had promised Alice to return in an hour.

"I won't be stupid if you insist," I said dryly. "But it's always an effort for me, Alice."

I heard a feeble snort.

"I don't want cute, neither." Alice struggled to sit up a little more on the pillows and winced. I silently handed her the control to electrically raise the head of the bed.

"Thanks. Flip that light back off, will you?" she asked. I assumed the overhead lights had been turned on so they could see the CT scan of Alice's head.

I turned off the lights and the room plunged into darkness. We stayed silent for a moment. The whine of the bed's motor had been loud but now there was only silence in the shadows.

"I don't remember a single thing," said Alice quietly. "Last I remember is bein' at my desk around lunch and even that's hazy."

"Do you remember calling me, asking me to meet you at Stedman?"

Alice started to shake her head no and winced. She waited for a second.

"No. Your Tom said that it's normal not to remember even what happened several hours before you get a conk on the head like this."

"Will you remember eventually?" I asked, and then wanted to bite my tongue. I was afraid Alice would think all I was interested in was whether she'd remember she'd seen the perp. But it turned out that was what Alice was interested in as well.

"Shit, I hope so," she said through clenched teeth. "I wanna remember who did this so bad and sock'em away for a million years." She had leaned forward a little in her wrath. Spent with even that small effort, she leaned back against the pillows and closed her eyes.

"And I want a cigarette so bad I can taste it in my lungs," she said to the ceiling.

"Where are they?" I asked. "I'll get them."

Alice cocked an eye at me.

"Boy, you musta been scared good if you're gonna get me a cigarette." She closed her eyes.

"But no dice. No cigarette. Raises the blood pressure or some damn fool thing like that. They said."

I waited in silence, the darkened room magnifying sounds from the hall. The clanging of carts taking away dirty dinner trays, the rumble of bed wheels, a sudden whoosh of a door.

"Kristin," Alice said after a minute, her eyes still closed. "I meant what I said about not gettin' stupid." Both eyes opened and their dark brown centers bored into me.

"I know you, girl. You think you can fix everythin' and if you don't everythin's your fault. You think you need to rush over to that basement, nose into it. Lots of good folks are gonna be goin' over that building, askin' questions, checkin' on that little bitch's stuff. And we don't even know this was about that. Probably not. Somebody hidin' in there where they're not supposed to be and I startle'd 'em by flippin' on the light."

Confession time.

"No, Alice. I called the ambulance and waited with you, but, well, you were out cold. I checked on you, but I also went through Carlyle's stuff. The boxes in her space were torn open, and books and papers were scattered on the floor. I assumed you hadn't made the mess and so I looked through her stuff."

"Christ," Alice said.

I waited. I was pretty sure she wasn't praying, but I also wasn't sure if that was directed at me or at the person who had hit her in order to search whatever of Carlyle's was stored in that basement.

"Did you touch anything?" Alice asked, her eyes slitted.

"I wore my gloves," I said, feeling like a worm. Lower than worm. The dirt under the worm.

"Huh," said Alice, her eyes boring into me.

"You didn't find anything or you'd have already told me," she went on in a monotone.

"No. I didn't find anything." I said. "The papers and books were spread out on the floor and they looked like schoolwork. The boxes were mostly clothes and some shoes. If there had been anything there, the perp got it. Or, there was nothing to find."

Alice closed her eyes. I shut up. She spoke without opening them.

"So who hit me then? That big girl roommate? Doesn't make sense. She packed the stuff up in the first place. She could have gotten rid of anything then. Doesn't make sense."

"I'd thought of that," I said slowly. "Maybe she gossiped with people at lunch about talking to us and somebody heard and figured they'd better get over there. The timing works."

"Possible," said Alice slowly. She partly opened her eyes, squinting at me. She was exhausted. What was I doing, tiring her out when she needed to rest? Had I just wanted to get my miserable confession in? Yeah, some. But we both wanted to know who'd hit her, maybe tried to kill her.

"Listen," I said firmly. "Forget it for now. If you remember, you remember. Meanwhile, like you said, there are good people working on this. We don't need to worry about it."

"You are the worst liar in the world, girl," said the tired voice from the bed.

"Just don't be stupid." Then Alice slept.

I let myself out. I was just glad she hadn't made me promise.

20

The sleep was deep
Finally he died
Family at his side
No war
No more
"The Vet Sleeps"
Daquon Williams, #1101
StreetWise

Saturday, May 19, 8 a.m.

My cell phone rang, jarring me out of the restless sleep I'd had after seeing Alice at the hospital.

"Alice!" I stabbed at the screen, fearing the worst. I cringed when I heard Tom's voice. I knew it. I knew it. She hadn't been fine.

"Kristin? This is Tom. Sorry to call so early."

"What? What is it?" I croaked through my lips that were stiff with fear. "Is it Alice?"

"No, no. She's fine. I just saw her. She's eating breakfast."

I could hear his words but my heart kept pounding in my ears. I struggled to sit up and not drop the phone at the same time.

"It's not that," Tom went on in the same calm voice. "It's the Carlyle woman. Her family's arrived and they have agreed to donate her organs. I told you about the neurological exam and she won't be here in the ICU much longer. I wondered if you wanted to come and say good-bye."

Tom's words woke me up completely. Say good-bye to a woman I'd barely met in life, but who would never leave my memory? And meet her parents when I'd failed to save their daughter? Did I want to do that? No, and yes. Maybe I could help the parents a little, and myself too, by showing up and bidding her farewell.

"Yes. I think I will. Yes." I had another thought. "And I think I'll call Adelaide Winters. I don't know. She might want to come too."

"Good idea. Be here by about 11, okay?" Tom hung up.

I'd said good idea. Was it? Now I regretted the impulse. That's what happens when you talk before having coffee.

I looked down at the screen of my phone. Now I could hear Saturday morning cartoons coming from downstairs. Normal sounds. Kid sounds. What I really wanted to do was drag a blanket down there and snuggle up to two little bodies and lose myself in Wile E. Coyote and the Road Runner. Instead, I thumbed through my directory to the W's and hit Adelaide's cell number.

She answered on the first ring. Her sandpaper voice softened when I said why I was calling. We agreed to meet in the main hospital lobby a little before 11. I hung up and headed downstairs toward the sound of the TV, dragging a blanket.

# # # #

Soft spring sunlight slid down between the branches of the trees in our front yard and lined our street. Flowering buds were popping out on the trees and some were even dropping off to make room for the coming leaves. No leaves as yet to block the sun in lime-green reflection on the sidewalks. The light was pure and new and it was everywhere. It didn't seem like a good day to let go of life. It was a day of new beginnings. The sweetness of the spring air was actually painful. Better to have had gloom and slush.

As I turned the corner to head toward campus and then on to the hospital, I noticed the new *StreetWise* vendor Dwayne was not on his corner. I thought they usually worked Saturdays. I looked across the street, but didn't see him. I hoped he was okay.

As I gazed across and then up the opposite side of the street, it occurred to me that anyone standing on Dwayne's corner would have a direct view of Stedman and especially the side where the emergency basement door was located. I wondered if Dwayne had seen anyone come in or go out of that door yesterday. I stopped and went back a little ways, looking in the window of the coffee shop to see if he was getting coffee. He wasn't in there. I went on, but also glanced in the copy shop window, though I couldn't imagine what he could have been doing in there. I moved on with a mental shrug. I wondered if he'd even remember he'd seen anything or if with being so shy he'd be willing to tell me. Besides, I thought as I passed Stedman and moved on down toward the main quad, anyone using that side door would have set off the alarm like I did when I'd opened the door. I decided to give my tired brain a break. I had no energy for investigating anything. I had to go watch a young life be over.

I met Adelaide in the main lobby. She was dressed all in gray. Good choice. The grayer the better. We silently rode up in the elevator together.

We got off at the ICU floor and I saw Tom at the far end of this lobby area. It was bisected by groupings of chairs and sofas in four quadrants and Adelaide and I had to negotiate among them, and the subdued families waiting there, to get to Tom. He was standing by a reception desk, talking on a house phone. We stood a little apart, waiting.

When he hung up, Tom turned and greeted us quietly. He was paler than usual and there was a tightness around his eyes. I wondered if he'd had any sleep at all.

With a nod of his head, he indicated a small room to the right of the entrance to the ICU.

"Karen Carlyle's family, Reverend and Mrs. Hecht, are in there with the organ coordinator, finishing up the paperwork for donating her organs. Her doctor will be here in a few minutes to tell them what to expect and then they will go in and say their farewells. After that, you both can go in."

"Hecht?" I asked. Their name's not Carlyle?"

"Stepfather, I think," Tom said.

The door of the small room opened and a young man holding a clipboard came out. Behind him emerged an older woman and man. The woman was looking down at the floor, her short gray hair falling slightly forward over wrinkled white cheeks. She had on an old-fashioned flowered dress that hung on her thin frame. It came well below her knees and had long sleeves and a high collar. Behind her was a man, not much taller, with very short blond hair, graying at the temples. The young man stepped away and then I saw the older man was wearing quite a well-cut dark suit topped off by a white clerical collar. Beside me, I felt Adelaide stiffen. She blames organized religion, and especially Christianity, for a lot of the ills in the world. She's not entirely wrong in that view.

The young man walked up to Tom.

"We're finished here, Dr. Grayson." He turned and said goodbye to the Hechts and then went into the ICU with the paperwork.

We all stood silently for a moment and then Tom spoke.

"Reverend and Mrs. Hecht, I'd like you to meet Professors Kristin Ginelli and Adelaide Winters. Kristin is the woman I told you about, who tried to save your daughter. Dr. Winters was one of Karen's teachers."

My stomach knotted at that description of me as someone who had 'tried to save' their daughter. The unspoken words were 'and failed.'

"How do you do?" I said, extending my hand to Mrs. Hecht, but she seemed not to see it. She stood, still looking down. I turned and extended my hand to Rev. Hecht.

He took it in both of his and patted it. I struggled not to jerk my hand away.

"I'm sure you did everything you could to save our little girl and I want to tell you how grateful we both are to you for your bravery. Why you could have been seriously injured yourself or even killed. Thank God only one life was lost."

I quickly extracted my hand. The tone had been sort of kindly, but the sentiment was skewed somehow. Why thank God only one life was lost? Had he meant it that way? I reminded myself this man was under tremendous strain and probably not thinking too clearly.

Adelaide merely nodded at the Hechts, though she did smile at Mrs. Hecht who did not see it as she was still looking at the floor.

Rev. Hecht looked at Adelaide. His eyes were quite arresting, light blue and heavily lashed. He gave her a broad smile. She did not smile back.

"And you were one of her teachers? And you came to say good-bye. Well that is going the second mile. I'm sure she was blessed to have such teachers. Thank you so much for being here."

"You're welcome," Adelaide said, not wasting any words. "Both of you."

"Thank you," said Mrs. Hecht softly, still not looking up.

Tom reached for his cell phone and when he looked at the screen, excused himself and walked away. Both Hechts barely seemed to register that he'd left.

"Reverend and Mrs. Hecht," I said. "I know this is a distressing time, but I wonder if you could tell me why your daughter quit school."

Adelaide drew in a sharp breath. Well, yeah, I knew it was tacky too, but this was the only time I might get to ask this question.

"Well, now," said Rev. Hecht quickly. "Karen found school to be a might difficult. I told her she should stay in Minnesota, live at home and help her mother and then maybe go to the community college some, but she had her heart set on trying this. She shouldn't have done that."

Adelaide was now glaring at Rev. Hecht.

"Really?" I said brightly, trying to cut off anything Adelaide might say. "From all we've heard, she was very academically talented. I don't think she left school for that reason. Do you know what she did after she quit?"

For a brief moment I saw Rev. Hecht's eyes flash with anger. Then his smile and his smooth preacher voice came on as though nothing had happened.

"You know how young people are, trying one thing and then trying another. I don't reckon she'd settled on any one thing. Do you, Mother?"

Mrs. Hecht started when he addressed her. She looked up, her face so pale she looked like she might faint.

"No. I have no idea," she said, tonelessly.

"Where was she living after she left school?" I asked, addressing both of them.

Rev. Hecht answered.

"Oh, Karen was staying with some girlfriends. I don't really recall their names. She had a lot of friends." He looked around the lobby like he might find some of his stepdaughter's friends lurking there.

Mrs. Hecht made a small sound, either a groan or a sob.

Rev. Hecht quickly took her arm and none too gently.

"Come on, Mother. You'll excuse us, please," he said through his teeth and he started moving away toward the door of the ICU.

"Certainly," I said quickly. "Just one more thing," I asked his retreating back. "Why did your daughter like to be called Courtney and not Karen?"

"Vanity," he said, over his shoulder. And they exited through the doors.

I looked after them for a moment, but rejected the idea of following. Behind me I heard a snort. For a moment, I thought it was Alice. But no, now my Department Chair had also taken to snorting at me. I turned to face her. She had folded her arms across her ample chest.

"Remind me to require you to take some sensitivity training," Adelaide said dryly.

"Yeah, well, only if the good Reverend takes them first. What did you think of that?"

"I don't think there's much good about that guy, Kristin, and I think he had no idea what his stepdaughter was doing. And I think that was definitely her choice."

"Yes," I said, thinking over the replies. "Still, it's not unusual for kids at that age to rebel against parents and refuse to stay in touch."

"No," said Adelaide, considering. "But what he said was too smooth, too friendly, in fact."

"Too friendly? What kind of criticism is that? Are you reacting negatively to him because he's a preacher?" Though I kind of agreed with her.

"Are you going to defend him just because he's wearing that dog collar and says 'God bless you' all the time?" Adelaide shot back, drawing herself up to her full height, which, while not much, made her look even more formidable than usual.

I try from time to time to persuade Adelaide that I didn't invent Christianity, I just teach it. But she still often saw me as a defender of the faith. And to some extent, that's true. It's not the faith I have trouble with, it's a lot of the faithful. But was Rev. Hecht lying or was that just his stock pastoral manner? His demeanor had been a little too smooth, I'd agree there. It had felt like an act. And there had definitely been flashes of anger.

"What did you think of Mrs. Hecht?" I asked, gazing at the closed doors of the ICU.

"Hard to say," Adelaide replied, considering. "I'd have to hear her say more than six or seven words."

"Well, why only a few words, then?"

"Kristin. Try to get a grip. Her daughter is brain dead and she's going to give her organs to other people and they're about to take her off life support. You can't judge a person's character at a time like that. Use some sense. That's probably true for him too."

This last was said grudgingly.

I looked across the lobby and saw Tom had reappeared and he was talking to another doctor, a slim, dark, wiry man. They parted and the other doctor entered the ICU.

Tom rejoined Adelaide and me.

"That's Karen's physician now, Dr. Gutierrez," Tom said, nodding in the direction Dr. Gutierrez had gone. "He's going to explain to the Hechts what will happen now. It is very hard on families. The patients look like they're breathing, like they could still wake up. They have to understand and accept that their daughter is dead. It can take a while."

"Excuse me," said Adelaide abruptly. "I need to make a phone call." She walked briskly away, but her shoulders were hunched and stiff.

"Let's sit a minute," Tom said, and gestured to the far side of the lobby. That section had emptied out of families. We sat down side-by-side for a minute. He didn't say any more. In fact, he seemed unusually subdued, even if he'd been up all night. Finally I spoke up.

"What is it, Tom?"

"Well, it's a couple of things. Gutierrez told me this morning. There's evidence of cocaine in the urine. That's one." Tom turned to look at me, his blue eyes flat behind his glasses.

Cocaine. As Alice and I had begun to suspect. The nervousness, the insomnia that Bonnie had described, even her being so thin. I wondered now if she'd just been so high she'd fallen into that elevator shaft. Maybe if someone had been with her and they'd both been using, that person would have been too scared to say anything. But then what about the bruises on her arms? And I remembered her behavior at the reception. She'd seemed purposeful but not high. I shook my head. I still thought it was murder, though I wondered what Williams was going to make of this information.

Tom looked at me pondering.

"You don't seem all that surprised," he said slowly.

"No. Alice and I talked to her former roommate this morning. It was pretty clear that Carlyle was on something, or several somethings from the former roommate's description of her behavior."

I had a thought.

"How can her organs be used for transplant if she'd been on drugs?"

"There's such a shortage of organs that we have started to expand the pool of what's acceptable. She's young and healthy and there didn't seem to be real damage yet. And the potential recipient will be informed and be able to decide if they want that organ or not."

Wow. Tough decision to have to make for someone needing a transplant.

Tom had fallen silent.

"You said a couple of things," I prompted. From his set face I could tell it wasn't good at all.

"There's scarring, more than just that one on her wrist. That's an old burn," Tom said slowly, looking across the room at the people waiting. A younger woman, slightly pregnant, was crying. An older man and woman were with her, the man awkwardly patting her on the back.

"The other scarring was in the pubic area. Small round scars."

Oh, God. I swallowed.

"How many?" I asked. Not that it mattered. One was too many.

"Seven." Tom cleared his throat. "It appears to be evidence of sexual abuse. Cigarette burns, you know. Gutierrez notified the authorities both about the cocaine and the scars. The coroner's office actually sent somebody to examine her and record the area. I don't know where that will go, but it's been done."

"Did anybody say how recent they thought those scars were?" I asked, thinking about the tragedies in Karen/Courtney's brief life.

"I asked Gutierrez that. The scars were fairly old, but it's difficult to tell exactly how old. And he didn't think they were all the same age, either. They had certainly turned from red and puckered to white and flat, but some, he said, seemed newer, and not all the red had faded. At least several years even on the newest ones, though."

"Then it's likely the scarring took place before she left home?"

"Apparently, though of course we don't know and she can't tell us."

We sat side by side looking at the ICU doors.

Then I saw Adelaide across the lobby. She stopped and looked around. Seeing us, she walked slowly over. Her face was lined and sober. I doubted she'd been making phone calls. She'd just needed to get away for a while. I was very glad she hadn't been with us when Tom had told me about the scarring. Though perhaps then he would have kept that, and even the drug use, to himself.

I looked at the entrance to the ICU again and thought about what Karen might have been running from when she'd left home. I thought about what Bonnie had said she had snapped out about her family. "You don't want to know." If she'd been being sexually abused at home, and perhaps even maltreated in other ways, that would go a long way to explaining not only her escape into college, but even her self-medicating with drugs. I pondered Rev. Hecht. I didn't share Adelaide's deep-seated prejudice against the clergy, but he had struck me as off. The smarmy holding of my hand came back to me. Had he been violently abusing his stepdaughter? Had her mother known or looked the other way as some did? Was she being abused as well? I hoped the city would follow up on what the coroner's office had recorded. I wanted to talk this over with Alice so badly that for a second I considered going to find her in her room after we'd seen Carlyle. Then I realized Adelaide was right. I could use some sensitivity training. Besides, I thought, with some self-mockery, Alice has probably been discharged. So I sat and stewed.

The pneumatic hiss of the ICU doors had made me look up several times before it was the Hechts returning, accompanied by Dr. Gutierrez. He ushered them back into the little private room where they had met with the organ coordinator and then he came over and told us we could go in.

Adelaide and I followed Tom and we entered the ICU. The science fiction look of the ICU with all its monitors, beeping sounds and metal frames holding more and more technology, was beginning to seem familiar to me and not as alien. But I had never visited an ICU before where the goal was to see a person who was already dead.

Tom opened the door of the glass-fronted room and we entered. The cubicle was lit with light the color of water and it made all the objects in the room seem further away than they were. Or perhaps that was just my fear affecting my vision. It seemed like I could feel the hum of the machines surrounding the bed on my skin, like an electric current lightly raising the hairs and stimulating the nerve endings.

The three of us stood there, silently. I gazed down at the little mound under the blankets. She seemed even smaller than when we'd last seen her. A monitor blinked, recording a heartbeat that went on pumping blood like a headless chicken still running in circles. I tried to focus on her face and connect with her humanity. The eyes were even partly open. She'd run from pain and fear, trying to use her beauty and her brains to save herself, but she'd not escaped. I bent my head, searching for the presence I sometimes felt, but it eluded me. I flung a silent 'why?' out into that void. It just echoed in an empty canyon and came back to me, unanswered. But I silently wished her peace.

I looked up and saw Tom and Adelaide were looking at me. Clearly they were more than ready to go.

I went home and took the boys to the playground for the afternoon. The bright morning sun had turned weak and watery, seeping through gauzy clouds, but it did not rain. The boys climbed and dug to their hearts' content. I watched them, wanting to encase them in glass to keep their joy pure and unsoiled with pain and I ached all over from the impossible task of keeping the stain of evil from these lives, or the lives of other children. How young had Karen been when she'd first been violated in that particularly cruel way? If I let myself, I could see the threat to young lives gathering in dark purple pools around the playground fence, seeping in under the gate.

I pushed the boys as high as I could on the swings until my arms were exhausted.

21

My grandma walks me to the school
I don't go without her
It's her rule
She tells me
If you hear a pop
We have to drop!
"Pop! Drop!"
Antonne Boisen, age 11

Saturday, May 19, 6 p.m.

I'd tried to beg off going to the Bulls game before I'd left Tom at the hospital. Not only was I emotionally exhausted, but also after Tom told me Kelly 'loved the boys' and 'loved coming over,' I was very suspicious. She was playing some game, I was sure of it. Did I want my boys exposed to that?

Tom kept saying we needed a break and finally I let him think he had persuaded me. But I wouldn't be taking a 'break,' I thought grimly as I looked through my closet to see what upscale, sporting event attire I owned. Tom had mentioned the guest list to me, and Dr. Russell Wagner, Karen/Courtney's date from the reception, was supposed to be there. All the surgery heads had been invited, in fact. Wagner was head of otolaryngology and supposedly a 'die-hard Bulls fan' according to Tom. I'd asked him what oto etc. was and learned that it was ear, nose and throat. I didn't even realize that was a surgical specialty. As I pulled on a silk blouse and tailored slacks, I tried to stifle the thought that I was also looking forward to seeing Cullen again. I added some earrings and pulled up my hair to show them off.

At the sound of a purring engine, I looked out the window and saw Tom and Kelly arriving in Tom's Porsche. I paused as I saw Tom's face was grim as he got out of the car. Then a stocking-clad leg about 15 feet long ending in a platform sandal emerged from the dark interior on the passenger side. Oh lord. Kelly tottered to her feet on the high sandals and I grimaced. Luckily she stayed on her feet. She was wearing a tube of some stretchy material that was now hiked up almost to her crotch and it pulled across her large breasts. Earrings dangled in her moussed hair. She looked awful.

Well, I thought as I left the window to head downstairs, if she wanted to pretend she had somewhere fancy to go, why not? I opened the front door and waited. It appeared Kelly was having trouble negotiating the uneven brick walkway in her high, platform shoes. Tom walked stiffly behind her. He really looked very angry. They must have had some fight over how she was dressed. Carol came up next to me with my purse and did a remarkable job of keeping a straight face when she caught sight of Kelly. I'd already said goodnight to the boys and when Kelly reached the front door, I said a quick 'hi' and walked down to meet Tom. He said nothing to Kelly and we walked silently to his car.

I settled myself in silence in the low car and Tom negotiated the maze of one-way streets to get us out of Hyde Park. I figured if he wanted to discuss Kelly, I'd just listen. Making a comment was a bad idea. Ordinarily I liked to watch his long, thin fingers move over the steering wheel like sensitive tendrils, but tonight I saw he was gripping the wheel so hard the tendons on the back of his hands stood out in ridged relief.

"You look wonderful," he said finally. His unspoken 'unlike Kelly' hung in the air.

"You too," I said, meaning it. He did look good. He had on a soft blue polo shirt with a dark blue blazer and gray slacks. Blue always brought out his Paul Newman eyes. Tom hardly ever paid attention to what he was wearing, and this carefully matched ensemble made me think that there were wheels within wheels at this surgery department outing. Or, these particular clothes had just been hanging next to each other in his closet.

"We've had some week, wouldn't you say?" said Tom glancing wryly at me as we waited at a light before getting on to Lake Shore Drive to approach the city. LSD, as it was nicknamed, was directly ahead of us now, jutting out aggressively at the lake as though trying to intimidate this unruly neighbor and keep the beach at its feet. This was a struggle LSD sometimes lost, as storms could drive waves up and over it. The city ahead had a just-washed look from the all the rain we'd had, and it seemed so near we could reach out and touch it. The light air of spring did not yet contain enough of the heavy ozone to create the brown haze of summer that would shroud the proud phallic architecture for several months.

"Yes, I'd say so," I replied, beginning to relax into the softly contoured seat.

"I'm not on tomorrow," Tom continued. "What do you say we have a real break and maybe take the kids on an outing?"

My spine stiffened against the seat and my senses went on alert at his use of the plural 'kids.' I didn't think he meant just my two.

"Oh?" I said, striving for a noncommittal tone.

"Yes," Tom hurried on, aware I was not showing much enthusiasm. "I'm not even on call, so I thought Kelly, Sam and Mike would all like to go to Great America," he said. I assumed he meant the huge amusement park north of the city, not the political slogan. My boys would be apoplectic with joy at the prospect and yet . . .

"Did you talk to Kelly about this plan yet?" I asked, again striving for a neutral tone.

"No, well, I meant to but then we got into the issue of how she was dressed and I got side-tracked. I think she'll want to go, though. She was very enthusiastic about seeing the boys again."

I sat silently for a moment, weighing my response. Attacking Kelly's credibility was not going to work and truly I did need to spend more time with the boys. I opted for the wait and see maneuver, and I'll always wonder what might have happened if I'd confronted the Kelly issue head on right then.

"Okay," I said. "You can ask her and I'll ask the boys and we'll see how they all feel." I knew exactly how my boys would feel, though I wasn't sure about Kelly. But I just kept my mouth shut.

Looking back on this exchange in the following days, I was amazed I'd had no sense of impending doom. If this had been a Greek drama, the chorus would have appeared over the lake to chant a rhythmic foreboding so we'd have had some notice of looming disaster. But instead, prosaically, we just took the exit for the United Center and followed a sign that pointed toward "Reserved Parking."

# # # #

The United Center resembles a large airplane hanger. That was entirely appropriate as the airline had paid millions to have its name on this huge stadium, at one time the largest in the country. It had opened in the early 1990's, I thought, as part of the clearing out of the poor from land near the lake that had become too valuable for merely warehousing them in huge tracts of public housing. The public housing tracts were almost all gone now. I thought the last of them had been torn down more than a decade ago. They were supposed to have been replaced by mixed income, scattered-site housing and what were called "Section 8" vouchers, subsidies for the poorer citizens of Chicago to pay for rental apartments. But the Bush administration had spent the federal money for that on their idiotic Iraq War and the war on the poor had continued at home. Even accelerated really. Now I'd heard McDonald's headquarters and Google were thinking of locating in this same area, completing the gentrification.

I looked with resentment at the huge gray and brown stadium as we joined the line of cars to get into the small reserved parking lot. I could see kids ahead of us with spray bottles of glass cleaner and dirty rags running up and starting to clean the windows of the cars. They washed the captive cars sometimes over the yelled protests of drivers, though most endured it in stony silence. A few windows would then roll down and a grudging dollar bill would flutter for a second before being expertly grabbed. Tom's car was next. A striped, stained tee shirt appeared and the windshield disappeared in a mist. The brief wipes left surprisingly few streaks. Tom looked wryly over at me while this was going on.

"How much is that worth?" he asked, getting out his wallet.

Outside his window, dark eyes watched his movements.

I thought it was actually worth more than we could afford, but said, "Give him a 5."

The bill was held out the window and it instantly disappeared into a hand that was too large for the thin arm that was attached to it. This is the city where sociologists have recorded kids saying not 'when I grow up,' but 'IF I grow up.' And yet the city had taken the land for these kids' housing and had placed a stadium that represented all they aspired to and could never have where they might otherwise have lived. Yes, the housing projects had been a giant mistake in terms of giving a haven to multiple gangs and drug traffickers, and the murder rate had been horrific. But after the projects were destroyed, the flow of drugs had become a firehose and Chicago now had a much higher murder rate than when the projects had stood. So had anything other than a land grab and an increase in homelessness been accomplished? No, I thought, no.

I realized I was not at all in the mood for a social event as we continued to inch forward and finally parked. Well, I had agreed to come for reasons of my own.

# # # #

Tom took out his cell phone before he locked the car and looked up his email.

"Gate 2 ½ ," he said, gazing at the little screen. "North side."

After we had gone through a TSA-type security screening, including metal detector, we looked at the numbers on the arched entryways. Gate 2 ½ was obvious, as it was also labeled, "Private Skybox Entrance." There was a security guard at that entrance as well who looked not only at our tickets but our drivers' licenses. More and more like TSA. Well, it was probably a good idea. Large gatherings of people in arenas were now targets for terrorists. We were told if we exited that area we would need to re-present our tickets and I.D.

We rode silently up in the private elevator indicated by the guard. It had a carpeted, mahogany-lined interior and the United Airlines theme, or really, Gershwin's *Rhapsody in Blue*, played, I assumed on a loop.

We exited on our assigned floor and before we could even look for Box 32, a uniformed usher met us, looked at our tickets, and escorted us to the box. It was a lot like the opera, though with metal detectors.

Tom took my jacket and gave it to an attendant standing just inside the door. I wondered just how many part-time jobs this stadium created and if they were just minimum wage. I'd bet they were and without any benefits.

We went down a short hallway and stood for a moment at the entrance to a large, well-appointed room. It had a men's club atmosphere, with a burgundy carpet flecked with green and a hunter green leather sectional sofa that followed the curve of one wall and then jutted out into the center of the room. Overstuffed armchairs in a small green and burgundy print faced the couch, but even as I watched, the short man with close-cropped sandy hair sitting in one swiveled it around to face the glass-walled front of the room. On a terrace beyond the glass, a row of at least a dozen seats was perched well above the floor seating. As I continued to scan the room, I saw the left side held a long buffet table complete with chef wearing a tall white hat. His dark face was impassive above a brilliantly white jacket buttoned to the neck.

As we stood there, a short man with dark, penetrating eyes and white, fluffy eyebrows came up to us. He seemed to be about 60, with deeply carved wrinkles radiating out from behind his wire-rimmed glasses.

"Tom, Tom, hahwahya?" he drawled out in a strong Boston accent. Made me feel a little homesick for New England, really.

"Fine, Harold, fine. Let me introduce Professor Kristin Ginelli. Kristin, this is Dr. Harold Weiss, Chief of Surgery."

I shook Harold's smooth hand and was in turn introduced to his wife Elizabeth, 'call me Beth,' Weiss, who was so short and thin I'd missed her standing behind her husband. Beth's wrinkled face was deeply tanned and she really was amazingly thin. She looked like a cigar wearing a gold choker necklace. Her silk dress and chunky jewelry screamed Florida to me. I was suddenly glad I'd worn earrings.

Then Dr. Weiss introduced us to the Chessons. Slightly younger, in their mid-forties I thought. He was introduced as a banker and a trustee. She, also stick-thin, was wearing what I thought was a Chanel jacket and so many gold chains you would think she had a side job as a rapper. She was not as tanned as Beth and was introduced as a 'club woman.' I had no idea what that meant and just nodded. Now I was really glad I'd worn the silk blouse and pants. Sandra Chesson had silk pants on too, only the crease in hers was so sharp she could slice meats at the buffet.

I stood with Beth and Sandra, towering over them as they chattered to each other about people I didn't know. I looked over their heads and saw that Harold Weiss was talking to Tom in short bursts of animation, rather like that robot I'd gotten the kids for Christmas. It moved frantically when they pressed the controls and then was stock-still. They'd played with it for about a week and then had lost interest.

I turned back and gazed down at Beth and Sandra, still dissecting various people they both knew. I realized my hostility had little to do with any of these people personally and more with the general obliviousness to poverty this structure, this event, this evening represented. Not even just obviousness. What Catholics called 'willful ignorance.' You have to actually want not to know whom you had crushed in order to make this kind of wealth and privilege work for you. And, to be honest, as I thought about it, my lousy mood was also due to the scene with Karen/Courtney's mother and stepfather this morning and what Tom had told me about the abuse she had suffered.

I excused myself to Beth and Sandra, who started a little when I spoke. They didn't seem to realize I was still standing with them. I turned away. Tom was still talking to Weiss, so I didn't want to go there. I thought maybe a little wine would help my mood and I moved toward where the bar was located.

As I crossed the room, snatches of conversation floated by. "*So when we couldn't do the anastomosis, we . . . and the prices, you've never seen anything like it . . . I don't care what he thinks, the market clearly won't . . .* "

As I approached the bar, I saw Russell Wagner at the adjacent buffet, getting the chef to carve him thick slabs of roast beef from the tenderloin on a carving block. I picked up one of the glasses of white wine on the end of the bar and walked up to him. It took him a second to tear his eyes away from his rapt consideration of the food.

But once he did look up, I felt a little like the tenderloin.

"Well, hello," he drawled, and his eyes were not exactly on my face.

"Hello," I said slowly, wondering if he'd get around to looking at my face and if so, if he would recognize me.

He did look up but I didn't see recognition on his face. What I saw was what I assumed he thought was a seductive smile. It was nauseating.

"You're a tall one, aren't you?" Wagner said, his little piggy eyes assessing me. 'A tall one of what?' I wanted to ask. But I didn't. I needed to get him to talk to me.

"I'm Kristin Ginelli," I said, holding out my hand.

Good ole Dr. Wagner took my outstretched hand in both of his. Just like good ole Rev. Hecht. I had to suppress a shudder.

"Well, well," he said, switching from holding my hand to patting my arm. "Pleased to see you. Real pleased. Have something here, why don't you? Like this beef. Hey, fella, get the lady some of that beef too." The face under the chef's hat didn't change a bit, but as he picked up the carving knife I saw a flash of contempt in his eyes.

"No, thanks," I said quickly. "I've just eaten."

I didn't mention he was making me nauseous.

"Sure. Sure. That's fine," he continued, reaching out for his own plate of beef.

I wasn't sure yet whether he recognized me or not. His manner was sickeningly friendly, but also oddly impersonal.

I thought I'd better try to clear things up.

"I don't know if you remember, but we've met before, at the Anderson Building reception. I'm Tom Grayson's friend."

Wagner's jowls slid down his face a little as he finally did actually look at my face. His eyes seemed to bore into mine and he released a breath.

"Oh, I see. Well, I'm glad you're here, like I said. Excuse me." Wagner closed his face and turned to focus on the buffet. He started stacking tomatoes and lettuce on to his five-inch pile of beef. Then he added a scoop of mayonnaise and topped it off with three bread rolls. His arms had to reach out around his stomach now. I could only imagine his girth after he finished all that food.

"Actually," I said to his back, "I wanted to talk to you about your date that night, Courtney Carlyle?"

Wagner turned, his heavily piled plate gripped in one hand. He brushed by me, and with his other hand he picked up a bottle of beer on the corner of the bar. Then he turned and, seeing I was still standing there, glared at me.

"Miss Ginellen, is it? I barely knew that young woman. I'd only met her the week before and I really knew nothing about her. She was a chance acquaintance. That's all." He turned, expertly balancing his enormous plate of food. I thought he'd had a lot of practice.

"Now, if you'll excuse me, I came here to see a basketball game." He walked away with a stiff-legged gate and out the glass doors to the balcony.

I took a sip of my wine, and watched him go. I'd let him think he'd gotten away from me. I waited about two minutes, and then I went out that door as well. The roar of the crowd hit me as I went out on the balcony. It was like some primitive beast. With a collective mouth they vented their pleasure as an electronically magnified voice overrode them. "The World Champion Chicago Bulls!"

I took a seat next to Wagner to his obvious discomfort, but I just sat there sipping my wine and waiting out the waves of noise as the individual players were introduced. Then the skating rink music started while the players warmed up on the court.

I turned to Wagner.

"I'm sure it's painful to remember, Dr. Wagner," I started, giving him an excuse for his rude behavior, "but I just watched along with her parents as she was taken off life support this morning. I can't help but feel a little responsible." I put a little whine into my words, as I learned how from my kids.

Wagner had stuck a slice of beef into his mouth and he munched, saying nothing. Then he took a long drink of beer. I thought he was going to ignore me completely. Finally, he turned toward me, still not meeting my eyes, but I didn't think this time he was trying to guess my bra size.

"I'm sure. But I can't help you."

"Oh, you never know what will help," I said slowly. "And you might know more than you realize. Whose party did you meet her at?" I asked, making a calculated guess.

Wagner had gone back to pretending to watch the players, but deep lines appeared around his mouth. He suddenly looked like he'd just realized his food had salmonella as a garnish.

"Who told you that?" he said angrily.

"It's what I thought you'd told the police right after the reception."

"And where did you hear that?" he barked, now really angry.

"I consult for the campus police. They told me."

Now the cat was out of the bag.

"Look, I don't know who you are and what you think you know, but you are absolutely wrong. I may have had trouble remembering where I met her in the shock of the moment, but I've made a statement and I've signed it."

Wagner had stopped eating. He looked determinedly at the basketball court as though fascinated by the play. I glanced down. A Bulls player was dribbling at center court, and then he passed to another Bulls player. Not a riveting moment in sports.

Was Wagner under the impression that making a statement was the same as telling the truth?

I waited.

He spoke slowly, carefully.

"I was shopping in that mall at 900 N. Michigan," said, naming the most upscale shopping area on the Chicago's 'Gold Coast.' "I went to eat in the food court. You know it?" He glanced over at me, more to see if I was buying this baloney, but I nodded. "It was crowded. This young woman asked if she could share my table. We got to talking. Said her name was Courtney. We talked more and well, that was it. I got her number and called her about the reception. End of story."

He concentrated on the basketball again and put a pickle in his mouth.

"Had you taken her out before the reception?"

"No, that was the first time," he mumbled around the pickle.

"Did you give her phone number to the police?"

"No, I'd lost it by then."

Right. And no checking Courtney's phone as it was likely encased in tons of concrete.

"And where did you pick her up to bring her to the reception?"

"She came in a cab. I had an emergency surgery and I didn't finish until right before the reception."

Sure. Emergency nose surgery. I bet. I also bet Williams never found the cab that had brought Carlyle to the reception.

"What was she like?" I asked, watching him pretend to watch the game.

"I don't know what you mean."

Well, what attracted you to her enough to ask her out?"

Wagner turned to look at me and for the first time he showed some humor.

"You're kidding, right?"

I wanted to slap that smirk off his face with the flat of my hand. I held on to the stem of my wine glass with both hands to keep from doing it. Good thing for him I'd finished the wine or he might have been wearing it. Of course, white wine doesn't stain, so that would have been a plus.

I stood up and looked down at him. He looked smug, thinking pretty well of himself for that last, snarky remark. Ironically enough, I thought, as I continued to look down at him, that had probably been the only time he'd been truthful with me.

"I hope you sleep well at night, Dr. Wagner," I said in as insulting a manner as I could manage. He flushed and turned deliberately to look at the game.

I turned and went back inside.

"Kristin!"

It took me a second to focus. It was Cullen and he was standing behind the chairs on the left. I confess I had looked for him when we'd come in and hadn't seen him. He was dressed in dark, tweed slacks and a black turtleneck with another beautifully cut cashmere sports coat, this one light gray. His red-gold head was flaming from the glare of the overhead lights and he looked every bit the upscale, jovial barbarian chief surveying his clan.

I walked over to him, pausing only to put my empty glass on the tray of a passing waiter.

"Hello, Cullen. Nice place for a party," I said as I came up to him. His eyes went from me to the windows and beyond to the action on the floor. I looked too. A pass down almost the length of the court was caught by a Bulls player and a basket scored right as the buzzer sounded. The Bulls were actually winning, I thought, though I'd been so preoccupied with Wagner I hadn't followed the game at all.

"That's a pretty sight, there," said Cullen, turning from watching the play. He focused his twinkly blue eyes on me.

"And you're a pretty sight up here," he said. The blarney was back, big time.

"Thank you," I said, somewhat primly and he laughed, his tan face breaking into grooves worn by decades of the same grin.

"What a world we live in now where complimentin' a girl's gonna get you in hot water if ye don't watch out."

I didn't rise to the bait and we just stood and watched the game for a few minutes. I saw Cullen glance out at Wagner a few times who was still sitting on the terrace. He was morosely drinking his beer.

"Have ye given any more thought to sailin' with me?" asked Cullen abruptly. Just as I opened my mouth to reply, Tom appeared at my side.

"Sailing?" he asked.

I made introductions and explained that Cullen had asked me to go sailing with him. I didn't elaborate.

"I didn't even know you knew each other," said Tom, his face carefully devoid of expression. A waiter appeared with a tray of wine. We all declined.

Even with that pause, I launched a little too quickly into a description of the concrete-dumped-into-the-car incident. I did not describe going up with Cullen to revisit the floor where the entrance to the elevator shaft was located. I tried to keep it light and Cullen and I were both laughing by the time I'd finished. Tom smiled with his mouth.

"Sounds like you had to have been there," Tom said, dryly. He glanced out toward the balcony. "How'd you do with Russell, there?" he said to me, clearly changing the topic.

"Oh, he's lying through his teeth," I said, not able to disguise my disgust for Dr. Wagner. "I hope the police give him another going over now that she's dead."

"What's all this, now?" Cullen asked abruptly.

Rats. I had honestly forgotten for a second that Cullen was there.

Tom jumped in before I could speak.

"Oh, Kristin's investigating that woman's death, the one who fell in the building you're putting up, and Dr. Wagner out there was the victim's date, apparently. Kristin wanted to come tonight to try to worm information out of him." I stared at him. Tom had just used more words than I heard him utter in a week.

I wished a waiter would come around with a tray of canapés so I could stuff one in his mouth.

"Ye don't say," said Cullen, looking at me, all the humor wiped from his face.

"Kristin was a policewoman, a detective, before she became a professor. Didn't she tell you?" said Tom with studied casualness. His 'I know her and you don't' attitude was straight out of high school. And I hate being spoken of in the third person when I'm standing right there.

"No, she didn't get around to it," I said with enough ice in my voice to re-stock the bar if they needed it. I turned my back on both of them.

"I'm going for some food. Excuse me." I walked quickly toward the buffet.

"Now ye've done it, lad," said Cullen to Tom. I think he thought he was whispering.

I stopped when I got to the buffet. I didn't really want food. And I didn't want more wine either. I was startled when a deep, accented voice spoke from behind my back.

"How are you tonight, Professor?"

I turned. Commander Stammos was standing directly behind me. He had moved so silently I hadn't even heard him approach.

He was wearing a dark, brown suit. He must not own any upscale sporting attire.

"All right, I guess." I paused, and then plunged ahead.

"Has there been any progress on discovering who hit Alice Matthews?" I asked.

Stammos narrowed his dark eyes and his lips compressed into a single line. Even though I was nearly a head taller than he, I felt like he was looking down on me, literally and figuratively.

"We are canvassing the area. It's been very slow. None of the campus police patrols were near there at the time, and the students have been no help at all, of course."

He drew his thick black eyebrows together so they made an almost continuous line as he frowned. I thought Stammos might like the university better without the students.

I thought for a minute.

"What about the guy who sells the street newspapers?" I asked. "He's standing down the street opposite Stedman almost all day. He might have seen something."

"Not the most reliable of witnesses, would you say?" Stammos thinned out the line of his lips in even more disapproval. I thought his lips might entirely disappear at this rate.

What an approach to investigation, I thought, my anger rising to choke off my speech for a second. Being speechless at that moment was probably a good thing, though, I thought, as I stared down at his closed-in face. I needed to try to sound reasonable. Good luck with that, I thought wryly. But the back and forth in my head helped me get control.

"I don't think so, " I said in as mild a voice as I could manage. Be specific, I told myself. Be specific. "I've spoken to him and while he has a mild speech impediment, he seems to watch the street very carefully. It's part of his job, really, to watch people and be ready to ask them to buy a paper."

"Not much of a job," Stammos said dismissively.

I looked at his face again, suspicious. He's trying to piss me off, I thought. Be careful. Then I became even more suspicious. Why try to piss me off? Is he trying to justify a shoddy investigation, or could it even be a cover-up?

"So what do you suspect happened?" I asked, again striving for a neutral tone. 'You will not piss me off. You will not piss me off,' I repeated in my head.

"It is very common on a college campus for people to hide in buildings and strike out when they are surprised. Police tend to follow the most common patterns of crime when doing an investigation." His condescending tone made me clamp my teeth together. 'Yes,' I thought, but didn't say it. 'I was a detective and you know it.'

"Besides," Stammos went on in his patronizing tone. "That Carlyle woman's belongings had been there for a long time. Why would anyone choose now to try to rifle through them?"

"Maybe whoever murdered Carlyle had not realized some of her personal items had been stored by the former roommate and that they were still there. Logically, when she left, she would most likely have thrown out what she didn't want and taken the rest with her. The murderer could have become alarmed there would have been notes or even a backup drive for her computer. That drive could have had pictures, for example. The stored items contained a ton of risk, I'd think."

"Her stored items have been given to the city police. So far they've found nothing," Stammos ground out.

I ground out my own reply. I'd been there. He hadn't.

"Then whatever it was that could have been incriminating was already removed. I saw her stuff had been seriously searched. The boxes were torn and a lot was strewn around on the floor."

Stammos's black eyes looked up at me, holding my gaze. He was not used to having his statements questioned and he clearly did not like it.

"'It?' What is 'it'? You can't make a case where there is no evidence. It is preferable to acquire evidence and then form a hypothesis. Better to protect our officers from crimes we know do happen, than to imagine connections to other crimes when there are none. Officer Matthews herself thinks that it could have been someone hiding in the basement, that it was just random."

I thought Alice couldn't remember anything.

"You've spoken to Officer Matthews?"

"Yes, this afternoon."

"How is she?"

"Improving. She'll have three more weeks disability leave with pay, then we'll see." Stammos's measured words had an ominous ring.

"You'll see what, Commander? Whether she still has a job?" I shouldn't have asked that, but he'd gotten to me. Damn. He'd gotten to me. I had tried to keep the fear out of my voice, but I didn't succeed. He looked as pleased as Williams at drawing blood.

"Whether she is the type of officer we want, one who can stick to the job for which she was hired." His flat, stony voice pounded out the words. Without raising his voice he had delivered the threat. Stay away from Alice Matthews and she might have a job to come back to.

I glared at him, but didn't dare say anything else.

He turned without another word and walked toward the hallway entrance to the box, maneuvering his wide shoulders through the knots of people standing around chatting and he disappeared.

Great. Jim was out of a job, and I'd managed to put Alice's job in jeopardy. I stood silently in the pool of eddying conversations and sunk down into my own self-recriminations. Behind me, the door to the balcony opened and the roar of thousands of throats came in behind me. They were the scream of frustration I did not dare utter.

I went to find Tom who'd moved over to a group of doctors. I told him I'd like to leave and he nodded. We thanked the Chief of Surgery. I looked around to say good-bye to Cullen, but didn't see him.

Tom was silent as he drove. I was glad for his silence. I didn't want to discuss the evening with him as it had been at times awkward and even troubling, but I couldn't keep from thinking about it. I needed to step away from Stammos and his barely veiled threat to fire Alice and I turned my thoughts to Wagner. His responses had struck me as off while I was talking to him, even for a guy who was a sexist dinosaur. Why change his story about how he'd met Courtney? Meeting a beautiful young girl at a party is not exactly a crime. Why fumble around and then obviously lie about meeting at an impersonal food court rather than at a party? Unless, I thought with a jolt, unless where he'd met her was a crime. What exactly had Courtney been doing to earn a living since she'd dropped out of school? I suddenly thought of the Latin term for prostitute, *meretrix*. 'She who earns.' It came up a lot, of course, in the diatribes by the so-called Church Fathers against the widespread and generally accepted forms of prostitution in the Roman Empire. To say nothing of the sexual exploitation of the huge number of Roman slaves. I was so lost in thought about these modern and ancient connections that it took me a moment to come back to the present and realize we had arrived at my house.

Tom walked with me up the path, but I had no sooner put my key into the lock of the front door than Kelly jerked open the door and dashed down the steps, brushing past her father and me. Her moussed hair had collapsed around her head and in the porch light I had seen her makeup smeared across her face. The black mascara had made lines down tearful cheeks. She ran to the car in stocking feet, holding her platform sandals in her hand, their wooden soles banging against her thigh.

Tom just raised a weary hand in farewell, and turned back to the car.

Carol came out on the porch with me with a very worried face. We stood for a moment and watched Tom and Kelly drive away. Then Carol said quietly, "I have a lot to tell you," and we entered the house.

We went into the den together and Carol shut the door. In her soft voice she told me that while she was putting the boys to bed, Giles had come upstairs to get her and he had been very upset. Kelly had flirted with him in the kitchen again and he said he had just left and come upstairs. 'I could think of nothing, nothing to say at this behavior,' he had told Carol miserably. Carol said she had left Giles with the boys and gone down to the kitchen to talk to Kelly, who had immediately started crying hysterically.

Then Kelly had run down the hall to the den and locked herself in. Carol said she had stayed by the door for a while, trying to get Kelly to unlock the door and talk to her, but while she could hear Kelly still crying, she had not responded to Carol's entreaties to open the door. Finally, Carol said, she had sat down in the adjacent dining room with her computer and waited. As soon as she had heard the car pull up, Carol said soberly, Kelly had unlocked the door and run outside.

I apologized to Carol, who of course thought that was unnecessary, and I told her to tell Giles I was sorry too. She left to go back upstairs and I sat in the darkened den for a while, debating whether to call Tom or not. I looked at my watch. It was after midnight. I thought not. Difficult conversations held after midnight are rarely productive.

I turned off the hall light and went upstairs. I stood in the boys' room for a while. They looked so small and sweet under their bunched up covers. I straightened the blankets and thought about the teenage storms yet to come.

Then I tip-toed out and went to bed. I had trouble sleeping, but I wouldn't have slept at all if I had realized what a mistake it was not to have called Tom right after Carol had spoken to me.

Kelly's Online Journal

Sunday, May 20, 1 a.m.

Who do they think they are? Shit. Shit. Shit. Shit. I hate them all. I hate her. Why oh why did Dad ever meet her??? They're all crap, all of them. That Carol. What a bullshitter. Oh, Kelly, talk to me, you'll feel better. Nobody is angry at you. What a load of bull. She doesn't care. She hates me. She's married to that whimp Giles. Got him tied up in knots. Runs to protect him. Who cares about them?

I gotta get away. I hate it here. I hate it. I hate it. At least in New York I had a life.

New York. How much does it cost to get to New York? Google knows. Wow. A lot.

Money. I need money.

Goodnight stinking journal. Gotta make plans.

22

On the street
On my feet
No stilettos now
I wear sneaks
They don't break my feets!
"Feet Don't Lie"
Mary Walsh, #1092
StreetWise

Sunday, May 20, 7 a.m.

I let Molly out into the yard. I watched her as I sipped my coffee and envied the single-minded attention she gave to each blade of grass. I could barely think straight I was so tired.

I'd waked early from a restless sleep. Once during the night I'd started awake, filled with dread over sinking and sinking down into concrete. And then I didn't want to sleep again and perhaps sink forever. Finally, I'd slept.

I'd checked my phone for messages from Tom as soon as I'd gotten up. Nothing.

I doubted any plans for Great America would be forthcoming, but I thought taking the boys on an outing was definitely a good idea. I'd see what they'd think about going to the Lincoln Park Zoo. It's an award-winning zoo right downtown and they loved it. We hadn't been there in a while. I looked at my watch. I'd better wake the boys. Parking is always at a premium in the zoo's small lot and the crowds are smaller in the morning. I gulped some more coffee and called Molly in.

The boys had been ecstatic about going to the zoo. They'd bolted their breakfast and we'd jumped in the car.

As soon as we entered the gates, they made straight for their favorite place, the Reptile House. I'm not that fond of snakes, actually, but I would not admit that to the boys or I'd never hear the end of it. Personally, I like the giraffes, and we'd eventually get around to them, but the snakes, especially the big ones, were the main attraction for the kids.

As we entered the Reptile House, the smell hit me as it always did. There was a kind of nasty, fishy odor under which was what I knew were the myriad smells coming from the tasty, slightly rotting treats for the reptiles the handlers hid in their enclosures to keep them entertained. The kids and I had learned that from a talk by a zookeeper at our last visit. We'd also learned that some snakes, like the King Snake, emit foul smells when they feel threatened. Did the masses of humans staring at them through the glass threaten them? I wondered. Add in the smell of the visitors packed into the long, humid enclosure, though, and it made for quite an aromatic stew.

The boys were already standing in front of the largest snake in the Reptile House, a huge boa constrictor. Mike was carefully recounting to Sam what the zookeeper had said about the boa, while Sam was ignoring him and making scary faces at the reptile, trying to get a rise out of it. The boa kept its eyes shut. It didn't care about scary faces from a kid. It knew it was the scary one. Its huge coils looped casually around on a rock, the intricate and cryptic patterns on its body a display of red, green and gray mimicking the colors and patterns of its natural environment. But on the cream-colored rock, the colors were in violent relief. I wondered if the boa thought it was still camouflaged.

Of course then my thoughts turned to Eve and the lying snake of Genesis that had tempted her. Is that what had happened to Courtney, I wondered? Had she been tempted by the money she could make from a certain kind of date? From the little I knew of high-end prostitution, there was a lot of camouflage provided so that especially the John could kid himself he was just giving gifts to an extraordinarily cooperative date. I looked around the Reptile House and thought with grim humor about all the possible snakes in this case that were telling lies and trying to blend in to their environment. Next to the flashy boa, I saw there was a puff adder. Deadly poisonous, but you could barely see it, it blended so well with the scattered rocks, sticks and leaves in its cage.

Mike had moved on to lecturing Sam about the puff adder, and Sam was trying to creep Mike out by making snake-fang faces. I tried to move the boys along so we could get out of the smelly, vaguely threatening Reptile House and on to something safer, like lions. We did, and we also finally got

to the giraffes. I greeted my favorite, a tall, stately female named "Morgan."
She was named after my long-time friend, Howard Morgan, who was a
dedicated zoo volunteer. Morgan was gently pulling leaves off branches high
in the trees in her enclosure, looking serene as she slowly munched them. I
envied her. Self- consciousness may have been too high a price to pay for a
larger, human frontal lobe. The boys stopped running around for a minute
to watch her too, but then they raced on to the adjacent elephants that were
spraying each other with water from a pond in their enclosure. If the boys
had trunks, I was sure they would try that.

As I drove us back to Hyde Park, the boys immediately fell asleep in the
backseat. I thought about how to find out more about high-end prostitution.

# # # #

After we got back, the kids flopped down on the couches in the TV room,
their sturdy arms and legs now amazingly flaccid and pliable. In fact, they
gave a good imitation of their favorite boa, relaxing on its rock, as they went
back to sleep.

I went into the den and opened my computer. I thought I'd read an
article in the campus newspaper a few months back about work the new
University Chaplain, Jane Miller-Gershman, was doing to expand student
volunteer opportunities. I'd met Jane when she'd been assigned to the liaison
committee with the campus police on which I also served, and which was,
apparently, the only concession to my 'working with the campus police' Adelaide Winters had been willing to make. Chaplain Jane's graying hair and
lined face had me assuming she was a 'take me or leave me' kind of person,
probably somewhere around fifty years of age, and her self-introduction to
the committee had been short and to the point. Originally from Kansas.
Harvard Divinity School. Worked as a pastor, then chaplain at a university
in Iowa. Then U of C. She'd said she was married to a woman rabbi who was
at a Chicago synagogue whose name I couldn't remember now. I'd liked her
self-possession.

I scrolled through online, back issues of the campus paper and finally
found the one I'd remembered. Yes, the article listed the "new and challenging outreach" opportunities for student volunteers Chaplain Jane Miller-
Gershman had initiated. There it was. One of the "new and challenging"
opportunities for students was with a not-for-profit, Magdalene House, that
worked with women in prostitution and seeking to leave prostitution.

I glanced at my watch. It was after 2. Sunday would be a workday for a
chaplain, I assumed, but I had no idea when Sunday services either started or
ended. Well, I could leave a voicemail asking her to call me back. The online

campus directory had a "Chaplain's Office" number. I got the expected 'leave a message' recording and I did, giving my name, cell number, and asking that Chaplain Jane Miller-Gershman call me back. I had no sooner peeked in and checked on the boys, who were still zonked, than my cell phone rang.

It was Jane. I briefly explained that I needed a contact at Magdalene House. She replied by asking me if I had time to come over and see her. It didn't seem she was inclined to just give out that information over the phone. She said she was in her office at the chapel now. I hesitated. I could just look up the number for Magdalene House, but it would probably be better to get some background from Jane, and importantly, an introduction.

I thanked her and asked her to hold on for a moment. I called upstairs and Giles answered. Carol was out, he said, but he was fine with my leaving the boys with him for an hour or so. I explained they were actually sleeping in the TV room. I heard him mutter to himself, "tout le meilleur," which was French for a general comment 'all the better they're asleep,' and then he called down and said he'd bring his computer and sit in the den. I got back on the phone with Chaplain Jane and said I'd be right over.

# # # #

The May days were getting longer and at 4 p.m. there was still plenty of sunshine. I walked along, enjoying the sun playing hide-and-seek with the budding trees. I had never been inside Rockefeller Chapel, but it dominated the campus, as John D. Rockefeller had required when he'd given the money to have it built. It had to remain the tallest building on campus. Everybody knew that, and many joked about how the tall tower on the side 'looked just like Rockefeller' and made other veiled and not so veiled references to phallic symbolism in architecture. It was still true, even with all the new building that had gone on, you couldn't help seeing the chapel from all directions and I guessed that was pretty much the point. It was in the same Gothic revival as the main campus, and I thought it looked as big as Chartres Cathedral in France, which I had been in, though Rockefeller appeared a lot more square and solid. No tall, lacy towers. This was the American version of the Gothic cathedral ethos that could be summed up as the church's message that 'we're in charge of everything.' But by the time Rockefeller had his cathedral built, cracks were appearing in that solid, medieval religious self-confidence both in Europe and in the United States. That's probably why Rockefeller Chapel was designed to look so solid. It didn't really explain the jutting tower, though, as medieval cathedrals had those too. Naturally. But in the late 1920's, even huge, solid-looking masses of stone couldn't stop the gathering forces that would ultimately decimate American Protestantism, and take a chunk out of Catholicism as well.

As I walked up to the side entrance, where a sign helpfully said "Chaplain's Office This Way," I felt dwarfed, as I guessed I was supposed to feel. And I realized I resented it looming over me. But no need to take that out on a chaplain who was doing her best to make this big pile of stone come alive to the needs of the city.

The inside hallway was paneled in dark, intricately carved wood, and so dim I was tempted to get out my cell phone and turn on the flashlight app. The arrows pointing to the Chaplain's Office were gilt, however, and they stood out in the gloom.

I dutifully followed the arrows and came to a door at the end. Chaplain's Office, I assumed. I knocked and Jane opened it. Her small, thin frame in a light, stone-colored suit was back-lit from the sun coming through the truly beautiful, stained glass windows that made up almost all of one wall of her office. These windows were much finer than the stained glass we had in our faculty conference room at Myerson. The multi-colored light lit her pale clothes and especially her graying hair as it stood out around her head. Not exactly a halo, but a good look for a minister, I thought wryly. Though since I figured people always wanted clergy to be angels on earth, and they weren't, it was actually something to be avoided. And from getting to know her, I knew she'd find my angel image quite ironic. It didn't take any detective work from me, given what she'd said introducing herself and mentioning her wife, to think that she'd probably had some pretty rough struggles to make her way as a Christian minister in the face of the cruel homophobia of both religion and society.

I realized Jane was holding out her hand and I quickly shook it and sat in a chair she indicated in a grouping of chairs on the side opposite her desk. She didn't sit.

"I was just about to have some tea. Can I bring you a cup? It's Chamomile."

Ick. Herb tea.

"Sure," I said, looking up at her. Though I didn't have to look up much. She really was quite short. I'd mostly seen her sitting at the meetings.

She carried over two cups of the steaming tea and handed me one. It smelled like hot grass clippings. Molly would love it. I put it down on a coaster on the small table in the middle of the circle of chairs.

"How can I help you?" she began, in her clear, measured voice.

I hesitated. Either I made up some excuse why I wanted to visit Magdalene House, or I told her the whole truth including my suspicions. It would have been easier to fudge what I really wanted over the phone. But I realized as I thought about it that I actually wanted to talk over with her all that had happened and my dawning suspicions about what Courtney had left school to do. Maybe what I had begun to suspect was, in fact, not all that likely.

So I told her. It took a while to tell what had been happening, from the reception, to pulling her out of the elevator shaft, to finding out she had been a student, to her angry, chaotic essay for Dr. Winters, and the fact that she'd dropped out, to the former roommate's comments, to Alice Matthews nearly getting killed searching her stored belongings, to meeting her mother and stepfather, and the questions that had raised for me. And then I stopped.

Jane looked steadily at me, but stayed silent. I absent-mindedly reached over, picked up the cup, and took a sip of the tea. I suppressed a shudder. It also tasted like I imagined warmed-up grass clippings would taste, with a few cooked flowers thrown in. But I was just buying time to think again. Mention the drugs and the scarring or not?

In for a penny, in for a pound. I put down the tea again and told Jane what Tom had said they'd found on examination.

Jane frowned, but still kept silent. It was an inviting kind of silence, as she seemed very present to what I was saying. Did they teach that in seminary or was it just her personality?

I plunged back in and got to how talking to Dr. Wagner had made me suspect his relationship with Carlyle had been, shall we say, arranged and not just an accidental meeting in a food court. And if it was the former, I concluded, I needed to know more about how those arrangements were made.

I automatically picked up the cup of tea again but didn't drink it. The warm cup did feel good in my hands.

"Yes, I can see why you called," she said slowly.

Hmm. Did that mean she thought I was in need of pastoral care, or did she mean she saw why I needed a contact to help me understand how high-end prostitution in Chicago worked? I tried not to squirm under her gaze.

"I know someone at Magdalene House who might know that aspect of the sex industry. It's not what they really deal with there, though. Most of those who come to Magdalene House work the streets and are struggling with poor health and various addictions. The women making thousands a night don't seek help. Not until they have aged out, if they are still alive, and have become the ones on the street."

"Sex industry?" I said, not able to keep the shock out of my voice.

"Yes," Jane said matter-of-factly. "Look. This is an enormously profitable industry that markets and sells sex. And sells it in multiple ways in multiple places. It helps to think more objectively about it if you realize it's an industry, and one where the profits are enormous and largely untaxed.

And if you call these women 'sex workers,' it really helps in debunking the 'Pretty Woman' myth, you know."

Well, I hadn't known. Made sense though.

I thought of something that didn't make sense and that, in fact, had irritated me since I'd first read the campus newspaper article.

"What's with the name of that place, though? Magdalene House? Mary Magdalene wasn't in the 'sex industry' as you call it. The Catholic Church framed her in the sixth century by deliberating faking that she was a prostitute. It's a travesty to keep perpetuating that slam on her and on women as the 'magna pecatrix,' like that Pope libeled her, the biggest sinner. Doesn't that just make people who go there for help continue to think of themselves as big sinners?"

I realized I was breathing hard.

Jane looked at me for a moment and took a sip of her own tea.

"I know Mary Magdalene wasn't a prostitute, and you know that, but what you don't know is these women already think of themselves as the biggest sinners. Since Mary Magdalene was a prostitute . . . " She stopped when she saw me stiffen. "Wait, let me finish. Since they believe she was a prostitute and then forgiven by Jesus and part of his ministry, they find that enormously comforting and even hopeful. Your biblical and historical reading is right and you are also dead wrong. They need Mary Magdalene to have been the forgiven prostitute."

Well, crap. I sat there silently, resenting what Jane had just said and realizing that she was likely right. Does the patriarchal church have to win every single damn time?

Jane looked like she knew I was struggling, and left me to it. She got up and went over to her desk and picked up her cell phone. She sat back down and started scrolling through what I assumed was her contacts directory.

"The director's name is Valentina Lopez. She was a nun, with the Sisters of Mercy, and she was a prison chaplain for quite a few years before she came to Chicago."

Yikes, I thought. Prison chaplain. Sister Lopez must be one tough lady.

Jane went on. "But she left the order, got a degree in social work here at the U of C and then was hired by Magdalene House."

Jane Addams had founded the U of C School of Social Work, and it had a great reputation. Carol loved it and sang its praises all the time.

"Are you free tomorrow morning? I can call and ask if she can see us."

Us? I didn't especially want Jane to go with me. I thought I'd do better with my pushy questions on my own.

"There's no need for you to put yourself out like that, Jane," I said quickly. "I can just go by myself."

"It's no trouble," she said calmly. She had this one expression that made me feel like the front of my brain was made of clear glass and she could look right in when she wanted to.

"Oh. Well. Thanks," I said, realizing there was no out. "Let me check my calendar. I think that should be okay."

I reached down and got my own cell phone out of my bag. I opened the calendar.

"I'm fine in the morning, but I need to be back by 1. I have student office hours."

Jane pressed the phone contact number and almost immediately started speaking. In Spanish. Apparently Ms. Lopez was in and picked up her own line. These religious types worked Sundays, I was realizing.

In about two minutes we had an appointment with her at 10 a.m. tomorrow.

I thanked Jane and stood up. She was still looking at me like she could read my mind. She knew perfectly well that was not the way I'd wanted to do this.

I said good-bye and departed.

I left my mostly undrunk tea on the table.

23

A house
A place
Where you feel safe
"Home"
Brandie Washington, #1623
StreetWise

Monday, May 21, 9:45 a.m.

I'd gotten an early morning text from Chaplain Jane that said she would meet me at Magdalene House and she'd included the address. I was now driving around looking for parking in the Lakeview area of the city in the little pocket called "Wrigleyville," located in the shadow of the baseball stadium, Wrigley Field, where the Chicago Cubs play. The Cubs were astonishingly beloved in Chicago whether as hapless fumblers or heroic champions. Not being a baseball fan, I'd never been to the stadium or this neighborhood for that matter. As I drove fruitlessly around, I started to notice this was another area where young professionals were pushing out the long-time and less affluent residents. Bars with cute names and clean glass fronts were jostling older bars with stained stucco fronts and flyspecked windows. Miller versus craft brews, I assumed.

I'd driven by Magdalene House several times now in my quest for street parking. It was a four-story, narrow, wooden structure. Not quite a shotgun house, but much longer front to back than it was wide. The gray paint was peeling, though not as badly as the paint on my house back in Hyde Park had been. Shades were drawn down on all the front windows, giving it a deserted look.

Suddenly, a car pulled out from a parking space right ahead of me and I wedged my car into a space that left me about six inches to spare front and back. Good thing I'd learned to parallel park in Boston where we certainly knew how to shoehorn any size car into a too-small parking space. I grabbed my purse and hustled up the front steps of Magdalene House. A security camera was very much in evidence above the door, and a notice said to ring the bell and state my name. I did. After about two minutes, the door opened.

# # # #

I had already stated to the intercom that I had an appointment with Director Lopez and the whippet-thin, African American woman who admitted me just told me to 'sit down' and then she walked down the central hallway to a kitchen I could see at the back of the house. I could hear some kind of blues playing softly, and then it suddenly cut off. Voices murmured.

I looked around and saw the front room to my immediate left was a kind of parlor with mismatched chairs around the walls. There was no one in the room. A small television sat on a stand in the far corner. I hesitantly sat on one of the chairs, a vinyl-covered kitchen chair with a scarred metal back and legs. Over the fireplace on the opposite wall there was a fairly large painting of a woman in a tight, red dress and those stiletto-type heels that just kill your feet. She was painted standing facing away from the viewer. An old-fashioned streetlight threw a harsh, yellow light down her back. She had one gloved hand on the pole of the streetlight, and another on a cocked hip. She was apparently looking at cars driving on a street in front of her. Her dark hair glistened and the ground around her was wet. It was raining.

I got up to see if the painting was signed. It was an arresting work, both amateurish on the one hand, and incredibly powerful on the other. I peered at the right corner and then stepped back when I read the signature. "Nobody" was written in a dripping scrawl.

I heard the buzz of the intercom and I turned to face the door. The same woman who had admitted me came unhurriedly from the back of the house and after talking through the intercom, admitted Jane. She and Jane spoke quietly for a minute and then she headed up the wooden stairs along the wall, the soft soles of her slippers making a sighing sound on the wooden treads.

I had no sooner said hello to Jane than another woman clattered rapidly down the stairs. Was this the Director, Valentina Lopez? She was very short, probably not much over five feet tall, with long black hair parted firmly in the middle and severely pulled back and tied with a brightly colored scarf. Her round face was a map of wrinkles.

She greeted Jane in Spanish and then turned to me. Dark eyes regarded me intently.

"Hello, I'm the director of Magdalene House, Valentina Lopez. You must be Professor Ginelli," she said pleasantly in barely accented English, and extended a small hand. Suddenly a wide smile spread over her whole face. The joy she conveyed followed the map of the wrinkles. Valentina Lopez had smiled a lot in her life, I thought.

"Please call me Kristin," I said, smiling back. Who could resist? "Thank you for taking time to see me," I continued.

"And me? I'm Valentina. An unlikely Valentine." And she chuckled. "Let's get to my office, shall we?" And she charged back up the stairs.

Jane followed in her usual measured way and I went behind her. She turned into a small room immediately on the right at the top of the stairs.

There were two wooden chairs placed facing a desk pushed into an alcove along the far wall. Jane immediately went over to sit in one of the chairs and I automatically took the other. The shades were drawn, as I had seen from outside, but they were apparently light filtering and the room was warmly illuminated by the diffused sunlight. Even so, and in such a small room, I did not immediately see Valentina Lopez.

"Coffee?" she said from behind us. I turned to see her bent over a small table pushed against a sidewall. A saucepan on a single-burner electric hot-plate was already starting to emit delicious smells of cinnamon, brown sugar and anise. Oh, wow. She was making traditional Mexican coffee.

"Oh, yes. Thank you," I said, trying not to drool.

"Don't worry, Jane," Valentina said as she stirred the water and spices in the pan. "The kettle is on for that tea you drink." She chuckled again. She continued to talk while stirring the mixture in the pan.

"The coffee is from my home in Tapachula, in Mexico. Grown high on the side of the mountains. Best coffee in the world. My aunt sends it to me." She continued to patiently stir the mixture and the smells of spice filled the room.

But I wasn't so distracted by the smell that I didn't register that she was from Chiapas, an area of Mexico near the border with Guatemala that is increasingly plagued with violent conflict among drug dealers, and where the lives of the indigenous people are being disrupted and deformed by crime and drug addiction. I realized from her small stature and round features she was likely of Mayan ancestry, and one of the indigenous people so horribly exploited over centuries from the Spanish invaders to today's Mexican military as well as the narcotraficantes. Indigenous women in particular have continuously been subject to tremendous violence and exploitation not only by invaders, but also by their own families and communities. The women were often short because they'd never been given enough to eat.

Valentina dispensed coffee beans from a sealed glass jar into a hand grinder and carefully turned the handle at the top. Then she poured the beans into a French press and added the contents of the saucepan. She took out a teabag from another container, put it in a mug and poured hot water from an electric kettle that had started to steam. Then she walked over and sat down in her desk chair and turned it to face us.

I realized that during the time she had taken to carefully prepare beverages for us, my nervousness had completely disappeared. I felt warmly welcomed and truly even cared for.

"So, Kristin. How can I help you?" Valentina said.

I glanced over at Jane and she lifted one shoulder as if to say, 'It's your party,' so I just repeated the whole story from the young woman drowning in concrete to finding out she had been a smart and very angry student who had dropped out, to the former roommate's revelations, to a campus police-woman nearly getting killed searching the student's stored belongings, to meeting her aggressive stepfather and subdued mother, and the questions the examination had raised for me, especially the evidence of drug use and the vaginal scarring, to how talking to Wagner had made me suspect his 'date' with Carlyle had been a professional one, and then my realization I knew very little about this business, not even knowing what to call it. I also asked Valentina directly what she thought of the pattern of behavior I was describing and whether the pattern justified my suspicions.

Valentina had listened intently as I was speaking, though during the description of the evidence of vaginal scarring and drug use she had shut her eyes. When I had finished, she got up without speaking and went over to the little table where our drinks were brewing. She pushed the plunger down on the French press and then removed Jane's teabag, brought the mug over and handed it to her. Going back, still silent, she poured out the coffee into two heavy pottery cups with matching saucers and carried them over. She handed me mine and sat back down. She sipped hers and I did the same.

The thick, rich, spiced coffee was almost syrupy in texture, and the spices stayed in my mouth after I had swallowed. It was impossible to do more than sip, as each mouthful stimulated every part of tongue and throat. I had taken two sips before I actually came back to an awareness of the room. I saw Valentina had been watching me, and she smiled with genuine pleasure. Then she sobered.

"Yes, to your question. I think there is reason for suspicion that the young woman you describe was involved in the sex industry, probably in some form of escort service or brothel or a combination of them."

Brothel? All I knew about brothels was that medieval theologians railed against them, likely because they were so popular with medieval men.

Valentina took a small sip of her coffee and continued more slowly.

"It's the scarring around the vagina that is the most telling. Here at Magdalene House, I do all the intake interviews and 90% of the women who come through that door," and she nodded her head at her own office entry, "tell me of child sexual abuse. Horrific things done to them as a child. The other 10% eventually tell me what was done to them as children. The helplessness and self-blame they learn makes them so vulnerable to recruitment into the sex industry."

Sex industry. I guessed it helped to think of it that way. It did seem to have a production line.

"That's different from the sex trafficking, where girls and women and even children are either sold, or kidnapped and sold, and often resold, multiple times. A lot of the time pimps will scoop up the runaways and the throwaways, the youngsters who run away from home because they are abused, or who are LGBTQ and maybe abused or thrown out for that, or ones that are just angry with their parents and decide the best way to handle that is to just 'get away.' So they come to the city. These pimps, they're smart and really good at becoming some kid's best friend right away. They cruise the streets in their cars, or they go hang around the bus station and look for them. Go there some evening and you'll learn to see them."

I shuddered and Valentina leaned forward.

"It's not the whole story, Kristin. You'll also see some good folks from organizations that try to help the kids too, get to them before the pimps do. The Night Ministry is one."

She paused, looked at Jane.

"There are some students volunteering for them too, right, Jane?"

Jane nodded, but added in her precise voice.

"Yes, Valentina, but only on the Night Ministry bus, where they aid the homeless too. Not at the bus station."

Good heavens, Jane had certainly expanded what the university students could learn if they had the courage.

Valentina went on, her kindly voice matter-of-factly describing horrors.

"So these pimps, the ones who run the prostitution rings, well, they get these youngsters, either directly or they buy them, and they traumatize them so much through repeated gang rapes, beatings and demands for absolute obedience that they create the same kind of helplessness and self-blame as childhood sexual abuse. They call it 'seasoning' them."

And she stopped and seemed to look inward. She was suddenly so lost in thought that the cup and saucer she was holding on her lap actually tilted. I tensed, wondering if I should take it, but I saw Jane put out a hand and cover one of Valentina's. They stayed like that for a minute.

"But it doesn't sound like that's what happened to your victim," Valentina resumed. Jane gave her hand one more pat and pulled back. "And remember, you can't discount the drug aspect. Young people start using drugs, and if there has been childhood abuse, often it is a form of self-medicating. It deadens the pain. But it's expensive and they can get into hooking just to pay for the habit. Or, those selling them the drugs, if they see someone they want to pull into the sex industry, they hook them up with Johns to pay for the stuff. And if like this Courtney child, they are very beautiful, there is a high, high fee. Then they are paid too, often thousands, and that itself is a drug. These ones, they love the cash and the drugs and the Johns are usually professional men who can treat them well. It pulls people in really fast."

I realized I had not thought of Courtney as a child. A beautiful young woman, an angry student, a patient on a ventilator, but not a child. But to Valentina she was. An exploited child.

"So how does that part of the industry usually work?" I asked, realizing I needed to get at the mechanics even while I was being emotionally rocked by this conversation.

Valentina sipped the last of her coffee slowly, and then took her cup over to the table. I looked at the cup and saucer I held and registered I had not finished mine. Sipping coffee and listening to what Valentina was both telling us and not telling us did not go together. But not to finish this beautifully prepared gift was unacceptable. I took a couple of sips, savored again, and then took my empty cup over to her. Then we sat back down.

"This is where we will need to ask someone else. We have a resident here. She likes to be called 'Mary.' Before she became so much an alcoholic, this was the part of the industry where she worked. I think she should be awake by now and I will go and ask her if she will join us."

I was surprised that someone might still be sleeping, as it must have been nearly 11 a.m. Valentina noticed my surprise, though I had said nothing. I realized again how very adept she was at reading people.

"Yes," she nodded to my unspoken comment. "The women here, they don't sleep much at night. Many because they have terrible nightmares, and also because they are used to working nights and sleeping days. If they need to sleep in the day, they get to sleep in the day. The Magdalene House mission is to be a place of hospitality. That means those who reside here are given warmth, kindness and respect, including respect for their chosen times of sleeping and waking."

She got up and left the room.

I looked at Jane. I knew now why Jane had come with me. Valentina had needed Jane to be here, and Jane had known it. But as much as Jane might have known about the sex industry, her normally pale face was actually pallid. Of course it was.

Suddenly, I had a thought. She was exposing students to this. It was, well, more intimate, being in this house with residents than being on a bus that went around and I assumed gave away food and clothes to the homeless.

"What do the students do when they volunteer here, Jane?"

Jane smiled a little.

"Cook."

"Cook?"

"Yes, cook. As well as shop for food, cook it, serve it to the residents and clean up. A lot of being hospitable to those who come through here is taking care of their physical needs. Preparing really good food and serving it to them is a way to show that hospitality without having to say a word. Of course after the food is served, the students sit down and eat with them. They volunteer in groups of three. Almost always just women students. Valentina interviews every student individually who wants to volunteer here. A few men have wanted to volunteer, but she's only accepted one so far. And he comes with two women. He's a lovely guy. Wants to go to seminary and become a pastor."

So probably one of our Philosophy and Religion students then.

"What's his name?"

"Well, we let students know their volunteer work will be kept in confidence unless they reveal it. Gives them some control."

I felt a little irritated. Fine. As a professor I could find out. Then I caught myself and cringed a little inside. I was thinking like the sort of privileged academic I so despised. Nope. I'd give the students their privacy like Jane did.

The door opened and both Jane and I stood up. Valentina had come back and a ghost of a woman I took to be 'Mary' came in behind her. Her paste-white face was broken in the center by the thread veins chronic alcoholism produces. Her red eyes, straw-dry light hair and emaciated body showed years of alcohol abuse. Now here was something I did know about. A whole lot about. Alcoholism rampages through some Scandinavian families, and especially mine. I looked closely at Mary, though trying not to be obvious about it. If she had once been beautiful, I could see nothing of it now.

Valentina shut the door behind Mary and introduced us to her as 'Jane and Kristin, friends of Magdalene House who want to find out more about how high-priced escort services work today.' Mary stood just inside the door and said nothing. Valentina did not seem disconcerted by this, she just gestured for Mary to take her own chair in front of the desk. Mary walked slowly over to the chair and stood in front of it. The baggy sweatshirt and pants she wore did not disguise her thin frame. When Valentina pulled up another chair from along the wall and sat in it, Mary sat too. We made a small circle. I looked at Mary with as friendly a face as I could manage. She was literally vibrating with tension; her hands were clenched so tightly in her lap, the veins on the back of her thin hands looked like cables.

Valentina spoke calmly into the void.

"Kristin, would you tell Mary a little about your former student and why you think she became an escort?"

I heard the "little" message loud and clear and just said that Karen Carlyle, who liked to be called Courtney, had been a very talented student but she had dropped out of school. When I had met her, she had been with a much older man. After she had had a serious and ultimately fatal accident, the older man had seemed very reluctant to say how he had met her and he had changed his story. It had made me suspicious of how they had met.

"That's all?" Mary asked in a voice so lovely it sounded like a violin softly playing in a minor key. Her appeal in her former life was now a little more apparent, not in what she looked like, but how she sounded.

Hmm. How to ask what I wanted to ask without really asking it?

"No, it's not really all, but I'm trying to get a picture of her after she had left school. Anything you can tell me about how the higher paid escorts work will be of help."

"That much you can get from Google," Mary pointed out.

"I don't always believe everything I read on the Internet," I immediately replied.

Mary gave a small smile. It was both charming and appalling as it exposed the gaps in her stained teeth.

"All too true," she said.

She paused.

"But today, these girls, and guys too, it's all about the Internet. They advertise online, they arrange hook-ups through cell phone apps, some even have a way to take credit cards on their phones—though a guy would be crazy to pay that way, of course."

"Even the really high paid ones, they just advertise?" I mean I'd heard that about Craigslist and so forth, but that didn't strike me as the whole of it.

"No. There are online clubs that are websites, really. You know, like that politician guy in New York got into big trouble for?"

I nodded. Sure. Eliot Spitzer. Attorney General. Governor. Idiot. What had I read he'd paid, thousands a night to escorts? And they'd caught up with him because of how the money was transferred, I thought.

"The ones who run the really classy clubs own apartments too where they throw parties and men can meet the women socially. Then they hook up from there," Mary continued.

Parties. Hadn't Wagner originally said he'd met Courtney at a party? But then he would have had to say what kind of party and where. So the meet had become a food court. Made perfect sense.

"Okay, got it. But how would a young woman who wanted to be an escort connect up with one of these classy ones, the kinds with websites? Well, actually like you said, the ones that are agencies, sort of, and also maybe have the apartments?"

"Research. And it's really hard work to wade through all the garbage that's out there. A really smart person, like the woman you name, she'd probably be able to do it, but it takes a whole lot of work and you have to be really smart about it. There are very few agencies that really screen clients and so forth. Most are barely disguised drug dealers and perhaps former sex workers and madams looking to make money off your back when they can't cut it any more."

Well, Courtney fit the bill for being smart, but she'd also ended up dead, so how smart had she really been about what she'd been doing? It did sound to me like Mary knew a lot about this. She was a recovering alcoholic, but may have also been addicted to other substances. And for Courtney, the drug dealer connection might make sense too. She'd really not been that smart at all.

"Is there any way to find out if she worked for one of these clubs and which one?" I asked.

"Did you search to see if she had her own website?" Mary said.

Her own website?

"No. I haven't. As I said, I know very little about this."

"Lucky you," said Mary contemptuously, her voice suddenly turning harsh and guttural.

How to reply to that? I realized there was no decent reply.

Valentina got up and went over to her computer, logged on.

"Courtney Carlyle, right? With an 'i' or a 'y'?"

I spelled it out and she typed.

"No. Nothing here that I see."

"She's dead so maybe no one is paying the fees for the website any more," Mary contributed, her voice now back to its lovely violin tone. She went on.

"I'll ask around a little. See what I can find. Maybe somebody knows what her agency was. If she had one. If she used that name. But dead girl, that should ring a few bells. Describe her."

The guttural tone crept back in at the words 'dead girl.'

I told her Courtney's approximate height, weight, hair color and length, eye color and so forth. And emphasized again that she was highly intelligent.

"That sells, you know?" Mary said softly. "You'd be surprised. More than real beauty. Guys forking out thousands a night want the high-end package. Education. Charm. Real brains. Classy clothes and manners. That can net you up to 10 even 15 thousand a night."

I started.

"Yes," Mary replied to the look on my face. "And more."

She rose and took out a cell phone from her pocket.

"Give me your cell number. If I find out anything, I'll text you."

I dictated it. She typed it in and then silently and rapidly walked out of the room.

Valentina rose and carried her chair back over to the wall.

Jane and I rose too.

I thanked Valentina warmly. She embraced me, her head coming up only to the middle of my chest. Then she put her arms around Jane and for a second put her head on Jane's shoulder. They spoke softly to each other and then Jane and I left.

After we got outside, I also thanked Jane for arranging this and coming with me.

"You got more than you bargained for, didn't you?" she said, looking up and assessing me.

"Yes. I did."

I turned back to look at the house, thinking of the hard, hard work done here. And by those other organizations, the ones that tried to keep the pimps from getting to the runaways and throwaways first.

"I will send a donation," I said, and was mentally making a list.

"Good," Jane said to my back. "But do it anonymously."

"Yeah. I know," I said not turning around to hide my shock that she might think otherwise. It made me wonder what Jane really thought of me.

I turned back and we each went our separate ways.

I don't remember the drive back to Hyde Park, but I somehow got there.

24

The streets are mean
They're not clean
I get to the underpass
There's lots of glass
But I rest.
Ellie Jenkins, #1622
StreetWise

Monday, May 21, 1:30 p.m.

I had to park my car in my own garage as there is nowhere else to park it at midday on the campus. I jogged over to my office, and made it only about 10 minutes late for office hours. As my head cleared the top of the stairs, I could see a woman student sitting on the floor outside my office totally absorbed in texting on her phone. Of course she was. I hoped she wasn't texting, 'Professor Ginelli late again for office hours.' Or rather, 'IDI PGen no show RME.' Emoticon, emoticon.

I said 'hi' in my cheeriest voice, came up the rest of the way, unlocked the door and invited her in. Amazingly enough, she stayed seated on the floor in the hall for about another 2 minutes, tapping away. Oh well. Gave me time to take a breath. I sat down and logged on to my computer. I had time to delete a dozen messages before she sauntered in. I struggled to place her. She wasn't in my class. Probably an advisee looking for approval for her schedule for next fall. That turned out to be the case and we had about a 60 second conversation where she told me the classes she wanted to take next fall and I said 'okay.'

Afterwards, having gotten my electronic approval entered into the faculty online portal, she departed, taking her cell phone out of her back pocket before she even reached the hall. I wondered, as I often did, what this constant cell phone use was doing to young brains. I had read that it fit the pattern of addiction. No, I told myself sternly, no more thinking about addiction today. Mary's deterioration from alcoholism had been way, way too close to memories of alcoholic family members, my mother in particular. Of course, my mother, as well as an an uncle and several cousins, had the advantage of very expensive health care and treatment facilities for their addictions that Mary hadn't had. Not that it helped my mother all that much. The cycle of getting clean and then drinking again still continued. As far as I knew. My communication with my family was down to about once a year.

Drop it, I told myself firmly.

I got up and went to the door and looked up and down the hall. No other students were waiting. I was briefly tempted by Adelaide's coffee bar down at the end of the hall, but with Valentina's Mexican coffee still percolating in me, and my agitated thoughts, I'd better wait a while.

Then I thought how Adelaide would love Valentina's Mexican coffee. I would try to learn to make it, though I bet the coffee beans her aunt sent would be hard to duplicate. For the next few minutes I distracted myself by looking online about how to make Mexican coffee and where to get all the ingredients in Chicago. I had actually made a little, written shopping list before the next student poked his head in. I didn't recognize him either. Another advisee, I assumed. I reluctantly turned from my Mexican coffee fantasies to invite him in.

# # # #

Seven students and nearly 2 hours later, I got up and shut my door. My posted office hours were 1-3 today and it was exactly 3. I was tired of entering an electronic signature on to a form for students I saw perhaps only twice a year. I didn't know them, they didn't know me, and they didn't particularly want anything but for me to tick off the box online. How could this be called 'advising'? It was electronic signing.

I turned back to the computer to finish deleting emails and my cell phone rang.

I took it out of my pocket and Tom's name was displayed on the screen. I answered.

"Kristin!" Tom's agitated voice startled me with just that one word. He was clearly upset.

"Yes. Tom, is something the matter?"

"Listen. Kelly's missing."

"What?" I exclaimed, my excess adrenaline from the morning and Tom's manifest anxiety causing my voice to rise sharply.

"The school called. She hasn't been there all day. She cut and I can't find her. I called her cell, no answer. Where could she be?"

I took a breath. Cutting school. I mean not the end of the world. Still.

"Did she say anything to you this morning?"

Tom exploded.

"She hasn't spoken to me since I picked her up at your house Saturday night. She ran to her room when we got home, locked herself in. She didn't come out once on Sunday. I had to go see a few patients, and when I got back the kitchen was a mess, so I knew she'd at least eaten, but the door was locked again and she wouldn't even answer when I knocked. I left her alone. This morning she got up and dressed in record time and just stormed out."

He paused.

"What the hell happened Saturday night, do you know?" Tom's voice had now taken on an accusatory tone.

I tried not to overreact to that. He was worried and upset. I tried for a short explanation.

"Well, what Carol said is that Kelly had spoken inappropriately to Giles when they were alone in the kitchen."

"Inappropriately?" Tom cut in. "What does that mean?"

I took a calming breath.

"Just wait a minute. What Carol told me is that Kelly, well . . . " I paused for a second. How to put it? "Kelly was trying to act older than she is. I mean you saw how she was dressed, right? Like she was going on a date? So when she spoke like that, Giles just left the kitchen and Carol came down to talk to Kelly and she ran and locked herself in the den until we got home."

"And you didn't think I needed to know this?" Tom said angrily.

He was starting to tick me off.

"I thought you would talk to your own daughter, frankly."

Silence. Then a change in tone. I'll say this for surgeons, they know how to focus.

"Look, it doesn't change anything right now. I need to find her. I need your help."

My anger drained away. Of course he did.

"Sure, Tom. Sure. Kelly is what matters."

I looked at my cell to check the time.

"It's after 3. School's out, I assume. Have you called any of her friends? Have they seen her?"

More silence.

"Tom?"

"I don't know any of her friends or how to get in touch with them," he said solemnly. A lot of self-blame there. Another thing to put aside for now.

"Okay. Then, have you called the police and reported her missing?"

"Ah, no. I thought you had to wait for that."

"No, Tom, not any more. She's under 18, so they'll take the report right away. If she were under 13, we might have been able to get an Amber Alert, but she is 14, right?"

"Yes." I thought Tom might be writing this down.

"The police will enter the information into a national database, but I can't tell you they'll start an active search right now. There's no evidence she's in danger. She's just humiliated and really angry too. She's rebelling against that. Running away feels like doing something about it."

Danger, I thought. How could I tell Tom she wasn't in danger when now I knew there were pimps crusing around looking for young runaways like Kelly? I felt sick and anxious.

"Look. I know a good guy from my time on the force. Let me give you his number. I even think I have his cell in my contacts. You'll get more action if you can have him take the report directly and then enter the information. Hold on."

I put him on hold and scrolled till I found the information for Anthony Walker. I texted the whole contact page to Tom's cell. I'd just been critical of cyberspace, but at times it could be a lifesaver. I swallowed. I hoped life and saving did not come in to this crisis with Kelly.

I pressed 'talk.'

"I just texted you his contact information. Anthony Walker. He's got teenagers himself. He's really the only one from my time on the force I keep up with. Use my name and tell him how upset she is. He needs you to read him in fully. Then give him a description and also, when you get him, you can text him a recent photo of Kelly. Tony's a lieutenant now, he'll have some clout."

"Got it," Tom said.

"Come to think of it, copy me on all that information too. I'll get in touch with that campus police guy I know. Alice is still on leave, but her usual partner, Mel Billman, is a really good guy too. You may have seen him. He came when you called in the Carlyle woman's fall. The campus police are out all around the area and if they have a photo of Kelly and her description they can look for her." How I missed Alice. I hoped Mel was working today.

"Yes, I will." He paused. "I only have one recent photo and it's not great. She hates having me take her photo." Tom was really beating himself up.

"It's what you have and the description will help too. I'll also call Carol and Giles. Giles can watch the boys and Carol and I will go out on the streets and start to look for her. What are her favorite hangout spots?"

"I don't know," Tom said in a monotone.

This was becoming a terrible parenting wake-up call for Tom. I hoped that was all it ended up to be.

I decided to be even more brisk.

"I'll walk by the school. It's just a block from my house. I'll see if I can find a middle school teacher and ask her or him where the kids tend to go. Then Carol and I will spread out."

Carol.

"And you know, Tom, Carol and Kelly have talked in the past. She may know of a friend or where she likes to go."

"Okay. And I'll get right on to Lieutenant Walker. Thanks."

"It's still light, Tom, and we have plenty of time. Also, alert your building doorman to call your cell if she comes home."

"Oh. Right. There's always someone there. Good idea."

Tom was sounding calmer.

I was not. The more I thought about Kelly and her vulnerability, the more panicked I became. To know, to really know that these pimps were cruising around looking for youngsters right this minute was nearly paralyzing. I thought of Kelly and wondered how she was dressed. With her height and the way she hunched her shoulders, she might as well have a sign on her saying 'I'm really needy, come get me.'

I shook myself. Get on with it.

I had Mel Billman's cell phone number in my contacts as well and I called him. I almost teared up I was so relieved when he picked up. He was on campus today and in his laconic way got all the information from me in record time. He promised to 'pass it around.' I tried to give him my cell, but he just said, 'Have it,' and hung up. I forwarded the photo of Kelly and Tom's description.

I called Carol. Giles had just left to get the kids at school. I explained what had happened and what I had told Tom to do. I said I would head to the school and then call her if I got any locations. I asked her if Kelly had mentioned any school friends to her, but Carol said no, no names. I said if I heard about any friends from a teacher, I'd try to get a number from the school and call them right away. I told her I was forwarding her a picture of Kelly and a description for her to use.

"And Carol, ask Giles if he'll just stay home with the boys, okay?"

"Yes," said Carol softly. "I know that."

I quickly left my office and jogged to the school. But try as I might, I found no teachers in the middle school building. It was now after 4 and they'd gone home. I found a swimming coach at the pool. He didn't know Kelly, and why would he, but he said sometimes kids hung out in the university student lounge in the basement of the building next to the school. I hustled over there, but it was nearly deserted and no one of Kelly's age was around.

I called Carol and told her I'd struck out. We discussed a grid pattern with three sections, north to south, east to west. I called Tom and told him I'd gotten no information at the school. He said he'd gotten through to Lieutenant Walker, and Kelly's information was now in the database. I told him I'd reached Mel Billman and the campus police were on it too. I suggested an area for him to start walking.

"Walking? Wouldn't it be more efficient to drive?"

"The cops are mostly driving; if we walk we can ask people on the street, show the photo. Try to talk to kids you think are her age especially."

"Okay."

"Tom, I'm starting out now. I have Kelly's photo on my phone to show people. Carol has it. We'll find her."

"Yeah. Thanks. I'm out of the hospital and already walking north. I'll let you know." And he hung up.

For 3 hours we all walked a grid up and down the streets of Hyde Park and then widened our search to adjoining neighborhoods. No one I showed the cell photo to had seen Kelly.

It was now dusk. I was really starting to panic.

I called Valentina and explained what was happening. I asked for her contact at the Night Ministry. She gave me the name and cell number of the director. I reached him right away and told him our problem. He had me send Kelly's photo to him. Volunteers would be out in a couple of hours, he said, and they could look too. I thanked him, hung up and then swallowed hard.

A couple of hours. Night.

I turned and made a loop south, debating whether to get the car and go to the bus station.

25

You gotta watch
The street
Hear the beat
Of the feet
Bad beat means
Run!
"Watch the Street!"
Dwayne Moorehouse, #2165
StreetWise

Monday, May 21, 7:15 p.m.

Gotta watch my street and guard my beat.

He went over it and over it in his head, trying to keep the bad thoughts out. Rhymes kept the bad thoughts out. That bad guy. Hurt somebody. Ambulance means somebody is hurt.

Beat. Feet. Street. That was good. No room for scared. Gotta eat.

Hey! Eat rhymes with beat, feet, street. Could he use it?

He sure needed to eat. Stayed off the corner two days. No money. No eating.

Stay late today, sell some more papers.

He carefully counted the papers he had left. Still 10. 10 was a lot.

Almost all the commuters were gone now. He sighed.

His head jerked up. A kid. A girl. Big girl. In the alley where he'd hid. Was she scared too?

He quivered. Stay and watch or run?

She was talking on her cell phone.

Okay. That was okay. She was fine. He didn't think she'd buy a paper, but he'd wait.

Nobody else on the street. Quiet.

Then the bad cop came by on his bike. He wanted to run. No. He froze. Better stay still. He glanced over at the girl. Maybe she'd help him if the cop wanted to hit him. But she'd disappeared.

Cop just rode his bike by, never even looked at him. Phew.

"Alison!" the girl said, really loud. She was back. Made him jump. She must have hidden in the shadows of the alley when the bad cop came by. She was smart.

He watched her. She was listening to her cell phone. He would like to have a cell phone.

"I gotta have it. How much have you got?" she said, in a really bad voice like she was mad at this Alison.

"Crap, that's not much."

She was swearing too. Oh, what Mama would have done to her. He didn't even like to think of it. Get that thought out.

Beat. Feet. Street. Eat. He said the rhyme in his head to drown out the girl. But it was no good.

"Meet up? Where? Cool Beans? You mean that coffee shop on 53rd? Sure. Be there as quick as I can. Gotta cut through alleys. All these cops around."

Drinking coffee too? That was bad. Mama always said drinking coffee was bad for you. He quivered with remembered pain and then he smiled. Fat lot Mama knew now. But a young girl. Coffee was bad for her. He thought about trying to tell her that, but she suddenly pushed on the phone, put it in her pocket and ran across the street to the alley opposite.

Five more minutes. He'd give it five more minutes. Till the bells rang on the big church. Then he'd go. Go to McD's. Maybe he had enough money.

Then he saw her. Glenda the Good Witch. She was standing down the street, looking around. Then she started coming right to him.

'StreetWise?' he said softly as she got near.

'Dwayne,' oh his name. His name again. But he knew her. She knew him. It was okay. She wasn't mad. She looked really really worried.

She took out her cell phone too. He looked at it. It seemed like a really nice one.

'Dwayne, I'm going to show you a picture of a young girl. Will you look and tell me if you've seen her?'

He just looked at her. Then gave a little nod.

She handed him the phone. Handed it to him! It felt nice.

'Dwayne,' she said in a soft voice. 'The picture there? Do you see it?'

He looked at the phone. Gave a start. It was the hiding girl, the one who made swears and drank coffee.

Glenda smiled a nice smile at him.

'I think you have seen her. Did you see her today?'

Oh. Oh. Just now. He said the words in his head. Just now. I saw her just now.

But he didn't speak.

'It's okay, Dwayne. Just nod. You saw her today?'

He nodded vigorously.

'Cccoffee!' he got the word out.

'Was she at this coffee shop?' Glenda pointed to the coffee shop on the corner of his street.

He shook his head no. No. No.

'You're doing fine. She wanted coffee but not here?' Glenda said again, smiling at him. He was doing fine. Fine.

He nodded again.

'Do you know where?'

Yes. Yes. I do. Hard words. Hard words. Glenda was worried. Should be. Young girl should not be drinking coffee.

He shut his eyes. Tried really hard.

'Kkkkk . . . kkk . . . oool. Bbbb . . . eeenss.'

He opened his eyes.

Glenda looked puzzled for a minute, then said, 'Cool Beans? The coffee shop on 53rd?'

He nodded a lot. Yes. Yes.

'How long ago? Could you show me on your fingers how many minutes?'

Oh. Easy. He handed back her phone and put up all five of his fingers.

'Five! Five minutes?'

He nodded again really really a lot.

She dialed her cell phone.

'Tom! The *StreetWise* vendor says he saw Kelly not five minutes ago heading to that coffee shop on 53rd. It's called Cool Beans. Where are you?' She waited. 'Oh that's great. You're only about two blocks away. I'll wait. Call me when you get there and let me know.'

She pushed a button on her phone but kept looking at it. The picture of the young girl was there.

'This young girl, Dwayne. She ran away from home. We're trying to find her.'

Oh. Oh. That was bad. Young girl on the streets. He shivered. Glenda saw him.

'Yes. It is scary. We have to find her.'

They stood together looking down at the phone. He was worried. He could see Glenda was really tired and she was worried too.

The cell phone rang.

'Yes. Oh, she's there? Oh wonderful. Good luck. Oh that's so good. Let's talk later.'

Glenda pushed on her phone and smiled at him. A really big smile.

'Dwayne. You're the best. We found her! And all because of you.'

He felt his face get really red. She was so happy.

'How many more papers do you have?' she said, taking out a wallet.

He held out the stack.

Glenda took them all and gave him two 20 dollar bills.

He shook his head. No only 10 papers. He held up 10 fingers.

Glenda smiled at him like she really really liked him.

'I know, but you're a hero. I'd like you to have all that money.'

He held the money in his hand and his head screamed no, no. Not a hero. Not like Jimmy Maddox. Jimmy Maddox tried to be a hero. He got killed.

She didn't seem to notice he was screaming in his head.

She smiled again and walked quickly away.

Not a hero. Jimmy Maddox got killed. Saw it. No. No. Get that thought right outta there. No. Not a hero. Saw nothing.

He ran.

26

I stand under the L
And yell
Nobody cares
I yell and yell
Like the guy with the cell
Can you hear me now?
No.
Jose Ramirez, #839
StreetWise

Tuesday, May 22, early morning to evening

The Gray City had returned.

As I walked toward campus to teach my class, the lowering sky and ground fog blotted out even the muted colors that passed for spring in Chicago. I could barely distinguish among the gray sky, gray stone buildings and gray street. I pulled my jacket closer around me, but the tendrils of fog still penetrated to my bones. I stopped for a second on the sidewalk and texted Carol that it was very chilly out and the boys would need their down jackets.

As I put my phone back in my pocket, I noticed Dwayne was not on his corner selling his papers. I had been looking forward to thanking him again for his help with Kelly and telling him that she was okay. At least, I hoped Kelly was okay. Tom had a long way to go there. And I hoped Dwayne was okay too. He had been very regular since he had taken over that corner from Jimmy Maddox after Jimmy had been murdered.

I walked along, wondering how the Maddox investigation was pro-ceeding. I was cut off from the campus cop grapevine with Alice Matthews being on medical leave, so I had heard nothing about how that investigation was proceeding. The Chicago papers had moved on to the many other murders that took place every day in this violent city.

My phone buzzed with an incoming text and I took it out, expecting a reply from Carol.

It wasn't from Carol.

"Mary" had texted me.

"Meet McD, Halsted & Rasin. 11. Got her."

Rasin? Maybe she meant Racine. I looked up that location and sure enough there were fast food restaurants on every corner of that intersection. 11 a.m. I'd never make it if I taught my class with Hercules this morning. It would take me at least an hour to get to that address in mid-morning traffic and I would have to go back home to get my car. It wasn't my turn to give the lecture, so that was a plus, but I hated ducking out on him at the last minute. I thought about what was best. I knew Hercules didn't text. In fact, while I thought he had a old flip phone, I was pretty sure he often left it at home. Better to see him in person.

I was almost to the office anyway. I started walking faster.

# # # #

Hercules had kindly conned me, there was no other verb that fit, into sitting in on the beginning of the class for his lecture and part of the discussion.

"Of course! Of course! It is fine with me," he had said when I'd knocked on his office door at 8:30 a.m. and explained I needed to be downtown by 11 so I would have to miss class. That was my first mistake. I'd let him know I had a full two hours.

"The students, though. They like to see you, I know. They like to see we are paying attention each of us to the other, to what we say. I think it helps them for themselves, you know, to listen to each other. But it is fine." Hercules normally bounced a little on his toes when he was standing, like a small balloon about to take flight, but as he said 'fine,' his heels went down and he deflated a little. The spidery wrinkles on his face also turned down and a wisp of a frown surrounded his mouth.

Oh rats. Then I'd heard myself say I could still make my appointment if I stayed for a while and while I was babbling about that he was nodding and smiling at me, bouncing on his toes again, and the spider wrinkles formed into their usual facial map of delight. I knew I'd been had in the most well-meaning sort of way.

And then I had gotten lost in the lecture. The reading for the week was by the psychiatrist Robert J. Lifton, from his chilling book "The Nazi Doctors." Lifton had taken the time to personally interview these despicable men who had committed atrocities on helpless men, women and children. Lifton, however, had concluded that they were not cruel, deranged and evil people. Instead, they were rather ordinary doctors who had rationalized their own behavior in horrific circumstances. They ultimately had suppressed the capacity to feel empathy, inducing what he came to call "psychic numbing." Lifton had seen the same kind of psychic numbing in survivors of Hiroshima and Nagasaki. I knew Lifton's work was foundational in the treatment of veterans suffering from PTSD.

Hands shot up around the room almost before Hercules had stopped speaking. Several students were outraged. The most evil monsters in history were supposed to stay evil monsters. How dare this psychiatrist try to understand them and compare them with survivors of nuclear war! Hercules patiently explained again and again how evil is not 'the large monsters you want them to be so you can see them so clearly,' but instead it is 'the little bad acts, the not wanting to see, that pile up and pile up.' I knew it, too. Little by little, evil creeps up on you. And there is no safe distance between you and the capacity for monstrous acts.

And then I looked at my watch. Yikes. It was already after 10.

As I raced down the stairs, I realized I was glad I had stayed. And I knew Hercules knew it. He knew I chased monsters by looking for the little slimy trails they left behind. I hoped Mary had information that would help me follow some of those slimy trails in the sex industry.

The sky had cleared while I'd been in class. Without the fog and if the traffic and parking gods were with me, I might still make it.

# # # #

I hadn't needed to rush to this appointment. I looked at my phone again. No text from Mary and it was 11:30. I had texted her when I'd arrived, using the full address of the 'McD' where I was waiting. No reply.

I had taken a table where I could clearly see the door and I was waiting. And waiting.

I could feel the grease in the air settling on my skin and hair. It left a fine sheen on the tables and chairs. The French fries burbled away in the fryers, adding that distinctive, steamy-starch smell topped off with overcooked meat and lots and lots of salt. I had risked buying a coffee after the first 15 minutes, not wanting to sit and wait without anything in front of me. I looked down at the cup. I'd not yet taken a drink. How bad could it be? I took a sip. It was kind of like a heated-up, liquid version of the thick, brown Chicago air of summer's worst days.

I scrolled through my email while I waited and found one from Adelaide Winters. She wanted to see me 'as soon as possible.' I typed that I'd come to her office as soon as I got to campus, probably around 1 p.m. But before I pressed send, I changed that to 2 p.m. I wasn't sure Mary was going to show at this point, but I'd hate to have to rush out as soon as she arrived.

In another 15 minutes, I was getting ready to leave when I saw her approaching the door. As soon as she entered, I stood up and waved. She turned sharply away and went to the counter. I sat back down. She placed an order. I had planned to get her something when she arrived. Not happening. So I waited some more.

Mary walked slowly between the tables toward me, a large soft drink in her hand. I realized she was not just weaving between the tables, she was weaving because she was not steady on her feet. She sat down next to me and the sweet, formaldehyde smell of the alcohol oozing out of her pores was nauseating. It brought back jarring memories of my mother smelling just like that at the breakfast table. I took a big gulp of the ghastly coffee to try to dilute the gorge rising in my throat.

Just forget it, I told myself. Just forget it. Focus.

"Hello, Mary. Thanks for getting in touch," I said quietly.

She took a long swallow of her soft drink and then sighed.

"Yeah. Okay," she said, not looking at me. Then she took another long drink.

Her lined face had that pulled look that comes from the dehydration and low blood sugar of heavy drinking. No wonder she was gulping the sugary soft drink.

I watched her, suspicious now why she had gotten in touch. I had wondered if I should offer to 'pay you for your time and trouble,' i.e. give her money. Now I was beginning to think that was all she had wanted when she'd gotten in touch.

Finally she turned blood-shot eyes to me, assessing. I tried to keep my disgust hidden, but I'm not sure I succeeded. She looked out the window, at first vaguely. Then she frowned.

I looked where she was looking and she stiffened.

"Don't. Don't look."

What?

I began to think that this jittery behavior meant she would not stay long and I had better jump in.

"Mary, you said you had found Courtney. What did you find?"

"She's dead."

Well, yeah. I knew that.

"Yes, she is. But did you find out whether she had been hooking and whether she was working for a specific group?"

I was being rude. I knew it. I couldn't seem to help it. I so wanted to get up and leave right then.

Silence. She took another long drink.

I waited, though in my mind I was already in my car driving home.

"Yeah. Couple people knew, knew she was dead. Talked some."

I kept quiet.

"She had a website. Called herself 'Silk.' It's down now. It had been linked to a service called 'YumYum.'"

"What do these services do? What does YumYum do?"

Mary looked anxiously out the window. Whatever was there or not there was clearly bothering her. She started to shake and her words broke up into little bullets.

"They have apartments. Nice ones. Gold Coast. Host parties. Courtney did a lot of parties. She was popular. People knew her. Picked up clients."

So Wagner's initial 'I met her at a party' was actually true. Until he realized what he'd said.

"Are there drugs at these parties?" I asked.

"Well, duh," Mary said derisively.

She took another long drink. I bet when she finished the drink she'd go. If I was going to offer money, I'd better do it now. She had come through with some information. Whether it was true was another question, but still, she'd made an effort. My purse was on my lap and I unzipped it and took out my wallet.

"Mary, I'd like to give you something . . . "

"Stop. Put it away. Don't!" she said, looking frightened. She took another quick look out the window.

This time there was somebody there. A guy, probably early thirties, in a cap pulled down low to shade his face, leather jacket, jeans and aviators, looking back at us. Was I imagining the bulge under his right arm? I didn't think so. When he saw me looking, he stepped away from the window and disappeared from view.

Was Mary being followed? Was I? Whatever else it is, the sex industry is a multi-billion dollar business especially when combined with the drug trade. Protecting the profits would be crucial. Was this guy connected to that?

Mary looked down at her drink and started to shake so much she moved back and forth on the chair. I didn't think it was just from her hangover.

"Mary, I saw a guy out the window just a minute ago. He seemed to be watching us. Are you being followed? Are you in danger? I could drive you back to Magdalene House if you think you are."

She froze and her mouth opened and then shut with an audible snap.

"Crap. Get away from me."

And she was up and out the door before I could even react.

I left too and outside I looked up and down the streets of the intersection to see if I could spot Mary and also leather jacket. They had both disappeared.

As I drove back to Hyde Park, I worried about Mary. About her safety. Then I pondered what to do with the information she'd given me. Did the police know about Courtney's website and her association with YumYum? The drug connections there? Then I cycled back to worrying about Mary. Should I tell Valentina that Mary might have been followed to her meeting with me? I didn't know this world at all. I wanted to talk to Alice so badly. Was she well enough for me to call? Maybe I should tell Stammos instead. Was that a good or a bad move?

Well, even if Mary considered it a betrayal, I thought I should let Valentina know my concerns that Mary might have been followed to a meeting with me. If she had been followed back, that could pose danger for the whole house, I thought. I called Valentina's number on the hands-free on my cell phone while I drove. Her voicemail picked up and I left a short message that I had met with Mary at her initiative and I was concerned someone had followed her to and from the meeting. And that Mary had seemed anxious as well. I left a call back-number and hung up.

# # # #

I parked in my garage and then walked slowly toward campus. I registered that Dwayne was still not on his corner, but I was too full of what I had just learned to spare him much thought. The bad coffee sloshed around in my empty stomach and I could feel it burn, but the thought of food was sickening. Anyway, it was almost 2 and I needed to keep my appointment with Adelaide.

When I got to the office, I could see Adelaide's door was open and she was at her desk. I walked directly down the hall and knocked on her doorframe.

She looked up and frowned. She followed that with a curt, "Come in, Kristin. Take a seat."

This didn't sound good.

Adelaide didn't get up or even look at me. She looked down at a pad in front of her.

"You're doing it again and this time you just need to stop." Adelaide's large shoulders were hunched and rigid as she continued to look down at whatever was on the pad. I could only see the top of her graying head.

I was not in the mood to be vaguely lectured and I could feel myself getting very angry.

"Doing what? Stop what?"

Adelaide looked up sharply and her tired, blood-shot eyes glinted with anger behind her glasses.

"Don't give me that. You know exactly what."

She tapped the pad.

"I've had irate phone calls from Commander Stammos of the campus police, and also from the Academic Dean. You have been talking to students about Karen's death, you put Officer Matthews in a situation without backup and she got hurt, and you have absolutely no authority to do any of this."

Blaming me for Alice getting hit over the head? The hell with that.

"You just wait a minute. Just wait a damn minute. Alice was investigating that on her own and I have no intention of getting slammed for it. I may have even saved her life by getting her medical help, so they can just stow that. Besides, I have an agreement with the Dean that I can 'consult' with the campus police and I even have release time to do that. So I have authority. You signed off on that and to blame me for what happened to Alice is just an outrage."

I was breathing so hard I needed to just stop talking or I'd choke.

"Well, that so-called agreement was made before Commander Stammos took over and he's not having any of it. And the Dean agrees." She took off her glasses and rubbed her forehead between her thick eyebrows. She didn't look at me.

I sat and looked at her for a moment, assessing. How much was this pressure from outside and how much did Adelaide agree or disagree?

I tried for a reasonable tone of voice.

"It's in writing, Adelaide. So unless they want to talk to my lawyer, who actually drafted that agreement, it's not a matter of who likes what. They may find it inconvenient, but then again the Dean was very happy that I did not sue after that fiasco last semester. I could still sue, you know."

Adelaide looked up and I plainly saw the pain in her eyes unshielded by the thick lenses of her glasses. I was sorry about that. She had suffered a lot from what I had just called a 'fiasco,' and I recognized it. But I was too angry to back down.

She looked at me for a second, willing me to listen.

"It's the talking to students, Kristin. You just can't run around doing that without at least clearing it first with the campus police, and with the Dean's office. Those students haven't complained, but they could. And then we'll see how much this so-called 'agreement' protects you."

"Well, then, why didn't the Dean or better yet, Commander Stammos, just talk to me directly? Why just push it off on to you?"

Adelaide rubbed her forehead again and then put her hands down flat on the desk. She looked hard at me.

"They want me to fire you."

"And what did you say to that?"

"I said I would talk to you."

I could understand why the Dean wanted to get rid of me. He was a buttoned-down, rigid administrator who was actually slightly afraid of me after what had happened last semester. But I wondered about Stammos. Why was he pushing to get rid of me now? I remembered he had been at the hospital reception where Courtney had been pushed or thrown into the el-evator shaft and that he had been right on the scene when I had been pulled up. I remembered those strong shoulders lifting me like I hardly weighed anything, and I actually weigh a lot. What was his role in all this? Was he aware of the river of drugs that flowed into Chicago and that some of it inevitably sloshed on to the college and university campuses? He had to be. How had he been so quickly and so conveniently on the scene? Stammos himself was not a direction I had thought about pursuing, but this effort to stop me from finding out about Courtney and how and why she died was raising my suspicions quite a bit. I also realized talking to Stammos about what Mary had said was a very bad idea.

"Kristin?"

I became aware I had been silent for some time. But I had made up my mind. Not only would I not quit, I had a new line to investigate. Often when people try to stop you cold like this, it's because they have something to hide.

"You can tell them you have talked to me. You can tell them we have a signed agreement and if they try to fire me for following that agreement, I will sue them. I will win. And not only that. I will also sue them for their massive failures that led to the tragedy last fall. My lawyer is one of the best in the city, Adelaide. You know I have the resources to fight them on this and I will use every one of them. And they really won't like the publicity."

Adelaide drew in a breath and then let it out slowly.

"That's what I thought you'd say. You never stop." She paused, her face grave. "But listen to me, Kristin. Are you sure?"

"Yes. You know me now, Adelaide. I am very sure."

And I got up and left.

# # # #

I didn't stop at my office. I needed to get away. I headed toward the boys' school. On the way, I called Carol and told her I'd pick them up today.

The boys came tumbling down the stairs, Sam in the lead as usual, dragging his backpack down the steps, his shirttail flapping where it had come untucked. "Mom! Mom!" he yelled and barreled into me. Mike followed more slowly, his dark chocolate eyes assessing. "Why are you picking us up today?" he asked as he walked up to us.

"I finished work early," I said. The assessing eyes continued to look at me. Alright. Some explanation was required.

"And you know what? I was just tired of being there, being at work, and so I just played a little hooky. Okay with you?"

Mike nodded thoughtfully. "Yeah, it's okay."

"Yeah, man, it's okay," Sam chimed in. "Can we go to the park before we go home?"

"Sure," I said, thinking I should play hooky more often and not just when I was sick to death of being at work. I should play hooky because these two were the most important things in my life.

We headed for the park, but as we got there my cell phone rang. I was going to let it ring, but I saw it was Valentina. She told me Mary had not come back to Magdalene House and had not been in touch with anyone there that she could find.

"She will do this often, Kristin. Do not worry. She finds her way back to us."

But while I was pushing the boys on the swings, I worried. What if this was a time she couldn't get back to Magdalene House?

# # # #

After the boys had gone to bed, tired from school and the playground, I sat in the den and didn't turn on the lights. The streetlights outside gave a blue glow to the room and I curled up in the corner of the couch with a soft throw. Molly came in and jumped up next to me, put her head on my knee and immediately started soft dog snores. Her warmth against me was comforting, but what I really wanted was a human to talk to, and that human, I realized, was Tom. I needed to talk about what I'd learned about Karen/Courtney and her life after she'd dropped out. My worry about Mary and the leather jacket guy. And the big-time pressure I was getting to drop the whole thing.

I looked at my watch. He might be home. I'd try the home number instead of his cell.

"Kristin!" Tom answered right away. "I'd just been thinking about calling you."

It felt good to talk to someone who wanted to talk to me.

"I'm glad," I said. "I really wanted to hear your voice, talk some things over with you."

"Right," Tom said. "So let me tell you about Kelly and about how we're trying to work that out. Your Carol has been a godsend, let me tell you. We have gone to the counselor she recommended and it's good. I mean, it's not good yet, but it's better."

I was quiet. The very last thing I wanted right now was to have to listen to Kelly troubles.

Tom went on about how he was taking a few days off at the counselor's recommendation and how Kelly was responding well to that and I just stopped listening.

Finally Tom seemed to wake up to the fact that I was not responding. "Kristin?"

I shook myself.

"That all sounds good, Tom." I paused. Equal time, right?

"I also wanted to tell you about some troubling things I've learned today about Courtney and all the flack I'm getting at work for that."

Tom's voice became flat and hard.

"I really wish you'd drop that, Kristin. Let the police handle it. Remember what happened the last time you started poking your nose into an investigation. You almost got killed. You have to learn to let these things go."

I sat up so abruptly on the couch Molly woofed a little in protest as her head fell off my knee.

"Don't give me that, Tom. Just don't. I can't take it after the day I've had today. If you can't listen to me like I listened to you then we have nothing. Nothing." I really hadn't listened to him, I thought, but I had at least shut up and let him talk.

Far from shutting up, Tom unwisely chose to lecture me.

"But it's stupid to keep on with this, Kristin. Don't you see that? Stupid and dangerous. It's not your job any more."

Stupid. That's what he thought. Stupid.

I needed to end this.

"Tom, I need to get off the phone. You not only don't support me, you actively work to undermine me. I can't take that. Truly, this is good-bye. Good luck with Kelly."

And I hung up. But not before I heard that suspicious second click. Kelly had been listening.

I realized I didn't care.

I started to head up to bed and my cell phone rang in my hand. Maybe Tom wanted to apologize.

It was Cullen O'Shea. I answered. His brand of sexy blarney was just what I needed.

"Kristin, me darlin'. Not too late, is it?"

Okay. That was a little thick. But still it made me smile.

"No, Cullen, I'm still awake."

"Good. I'm takin' the boat out tomorrow, need to start some shake-down for the race. I wondered if you'd be me crew? We can have a bite at the club and sail for a few hours."

Just what I needed. Sailing. Getting away.

"Yes, Cullen. I'll come. How do I get there?"

"No, no need for that. I'll pick you up at your house around 11, okay?"

"Yes, that's fine. See you then."

A sail with Cullen would be fun. Of that I was sure. Fun and a little risky, but right now I was more than okay with risky.

27

Secrets
So many secrets
On the street
Just when they think
Their secret is safe
I got it.
"No Secrets"
James Maddox, #965
StreetWise

Wednesday, May 23, dawn

His bones hurt in the cold, damp air. Shoulda worn that jacket. Warm jacket. Cold cold wind and a guy had just come up to him on the corner, a regular, and handed it to him. 'Here, Dwayne. Take this.' Guy looked kinda like Jesus, beard and all. Nice eyes. Not like that cop on the bicycle. Mean. Mean cop eyes, lookin' all the time. He knew. Jimmy knew. Passing stuff to students. No. Stop.

Cold. Shoulda worn the jacket.

Shelter had been loud last night. Not much sleep. Why keep yelling all night long? Stupid. Scary. He'd stayed awake mostly, laying on his stuff. But somebody had stolen his money anyway. Taken it when he'd slept a little. No money under his pillow this morning. Mad and sad and too tired to walk but gotta sell some papers. Gotta get something to eat. He jingled the coins in his pocket. Almost enough for coffee. Couldn't live on coffee. He chuckled. Mama'd be pissed.

Cut through where that building was getting built. Not so much walking. Short cut. He'd done it before. There was a hole in the fence at the back. Save some time. Nobody around this early, he hoped.

He just fit through where the chain link of the fence was loose. Took care not to tear his papers. Got to sell some this morning. Got to eat.

He turned the corner around the big building. He looked up. Getting higher and higher. He looked down. Oh no. A truck. A truck was there. Not a big one. Medium. Open at the back. Delivery. He hid behind a stack of lumber. When they finished he could go. Nobody would see him.

He watched. A guy came around the back and picked up one of the bundles. Looked like the way they wrapped up a bunch of papers when he went to buy new ones. Wrapping stuff all around. The guy reached in the back of the truck and pulled at a bundle. He grunted, pulled again hard and it fell. The wrapping broke and all these little boxes fell on the ground. Little white boxes. His eyes were real good. He could see real well. Little boxes with writing on them. Guy said a lot of swears. A lot of swears. He tried not to listen.

Suddenly he was grabbed from behind, spun around.

"What the hell are you doing here?" It was a giant. A giant with big shoulders and arms and red hair like, like, oh, like his hair was on fire.

The giant put a big hand on his shoulder and shook him.

"Get out of here. Never come here, got it?" The giant grabbed his arm and dragged him away from the truck toward a gate in the fence.

The giant pulled the gate open some with his other hand and then shoved him through. He fell. His papers scattered.

"Stay away if you know what's good for you!" The giant slammed the gate and stormed away.

Oh, no. Some of the papers had gotten dirty. He picked them up with shaking hands. He had to get away. He could brush them off later. Now get away. Get away.

He hurried down the street toward his corner. Oh, Jimmy. Did you see something you weren't supposed to? I saw, but I won't tell. I swear.

# # # #

He hid in the alley by his corner. He wanted to run away but he was hungry. He saw some early commuters walk by on the sidewalk at the end of the alley. Coulda bought. After a while he came out of the shadows, but he stood on his toes on his corner, ready to run. A few regulars came by early. Bought papers. Smiled. Okay. Okay. He wanted to go to the coffee shop on the corner so bad, but lots of commuters now. Sun was making the windows on the shops sparkle. Commuters were happy. Bought more papers. He kept his spot, selling papers. He counted his papers. He could sell out!

Then it slowed down. Way down. He felt in his pocket. He had a lot of bills. A lot of coins. Felt good. Time to get coffee and something to eat. He went into the coffee shop on the corner and got a big sweet muffin thing that looked so good. And a big coffee. He took some big bites of the muffin before he even went outside. The sun was still shining and he walked a little. He stuffed the rest of the sweet, sweet tasty thing into his mouth. He chewed it all up and took a drink of his coffee. He turned the corner.

She was there. Down the block. Glenda. He thought it was her. She was bending over, pulling at some flowers. Her long blonde hair sparkled in the sun. Like the Madonna. NO. Not like the Madonna. Like Glenda. He squinted so he could see her shoes. He sighed. Sneakers. Just like his. He looked down. His sneakers were a little dirty from when he fell. No. No thinking about that.

"Dwayne!"

He looked up. She was calling his name and walking toward him. Maybe she wanted a paper. He had one left. It was a lucky sign.

He walked slowly toward her.

"Hey, Dwayne. It's Kristin. I'm so glad to see you. Are you working today?"

He nodded and held out his last paper.

She smiled too.

"Yeah. Okay. I'll take it. Thanks." She reached into her pocket and brought out two dollars. Handed them over. He gave her the paper. Sold out!

"I wanted to tell you that Kelly, the young girl you helped us find, is doing okay. Her Dad told me. Thanks again for your help."

He stiffened a little, remembering. Not a hero.

She went on talking.

"I'm waiting for a friend to take me out on a sailboat on Lake Michigan."

He pointed east, where he knew the lake was. He liked the lake when it was flat and still. Sometimes when it was warm and nobody was around he'd go in and swim some. He liked swimmng.

"Yes, right," she nodded when he pointed. "But we're going up a little north, to the Chicago Yacht Club."

Yacht. New word. He frowned. He thought maybe he'd try it. Sounded okay in his head.

"Yachtt."

She smiled.

"Yep, and yacht just means a big boat."

Yacht was better than big boat. Too many b's. He hated b's.

He nodded.

"The boat has a name, too. It's named after the flag." She pointed to a flag on a flagpole at the school way up the other end of the street.

He turned so he could see the flag.

"The boat's name is 'Stars and Bars.'"

The worst. An s sound and a b sound. No way he'd try that.

Just then a huge black car came up the street from the other direction.

"Here's my ride," she said. "Bye." She smiled and turned to walk toward where the car was stopping.

He turned too. He had no more papers to sell. He had to catch a bus and go to the center where he could get more.

He walked back down the street and started to turn the corner. He looked back one more time. She was really his friend. They'd talked like friends.

And then he stiffened and ducked around the corner to hide. It was the giant. The big, huge, red-haired giant. The giant had gotten out of the big black car. He was holding the door for her. She was getting into the car with the giant who'd pushed him, pulled him, hurt him. That giant was bad. He was very bad.

He froze. He wanted to run back down the street and yell at her not to get in that car. Not to go. He was scared. She was his friend.

Then he saw the big black car go on up the street. He hid his face against the wall of the coffee shop. Too late.

# # # #

He had no papers to sell but he stood on his corner trembling with fear for his friend.

What to do? What to do?

He looked over at the copy shop. Was the nice copy shop guy there? Could he tell him? He went over and looked in the window, but he didn't see him.

He stood by the copy shop window. Couldn't tell cops. Cops were bad too.

Just then he saw her. The girl. The one from the picture who had run away. He was sure it was her. She and another girl, short with really curly hair, were coming down the sidewalk. He had to tell.

Her name. Kelly.

When they got near him, he pushed the word out.

"Kell-ly. Kell-ly."

She stopped and stared at him. Her friend laughed.

"How come this retard knows you?"

Not a retard. Mama said. Not a retard.

"Dunno. Come on, we need to get back to class in a few."

They were leaving.

"Kell-ly. Need help."

She stopped.

"Listen, man. I don't have any change, sorry," she said, not in a mean way.

He shook his head a lot.

"No. No. Help for KKKris-tin."

"What? What did you just say?"

Her friend pulled at her arm but Kelly didn't go.

"Listen. Forget this. We need to go."

"You go. Go ahead," Kelly said.

The friend said a swear and left.

Kelly stared at him.

"What do you mean, Kristin needs help? You mean Kristin the big tall blonde lady who lives over there?" She pointed to the street where his friend lived. He nodded a lot. Yes. Yes.

"So, what? Come on. I gotta go."

"Bbb—ad man. Took her. Bbb-lack car. Took her. Go on boat. Yach-th club. Sssssaw it. Ssssaw it. Go. Go get her."

He stopped, exhausted.

"She was kidnapped? You saw her get kidnapped? Are you kidding? Nah. Not possible. Trust me. She can take care of herself."

She started to walk away.

"Hurt her. Hurt her."

She turned back.

"Seriously?"

He nodded and nodded.

"You should tell a cop, not me."

He backed up, stiff with fear.

Then he turned and ran.

Behind him he heard Kelly say some bad, bad swears.

Kelly

"Dad?"

"Yes, Kelly. Are you okay?"

The cell connection was really good and she could hear he was like getting all worried. She sighed.

"Yeah. Sure. I'm fine. I thought I'd call you because a really weird thing just happened and, well, I thought you should know."

"Oh, okay."

"Well, it's like really really weird but you know that guy who sells the papers on the street?"

"Do you mean the one by Kristin's house? The one who recognized your photo?"

"Yeah. I think that's the guy. Little dweeb, stutters, but he's also kind of cute like a sort of a cartoon guy."

"Okay," her Dad said, but she could tell he was getting tense again.

"Well he just tried to tell me he saw Kristin get kidnapped."

"What? What do you mean, kidnapped?" Dad was like going ballistic.

"Yeah. Look. I said it was totally weird. Well he was all jittery and wacked and stuff and he can hardly talk but best as I can make out he was trying to tell me he'd seen Kristin get into a big black car and there was a boat some guy was going to take her on, a boat at a yacht club. But he kept saying 'hurt her, hurt her' and like getting totally bent and I said, 'no way' and he kept on it."

"He needs to tell the police what he saw."

"Totally. I said that and he just ran away."

Silence.

"Dad?"

"Where are you now?"

"I'm outside the school. Alison and I went to get some candy at that market by the school."

"You cut class?"

Kelly sighed. It had been a bad idea all around to call her Dad.

"No. Don't get bent yourself. I have a free period."

"I'm at home. I'll come over there and I'll try to figure out something on the way. Maybe we can find that guy and I can ask him about what he saw, get him to tell the right people. I'll need your help though. I've never seen him."

"Yeah. Okay. Yeah. I'll go back and wait by the copy shop. You know that place?"

"Yes. I do. Be right there."

Kelly sighed a little inside. Need you. But for what? Find the Amazon.

# # # #

"Well, we're wasting time," her Dad said after they'd walked the blocks around where the vendor was usually found. Totally.

"Yeah. I think so too," Kelly agreed. She was getting tired of this and she needed to get to her next class. It was also getting real cloudy and colder. She hoped it didn't rain. She'd look like hell if her hair got all wet.

Her Dad had stopped walking.

"Maybe I should call the campus police. They know the area and they were really helpful with, well, you know."

"Yeah. No kidding," said Kelly. "There was a campus cop car on every corner. It made it tough to get around."

She chuckled a little and then looked at her Dad's face. He had that look on like he'd had when he'd come to get her in the coffee shop, or like at her Mom's funeral. Oh shit. The counselor had told her that her Dad would take a long time to get over the fear of losing her. She felt bad for making a joke.

But before she could say 'sorry' he was talking again.

"The head guy. His name is Nicolas Stammos. I've met him. I could call him. Ask his advice. I don't know what else to do."

"Yeah. Yeah. Fine. That sounds okay but we need to start walking toward the school. I am totally going to be late for science."

"Alright. But if I get him he may want to talk to you."

Kelly sighed. Worst idea in the world to have called her Dad.

They turned and started walking back toward the school while he called campus information, asked for Commander Stammos.

Kelly listened to her Dad use his doctor voice to get through a couple of people to try to get to the head guy. She glanced at him while he worked at it. He was important, she realized. And he cared about people. She looked away. He was okay for a Dad. Parents were all weird anyway, right?

Suddenly he stopped.

"Yes, thank you. Hello, Commander Stammos? This is Dr. Tom Grayson. Yes. Right. At the game. I wanted to tell you that my daughter had an encounter on the street today and she consulted me. No. No. She's fine. One of the people who sell the street papers told her that he'd seen Kristin Ginelli get into a black car and he was alarmed. Very alarmed. The vendor told my daughter he thought Kristin had been kidnapped."

Tom listened.

"No. We've looked together but we can't find him. But he was insistent enough that my daughter called me. The guy doesn't talk much, apparently, but kept saying 'go on a boat,' and 'hurt her.' We wanted advice about what to do with this information, if anything."

"Oh. Oh, no."

Kelly looked at him in alarm. His face was like totally white and he was staring at nothing.

"Yes. Certainly. We'll come. Yes. Right now. It's not far. Ten minutes tops."

He ended the call and looked down at her.

"It's not good, honey. Not good. The guy she went with, the cops are investigating him. She could actually be in danger. They want us to both come to the campus police station. They want to talk to you."

Holy crap, Kelly thought. Leave it to the Amazon to get kidnapped.

Her Dad turned to start walking toward the campus police station.

"Dad, you better call the school and let them know I'll miss class."

"Yeah. Yeah. Right."

His eyes looked sort of funny, like he didn't see her.

# # # #

When they got to the campus police station, a guy in uniform met them by the door like he was waiting for them and took them right upstairs to a big office.

Kelly took her Dad's hand. This was no joke. This was scary real.

"It'll be okay," Dad said. But it sounded like he was telling himself too.

They went right through a small room and into a big office. A whole lot of people in uniform and some in like khakis and shirts and jackets that said FBI on them were standing around. Other jackets said DEA, whatever that was.

But whoa. FBI.

A guy with like huge shoulders, like a wrestler type guy but in a cop uniform came over to them.

"Dr. Grayson, thanks for coming. And you must be Kelly."

He shook hands with her Dad.

Kelly just nodded.

"Kelly, it is really important for you to tell me what you heard the guy on the street say about Kristin Ginelli."

Kelly nodded again. She was really nervous.

Her Dad squeezed her hand and she started to talk in a low, whispery voice.

She tried hard to be really careful and say exactly what the little guy had said to her. She thought she should use regular words and not like mimic him as that would be like weird and kind of insulting to him but she told them he had a stutter so these were the words she thought he had said.

When she finished, the wrestler guy nodded.

"Thanks. That is really helpful."

He turned to one of the FBI jacket guys.

"You better tell them. He has a hostage."

Her Dad squeezed her hand so hard it like hurt.

Hostage.

This wasn't some stupid TV show. This was real.

She squeezed his hand back.

28

It sighs
It growls
It whispers
It shouts
It doesn't stay still
The lake is a living thing
And it can swallow you whole
If you don't watch out
Anonymous
StreetWise

Wednesday, May 29, 11 a.m.

I sat down on the butter-soft leather seat in the back of Cullen's limo and felt the deep padding close around me. I sighed with delight. Now this was playing hooky.

Cullen sat beside me and put his long arm on the back of my seat and spoke over his shoulder to the driver.

"We're ready."

The big car made almost no sound as it pulled away from the curb.

Cullen turned and smiled his big, tabby cat smile at me, and he lowered his arm so it was just above my shoulders.

I felt like we were teenagers in the back row of a movie.

I turned and looked him full in the face, gazing at the faint, red stubble of his beard and his full, smiling lips. I didn't want to check in with my rational self. I just looked and enjoyed it. Cullen's arm came fully around me and he bent his head. I wasn't ready for that. Hooky is one thing. This was a signal I was not ready to give. I pushed away a little. He raised his head.

He said something totally unintelligible in what I assumed was Irish while he began to play with my hair.

I laughed at how Cullen suddenly became all Irish when he wanted something.

"What the heck does that mean?" I asked, chuckling a little.

"I said 'don't pretend to be so innocent, little one.'"

"I'm not little, Cullen. That much I know," I said wryly.

Suddenly my phone buzzed in my pocket with an incoming text.

I leaned forward and got out from under his big arm. The arm didn't retract, it slid down behind me and around my hips.

"Must ya do that now?" Cullen said in a low voice.

"It might be about one of the kids. Yes, I do have to check."

He sat back, a little disgruntled. I shifted over to the seat opposite him.

I read the text. It was from Valentina. "Mary came back last night. We took her to rehab this morning."

I sat back and frowned at the screen. Had looking for Courtney brought on Mary's relapse? Then I mentally shook myself. Don't do it. Don't let an addict make their addiction your fault. How many times had I heard that at Alateen when I was a kid? 'Your parents' problems are theirs not yours.' Yeah. Yeah. But old habits die hard.

"Bad news?" Cullen asked softly.

I'd actually forgotten he was there.

"Well, sort of," I said. "This is about that woman who fell into the elevator shaft in your building."

He nodded slowly.

"I managed to trace her. She'd been a student and dropped out and I found out she'd become a high-end call girl here in Chicago."

"She had the looks for it, I'll gie ye that."

I looked over at him.

"I didn't know you knew her."

"Ye mind, lassie, I was at that do like you were, and I saw her, same as any man. I was makin' up my mind to go over where she was gettin' herself a drink, all alone, puir thing, and then some little asshole grabs me and starts blathering about more operating rooms. Missed me chance." He paused, seeming to reflect. "Maybe if she'd been with me now . . . "

He shook himself.

"Now what're we doin', spoilin' things with talk like that? We have some sailin' to do."

"Right," I said, trying to shake off my mood. But that reminded me. I held up my phone. "Do you want me to do a weather check? I confess I didn't look this morning."

Cullen reached over, took the phone out my hand with one arm, and pulled me back next to him with the other.

"I checked. We'll have a bit of weather later but nothin' to worry two sailors like us." He grinned at me.

"But I tell ye what. Let's get the food from the club to go and get right out on the water. Then, if there's weather, we'll still have had time to run about."

"Okay," I said, "but give me back my own phone."

He hesitated for a second and I started to get annoyed. I think he saw it and handed me my phone. I took it, turned it off and pocketed it. There wouldn't be any cell reception out on the water anyway. I'd put it in the duffle I'd brought, in a dry bag.

Cullen called up to the driver to connect him to the Chicago Yacht Club restaurant. In a couple of minutes we had two to-go orders.

Then he lowered his head again.

Before I met his lips, I glanced out the window. We were pulling into the parking lot. A few kisses couldn't hurt. Right?

# # # #

I struggled up out of the limo. Amazing what those big arms and hands could do in just a couple of seconds. Acting like a rebellious teenager was not without its risks, and Cullen, for all his charm, was no one to toy with. It was a good thing sailing a 12-meter on Lake Michigan with just two people would mean both hands on deck all the time. Literally both hands on deck.

Cullen had sent the limo driver to pick up our lunches and he was already striding rapidly toward the gate that protected the private moorings, carrying his duffle and mine. I picked up my pace and caught up with him.

Only three berths down the ramp, he turned and grinned at me. I looked at the magnificent creature moored there. It was so sleek, it seemed like a living thing, its very breathing causing it to bob gently up and down. The sky-blue hull, picked out with white and red trim, was spotless. I turned, entranced.

"How much sail?"

"When we pop the spinnaker, it's a full 165 square meters. She has only a 9-foot draft and ye can see how skinny she is. Cuts through the water like a butter knife. Come on board."

He gestured me to the plank and I hopped up on board. How I had missed sailing. Cullen turned to receive a cooler of food from the chauffeur and then he clamored aboard.

I walked all around the deck, looking at the fittings. We two should be able to manage it, especially if we just used the mainsail. I noticed there was a small dingy covered in canvas strapped down on the bow. Kind of spoiled the lines, but probably a good idea for sailing on Lake Michigan. The lake was no joke for sailors, no matter how experienced. I had heard it described as a 'sea with a mean streak.'

I stood on the bow until I heard the engine turn over. Then I turned to Cullen.

"Shall I cast off the bowline?"

"Just a mo." I waited. "Okay, now."

I leaned over and freed the line from the cleat on the dock and coiled it around the cleat on the bow.

"Done."

Cullen did the same with the stern line and we motored smoothly out of the harbor and around the breakwater. I looked back at the city behind me. Maggie Daley Park, named for the former mayor's wife, was directly opposite us on shore. I realized it was rapidly shrinking in size. We were really moving and throwing up some wake. I glanced at the "NO WAKE" sign as we blew by it. Cullen was in a hurry.

I walked back and headed toward the seats in the stern. These were not the fancy, padded seats of recreational yachts. They were molded benches with non-slip stripes on the seats and even on the backs. They were hinged at the back, forming storage compartments. Before I sat down, I looked inside. Plenty of life preservers. I closed the compartment and sat down. In the race, Cullen's crew of 7 would need them, though they'd be standing a lot of the time, not sitting leisurely.

As we reached open water, it got noticeably colder and I zipped up my waterproof jacket, pulled a wool cap from my pocket and put it on. I was still a little cold, so I opened the small bag I'd brought and got out my waterproof pants. I pulled them on over my khakis, and took the time to stow my cell phone in the waterproof bag I'd brought.

I looked at the sky. Dark clouds were gathering to the north. I thought we might end up having a short sail.

"Let's get the mainsail up, Kristin," Cullen said.

I nodded and started undoing the line that held the mainsail tied to the boom. Cullen stayed at the wheel. When I had all the line off and stowed, I looked at him.

"Wind is from the north, so we'll tack for a while." He turned the wheel. "Let's raise 'er."

I went to the winch. It had an incredibly smooth action and the big sail started to rise. It started to luff in the freshening wind.

"Do you want it all up?" I called back to Cullen.

"Yes, do. Let's get goin' here."

I turned the handle of the winch and the big sail rose to the top of the mast. I tied off the line, but kept low.

Cullen turned the wheel and the wind immediately filled the enormous bulk of the canvas and it swung out. I felt the deck jump beneath my feet. That was always a thrilling moment in sailing, when the craft takes flight. I heard Cullen cut the engine and the throaty sound of the wind was all I heard.

I glanced back at Cullen, his legs braced on the deck, the big wheel held lightly as he grinned at me and then he looked down at the compass. I sat down and enjoyed being out sailing again. I gazed back at the city that had amazingly all but disappeared. We were flying.

After a while, I realized I had to go to the head and I just pulled open the door to the cabin and hurried down the stairs. I flipped on a light to my right, and saw a bank of instrument panels, and then, instead of the regular fixtures of a cabin beyond there was, well, nothing. The whole hull was empty as far as I could see into the gloom. There wasn't even a head. Some netting was attached to cleats spaced along the walls. I went further in and looked around. Caught in one of the nets was a little box. I bent over and freed it. I read the label. "Adderall."

I stood for a minute, stupidly looking at the little box in my hand.

Then it came together. What an idiot I had been. Cullen was the drug connection. He was using his boat to bring prescription drugs into Chicago, probably employing the construction site as a distribution center. He had known what Courtney had looked like, not because he'd gone catting after her at the reception, but because he'd killed her. Had she discovered what he was ferrying back and forth across the lake to avoid truck inspections at the Indiana/Illinois border?

"I had hoped to get a little further out in the lake before you stuck your nose where it doesn't belong. Again."

Cullen's voice came from behind me. Gone was the sexy blarney. In its place was a guttural sound, almost a growl.

"No matter," he ground out. "We can still have some fun before you have to swim for it. Then I'll scuttle this little beauty and get goin' to shore."

I kept my back to him. So, rape, murder, and then he planned to escape.

Not if I had anything to do with it. I'd screwed up to this point, but damned if I'd screw up now.

"You killed her, didn't you, you drug-smuggling bastard?" I said, still not turning around.

"What? The little, blond whore? Sure I did. She was a distributor for me and made damn good money too. The idiot students want to stay up all the time. They'll gobble those pills like candy. And the ones she was fucking too. They gobbled it up. Gobbled her up. She made a fortune and then she tries to blackmail me to get more? Sure I threw her in there."

I heard him move closer to me.

"And then you, you had to drag her up. She would never have been found if you hadn't interfered. I almost killed you that day you came to the construction site. I wanted to. Saints alive. I wanted to."

And I heard him take another step.

I took a deep breath, whirled around and kicked out as hard as I could with my right foot in a front kick, aiming directly at his crotch. He'd been erect, as I'd suspected, and that had to hurt quite a bit. He actually screamed as he fell to his knees. I have always found having a black belt in Tae Kwon Do to be a big help in my life. I don't know how I managed it, exactly, but I ran into a fair number of murdering bastards and had to defend myself.

I followed that with a backhand chop to his neck and he fell forward. He wasn't out though. He was struggling back up, swearing in English and what I assumed was Irish. How to put him down? I looked around. There was nothing in the empty hold that I could see to use as a weapon. Maybe the nets. Try to get him tangled up in a net. But as I grabbed for one on the wall, a hand reached out and took hold of my leg. No good. I'd have to get on deck and see what I could find.

I stomped on the forearm of the hand that was holding me and I heard a satisfying crack. Another scream.

I ran up the stairs, got out of the cabin and closed the doors behind me. There was a small deadbolt on the cabin door on the outside. I latched it.

I looked around. What to use? I wondered if Cullen had brought a gun in his duffle. I ran to where it was stowed under a seat in the stern and pulled it out. I unzipped it and felt around inside. No. No gun. Just clothes in a dry bag.

I looked up. I could hear Cullen starting to pound at the cabin door. It wouldn't stay locked for long.

The dingy! There might be oars. I pulled myself up and over the cabin to get to the bow. I didn't want to risk going around on the narrow deck. The craft was really rocking. Before he'd come down into the cabin, Cullen must have turned us into the wind again and tied off the wheel. The mainsail was luffing crazily above my head and the waves had become noticeably higher. The shifting winds of what was obviously an approaching storm were tearing at the sail. I realized we could capsize if the wind suddenly changed direction. As it would surely do on this unpredictable lake.

Well, nothing to be done about that now.

First things first. Try not to get murdered.

I reached the dingy and pulled back the canvas covering it. And I got the shock of my life. Dwayne was huddled in the bottom of the small boat, soaking wet, shivering and looking scared to death.

"Dwayne! What are you doing here?" I shouted, trying to be heard over the wind.

He looked so stunned I wasn't sure he'd heard me. His little round face was completely without color.

"Help. Help you," he managed through chattering teeth.

Good grief.

I saw an oar and pulled it out.

"Listen, Dwayne. You can help me. When you hear the bad man come near, make a big noise, okay? Have you got that?"

Dwayne's light blue eyes looked so like a rabbit's I had little confidence he had understood.

I repeated it one more time and then covered him up with the canvas.

I retreated to where the cabin rose in the middle of the deck and took as much cover as I could in its shadow. I gripped the oar in both hands. I heard the splintering of the cabin door and a roar from Cullen.

I heard him continuing to swear a blue streak. It helped me locate him. He was coming around the side of the deck, not over the cabin. Good. I saw his legs go by and he was still yelling curses.

Suddenly, the canvas covering the dingy started moving.

"Ah got ya, ya whore," Cullen yelled and bent to pull the canvas off.

I stood up and swung the oar. I hit him square on the side of his head and he dropped like a stone. Unfortunately, he dropped right down on top of the dingy. I heard an 'oomph' from Dwayne.

I grabbed the mooring line that I had so neatly stowed when we had cast off from the dock. It seemed like days ago.

I pulled Cullen part of the way off of the dingy and I secured his hands in front of him. Only then did I feel for a pulse. Fortunately, it seemed I hadn't killed him, but that meant he could wake up. I started yanking his bulk to the side to free Dwayne who was scrabbling around under the canvas like a manic mole. Cullen's bulk suddenly fell to the deck and Dwayne popped up.

"Dwayne, you okay?" I asked anxiously.

He nodded, looking anywhere but at where Cullen was lying on his side down on the deck.

"Dwayne. Help me get the bad man turned over so we can tie him up more."

Dwayne shivered and didn't move.

"Come on Dwayne. There's a storm and we need to tie him down."

We started shoving at Cullen's right side and eventually got him flat on his back. If I'd tied him to the deck in the storm on his side, he might drown just from the water on the bow. He might drown anyway lying flat on his back, but there was no way Dwayne and I could move his huge bulk. I used the rest of the bowline to secure his feet and I tied the end of that line to the bow cleat.

I'd finish up with the netting to hold him down, but first I needed to get Dwayne inside and a little warmer.

I took Dwayne by the arm and guided him over the top of the cabin. He kept stopping and staring at the rising waves. I crawled over him and then pulled him along. When I got him down to the deck, I kept one hand on his head so the swinging boom didn't hit him, and I used the other to grab two life jackets from inside the seat locker. I had to push the splintered wood of the cabin door aside, and then I took Dwayne's hand and led him inside. I hurriedly put on one of the life jackets. Dwayne was shivering violently. He needed to get dry clothes on. He could get hypothermia at this rate. I went back out to the deck and staggered over to get Cullen's duffle. I could get Dwayne to put on the dry clothes, the clothes I assumed Cullen had brought for making his escape.

I went back down into the cabin.

"Dwayne. Dwayne!" He looked up at me. I held out the clothes.

"Put these on. You'll be warmer. Quick. Do it now."

I went down into the hold and freed one of the large nets. I'd use it to secure Cullen and then I had to figure out how to avoid sinking this beautiful boat.

When I came up, Dwayne had on a sweater and pants that could have fit three of him, but he looked a little better. I strapped the other life jacket on him and told him to stay in the cabin. There were small benches built in to each side of the cabin, as well as two, taller, metal chairs bolted to the floor. I pushed him gently down onto a bench.

I dragged the net outside and up over the cabin and put it over Cullen. I tied it as best I could to the cleats on either side of the bow.

Then I crawled back over the cabin. I needed to drop the mainsail as fast as I could and get the motor going.

When Cullen had started the motor, he'd reached down somewhere near the wheel. I had trouble keeping my footing now as the deck below my feet was rocking like a ride at Disney World.

I looked around and then saw an obvious starter button. I pressed it and the reassuring sound of the motor came on. I took a look at the lake, the waves now at least 5 to 6 feet high. Maybe more. I untied the wheel and corrected course a little more so we were again heading directly into the wind. Then I tied it off again. Overhead, the huge sail flapped, the wind dumping out of it.

I went to the winch and started to lower the big sail. Some gusts would catch it and lowering it now was a lot tougher than raising it. I wondered if I should leave a little sail and reef it, but decided against it. I let go of the winch and the huge canvas dropped completely to the deck. I thought about trying to tie it up, but decided I had bigger problems than a messy deck.

I went back to the wheel and looked at the compass. Northwest. The boat was now shuddering as some of the larger waves plowed into us. These were not smooth 3 to 4 footers, more like flat-faced, hard, liquid walls, breaking spray at the crest. Where the hell did they come from? Was it going to get worse? When we went up, the motor sputtered a little, but it kicked in as we came down. I tied the wheel again and crawled toward the ruined door of the cabin.

Inside, Dwayne was practically catatonic, slumped sideways on the small bench. I felt the pulse in his neck and he didn't even move. Okay. His pulse was reedy but there.

I turned to the instruments. I needed to send a distress signal. I turned on the panel and the radio crackled. I looked for the emergency distress beacon, the GPS device that would enable the Marine Police to find us. I saw it on the upper right of the panel, and realized instead of the usual blinking green light, it was dark. I bet Cullen had disabled it, since he had apparently planned to escape.

I thought for a minute, though the pounding of my heart made it difficult for me to hear my own thoughts. There had to be a way to turn it on. I knelt down and looked under the instrument panel. There was a wire hanging down below where the distress signal light was located on the panel above. I grabbed it and looked for a place to connect it. It had not been cut, I saw with relief, just pulled out from the board above. In the dim light, I saw what could be the outlet for the device. I pushed the prongs at the end of the wire into what looked like the matching configuration. It fit. I stood up. The beacon light was on.

Now the distress call.

"Mayday. Mayday. This is the Stars and Bars. We are in distress. I have activated our emergency beacon."

I repeated the call several times.

I switched the dial on the radio, wondering if I had the right channel. I repeated the message on different channels. Then a tone sounded and a message came across one of the screens on the console.

> THE NATIONAL WEATHER SERVICE HAS ISSUED A SE-VERE STORM WARNING FOR LAKE MICHIGAN TODAY. NORTHWEST GALES TO 25 KT QUICKLY INCREASING TO STORM FORCE WINDS OF 35 KT THROUGH THE AFTERNOON. WAVES 5 TO 7 FT INCREASING TO 9-12 FT. OCCASIONAL WAVES AS HIGH AS 20 FT ARE POSSIBLE.

Occasional? I swallowed rising gorge. That meant a 20 foot rogue wave might come roaring over us any time!

That forecast certainly explained why Cullen had not wanted me to check the weather on my phone. Scuttling a boat in a huge storm on the lake would have given him perfect cover. Plus a sure thing on murdering me.

Suddenly the whole sailboat rose in the air and then crashed down. Water came cascading through the broken cabin door and pooled at my feet. I glanced at Dwayne. He was still on the small side bench, but he was sitting up and actually looked more alert, though terrified. I put my hands under his arms and moved him into the metal chair that was bolted to the cabin floor on that side. He started immediately holding on to the metal chair for dear life. Well, good.

Now that the beacon was working, I could see what I thought was the Stars and Bars on the radar screen. We were not that far out into the lake, and not as far from the city as I'd feared.

I thought I'd take a chance and at least peer out on deck and see what was happening. But as I started for the stairs, another sickening rise and fall of the boat knocked me to my knees and another, larger amount of water came down the stairs. It ran down into the empty hull where I could dimly see it sloshing around.

The bilge pump. Was it on?

I scanned the panel again and saw the bilge pump plainly labeled. I flipped the switch and heard the reassuring ka-chunk, ka-chunk of the pumps turning on.

I decided I had better sit down and hold on like Dwayne. If I got knocked out, we would surely be in an even bigger mess. I took the captain's chair in front of the console and grabbed the arms.

I listened to the engine sputtering and the bilge pumps working and wondered how much gas we had. I struggled against a feeling of claustrophobia. Would I be trapped in the cabin if we capsized? I would have to get Dwayne out. I felt so alone and trapped and I tried to not let fear take over. I hung on for dear life just like Dwayne. It was all I could do.

# # # #

My arms were sore from clutching the arms of the captain's chair. I had completely lost track of time. I began to notice that the sharp rise and sickening fall of the boat had lessened some. I wondered if I dared climb up to the deck and look around. Maybe if I tied a line on my waist, I could venture out a little ways. I checked our position on the screen. If I could head us a little more to the west, we would be heading for the Chicago shoreline.

I got up and my legs nearly gave way under me. I held on to the chair back and stretched them. Then, when I thought I could walk, I looked in some of the cabinets in this part of the cabin. One pullout drawer had several coiled ropes and I took one. I tied one end to the chair and looped the other about my waist and tied it with a slipknot. I didn't want to be attached to this chair if we did capsize. I saw Dwayne looking at me curiously. He was less dazed, I thought.

"Dwayne, there's nothing to worry about. I am just going to go up on the deck and look around. See where we are. You stay put."

He nodded and continued to hang on to his chair.

I crept up the stairs. The waves were still about 5 to 6 feet high, but not nearly what I thought they had been when Dwayne and I had been being knocked up and down in the cabin. I gave a thought to Cullen, tied to the deck. I glanced over the roof of the cabin and I could just see his head, encased in the netting. Well, he was still there at least.

I went further out on the deck and then, as it seemed safe to do so, went to the wheel.

I went behind the wheel and grabbed on. I checked the compass and then I untied the wheel and did a small course correction. I still wanted to hit those waves as directly as I could and yet turn us more to the west. If I turned too far, the waves would hit us on the starboard side and they could quickly swamp us.

Suddenly, in the distance, I saw a fairly large craft coming right toward us. I felt weak in the knees with relief. As I watched it through the rain, I could see its course continued in our direction. It was heading for us.

When we were in hailing distance, I heard a voice magnified through a bullhorn.

"Chicago Marine Police. You will be boarded."

I waved and throttled way down. I didn't dare shut off the motor completely as we would be turned by the waves. As they came alongside, two guys in dark blue slickers each holding guns in one hand jumped aboard. They were holding lines in their other hands. I put one hand up, but kept hold of the wheel with the other. They both looked at me for a second and then one holstered his gun under his rain slicker and quickly used one of the lines to secure us to the side of the cruiser. I was pretty sure they weren't going to shoot me, so I stopped holding my one hand up, reached over and cut the engine completely.

The taller of the two men came rapidly over to me. He gripped the wheel as well.

"Are you named Ginelli?"

I nodded. He had not holstered his gun.

"We have an arrest warrant for a Cullen O'Shea. Is he on board?"

"Yes. I have him tied down on the bow. He tried to kill me."

To his credit, the officer did not look all that surprised. He went over to the side of the deck, stepped up on the gunnel and looked up toward the bow.

"Is he alive?" he asked as he stepped back down. He holstered his gun.

"I don't know. He was after I knocked him out. I'm sure he will need medical attention."

"Mack!" he called to the other officer who was standing near what remained of the cabin door, looking at it hanging from its hinges and listening to his radio. Mack started and looked up.

"Tell'em O'Shea is on board. He's tied up and needs medical attention. Then get up to the bow and secure a bow line. Watch yourself."

He started to turn toward the cabin.

"Officer," I said loudly, "there's a passenger in the cabin. He helped me with O'Shea. He is really cold and frightened. Let me be the one to speak to him."

He bent and looked into the cabin. I think he must have seen Dwayne posed no threat and he stood up.

"He looks like he could use some medical attention too." He came over and peered at me. "Are you okay?"

"Yes, I'm fine."

He took out his own radio from underneath his slicker.

"This is Parker. Yes, Mack said. Right. We need the medical team over here." Pause. "Yes, right away. For O'Shea. But use handcuffs. The woman seems fine. And there's another guy, sort of a passenger. Right."

I went down into the cabin to tell Dwayne not to worry, the Chicago Marine Police had arrived. It was a mistake to say the word 'police,' I realized, when Dwayne shrank back in his chair and refused to look at me. He just shook his head.

"They're nice people, Dwayne. Don't worry. I'll be with you."

He didn't look up.

Other than being terrified, I thought he looked better so I didn't push it.

I went back up on deck and looked over the cabin to the bow. I saw Cullen being strapped into a metal basket. When they had him secured, they lifted him over to the police boat.

Parker turned to me.

"We'll tow this craft in behind us. After that guy is stowed," he jerked his head to where Cullen's body was now being carried below decks on the police craft, "we can get you aboard too."

I looked at him for a second and then I looked out over the beautiful sailboat that had been about to be scuttled. I shook my head no.

"I'll stay here, work the wheel. I can turn the engine on low and we'll be steadier that way," I said. "The tow still needs a captain here, and now that's me."

"Really, ma'am, that's not necessary. We can do that."

"I'm an experienced sailor, sir, and I'd prefer to do it. And I think my passenger will have a panic attack if you try to move him. If I could just have a couple of blankets for him, we're good to go when you are."

To Parker's ever-lasting credit, he didn't argue. He just radioed for some blankets to be handed over. When I got them, I took them down and tucked Dwayne into his chair.

"We're going to go back to shore now, Dwayne. Stay warm and I will be right up there." I nodded my head in the direction of the wheel.

"Okay," Dwayne said. He was actually looking sleepy. I felt his neck again and his pulse was steady. If he dozed, that would be best.

I went back on deck, stepping over the mainsail still lying on the deck. There was nothing I could do to get the big sail up and secured on the boom by myself, but I could secure the flapping lines so they didn't accidentally catch someone around the neck. I did that and the clanging noise of the loose lines subsided. I made sure the boom was tightly secured.

I looked over. The Marine Police craft was a pretty good size, I noted. Must be more than 40 feet.

Parker went up to the bow and caught a line thrown from the stern of the police craft. He affixed the tow, but stayed in the bow, holding on to a line. He signaled we were secure and the police vessel started to churn away.

The towrope tightened and we began to move through the waves. I started the engine and we moved securely behind.

# # # #

As the blue roof of the Chicago Marine headquarters came into view, the clouds cleared to the west and a shaft of pure gold spread over the city. The wind had dropped closer to shore.

We went through the lock and up into the protected harbor where the Chicago Marine Police fleet was housed.

Parker released the towline and I took the Stars and Bars in under her own power. I pulled it into a slip next to the police boat and killed the engine.

I heard "Kristin!" and looked up.

Tom was standing on the dock waiting. And of all things, Kelly was next to him.

I waved and went down into the cabin to get Dwayne. He came without trouble, trailing his blankets.

I helped him on to the dock and a very sweet young woman in a rain jacket with a red cross on it met us. She spoke softly to Dwayne and he went quietly with her.

I ran to Tom and threw myself into his arms. They closed around me.

"I thought I'd lost you," he said, brokenly.

"You won't lose me, Tom. I may be an idiot at times, but I'm an idiot who loves you." I sighed into his chest. I'd had plenty of time to think about my feelings for Tom when I'd been scared to death in the cabin.

His arms tightened.

"I love you too, so much it makes me insane."

Kelly put her arms around both of us.

"It does make him insane," she contributed.

And all three of us laughed hysterically like the idiots we were.

29

The peace of the day descends
Tired children are collected
From the playground across the street
The sky revolves and blue turns to gray
Good-night
Sleep well.
"The City Sleeps"
James Maddox, #965
StreetWise

A Week Later

I was sitting in the plush anteroom of Commander Stammos's office, waiting to meet with him.

Things had been hectic, to say the least, for the last week and it was unlikely that would subside any time soon. As soon as Tom, Kelly and I had entered the Marine Police building, both a DEA and an FBI agent had met me. Needless to say, they wanted to talk with me. I didn't seem to be under arrest, so I asked them to wait a minute and walked over to where Tom and Kelly were standing near where the young woman from the medical team seemed to be finishing up with Dwayne.

I put my arm through Tom's just to feel his warmth and secure presence again. He had filled me in on how they'd gotten there.

"Would you and Kelly take Dwayne to his shelter?" I asked. "Apparently I'm going to have to go with those guys over there." I pointed to the two agents who were clearly keeping an eye on me.

"Of course," Tom said. "Are you okay? Really?"

I kind of checked in with myself before I answered. My right hand, where I had chopped down on O'Shea's neck, was a little swollen, but my fingers worked okay. Other than that, I did seem to feel fine, though I was sure I'd crash later.

"Actually, I do. I hurt him before he had a chance to hurt me."

Kelly was staring at me with a hero-worship kind of look. Oh, good grief. I'd read that the new Wonder Woman movie was having a big impact on girls. A new vista of different Kelly problems spread out in front of me.

The medical person seemed to be finished with Dwayne. They had taken away O'Shea's clothes, I assume for evidence, and given him dark blue sweatpants and a hooded sweatshirt with CMP on the front. He was looking at me.

I went over and explained that my friend, I pointed to Tom, was going to give him a ride back to the shelter. He put his head down and mumbled 'no.'

Oh dear.

Kelly came up next to me and then just sat down in the chair next to Dwayne.

Dwayne looked over at her, his Disney Mouse smile returning.

"Kel-ly."

She smiled back at him, but still wisely said nothing.

I walked softly away and went back to Tom.

He was looking at his daughter like he'd not seen her before. Well, he hadn't seen Kelly, really, and neither had I. We'd seen a ticking, teenage bomb, ready to go off at any moment. Neither of us had seen this compassionate young woman, this Kelly, the one who had cared about Dwayne enough to listen to him. And, cared about me, I thought. Maybe Kelly hadn't seen this side of herself before, either, but now she was taking charge and doing a good job, apparently.

Kelly got up and Dwayne followed her.

"We'll go now, okay, Dad?" Kelly said quietly.

"Bye, Dwayne," I said. "Thank you for helping me."

He nodded, and then followed Kelly and Tom. Tom looked back at me with a dazed look on his face. He'd get used to it. Two Wonder Women in his life.

I would do something for Dwayne, I thought as I watched him walk down the dock toward the parking lot. But before I did anything, I'd consult with the *StreetWise* staff about what was best, though. Should I set up a trust fund for Dwayne with an administrator so he could have a small apartment, some money of his own, maybe even for some vocational training? Good idea? Bad idea?

In this past week, I had made an appointment to see one of their senior outreach workers, and also donated some money to them directly for operations and some to tide Dwayne over until he felt like selling his papers again.

After Kelly, Dwayne and Tom had left, I had gone back to the two agents and asked them where they wanted to talk. When the FBI agent had indicated they wanted to take me to their main Chicago offices, I'd called my lawyer, Anna Feldman, on her cell phone. Thank heavens she picked up. She listened quietly to my short explanation and said she would meet us at the FBI office. I'd relayed the address.

O'Shea was alive when he was taken away by police ambulance. Parker had told me that while I was waiting for the agents. That was good. Good for him, certainly, but also good for me. I'd killed someone in self-defense only last year, and I thought it might look a tad suspicious if I claimed I'd done it again.

I was taken directly to a windowless conference room at the Chicago FBI office. It smelled of some kind of pine air freshener that didn't exactly cover the smell of years of dried sweat. There were two FBI agents, three DEA agents, Anna and me, and it went on for nearly three hours. Anna sat there in her St. John's suit and a gold and diamond starburst pin on her shoulder that was so big and so bright you really couldn't look at it for any length of time or you'd start to see spots before your eyes. I didn't say anything until Anna had made sure that I was not being charged with any crime. She actually got that in writing before she let me proceed. And then I'd given them all I knew, from the moment Tom and I had heard the scream and the thud at the hospital reception up until I'd hit O'Shea with the oar. One of the agents actually quizzed me several times on how I'd managed to disable O'Shea. He'd been openly sarcastic at first, convinced I was exaggerating my Tae Kwon Do skills. He'd seen the size of O'Shea before they carted him away to the ambulance. How exactly had I pulled that off, he wanted to know? By the third time he'd asked me that, I was contemplating offering him a demonstration, but I was just too tired. Finally, he let it go.

I kept Valentina, Magdalene House, and Mary out of it though. I just said I had suspected Courtney's activities. I also kept Dwayne out of it as much as I could. I said I had told him I was going on a boat on Lake Michigan and had even told him the name (true), I said that I thought he had followed me by bus and had swum out to the yacht and hidden himself in the dingy (I thought that was true) in order to go on a boat ride (not true). I said he had not seen me hit O'Shea with the oar as he had been under the canvas (true). I also lectured them about not speaking to him without an attorney, and I indicated that Anna was representing him. She raised her eyebrows, but did not object. She'd been good on that. Over this past week, she had managed to keep the agents away from Dwayne. I was very grateful.

After a couple of hours, and despite a few cups of bad coffee, I had started to fade. Anna had ended the meeting, but as I stood up to go, I asked what would happen to the Stars and Bars after all the evidence had been collected from it. I was told it would be sold at auction. I asked to be notified when that would be as I wanted to buy it. That produced dead silence around the table, and then the lead agent had mumbled, 'We'll let you know.' I knew we had miles to go together before that, including my testimony at O'Shea's trial, but I wanted that boat. I could have it renovated, and then I could teach the boys to sail. I wondered what Carol and Giles would think about sailing.

Anna and I left and she put me in a waiting limo. Anna never drove. She had a limo service on call. Another one was pulling up as she gave me a brisk hug on the sidewalk and pushed me into the first one. As I got into another beautifully appointed luxury car, I reflected the day had started and ended with these big cars, and had gone to hell in between. I had slept on the way home.

Early the next morning, I called Hercules on his home phone. I needed a day off. He was touchingly sympathetic and I lounged around the house in my pajamas until after lunch. My cell rang at about 2. It was Jane. I picked up. She asked how I was and if she could come over. I took it that this was a pastoral call and I realized I'd like to see her. We sat in the den. I didn't have any herb tea, so she made do with warm water and a slice of lemon. I was aghast, but hid it.

I looked over at her, sitting so still, waiting, her gray eyes and lightly lined, pale face lending her a quiet dignity. I started talking about what was bothering me the most. My mother. And Mary. And my deepest fear that I too had an addictive personality. I told Jane I feared I was addicted to violence. And she listened, and she shared that she was a recovering alcoholic. We talked for a long time as the sun moved across the bay windows in the den, light and shadow trading places in the room, as light and shadow traded places so often in human life.

# # # #

Before I had made this appointment with Commander Stammos, I'd called Alice at home to ask her if she felt well enough to come to the meeting, and if she were willing.

"About time you got that mess cleared up," she'd said flatly, and added that she'd come.

I called Stammos's office and asked for a time for him to meet with me and I said that Officer Alice Matthews would be joining me. When asked what the meeting would be about, I said I wanted to clarify my status with the campus police. The officer who had taken my message had called back promptly, and he had indicated that the Commander also wanted to see me as well as Officer Matthews. Good news? I didn't know.

I did know I wanted to clarify my status with the campus police. I was finished with this nonsense where I was called on the carpet and even threatened with dismissal for doing what I had a signed letter of appointment to do. And I wouldn't be content with just being the faculty liaison to the campus security committee either.

When I'd stepped into Adelaide's office a couple of days ago to tell her I was going to force the issue myself, she'd not said anything when she saw me, she just came out from behind her desk and put her arms around my waist.

"Thank you, Kristin," she said, actually squeezing me. "Thank you for finding justice for Karen."

Wow. I didn't know what to say.

I patted her on her back and mumbled something inane like, 'that's okay.'

Then she pushed away from me, almost knocking me down as I wasn't expecting it, and she moved her bulk back behind her desk as quickly as she had come out. She briskly changed the subject to the progress on the new faculty searches. Apparently we had some promising candidates.

I sat down in the chair opposite her desk before I fell down.

# # # #

So now I was waiting for my appointment with Commander Stammos. Alice Matthews opened the door to the anteroom, walked directly toward the secretary sitting there, and identified herself. Her brown, lace-up cop shoes made no sound on the plush carpet. She was wearing khakis and a blue, button-down collar shirt. Alice could look like she was in uniform even when she was not in uniform. She came over and sat down next to me.

She looked really good. Her color was normal and her bright, dark eyes scanned me, the way I was looking at her, trying to see beneath the surface. She was also frowning at me as usual. I found that very reassuring.

"Huh," she said.

"Huh yourself," I said, grinning at her.

"Cute. Always cute," she said, but she couldn't quite keep the frown going.

Then the door opened and the bulk of Commander Stammos filled the doorway.

"Please come in," he said formally.

We did, and when we were seated in front of his enormous desk, I jumped right in. I was nervous, I realized, and I wanted to get my little speech over before I chickened out.

I explained about the arrangement I had negotiated last year and I pulled out a hard copy from my purse and handed it to him. He put on some reading glasses and read it.

When he looked up, I said I wanted to get clarity on what 'consulting with the campus police' actually meant so there would be no more misunderstandings.

Alice snorted softly, but didn't comment.

"Well, you won't get that clarity from me," Stammos said point-blank.

What? That was kind of abrupt, even for him.

"I'm leaving in about two more weeks. What I mean is that someone else will have to give you that clarity. Besides which, I'm not actually with the campus police. I have been working here undercover to discover and stop the tide of prescription drugs coming on to the campus."

Alice and I looked at each other. I saw she was shocked too. Her dark eyebrows were up so high they almost met the fringe of her hair. She hadn't known.

Stammos put his elbows on the desk, steepled his large, stubby fingers and addressed Alice.

"I regret, Officer, that you and so many were kept in the dark here about my role, but since there was no way of knowing if there was corruption in the department itself, I could take no one into my confidence. I will, of course, be letting the rest of the officers know before I leave. The only person who knew was the President of the University, who had actually asked the DEA for help. They contacted me."

"Do you know who killed Jimmy Maddox?" I asked. "Was it O'Shea?"

"No. Not O'Shea," Stammos said grimly, "though there is plenty to lay at that boy's door, let me tell you. Plenty, and for a long time.

"No, it was a young man who worked for O'Shea and who rode around campus on a bicycle wearing a campus police uniform disguise and running a kind of drug delivery service." He grimaced. "It took an unconscionably long time for us to catch on to that. He was really clever about where and when he did his act. We have him in custody."

"What? Did Maddox see him and suspect?" Alice asked in a clipped voice.

Stammos turned back to her.

"Yes. That's what we think happened. Maddox had kicked a drug habit, but he knew what street distribution looked like. He should have reported what he'd seen to us, but I wonder if he wasn't sure who was clean and who it was safe to tell." Stammos sighed hugely. "And he was a vet, a brave man. I bet he thought he could just take care of it himself. And he was killed for it."

We sat in silence, remembering a good man.

Stammos turned again to Alice.

"That pretend campus cop is also the one who hit you in the dormitory storage room, Officer Matthews. I regret that our surveillance of him did not pick him up going into that building. We believe he had been told to remove anything incriminating from the Carlyle woman's stored items. He has admitted being the one who hit you. You never saw anyone, correct?"

Alice didn't hesitate.

"No, I didn't. I wish I had."

"Then I doubt you will be asked to testify in his trial, but that is up to the District Attorney."

Stammos turned his penetrating gaze on me.

I tried not to squirm.

"Professor, I tried everything I could to get you to quit investigating on your own. We had begun to suspect O'Shea and his role not only in the drug trafficking, but also in murder. We wanted to protect you."

His Greek resistance-fighter face took on a look of grim humor.

"But, I know now you brought down O'Shea. By yourself. That is no mean feat, young lady. I have known him for many years. He is one tough *diaolou*, devil you would say." I knew enough Greek to know that. And now that I knew what O'Shea was really like, it was apt.

"And you saved the evidence, and kept O'Shea from getting away from the justice that is due him. I wonder now why I tried to stop you, when you literally pulled our bacon out of the fire."

Stammos chuckled a little, shaking his big head. Then his voice dropped, and he went on ruefully.

"In the beginning, I did not suspect him of drug-running and murder. Some shady construction practices, yes, but not that. But once we toppled to the lad on the bicycle being a sham, we had him followed and he came too often to that construction site. Trucks would come in and go out, and that's normal for a construction zone. That's what made it hard to spot. Once Cullen got the stuff across the lake on his boat, he'd bring it bold as brass to his own building site and it would go out, not just to the campus but to the whole city from there.

"And not just the prescription stuff I heard you saw on the boat, Professor. Cocaine sometimes and heroin too. Filthy stuff. I heard they found traces of all of that in the hold of the vessel you kept him from scuttling. He could have killed you, sunk the boat and gotten away. He had plenty of money stashed all around the world I'm sure. O'Shea is truly an evil man."

"I know," I said, remembering O'Shea's matter-of-fact voice describing murder and drug distribution to me.

I realized I was really looking forward to testifying at his trial. As long as Anna coached me, that is.

I glanced over at Alice again, and we both stood. We each shook the Commander's hand.

"Thank you for your service to our university," Alice said warmly. Stammos actually flushed a little, and he nodded.

"Yes," I added. "Thank you. I assume I will see you at the trial?"

"Oh yes," Stammos said sternly. "You surely will."

Alice and I walked out together and went quickly down the stairs. By unspoken agreement, we headed to a little pocket park down the street from the station.

We sat in silence for a few minutes, both fairly stunned.

"When do you start work again?" I asked.

"Right after graduation," she said. Graduation was in two weeks. Next week was the last week of classes.

"I've missed you," I said softly.

"Girl, I have missed you too, but let's try to have a quiet few months, okay?"

She got up, punched me lightly on the arm and strode away on her sturdy cop shoes.

I sat there for a moment, a little resentful. I don't invent these murdering bastards. They just seem to come out of the woodwork, like cockroaches.

I walked home to have dinner with my kids. Carol and Giles were going out to a grad student party and it was my turn to cook.

Macaroni and cheese. My go-to dinner.

In fact, the only recipe I knew.

# # # #

Later that night, after I had read "Goodnight Moon" six times, and the boys and Molly had fallen into a deep sleep, Tom called.

"Kristin, how did the meeting with Stammos go?" he asked, with genuine interest.

"Well . . . ," I said. It took me a while to bring Tom up to speed on all the stunning revelations of that meeting.

Tom whistled through his teeth.

"Wow. And poor Jimmy Maddox. I'm glad they got that guy who killed him."

"Yes, me too," I said. I still wondered what Dwayne had known about that. Had he seen it? Had he always been afraid of cops or had he seen the fake cop murder Jimmy and that had caused his fear?

"Listen, Kristin," Tom began, somewhat hesitantly.

"Yes?"

"I, well, I'd like to go away with you, just the two of us, for a long weekend."

I thought about that for all of 10 seconds.

"Yes, Tom, I'd like that." And to myself, I said, 'it's time.' I still mourned my dead husband, Marco, but I would always mourn. I realized I wanted this relationship with Tom very much.

"Oh, good. Yes, well." Tom had apparently planned to have to convince me for a while and he was a little taken aback.

While he mumbled a little more, I asked about Kelly.

"Have you talked to Kelly? Is she okay with that?"

"I actually brought it up at counseling this evening."

"Really?" Tom had come a long way.

"Kelly said she was 'cool with it' and would like to stay with Alison if it was okay with Alison's parents. The counselor told me on the phone later that he thought this was a very positive sign. And I just got off the phone with Alison's parents and they are fine with her coming to stay."

Oh, good. No drama about Carol and Giles.

"So where and when?" I asked, getting more into the idea by the minute.

"I have some days coming to me, so I thought the weekend after graduation, leaving Thursday, coming back Tuesday."

That was indeed a very long weekend.

"Let me look at my calendar for a minute." I put him on hold and checked.

"Yes, that's good by me."

"So I think Paris. I have a friend who will lend us a little apartment he has there."

Paris. Apartment.

"I love Paris. Sure." And I love you, I said, but silently. I'd say it out loud later, I thought, probably starting on the Pont Neuf.

Yippee!

30

For our struggle is not against enemies of blood and flesh,
but against the rulers, against the authorities, against the
cosmic powers of this present darkness, against the spiritual
forces of evil in the heavenly places.
Ephesians 6:12

Thursday, May 31, 8:30 a.m.

This was the last day of class and I was giving the last lecture. I glanced down at my tablet lying on my desk. I had worked over the lecture outline for days, but I knew what I was going to say. The title of the lecture was "Wickedness."

There was a firm knock on the door.

I called 'come in,' and Edwin Porterman stepped into my office. He had a small envelope in his large hand.

"Professor," he said politely.

"Hello, Edwin, what can I do for you?" I asked, though my mind was really on what else I needed to bring to class and I looked down at my desk.

He didn't reply.

I looked up and his normally serious face seemed even more so. I waited.

"First, I wanted to say that I am glad you got the guy who killed Karen."

He looked down and it was a long way down to his polished, wing-tip shoes.

"A horrible way to die," he said, finally.

"Yes," I agreed and tried not to visibly shudder. I still had occasional nightmares about deep elevator shafts and still wet concrete.

Edwin visibly shifted gears and stepped forward to hand me the little envelope.

"This is an invitation to graduation. I hope you can come and see my Aunt Melda."

I thanked him gravely, though I did not need the invitation. Faculty normally marched at graduation.

"I will make sure to find both of you after the ceremony. I'd love to see her." I meant it. Aunt Melda had done a wonderful job of raising Edwin.

"Good. I am heading to the London School of Economics later this summer. I have enough credits to graduate early, and I decided it was time."

I thought he was right. There were too many unhappy memories for him here. In the checks and balances economic mind of Edwin Porterman, that would add up.

"You will wow them, I'm sure," I said, smiling at him.

He nodded, a tiny smile holding up the ends of his firm mouth for a brief second. He nodded, thanked me gravely, and then left.

I thought about Edwin, his talents and his private griefs and I realized I was glad he was going abroad right now. There was no safe place in this country these days for a young, handsome and brilliant African American man. Perhaps there never had been, but I was newly aware of it.

I gathered up my things, and walked down to the seminar room.

# # # #

I stood up at one end of the conference table. This was not a lecture to give sitting down.

"Joseph Conrad, in his novel 'Under Western Eyes,' wrote, 'a belief in a supernatural source of evil is not necessary; men alone are quite capable of every wickedness.' Conrad nearly lost his mind writing that brilliant work. In the story, he pushes back at those inane ideas, the same ones that biblical Job is refuting, that 'everything happens for the best' or even more ridiculous, that ultimately evil does not prevail and the innocent can stay innocent. Life is actually irrational, Conrad thought, and suffering is frequently inflicted on the innocent and the poor with no risk of retribution. Human lives are just callously cast away. That's existence, Conrad realized, and he could hardly face it.

"Religion often doesn't help us understand this underbelly of existence. In fact, a lot of religion is designed to hide the reality of evil at the heart of human life. Some would argue that's the purpose of religion, to 'clean it up' by pushing evil off of earth and into heaven. It is a way to try to make the intolerable, tolerable."

I stopped and looked over at Hercules sitting at the far end of the table. He seemed to be lost in his own memories of intolerable loss. The students, all of them, were staring at me. The campus rumor mill had worked overtime and they knew I had helped find a murderer and uncover a drug trafficking ring. There was probably plenty more being churned out by the rumor mill, and most of that untrue. But the basics were out there. I planned to use it.

"What Conrad means is it is a mistake to attribute evil in this world to a supernatural guy in a red suit carrying a pitchfork. That guy, the devil, is definitely not supernatural. He's human." I thought of what Stammos had said of O'Shea. A devil. A very human devil.

"Evil is a human endeavor and it is not a single thing, a thing we can isolate and say, 'there it is, that's evil.' No, not at all. Evil is made up of all the little bad acts, all connecting to each other, all reinforcing each other, but all claiming to be innocent, or, even worse, cloaked as 'not so bad, really.'"

I walked around the room, silently looking directly into the faces of each of them.

"How bad is it, really, to buy some pills from somebody so you can stay up all night to cram for that Calculus test? Better not think of how those pills got to you. Don't think about the sheaf of prescriptions some doctor provided, the pharmacies that fill dozens of prescriptions knowing they will be trafficked, and don't think about who gets those pills so conveniently into your hand. You might think it's just a sale. It's not and you, in that act, are not innocent." To a person they all looked anywhere but at me.

"Or what about sex?" Heads went back up around the room.

"Is it bad to download an app, scroll down and pick a beautiful young woman almost at random, and meet her at a hotel? It's just sex right? Nobody gets hurt. Just some fun. Just a way she makes her living. Except young women in the sex industry have been known to say, 'it kind of kills you inside, but then it's over.' Little kills, little deaths. They add up."

Now they were back to looking down at their computers or tablets, but they were not taking notes. They had gone inward, as I hoped, examining themselves, not only their attitudes, but also perhaps some of their own actions.

"That's wickedness. All those interconnected bad acts that get covered up, renamed, filed away in the 'don't think about it just do it' part of your mind. And those bad acts enable others so that whole systems develop where sometimes the outcome can even be coma or death from an overdose, or the occasional murder.

"We don't need a supernatural devil to explain that. In fact, he only gets in the way, blows smoke at evil and gives us a convenient way out. No, no. Human beings alone are capable of every wickedness."

I stopped there.

Questions for Discussion Groups

1. Kristin always "rushes in where angels fear to tread." Why does she do this, and do you think she is justified, as a widow and a single mother of two young children, in risking her life so often?

2. Was there anything Professor Adelaide Winters could have done to reach her student, Karen Carlyle, and help that young woman see that she was trapped by her own beauty? Does society make women and girls feel badly about how they look, and why?

3. The street newspaper vendor, Dwayne Moorehouse, appears to have been abused as a child, and thus has developed a speech impediment. Often people turn to drugs and alcohol to self-mediate for a lack of care. How much do you think this contributes to struggles with homelessness?

4. Why do you think Kristin admires the teaching style of her colleague, Hercules Abraham?

5. Talk in your group about Kelly. What do you think is going on with her in this book? What advice would you give to her Dad? To Kristin?

6. What do you think Kristin sees in Tom and what issues do you see emerging in their relationship?

7. What do you think about the term "sex industry" versus the more common "prostitution"? Is it a good idea to see this issue as an industry? Will it help promote change, or normalize it even more?

8. What do you know about the opioid crisis in the U.S.? What should we as a nation be doing about it and where do you think we are failing?

9. Is Kristin right to keep pushing to blend her life as a former cop and her new life as a professor? Do you think she will ever get them to work together?

10. Kristin and Hercules are trying to help their class see that evil as well as good are not supernatural, but very human productions. Do you agree or disagree and why?

If you would like to know more about the issues informing this novel, here are a few resources to help you:

First, the sex industry is vast and poorly understood. For a theological interpretation of the sex industry, read Rita Nakashima Brock and Susan Brooks Thistlethwaite, *Casting Stones: Prostitution and Liberation in Asia and the United States* (Fortress Press, 1996).

Second, it is important to understand the cause and effects of the flood of pain medications (opiates) into American society that began during 1990's and its relationship to other drug trafficking such as heroin, cocaine and the new designer-type drugs. From major cities to small towns, we are reeling from this catastrophe. For a good presentation on these complexities, see Sam Quinones, *Dreamland: The True Tale of America's Opiate Epidemic* (Bloomsbury Press, 2015).

Finally, it is crucial to grasp the crisis of poverty and homelessness in this country. Read Sasha Abramsky, *The American Way of Poverty: How the Other Half Lives* (Nation Books, 2013).